D0060103

ALSO BY PATRICE NGANANG

Fiction

When the Plums Are Ripe

Mount Pleasant

Dog Days

Poetry

elobi

A Trail of Crab Tracks

A Trail of Crab Tracks

PATRICE NGANANG

Translated from the French by Amy B. Reid

FARRAR, STRAUS AND GIROUX | NEW YORK

Farrar, Straus and Giroux
120 Broadway, New York 10271

Printed in the United States of America
Originally published in French in 2018 by Jean-Claude Lattès, France, as *Empreintes de crabe*
English translation published in the United States by Farrar, Straus and Giroux
First American edition, 2022

Crab ornament image by barka / Shutterstock.com.

Library of Congress Cataloging-in-Publication Data
Title: A trail of crab tracks : a novel / Patrice Nganang ; translated from the French by Amy B. Reid.
Other titles: Empreintes de crabe. English
Description: First American edition. | New York : Farrar, Straus and Giroux, 2022.
Identifiers: LCCN 2021060835 | ISBN 9780374602987 (hardback)
Subjects: LCGFT: Novels.
Classification: LCC PQ3989.2.N4623 E4713 2022 | DDC 843/.92—dc23/eng/20211228
LC record available at https://lccn.loc.gov/2021060835

Designed by Janet Evans-Scanlon

10 9 8 7 6 5 4 3 2 1

This novel is dedicated to Nomsa, my Bwonda'

Cameroon, such as we know it today, has changed forms several times, and it gained independence in 1960 and 1961. But all those who fought for a true Independence were assassinated: namely, the leaders of the Union of the Peoples of Cameroon, Ruben Um Nyobè, Félix Moumié, and the hero of this novel, Ernest Ouandié. The country experienced a terrible civil war from 1960 to 1970. Its leaders do not like those who remind them of it. In the face of such censure, writers and intellectuals developed various writing systems, including the Bagam writing—in other words, Bamileke writing—used by several characters in this novel. These writers, if they aren't dismissed as fools, are thrown in prison or have simply left the country.

Three Letters

1

This must be what death is like, what else could it be? Waking up groggy on a day when the sun is slow to rise. Slowly, ever so slowly, stretching, extracting oneself from the warm covers like a snail emerging from its shell. Tentatively reaching for the floor with one foot and then the other, the damp feel of bare boards. Feeling around tentatively for the slippers that he'll never get used to, but are so warm once they're on. Yawning, trying to conjure up some warmth to compensate for what the body is losing. Standing up. Opening the curtains to see the endless white stretch of the world, suddenly so different than the night before: the trees, their leaves, the bushes scattered around the yard, yes, the whole yard and even the sky itself, the horizon, shrouded by death. And it was of death that Nithap thought, of his own. Who could say, who could tell him, tell us, any of us, that death isn't waking up to a snow-covered world?

This fluttering of his mind, this fog blurring his brain, this cloud covering his consciousness, this sense of doubt, there's no way that his son—whose name was Nithap Salomon, Sal for the Americans, Tanou for his family—could help him in his struggle against it. Tanou had already left for work, as had his wife, and the little one was at school, like every day of the week, leaving him, the grandfather, alone with this ill-defined, vaporous feeling that he'd never before felt so keenly: it was suffocating. Yet suddenly a burst of energy, a flood of warm blood through his veins, reminded him that there is no age at which one should cease to explore or stop learning. That's what he always said, what he had said to everyone there in Bangwa the day he left. That lesson, renewed each day, was now taking shape in the flakes he watched gently floating down from the sky, carried by the wind that, in the warmth of his room, he could not feel, but that he knew to be cold, so very cold, a cold that had deadened his body, all the way to the tips of his ears, and cracked his lips, which he now had to cover with cream.

He didn't brush his teeth or take a shower, but headed downstairs in his pajamas, shuffling his slippered feet, egged on by his curiosity. His eyes brightened only when Marie, the little one, gave him English lessons, shaping her lips into rounds to show him how to pronounce the words.

"Grandpa, *snow*," she said in English.

"Why aren't you at school?"

The little one took the hand of her Old Papa—that was her nickname for him—and dragged him off, without answering his question, or perhaps answering it in her own way. She dragged him outside, under the watchful eye of her mother, who was busily cleaning off her own shoes.

"What about school?"

"Snow!"

What child doesn't like snow? This child, Marie, six years old, wanted to teach something to her seventy-five-year-old grandfather. She had jumped quickly out of the car, a Jeep Cherokee, angry with her mother, Angela, who was "wasting time"; she'd run into the living room, heading toward the stairs, where she met her Old Papa coming down. He was the one she wanted to teach something: *snow*. Her enthusiasm was so contagious that her grandfather didn't even think to put on a coat, especially since Marie, already outside, was disappearing into the flurry of white falling from the sky, joining the universe in its dance. Suddenly remembering her duties—that she needed to introduce him to this new world, her realm—Marie grabbed two fluffy handfuls that she let fall, sprinkling down in front of Nithap's astounded face. "Snow," she said, as her own face lit up. She rounded her lips, emphasizing the right pronunciation: *snow*.

"You're going to catch cold!"

Her mother's voice interrupted their dream.

And her mother was right, because her father-in-law was out there, in the middle of winter, wearing only his pajamas and slippers. He didn't notice that his little one was dressed for the weather. School was closed but they'd heard the news too late, only after they were on their way. Angela came out with an overcoat and boots, since the grandfather was clearly carried away by his granddaughter's enthusiasm, becoming his granddaughter in some sense, repeating what she wanted him to say, just like in their English lessons, holding out his hands and showing the clump of white: *snow*.

The mother shut the door on this literacy lesson in reverse, shutting out the cold and the promise the little girl had made to educate her grandfather by assigning a word to each thing around. With one eye on the screen of her phone, the mother turned on the stove to make hot chocolate, indispensable "after that crazy escapade," as she heard shouts of joy outside. The little one was thrilled, as was her grandfather: you'd think the two had invented snow. As for the mother, she was getting worried: "Always such cheapskates," she murmured. She was thinking about the place where she worked, and the university that had sent her husband out on the road so early that morning. She was sure the campus would announce it was closing once he was halfway to his office. "They are going to kill my husband one day!" Through the windowpane she watched the grandfather, who, following the little one's orders, was both discovering the United States for the first time and coming back to life himself; she shook her head at the sight of them, but used her phone to capture the moment, taking pictures and even a short video—that was what led her to head outside again and join in the dance.

The snow had caught them all off guard, Tanou even more than the others, as he drove along I-95. Each time he had to stop, he took a quick glance at his phone, hoping to see a message, an announcement from the university. It didn't arrive until he'd made it onto Route 13, heading toward the Verrazzano Bridge and Brooklyn. *Campus closed today; all classes canceled*: a simple phrase that he had hoped to see the night before, and then in the morning, and even as he anxiously drove to work. Feeling relieved, he had his left hand on the wheel and in his right the phone when his wife's name popped up on the screen.

"Finally," he said, barely masking his frustration.

"Same thing here."

"I was just about to call you."

Angela knew that he had once again made the drive for nothing, and so early in the morning, too, because he was headstrong and reluctant to heed her advice, as she often reminded him. "If only you'd listened to me."

But this wasn't the time for a family squabble, and she knew it, too. She looked through the pictures she'd taken in the yard and sent him one.

"Baby," she said, "you should pull over if the roads are bad."

"Papa, school is closed." The little one's voice. Her excitement broke through the ice on the windows, cleared the snow off the roads. "Grandfather and I, we were outside."

The anxiety that he had inherited from his mother, Ngountchou.

"Marie . . ." he began, but then he stopped, certain that she had already told her grandfather to be careful, to come in.

"We're all at home." His wife's voice was reassuring. "We're waiting for you here."

"Papa, are you coming home? Your hot chocolate is getting cold."

"I sent you a picture—"

"Baby, how can I look at the picture you sent, you know I'm trying to drive, and the roads are slippery."

"You didn't let me finish."

Taking out his stress on his wife, just like his father had done!

"Finish what?"

"You don't have to rush home, I sent you pictures."

"Baby."

"I'll send you a video, too."

"And what am I supposed to do with it?"

His iPhone vibrated.

"That way you can stop and see what we're doing."

And then what?

"You don't have to be here."

So that's what he did. After turning back toward home, he pulled off at Exit 9 and stopped at a gas station. Then he called his wife to tell her the details of his trip, complaining about the tanker trucks, "those idiots," telling her about an accident, "nothing serious," on Route 27, and uttering the phrase, "I'm sorry," which was necessary—absolutely necessary—to hold her attention, so that he could start again to explain his worries, now that she was really listening. He told her that, yes, he was safe and warm, that he wasn't going to leave the gas station anytime soon, and that the highway would be sanded before long—the plows were hard at work. He added that the Volvo drove just fine in the snow, that the video had arrived—"yes, yes," he'd had a chance to watch it—and that what the little one was doing with her grandfather was *terrific* (he said that in English), but they needed to be careful not to get frozen, "especially not Old Papa, you know, he's not used to snow."

"Yes, yes," Angela reassured him. "We're all safe and warm."

Get frozen. The phrase, the image of food in the freezer, made him smile when he hung up and noticed the somber faces around him, all the people who'd taken shelter together and whose minds were elsewhere, like his, one eye fixed on the image of a grandfather in a snow flurry, there on the iPhone screen. Beneath the overcoat—his own—he recognized the colors of a pair of pajamas and jumped. "Old Papa is gonna freeze!" He tapped on Angela's number and, as soon as she answered, realized how silly he was being: she had already told him that they were safe and warm, in the living room, and so he was the only one out on the snowy roads.

"I love you," he said.

"Me, too."

2

*Of those who had been surprised by the snow, Nithap was certainly the happi-*est. His son Tanou found him comfortably ensconced in the living room: looking outside, but safe and warm. The last FaceTime session had reassured him. He hadn't been able to keep himself from calling one last time. Just as his wife had also called to make sure he was okay—"You'd said there were accidents on Route 27." Or worse: he could have been killed by the police. "*Black lives matter*, you know," she added, in English. The grandfather was sitting in front of the television with the little one, wearing out his eyes on a cartoon whose noisy twists and turns had the child so entranced that she didn't even look up when her father opened the door.

"Is anyone happy that I escaped *death*?" he tossed out.

"Death?" Angela gave him a kiss. "Watch what you're saying, baby."

His father was the one to welcome him home.

"Do you want a coffee?"

"This is your first snow," he said to Old Papa as he took off his coat and shoes, and rubbed his hands, his breath still rising up in a cloud from his lips. "You can see what we were trying to avoid. And yes, I'd love a coffee."

"Avoid the snow," that had been his mantra a few months ago when he'd gone to pick up his father at the airport. "At all cost, avoid the snow." That meant avoiding the month of December. But his father's illness had thrown a wrench in their plans and now it was January. What had started as a family reunion, "a chance to see your granddaughter," had morphed first into a series of trips to the hospital, and then into a full schedule of appointments, one after the other, various moments where someone expressed surprise that Old Papa was still standing, a ritual chanting of all of his ills. The doctor would look up from his notebook.

"Tell him," Nithap insisted, "that I was a nurse."

"I already told him, Papa."

"Tell him again," Old Papa insisted.

He wasn't convinced until the doctor turned to him with a smile:

"A nurse, you say?"

"I retired from the referral hospital in Bangwa in 1990."

He stressed the word *referral.*

"Your father has insurance?"

That's the only thing that the young Indian doctor was worried about. The retired nurse couldn't know that. His son didn't translate his ensuing exchange with the doctor, during which he admitted that his father didn't have health insurance; they'd pay out of pocket. His father, meanwhile, pressed his son to explain to the doctor the difficulties he'd been having each time he went to the bank.

"Tell him how hard it was for me to sign all the forms."

The father described the absurd procedure imposed by his banker, "a young man who has known me for years": he kept asking him to sign documents one after another, and once he'd signed, he refused to give him the money from his pension, "because the signature on file wasn't the same."

"No joke."

This story elicited an unexpected laugh from his son and, once it had been translated, a smile from the doctor, but Nithap didn't find it funny at all. He found it much more worrisome than his fainting spells, those "syncopes," as he called them, which were the recurring symptom of his illness and the start of all these visits, the reason why he had extended his stay in the United States, even before the accident. The story had him so worried that he repeated it at least three times: first to the doctor, then at his next visit, when he nudged his son, "Don't forget to ask him to prescribe something for me," and then later to Marie. Four times, if you count the allusion he made to it when Big stopped by for a visit.

Big, that's what we called the poet, the renowned poet. He lived at number 26, they at number 13. Nithap had first met him when the poet was taking his dog, Sahara, out for his daily walk, back when the weather still allowed it. And then he'd gotten to know him over a dinner organized by his son—"a dinner to welcome my father." It was Sahara who had really brought them together.

"What's her name?"

"*His* name is Sahara."

"That's an African name! Have you been to Africa?"

"Yes, to Senegal."

"Really?"

"Yes, and Morocco, too."

"I went to Senegal, but a long time ago."

The grandfather hated all those signs that gave away his age, even as he claimed the rights due him because of it. That day Tanou was really amused when his father found out that Big was two years older than he.

"I am in much worse shape than you are," Big had said, smiling at a story about a tremor in his fingers.

"Writing is a whole other story."

"Significant memory loss." The doctor's diagnosis, given after numerous visits, was cut-and-dried. "I'd like to see him again in two weeks."

After those two weeks came a month and then another, bringing Grandfather right into the middle of winter.

"I'm not going to keep things from you," Tanou told Marianne, who was like a sister to him, when he called the old country to tell her about the doctor's appointment. "I think that the old guy is developing symptoms of Alzheimer's."

"Alzheimer's?"

"Oh, what do I know?"

"When he left here, he was just fine."

"Now you, too, Marianne! Ugh!"

Big was a writer. Robert Adams—a poet, author of some twenty books— didn't look like the walking library he actually was. Despite his years, he still stood straight and tall like the basketball player he claimed to have been in his younger days. The black-and-white photos he showed everyone revealed a very different man, in shorts, svelte, holding a ball with both hands, his eyes fixed overhead.

"What year was that?"

"I think it was 1959."

"Yes, 1959," his wife, Céline, chimed in.

Suddenly lost in his own thoughts, Nithap picked up the photo. He turned it over as if expecting to find on the back an inscription predicting the future, details hinting at a larger story, something larger than life.

"I was a student."

"1959."

He repeated the year two more times.

"I wasn't even born yet," said little Marie, bringing a smile to everyone's lips.

"Of course not, my little one," Big said, patting her head gently. "Your father wasn't even born then."

Then the little one took hold of the photo, staring at it as if it were another of the cartoons that filled her days, or a picture from one of her storybooks. She snuggled into her grandfather's arms, still gazing at the photo, before imitating its pose—much to everyone's amusement.

"I was just starting my work in Bangwa."

"Bangwa?"

"At the hospital in Bangwa."

The details: first, explaining that Bangwa was in the west of Cameroon, in Bamileke land; then that the Bamilekes were one of the peoples of Cameroon—*not a tribe, okay?*—and that they were Bamileke. Those details, it fell to Tanou to fill them in.

"Papa, am I Bamileke?"

The little one's question roused her father and made everyone stop and consider its perplexing implications. Marie had asked the question in English, because that's the language she used when talking with her father, although the conversation around the table that day had been in French—which created an intimate space within the intimacy of the home that reassured Nithap. Language was a cord strong enough to bind together this eccentric group, but English, no, he didn't understand it. At the start of his stay he had tried to use Pidgin, but had realized that nobody understood.

In the end it was Céline, Big's wife, who answered her question, and in English, although she was French herself. ("My name is Céline," she always said, "like the author, but on the Left.") Better to say that she tried to answer, actually, because just then the dog, Sahara, had started scratching meaningfully at the foyer door, barking sharply, insistently, letting everyone know he'd been kept away too long—far too long—from the action. Céline got up to open the door and the dog came gamboling into the kitchen, happy to be free, even as Marie, who was scared, jumped onto her father's lap.

"Don't be afraid, my dear," Céline said, as she gently tried to grab hold of Sahara, who, skilled at evasion, slid under the table and soon poked his nose out in front of Tanou and the little girl. "Sahara is happy to see you."

"I'm not afraid."

But the child looked on the edge of tears, and her body had gone limp, except for her frantically waving hands.

"Don't be afraid," her father said. "He won't hurt you."

"I'm not afraid."

"Look," said the poet, who put his hand down in front of Sahara's mouth. The dog began to lick, his tail wagging, and then Céline managed to grab him. "Look, he wants to play."

"It's okay, Sahara."

Then the dog got a treat. But Marie had already clambered up first onto her father's lap and then into his arms, wrapping her legs tightly around his chest, as if she were climbing a palm tree. When she tried to climb higher, he lifted her swiftly onto his shoulders and then stood up. Still, the child tried to climb even higher, lifting her feet, as if to fly away from this place, from this dog, who saw her antics as an invitation to play and kept barking happily.

"Céline, maybe Sahara should go back out?"

"No need," said Tanou. "We've already been here awhile. We should go."

"No, no . . ."

"Oh yes," Grandfather chimed in. "We *ought* to go."

He stressed the word *ought*, as if it weren't a bit of a lie, one of those phrases said to fill up the empty space that the dog's arrival had created, even though they were in the dog's kitchen.

With Marie still sitting on his shoulders, Tanou moved toward the front door, followed by the poet and his wife, who was still holding on to Sahara's neck. But then he suddenly realized that his father had sat back down.

"Papa?"

He looked at him, sitting there at the kitchen table, as if everything that had just taken place—Sahara's barking interruption of the conversation, Marie's flight, the end of the conversation—really didn't concern him, as if this house, and not his son's, were where he belonged, as if he had known the poet since that basketball game long ago, captured in a black-and-white photo that, due to an unexpected turn of events, he'd happened to see.

"Of course," said the poet softly, "Sakio, stay a little longer."

He phrased it as a polite invitation, but it was more of a factual description: *Sakio is staying a little longer.*

"Of course."

His phrasing, so careful, and yet familiar—like his use of the name Sakio—did not escape Tanou; he understood it meant, *Not you.*

"Papa," Marie said as soon as the door had shut behind them, keeping the dog in. "I want to stay with Grandfather."

"Are you sure?"

One more bark from the dog inside the house, and the little girl quickly changed her mind.

"No, let's go home."

That made her father laugh.

"Yes, let's go home."

A few minutes later Grandfather rejoined them and, of course, Tanou asked what they had talked about. But that just brought out his father's bad mood. That was something that had always exasperated him: his father's secretive nature, the habit he had of never talking to him about the things he wanted to know. Tanou realized not only how ridiculous he'd been to think his father would finally share his own secrets, but also how much more relaxed his father was with those he considered his friends. He was sure that his father had just opened up and told them his whole story.

Tanou was much more of a stranger to his father than was the poet.

3

One day when his wife arrived home, she told him that she had seen Grandfather in town, a cap on his head and a jacket over his shoulders, walking a dog.

"I'm not sure that it was Sahara, but it looked like it."

"What do you mean?" He couldn't believe his ears. "So why didn't you bring them back in your car?"

"I was driving and didn't recognize them at first," she admitted. "But then I checked in the rearview mirror."

"And you didn't stop?"

"Are we going to have an argument about this?"

"No. I'm just asking."

She shook her head and walked off to her office. Tanou paused for a minute in the living room, scratching his head, his eyes fixed on the television that was keeping Marie entertained; he'd picked her up from school that day. Then, as if spurred on by a guilty conscience, he got up, headed toward Angela's office, and opened the door, a question on his lips. She didn't let him get the question out; with her arms crossed over her chest, her angry glare hit him hard.

"Tanou," she asked, "why are you always looking for problems where there aren't any?" Then she laughed, with that snarky, exasperated laugh of hers, and slapped her forehead with the palm of her hand. "Are we going to get into a debate about stoplights now?"

"No, obviously not."

When Grandfather returned, just in time for dinner, he broke the silence by telling a joke.

"I took the poet's dog for a walk today."

That was his joke.

"Sahara?"

It is best to feign ignorance when faced with the absurd. But that wasn't Angela's way.

"Yes, I saw you. On Main Street."

"We went all around town."

Pennington was a small town; you could walk all around it in less than an hour. Even Bangangte* was bigger. Now he lived in Bangwa, which was the largest town in the region. Since he'd arrived in Pennington, Grandfather had gotten into the habit of walking—there was nothing else for him to do, really, and he certainly wasn't going to spend his days in front of the television. His whole life he had railed against his children's love for Cameroonian television. It was summer then. The greenery made the village look like a bouquet, and after a week, he knew every corner of it, as if it were his own. Usually he waited until his "children"—as he called them—had left for work or school; and then he filled his days as a retiree with the scent of the town.

Big and his wife were also retired—he from the teaching positions he'd held at various universities, and Céline from her career as a stage designer, even if she kept busy with a thousand things she had trouble describing.

"I restore antique clothing," she often said.

Or, "I'm a seamstress."

Grandfather perked up his ears; his wife had been a seamstress for years.

---

* Let's take a moment to go over the lay of the land: Bangangte is made up of villages or *ntang la'*, namely: Bangangte (the main town in question here), Bangwa, Bangoulap, Bamena, Bazou, Balengou, Bawouok, Bassamba, Bandounga, Bantoum, Bangangfoukong, Badiangseu, Ntonga, Bakong, Banyoun, Bamac; and these are connected, as if by osmosis, with the Bangangte neighborhoods in cities like Mbanga, Douala (New Bell–Kassalafam), Yaounde, and even Paris and New York.

But she also said, "I sew outfits from a century ago for parades."

"For men or for women?"

"It doesn't matter."

"What parades?"

Visibly embarrassed, she searched for the right words and then fell silent, turning to look at her husband.

"For reenactments of the Civil War."

Would she really have to explain what that meant?

"Which civil war?"

"The American Civil War."

Then her husband, who was American, piped up with an explanation.

"You see, we Americans haven't had a war on our territory for more than a hundred years, even if the United States has instigated many civil wars around the world. Even if the United States wages war all around the world, almost every year, and even if this is the most belligerent country of all. Look at Syria and Iraq; even Obama didn't change anything in the end." He gave a big sigh, as if exhausted by it all. "Well, because the memory of war on our own territory is so distant, people have grown sort of nostalgic, and so each year they stage episodes from the war. From the American Civil War."

"So, it's a game?"

Grandfather was really interested now.

"Not a game," Céline said. "My customers take this very seriously; it's not fun and games."

"Maneuvers?"

"*Well*," the poet began in English, out of habit, but then quickly switched back to French. "I'd say it's theater."

"Yes, Sakio, it's a sort of popular theater."

"A theater of war?"

"It keeps me busy," Céline continued. "What else can a French seamstress do in New Jersey?"

Her eyes suggested a wounded bird on a deserted path, a turtledove caught in a devilish trap, and yet she hadn't finished her sentence as she would have liked: *I'm retired, too, and it keeps me busy.*

"Sitting around with nothing to do," Grandfather said, "that's not my way, either."

Keeping busy was a religion for him, and Tanou had quickly realized that it was a religion his father shared with these two friends: a religion of movement, a religion of uninterrupted activity, a religion of any and all kinds of action.

"I had a salon in France," Céline said, "in Paris."

"Really?"

"On rue des Prairies."

Silence fell.

"In the twentieth arrondissement," she continued, as if everyone there had a map of Paris in their pocket.

Grandfather tried to imagine a seamstress's salon in Paris, a city he'd never visited, *in the twentieth arrondissement*, on a street with several shops, with cars parked in front and people hurrying by; the vision was evident on his face, which lit up with a broad smile. He laughed more easily here—much more easily, his son noted—with a smile that showed all his teeth.

"That's where we met."

Another moment of silence.

"Bob had come to buy an outfit for his wife."

The poet smiled and looked up. *How can a man so big be called Bob?* Tanou had wondered, tickled by the thought, the day his neighbor had introduced himself. "Call me Bob." Tanou preferred Big. The open-heartedness of this couple, together now for forty-six years, left him speechless. His father never spoke like this about himself, never even mentioned Tanou's mother, truth be told, although they'd been married for fifty years.

"Forty-six years of adultery," the poet stressed; that thought still amused him, even made him laugh.

Céline was also the poet's muse and appeared in several of his poems. And there in front of him stood the stoic grandfather, the impassive man he'd become, by which I mean an assiduous reader of one, and only one, book, the Bible. Tanou often found him in his room reading, his finger moving softly along each line, his lips murmuring enigmatic words. His eyes had barely registered the tenderness on display before him, the expression of a couple joined for so long by a love that had given them two sons, each already an adult. His own son suddenly realized how strange the world his father inhabited was, and how tightly it was closed off to him. It was a world of silence, the sort of silence that relies on all sorts of subterfuges, including proverbs, to justify its *lock nshou*.*

It's part of his character, Tanou told himself, and he accepted it as his destiny, like a film script that left him perplexed, but that, without even realizing it, he kept on acting out, that he'd adopted as part of his own routine. His wife reminded him of it at every chance, triggering another of those "useless quarrels" that erupted whenever Old Papa experienced one of his lapses. To tell the truth, that's really what they were all about.

"You know how difficult you are," Angela would say.

At times it seemed the couple was engaged in a sort of trench warfare: for each millimeter gained, one of the two planted a flag to mark their advance.

Bob had given a reading in Arizona. He returned buoyed up by the words of praise from the president of the university the day of his talk. "He's read some of my poems." His wife had gone with him on the trip and the two had rounded out their stay with visits to several tourist sites, since Céline had never been to that part of the country before. They had needed someone to take care of Sahara while they were gone, and also to water their plants. Usually they hired someone to do this—someone they didn't really know, often a student recruited on the internet. It took a long time to arrange, because they interviewed everyone, and it wasn't without risk. "We're old folks, you know."

"I told them I'd do it."

Tanou and his wife exchanged glances.

**Lock nshou* = "Shut your mouth!"; a combination of the Pidgin *lock*, key or to shut, and the Medumba *nshou*, or mouth, which means silence.

"That's all?"

"That's all."

Tanou wouldn't have been Tanou had he not asked the next question:

"And did they pay you?"

"Tanou!" Angela exclaimed in embarrassment.

"Well, you know," her husband replied, "it's depriving students of earning a little extra."

The sound of the television filled the void in their conversation while Tanou set the dinner table.

"The students will find some other way to make money; there's no shortage of odd jobs. Marie, it's time for dinner."

"Who knows if those students have enough to make it through the summer, do you see what I mean?"

"No, I don't."

"Listen . . ."

But Angela didn't listen, no one did, really, because, without their realizing it, the sounds of the television had grown louder and louder, filling up the space of their lives with screechy cartoon voices.

"Marie!"

"Anyway, they're not poor, those students of yours."

4

Tanou was worried about what people in Pennington might say about them. The sight of his father walking Sahara was rather comical. Old Papa saw nothing wrong with it, but the son imagined how people might look askance at him. In truth, the two men really didn't know each other anymore, but were finding out about one another bit by bit, with each new trap life set up for them. *Grandfather is walking a dog. So what?* That English phrase wasn't yet part of Tanou's vocabulary. He had forgotten that his father had always had a dog, that he'd had to walk a dog himself when he was growing up. Still, the familiarity with which Grandfather greeted Céline had surprised him.

He must be making fun of me, the son told himself.

He didn't realize how unfair he was being to his father, or maybe he did but, feeling embarrassed, tried to erase that thought from his mind.

He was surprised by how easily Nithap had struck up a friendship with his neighbors, Céline and her husband. It was as if they'd known one another since the dawn of time. It seemed to mean that, "in the end, the colonists are our friends." Then Tanou murmured, "It doesn't matter if they're white or Black." And yet, even to him, that phrase seemed really unjustified: *the colonists*? Happily, he hadn't actually expressed his thoughts out loud, because those around him—his father, his wife, and even Marie—would all have told him he was being absurd, illogical, that his imagination was twisted. *Leave him be, will you?* That is certainly what his wife would have answered, and she'd have been right. *Leave him be.*

One evening, when Céline mentioned she was from Provence, Grandfather's face lit up.

"Provence," he'd said, obviously enchanted. Then, all of a sudden, he began to recite the names of French rivers.

"The Rhône, the Paillon, the Argens, the Touloubre."

"My, my . . ."

"The Loup, the Brague."

He recited the names, counting them off on his fingers, his old schoolboy reflexes flooding back. Digging deep into his memories, he recalled the time spent in a school hidden away in the depths of Bangangte.

"We learned the names of all the rivers in France."

Tanou couldn't keep himself from interjecting, "And those of Cameroon as well?"

Then he began to wonder: Did his father know the names of as many Cameroonian rivers? Did he himself know as many?

But there was no room for his irony in Nithap's eyes, nor in Céline's; they were discovering each other in the intoxicating thrill of a sublime instant, an unanticipated glimmer of recognition.

"And the poems, too."

Then Old Papa rose to his feet, like the child he had been so long ago. With his chest puffed out he struck the familiar pose of an orator, and the kitchen was transformed into a classroom. He raised one hand.

"'The Grasshopper and the Ant.' A Grasshopper gay / Sang the summer away, / And found herself poor / By the winter's first roar. / Of meat or of bread, / Not a morsel she had!"

Then he paused.

"I'm getting a little tripped up."

The poet—one elbow leaning on *The New York Times* while with the other hand he stroked Sahara, lying on the floor at his feet—was wholly caught up in the scene.

Céline, with a smile, whispered the next line, "So a begging she went . . ."

And the forgetful orator continued on before pausing once more so his friends could again chime in, continuing this game of verbal ping-pong.

"So a begging she went, / To her neighbour the ant, / For the loan . . ."

After another pause he continued, confident in the ballast of his memory, the words of the poem flowing as smoothly as a limpid stream, until he came to the final verses that he and Céline recited together.

"You sang! I'm at ease; / For 'tis plain at a glance, / Now, ma'am, you must dance."

The poet was quite impressed and applauded, as did Tanou. Even the dog barked. It was impossible not to respond to the beauty of the reunion taking place in this home, in this living room. The son felt his father's joy as his own. Grandfather congratulated himself on his memory—that he hadn't forgotten the verses of that poem from his childhood, didn't that prove he was in good health? "What does that Indian doctor really know, anyhow?" Tanou smiled, but he was really thinking about his own childhood, about recitations in the public school in Bangwa, about the young boy, whose smoothly shaved head had earned him the nickname Congolibong,* who always concluded his recitation with the full citation: "Jean de La Fontaine, *Fables*, Book One, Paris, 1965, page fifty-six."

Amused by it all, Big had smiled; he wasn't used to reciting poems. Once, when the son, his neighbor, had asked him to *say* one of his poems, he had replied, "I don't recite my poems, I read them," and he made no exception then! Happily, YouTube had saved recordings of several of his readings. That day they talked about everything: how poetry is taught in schools, if American students memorize poems "by heart" (he loved that expression so, "by heart"!), and if he knew *by heart* any verses of his favorite poet, Walt Whitman, or of Césaire.

If he were a poet, if he were generous—and, frankly, he was both—how could he not open up and join in this free-flowing poetic effusion, even though it made the son uncomfortable?

"We also learned that in school," he'd said.

"Us, too," Céline chimed in. "Always La Fontaine in school."

"Everywhere."

---

* *Congolibong*: a Camfranglais expression children use, meaning "smooth head."

"Us, too."

"Everywhere in Africa."

"And in France."

Things hadn't changed. Father and son had both learned La Fontaine's fables in school, from the same book, *Mamadou et Bineta**; yet a sense of discomfort he couldn't explain had kept the son from joining in. Why? the poet asked him. In return, he asked why the poet had refused when asked to recite one of his own poems. They looked at each other warily.

"I wasn't sure I'd remember."

That was a lie.

"I'm a bit hoarse," the poet said, so Céline had read the poem for him.

She loved poetry, although certainly not as much as she loved her husband. Still, it was clear that she was his reader; it was likely in her voice that his poems resonated through the house when they were alone.

"My memory isn't as good as Sakio's," Céline added gaily.

That made Grandfather smile, lighting up his face with what was really a silent laugh, a moment of illumination. And then he remembered a story that a friend had told him: the friend was in Sweden, at an international conference, and he saw three Africans and a white man talking in a corner. He moved closer and closer to them. The four didn't lower their voices because they knew no one understood what they were saying, they knew they were protected by the borders of an extraordinary complicity: they were speaking in French.

Their refuge.

---

* A veritable transgenerational bible, published in two volumes in 1950 and still used in some countries as of 2005, *Mamadou et Bineta* and *Mamadou et Bineta sont devenus grands*, by André Davesne, taught Africa how to speak French. You'll meet very few who are as critical of these books as they are of the CFA franc; quite the contrary. It would seem that grammar has been eternally sanctified in their concordance of verb tenses . . .

5

Later, it occurred to Tanou that that was only the second time he'd seen his father express such complete happiness. The house next door to his own—there in Big's kitchen, the poet's kitchen—was also the only place he'd ever heard his father called by his first name: Sakio. The first time he'd ever seen him that happy was in a mall. They'd gone there to meet two women who were raising money to build a girls' school in Cameroon, in Bamenda. Tanou had struck up a conversation with them in the church where they'd come to pitch their project.

The coincidence was too great, and he was carried away as much by the idea of finding something for his father to do as by helping the kids. The meeting had been a catastrophe, for as the women tried to explain the Cameroonian contradictions that made it difficult to build a school, even in a country where children were crammed by the hundreds into small rooms, his father was goofing around, first bending over to pick up the scarf one of the women had let fall by her feet and taking the chance to flirt with her, then twirling his coffee spoon and playing with the menu, and soon after starting to whistle.

"Papa, will you stop?" Tanou had said in Medumba.

Later, in the car, he had asked Old Papa what had gotten into him, but was met with silence. "Are you making fun of me?" Tanou had worked through his own exasperation in silence, with the determination of a marathon runner, struggling to find the right words to express his indignation.

"You'd think you don't want them to build that school."

Silence.

"But it's going to help our children."

Silence.

"And its Americans who are going to pay for it."

Silence.

Was it even worth the trouble to continue this monologue? he wondered, as his eyes scanned the parade of billboards filing past, announcements of public works projects, ads for businesses and sales. When his father had first arrived, back in 2013, he had taken him to Macy's, spread his arms out wide, and told him to choose the clothes he wanted. Old Papa had looked at him in disbelief; for so many years he'd been the one who bought clothes for his kids.

"I hope it's not too expensive," he'd said.

"Papa!"

To distract himself a bit, he turned on the radio, bobbing his head to the beat of an insipid song, then changed stations, only to hear another insipid tune; he let the refrain fill the silence that had taken over the vehicle, as if it were its only occupant.

Moving through a world where he didn't understand the language, where he didn't understand everything that is taken for granted, where the basic logic escaped him and everyday life was too complicated: Was Old Papa even happy to be in the United States? *Silence*. Did he appreciate the beauty of these places that made more than a few young people back home jealous? The United States, *bebela*!* New York! Bringing his father over had been the gift he'd given himself when he'd become a citizen. He'd been waiting ten long years, and then—it was unbelievable—he'd had to work hard to convince him to come and visit, "just for a month." "Why don't you choose one of your cousins?" Old Papa had said. "One of your nephews, maybe."

Because I miss you, old man, he'd thought.

---

* *Bebela*: an Ewondo term, commonly used in Yaounde's Camfranglais, that means "really."

He hadn't said it, of course. *Sentiments are the expression of laws rather than of hearts*, that's what he taught his students. *We are in fact the product of jurisdictions, laws, and decrees.* He could still see that neighbor of his from Kansas, smitten by everything African because he'd spent a year as a volunteer in a village in Kenya, who, when he'd been invited for dinner one evening, noticed Tanou's doctoral thesis and took it home with him. "A little bedtime reading," he'd said; Tanou had laughed. The next day he'd returned it, admitting sheepishly that he hadn't gotten past the title: *The Construction of the Subject in the Early Writings of Frantz Fanon and Michel Foucault: A Comparative Study.*

Just like the voice of that neighbor, his father's distant voice echoed in his mind, reminding him just how crazy what he spent his time on was; now he was there, huddled down in the seat next to him, a beaten man. All those expensive exchanges on the phone, long-distance, were over. You try to tell his father to use the more affordable means of communication available in Bangwa! As far as he was concerned, that old Nokia 3360 cell phone was a big improvement on witchcraft!

Tanou went through all the little things that irritated him, like talking for free to a friend on vacation in Vanuatu, but $2.50 a minute to talk to his father, because he refused to try to use anything besides that damned Neanderthal of a phone! Or having to shout into the phone as if he were trying to be heard by a whole soccer stadium: "Yes, do you hear me? Do you hear me? So, as I was saying . . . Huh?" Or having to work around the endless problems with "bad connections," just to hear his father say, "Bring your nephew instead." What he saw parading before his eyes, instead of the billboards, were the names of all of those cousins, nephews, and nieces who certainly would have exploded with joy to be the beneficiary of Old Papa's suggestion.

"But it's you and only you who can get a visa quickly."

Silence.

". . . Won't you come visit me?"

What he heard coming through the phone were words full of resentment, from his nephews mostly: "He's old, he doesn't need to go to the United States, but me . . . !" Each one had some need greater than the other, it was like triage in a doctor's office where one after another in a line you have gangrene and cancer, an embolism, diarrhea, an ever-growing slew of pains that all start to sound the same, all ending with the father's memory lapses. Except that the nurse was Nithap, and there in the car, all the way home, his father kept quiet.

"And what about *me*, then?" he'd say.

The man starved for love that you become after spending years so far away from home, especially when your family doesn't understand!

"You're not a child anymore," he'd reply. "Why should I go see you?"

"Because you are sick, so just maybe we could get you taken care of."

"But I'm not sick!"

"That's just what the doctor said so we can get you the visa."

"Really?"

"Okay, really, *I'm* the one who wants to see you. That's the truth."

He'd put his hand over the speaker on the phone and sob.

"Son, are you still there?"

Finally, in one of their conversations he'd said, "Papa, it's a lot more complicated with people who aren't immediate family."

*Now, in the car, he silently went through each of their previous misunderstand-*ings; those exchanges had left him breathless and bloodied, but the fact that they were both there in the car together was proof of his victory over Old Papa's stubbornness.

"But they're your family, too!"

Shit, why are old people so stubborn?

"Papa, it's not up to me!"

"They're your nephews!"

"You tell immigration that."

"Your cousins!"

"I know."

"Your children," he added. "Besides, did you know that Marianne just had a baby boy?"

"She told me."

Try explaining to his father that the Americans—out of habit he still said "the Americans," even though he'd now become one himself and was, in fact, exercising one of the privileges of citizenship by inviting his father—that the Americans had refused to give a visa to Ngountchou in 2009—"to my own mother!"—even though she was gravely ill. "Precisely because she was so sick," Marianne retorted. "That's how they are in those countries! They don't want the sick. They don't want the young kids! Just what do they want, huh?" "Trump said it: they don't want anyone anymore!" He really didn't want to rehash all those sad stories that his father seemed to have forgotten, or was trying to forget, especially since his mother's visa had been denied "under Obama." Several times during these difficult conversations he'd had to call on his wife, on flattery, even if in the end it was only the sound of Marie's voice that had convinced Old Papa: "Grandfather, when are you coming? Are you coming this summer?"

"Yes, my little one!"

As they sat in deafening silence, all the promises of this country paraded by on the left and the right, promises written in big letters on brightly colored billboards, letters in yellow, blue, and red, Sears, Macy's, a Honda car dealership; promises that, the son finally realized, were losing their polish, becoming comical. He burst out laughing.

Old Papa looked at him and smiled.

"I know," the son had said, "all of this is strange to you."

Even him, hadn't he become strange? He remembered that time when his father had insisted on going to see him teach. He sat in the back of the lecture hall. That day, he was talking about gender; he had made photocopies of the important points of the lecture and distributed them to the students. In the shadows of the corner where he sat, Nithap watched his son lecture to two hundred students, with a PowerPoint projected onto a screen; he watched as, with a simple gesture, he made his teaching assistant, a white man, stand, and with another had the second assistant, a Chinese student, crisscross the room, without ever losing a beat in his lecture; at least that's how Old Papa described it later.

Even though he'd gotten caught up in the elaboration of his argument, Tanou never took his eyes off that dark corner where he hoped, wished, that his father had fallen asleep. He just didn't have the courage to face his stony stare, or to answer the questions he might have. Yet as the room emptied out, once the lecture was over, and he saw his father on the far side of the room, standing tall and proud, a big smile on his face, he dragged his feet a little. Maybe he actually got it all? He came up to his father with an excuse on his lips, "I know it was in English," and his mother Ngountchou's words echoing in his ear, "When you aren't born into a good family, it's up to you to find your own path." Had he discovered his path there in the lecture hall? His father didn't give him a chance to say anything more in that room that had been filled with his voice for the last fifty minutes. He wrapped Tanou in his arms and gave him a kiss, as his feet began a dance that shook him from head to toe.

"Tanou," he'd said, "I'm so proud of you."

Old Papa was clutching the handout the assistant had distributed.

"What are you going to do with that?"

"It's a souvenir. A precious one. I want to frame it and hang it up in the living room, in Bangwa."

"Why?"

"Because this is what you teach the whites."

"But you didn't even read it. If anyone asks, what are you going to say?"

"It doesn't matter, you can explain it to me."

The son gave a start, for this is what the document said:

> Salomon Nithap, Professor
> Synthesis
> *The range of human genders: male, female, gender-neutral, androgynous, bigender, cisgender, gender-fluid, genderqueer, intersex, transsexual, two-spirit, but also, and it's possible, with no identifiable gender.*

He imagined this text framed and hanging on the living room wall, next to the clichéd portrait of a pair of children* inscribed with the phrase: *Jesus Christ Is the Master of This Home*. Tanou stared at Old Papa, so sublime in his pride, and he suddenly remembered the day he'd gone to the wedding of one of his students, Adam. He was, at that point, teaching in rural Pennsylvania. It was his first year teaching there and he'd seen nothing but kindness in the faces of the people around him. Especially those who had welcomed him—him, his father's son—as if he were their own. He wanted to offer the young couple a gift that reflected who he was in his student's eyes: the respected professor. In the bookstore in the mall, he looked over several rows of shelves, pausing to consider various insignificant books; he leafed through a number of biographies, of shallow novels, and then noticed two copies of a book with a black cover, its title inscribed in a strange font. He moved closer, and the sparkling letters of the title were forever burned into his eyes: *Hitler, Mein Kampf*. He bought something else but left distraught, because he was teaching German then.

The radio was playing Alanis Morissette.

"I know," Tanou said, "even the music is strange. Even the toilets are strange here," he added, "because a people that decides to watch each day, sometimes several times each day, their own excrement spin around in concentric circles, sucked down in a centripetal swirl of water, before disappearing in a whoosh, surely has a lot of secrets to drown."

Tanou couldn't help thinking about the two women who wanted to build a school in Bamenda.

"It was for the country back home!" he finally burst out.

He had wanted to add, *for you*, but managed to catch his tongue. He remembered Old Papa's mirth back in the mall, which made him see

* These images, portraits of a boy and a girl, are standard in Cameroonian living rooms. Since the painter is unknown, no royalties are paid.

the ridiculousness of his own thoughts. He burst out laughing. What really made him laugh were the words he'd said, "the country back home."

All the funny stories of his ten American years paraded through his mind.

6

His conversations with Aunt Mensa' were more than just a welcome relief. One day by Skype, the next by Messenger or WhatsApp. Everyone thought of Mensa' as "Grandma Skype." Marie knew her only as an image on a computer screen. A grandmother without a body, without bones, discarnate: A Voice. It wasn't important to know where she lived, because she was really more of a guardian angel, somewhere up in the clouds, near the sun, in the ether. Sometimes the son compared her vitality to his father's, and each time the thought made him cover his face with his hands, because the woman was still as lively as an adolescent.

"Mama," he always said, "please ask Grandfather not to turn off his phone."

Yes, it was that bad, ridiculous.

"You still haven't called Marianne."

"Of course I have."

Mensa' lived in Yaounde, in the neighborhood of Melen. She was Tanou's aunt. She was a widow, and had been married three times. Each of her marriages, after the one to "the Deputy" (because no one even dared mention his infamous name), had produced children, and each had plunged her further down the social ladder, as was obvious from the turbulent noise of the marketplace always present in the background of their conversations. And yet she was categorical: "I don't like Bangangte," and she said so repeatedly.

"Hello, Grandmother."

"Ah, my little one."

Marie picked up the laptop.

"Marie," her mother scolded, "be respectful."

"I want to talk to my little one."

"Grandmother," Marie said, "Papa never lets me use his computer."

"Is that true?"

"Yes."

"Call him here, then."

Marie called her father, who took back the computer. Mensa' was already talking about something else, as Marie looked on somberly.

"Tanou," she said, "you're taking good care of your father, yes? You know, he doesn't eat much."

"Grandmother," Marie insisted, "tell him to give me his computer."

"I will, I will," Tanou interjected.

Just a little earlier, Old Papa had said on the phone that he'd eaten *baguettes*, which had scandalized everyone.

"Don't you cook anything?" Mensa' asked.

Tanou's wife did most of the cooking, and too often saw the fruits of her efforts—which came after a hard day at work—tossed into the garbage. But no one in the house expressed their exasperation about it as much as the son, who took it personally, who always took everything personally. As if he wanted to prove something, to show his Old Papa not just all that the country had to offer but his own success. So all he would eat was *baguettes*?

"I was very surprised to find that they have baguettes here," Old Papa had said.

Because his son had asked.

"Papa, tell Mensa' that you are doing well here, because it's the truth. Tell her that you have everything you need, that we're taking very good care of you. Tell her that this country has everything, that no one is dying of hunger, tell her what's really going on."

There were so many things he could talk about: visits to New York, Philadelphia, and so many other places; the Statue of Liberty, the bright lights of Times Square, the statue of Rocky; and their walks around the mall as they waited for the stores to open, because he was too impatient to wait, in a hurry to buy more razor blades ("Who even uses them anymore, Papa?" "Your Old Papa of course"); his discovery of men his age who walked for exercise; the eight-lane highways; so much that was actually interesting—so why "baguettes"?

Even Grandmother was surprised.

"All you're eating there is *bread*?"

Then a cousin took advantage of the generalized shock and the protests from the mistress of the house to interrupt:

"Uncle, hello . . . Bread, really?"

Tanou couldn't escape.

"Hello, Bagam."

Bagam, then twenty years old, had become one of Mensa''s seven children.

"You haven't forgotten about me, have you?"

Bagam took over the computer, his face filling the whole screen from then on. How to sum up several months in a few sentences, all the while carefully avoiding words that might offend? This was the tête-à-tête Tanou had hoped to avoid.

"Let me finish up with Mensa'," he said, already on the defensive. "Did I promise you anything?"

"Of course you did, don't you remember?"

"Go on, remind me."

"My application."

"What application?"

From somewhere behind him, Tanou's wife whispered something in his ear.

"Just a second," he told his nephew.

"Bagam sent me his application for your university. I forwarded it to you a few weeks ago. Are you still using your Gmail account?"

"Oh, I see, I see," he said.

"Hello, Auntie!" said Bagam.

"Hello, Bagam."

These multiple threads of crisscrossed conversations, this traffic jam of mixed-up plots.

"How are things at the university?"

"It's awful, everything is awful here."

"Everything in Cameroon can't be awful," Tanou interrupted. "That's impossible."

"You don't live here."

"You're right about that."

"Let him talk," the wife insisted.

"Biya* is screwing everything up," Bagam said. "This country has gone down the drain—it's in the *watarout*."

Tanou agreed with him, "A young man can't fight the battles of his parents and grandparents on his own," but they weren't going to open up the floor for political debate in the middle of the virtual family council. Still, Tanou had to admit that of all his cousins, Bagam was the one he understood the best.

"You know I keep up on everything that's happening there," Tanou reminded him, "twenty-four hours a day."

"Facebook."

They were "friends," and Tanou always read Bagam's highly charged posts on the internet. He didn't say it, but he relied on "Little Papa's" posts—that's what everyone called him—to keep up with what was really going on in the country.

"How are you kids?"

That was Mensa''s voice.

"Everything's fine, Mama," said the wife. "When are you coming to visit us?"

"I see already how you are taking care of *mon beau*!"

After all these years, she still said *mon beau* in French.

"Papa," said the wife, "are we taking good care of you?"

"Excellent! Excellent! Yesterday we even ate . . . what was it we ate yesterday?"

* Paul Biya, who in 2018 was still president of Cameroon.

Everyone burst out laughing. Yesterday, that was in the past. Now it was getting to be dinnertime. Only one person was worried about what to make for dinner, and she muttered something about "gender relations." There was a knock at the door. Tanou went to open it and found Céline, smiling and holding out a small envelope.

"For Sakio."

He went back to the living room and handed it to his father. He fixed his curious eyes on Old Papa, who just stared at the envelope, front and back, without opening it. The son couldn't ask what was going on, because the conversation just kept on going. Everybody had to chime in, show their face in front of the camera, tell some little bit of their life, the hidden details of their day-to-day. Soon he was caught up in this unpredictable back-and-forth. Even if it was just to repeat himself, to hear himself saying what had already been said. Responsibilities, promises, words from long ago, things close at hand and forgotten, all the typical family banter. Old Papa was clearly distracted; he was looking at his children, answering questions here and there with a "Yes, everything is fine," or a "Tanou will take care of it," but adding nothing more.

One week later, they were headed to Fredericksburg, in Pennsylvania, to see a reenactment of a battle from the Civil War.

7

Grandfather had arrived in the United States in 2013 after a series of very hard months. It had started when he retired from the hospital in Bangwa. He had thought a lot about it beforehand, but it still hit him like a ton of bricks. He had gotten out of bed, as if nothing had changed, put on his nurse's smock, and left the house. Yet he didn't head back to the hospital, because his ears were still ringing with the sounds of the farewell party his colleagues, all younger than he, had thrown for him. No, he simply kept putting one foot in front of the other, as if nothing had changed; he walked down the paved road all the way to Bangangte, just as usual. There he went to his wife's family's home, where he found a group of women—cousins, really—and nephews. Then one of them called Ngountchou.

Once back in Bangwa, he seemed stunned. He went into his room, covered his face with his hands, and then tears flowed down his cheeks. That was when Ngountchou realized how much his career as a nurse had defined him. She tried not to upset him and even accepted that he wore his smock around the house from time to time. Only the neighbors, looking on from a distance, found it amusing. She waited a while before telling Tanou that he needed to do something for his father. Grandfather hadn't said anything when Tanou had called and asked him what he planned to do now that he was retired. Just a heavy silence, which made the son think that they'd been disconnected. That was before the Nokia. They would call on their neighbor's phone.

"Are you there, Papa?"

"What do you plan to do?" was too weighty a question for that man whom the hospital had thanked and sent off to pasture; and too similar to the question Tanou asked his students. They would stammer something in response, but his father, he just stayed silent. Ngountchou hadn't told Tanou about Old Papa taking walks dressed in his nurse's uniform. He hadn't understood how serious it was, that for his father retirement was a leap into the unknown, even if he tried to suggest a few things he could do. What he'd really noticed was that Nithap Sr. didn't want to just sit and do nothing, like his friends.

"Trowel just stays at home," his father muttered.

Trowel was one of Old Papa's childhood friends. He'd earned his nickname because, in addition to being a nurse, he was a mason. He had retired from the hospital two years before Nithap, and curiously, he had stopped working as a mason at the same time. It was as if he couldn't do one without the other. Now even routine repairs around the house were left to others.

"I have worked too long in my life," Trowel said, "it's time for me to rest."

As for Nithap, he didn't want to rest, and his excursion the day after his retirement—all dressed up for work, as if nothing had changed—was proof of it. He didn't want his life to change. He was ready to keep up with his routine, even if it was an illusion. The idea that he might open a bar came from Ngountchou, who wasn't afraid he would sink into dementia, but rather wanted to put an end to the bad mood caused by his inactivity. What she didn't need, and all her children agreed, Tanou first among them, was to end up divorced.

"Not at this age," she said.

There was one clear consequence of his inactivity: nonstop complaining.

"He criticizes everything."

Nothing was right, as far as he was concerned. If one of his grandchildren swept the courtyard, as soon as the job was done he'd get up, take the broom, and sweep it himself. Sometimes, as he walked by the clothesline, he'd quickly readjust the sheets and dresses hanging there to dry. There were so many examples, but all of them irked Ngountchou, who, for some time now, had been forced to slow down because of Old Papa's declining health, sometimes spending whole days sitting on the veranda. From the stoop, she'd watch her husband rearrange their well-ordered world, straighten up things that were already in place. The truth is that in all of their married life, they'd never spent a whole day together, and suddenly the perspective of doing nothing but that until death do them part seemed like hell.

Ngountchou's first reaction to the avalanche of criticism from Old Papa had been to go spend a few days in Yaounde, at her sister's, days that soon became weeks and then months. Her illness gave her the excuse she needed: "My heart."

"I don't understand," her husband said. "Why don't you continue your treatment at the hospital in Bangwa?"

He couldn't understand. Had he ever understood his wife? Had he ever even listened to her?

"Mensa' will take care of me."

That was a stinging critique, one that Nithap didn't hear. She came back to Bangwa a month later. He was no longer so critical, having refocused his attention on the eight o'clock news on CRTV and on his *Mandjo** (which only met once a month, on the first Saturday), which meant that his whole day was organized around, and only found its meaning, at eight o'clock at night. That just wasn't enough: any sane person would lose their mind if they spent their days with such a man. Ngountchou went back to her sister's, and that was before he developed a morbid interest and decided to invest his pension in a funeral home; before he started calling his contacts at the hospital to help get his name out to the families of the deceased. "Just hand out my business card," he said to his young former colleagues, "that's all." He'd had cards printed:

---

* A mutual-aid association among the Bangangtes, composed mostly of men, and different from the *tontine*, or *nshe'de*, which is made of primarily women and poorer people.

EVERYTHING YOU NEED FOR FUNERALS

Sakio Nithap, licensed nurse, retired
Formerly on staff at the Bangwa Hospital
Services include: tarpaulin, drinks, chairs, etc.

Contact: 67326734

"Death is the biggest business going in this town!" now said the man who'd spent his life trying to keep it at bay.

"Is that true?"

"All you have to do is sit and watch the street." And that's what he did, alongside the cigarette vendor who filled his days with the chatter his wife refused to provide. "All you see going by are coffins and more coffins."

"The dead, they come from all over, that's for sure."

"And all of them come back to Bangwa."

"This one from Paris."

"Another from Libreville."

"Do you know where the dead man came from the other day?"

"Which day?"

"Oh, I remember. From China."

"Going all the way to China, just to die."

"And then coming back to Bangwa, just to be buried."

Ngountchou wasn't there to listen to him anymore. How could she have known he'd pick up the trade of burying people? The one taking care of her was Bagam, her "nephew," a student at the University of Yaounde; she'd nicknamed him Little Papa, because in every little detail, he reminded her of her father.

8

Bagam was just one of Léonard's nicknames; his friends also called him "Prez." He was clearly in charge of his group and bossed everyone around. A trim young man, with a quick wit and a way with words, always wearing tight jeans and a T-shirt adorned with the face of some pop singer, as was the fashion of the day. On this specific day he wore a T-shirt with the picture of a band, X-Maleya. He studied physics, but you'd never have guessed, because what took up his days was organizing. There was the League for the Defense of Students' Rights, of which he'd been secretary general twice, until he ran into a clause about term limits: one could serve no more than two terms, "to set a good example." But most importantly, there was the Bagam Student Association; he was its president. Actually, he'd founded it with just three members after a visit from his aunt and because of his relationship to Pastor Elie Tbongo.

Bagam's involvement in those groups didn't give him power, it just made it official: he was a born leader. Calling him "Prez" was the consecration of his activism, even if, according to his aunt Ngountchou, Little Papa's vitality was proof that her father's spirit was reincarnated in him. One day, when he was helping her wash her dresses (a task that the nephews were always eager to take on, although less out of duty or respect for this woman, who'd been injured in an accident when the car she was in had rolled over on the road from Bazou, than because they hoped to find a few forgotten bills among her things), Bagam had found some papers on which illegible signs had been scribbled. Illegible to him, perhaps, but once he showed them to his aunt, her lips opened in a confident smile.

"What is this?" he asked.

Ngountchou had thought for a moment, then said, "A letter from your grandfather."

"A letter?"

The eyes of the young man who hadn't yet become the Prez, who hadn't yet become Bagam, opened wide as he stared at those figures that would transform his life, metamorphose his spirit, and reshape his relationship with Ngountchou.

Translation: *The toad who wanders will have nothing.*

It was enough to turn the young man into the mother's pupil, to make him sit by her feet during each of her visits, his eyes fixed on the puzzle of symbols he couldn't decode, but that Ngountchou—carefully posing a finger on each one in turn, the hesitancy of her fingers recalling the certainty of a distant voice—brought to life as captivating phrases.

"Grandfather wrote this?"

There in the courtyard where they sat, the wind swathed them in silence, muting the sounds of the marketplace, which until then had been for him just noise, and created a space for what would become their ritual: Bagam sitting at the feet of the temple. This ritual, which he described as his "new birth," would take him back to the hills of western Cameroon, would make him empty Pastor Elie Tbongo's blackened trunks, spreading out at his feet piles of parchments, documents covered in dust, some nibbled away by cockroaches or by fire; he'd look up at the sky and hit his own forehead, expressing the surprise of a man who suddenly realizes the extent of his folly, even as he swears that he'll find the strength, the power, to transform these seeds into knowledge.

Bagam discovered his name at the same time as his vocation as an organizer. What he really needed to do was to tell the world—which, like this marketplace, shouted in order to silence intimate truths, bellowed so as to leave what really mattered unspoken, and roared only to remain speechless about the heart of the matter—he needed to tell this distracted world that there was a treasure hidden in the depths of the poor neighborhoods, in the miasmas of their colorless existence. The best way to do it was to create alliances among young people, to teach them to march, if necessary, to show them the way to this archive hidden beneath the *kaba ngondo* of an old mama, stashed in the bottom of an old man's trunk, and in signs drawn with arabesques. He needed to shed light on these scribblings that fools knew nothing about. So Bagam sat there to encourage others to sit; he began his studies, unsure of where they would lead, in order to school his friends, whom he had no trouble making his disciples. Obviously, this was before he got a Facebook account and found hundreds, and then thousands, of followers. Salomon Nithap was just one of the followers of the enigmatically named page, Bagam, even though it was telling his own story, his family's story.

Following Bagam allowed Tanou to keep up on his nephew's intellectual evolution, as well as the news of the country. What didn't appear in its posts, however, because the page wasn't private, was news about family, the little details about what was going on in Bangangte that Tanou was dying to know, especially since his father's retirement. What else didn't appear were the circumstances surrounding his mother's death. On that fateful day, Bagam had replaced his profile picture with a simple black square, which led to many questions posted in the comments and, after he added the words "The Mater is no more," to many RIPs. It was on the phone that he gave his perplexed uncle the details of the death of the woman who would always ask her son, each time they spoke, to "bring your cousin over."

"He's really quite smart," she'd say, using her most insistent voice, "but he has no future in this country."

Old Papa joined in as well, as we know.

Later, much later, the professor finally understood that this was the only way Ngountchou had to preserve her father's memory from oblivion. Finding among the fifteen or so grandchildren of Elie Tbongo one who was his mirror image, that is what had brought to Ngountchou's lips the smile Bagam saw the day he spread out before her the scribbled words that were going to transform his life. On that fateful Friday, however, what he saw on Ngountchou's face was something other than a moment of illumination. It was the emptiness of a gaze that was searching for something within itself, that got lost and hesitated, then got lost again, even as the mother's hands and feet moved about in all directions. The young man with thousands of Facebook friends, the president of many associations, the charismatic leader, was standing there alone when his aunt had a heart attack.

He trembled.

On the phone later, Tanou asked him to calm down and describe everything that had happened.

"She was coming back from the hospital."

"What do you mean?"

"I took her there myself. She got up early that morning, complaining about chest pain."

"What sort of pain?"

"A weight. Her right arm, on the side where she'd broken her shoulder blade in that car accident, was really hurting."

Tanou didn't understand.

"Her chest or her shoulder?"

"Listen, Uncle. I'm just telling you what she told me. It was so painful she couldn't even take her bath."

Taking a bath meant getting a bucketful of water and using a cup to pour it, since the water had been cut in the neighborhood quite a while back.

Skype cut in to ask if he wanted to replenish his account, to add $20, but with his eyes filled with tears, he hadn't noticed. He always added to it in small amounts, to keep some control over his phone bill, because even if the expenses, which really weren't that high, were necessary to keep the connection alive with his far-flung family, he was convinced that phone bills were a luxury, "like throwing money into the river," an opinion he shared with his parents, who only answered, "Things are okay," each time he asked them to tell him about their lives.

"This is too expensive," Ngountchou would say. "You shouldn't spend all your money on the phone!"

And that let him play Mister Magnanimous about the price of the spoken word.

"Mama, it's barely the cost of a meal."

"Precisely, use that money to feed my baby."

She was talking about Marie.

"Tell me," Tanou said to Bagam, still in disbelief, as tears filled his eyes.

But the line had been cut. He refilled his account.

"It's me."

"Yes, I was saying, we went to the hospital together."

"And what did the doctor there say?"

"Nothing."

"Nothing?"

"He gave her a few painkillers. A few standard pills. Acetaminophen, and stuff like that. You know that Ngountchou didn't like to take medicine."

The obstinacy of old folks!

"Wait, is it that she didn't take the medicine or that the doctor didn't really examine her or give her the right diagnosis?"

"I'm just adding that in."

Don't add anything, Little Papa. Just tell it like it was.

"We waited three hours at the hospital."

Three hours!

"And the doctor barely looked at her. In fact, it wasn't really a doctor, but a young guy. You know, now if you go to the hospital in Yaounde, all you see are interns from the medical school."

"So he was an intern?"

Tanou saw the images, those viral images of a woman who, tired of waiting at the door of the hospital for her dying sister to see a doctor, had taken a knife and cut open her sister's belly to free the baby she was carrying; once she was holding the dead body of the infant in her hands, dripping with blood, she had cried out again, her pain-stricken voice amplified by the cries of the horrified crowd gathered around her, "Doctor! Doctor!" Only then had the physician come out from hiding.

"The intern, you mean?"

"That's what he seemed like to me. He's the one who wrote the prescription. But we'd barely gotten back home when Ngountchou said she needed to sit down. We came across the courtyard. I was holding her hand so she wouldn't fall. Her face was dripping with sweat and she was breathing really fast. I ran to the living room and got a chair. I had her sit down right in the doorway. The house was empty. Mensa' was at the market, you know, and the kids were already at school."

By "the kids," he meant Mensa''s three small grandchildren, whose parents had left them at the maternal compound so they could continue on with their private little war, "their brawls," which hadn't yet resulted in a divorce. Tanou was furious. "That's what's making your mama sick"; she wasn't used to taking care of little kids anymore, and besides, "It's not up to her to raise your children, good god!" "It's none of your business": Mensa' had been quite categorical about it. She knew how to protect her little family when she needed to. "You talk to them," said Little Papa, "talk to them yourself."

Little Papa was the gossip in the family, the point of connection for so many conversations that would have been impossible without him, the one who filled the role that, due to his absence, Tanou failed to fill: the role of the son, the heir. Tanou sighed, relieved that at least the attack hadn't occurred in front of the little kids, the oldest of whom, a precocious little boy, was a bit younger than Marie. He never had anything to say to his other cousin, the kids' mother, during those family conversations via Skype, despite everyone's prompting.

"Why didn't you go back to the hospital?"

"And leave her there?"

"No, with her, of course." He grew insistent. "*Why didn't you go back there?*"

"Wait. We didn't know it was that serious. I thought it would be just like the other times."

"The other times?"

His Skype account was empty again.

"Do you want to switch to Messenger?"

He'd forgotten about that option.

9

Your parents' health is a topic that just doesn't work over Skype. "Things are okay": such was the leitmotif repeated in each of the conversations he'd had with Ngountchou in recent years. "How are you doing, Mama?" "Things are okay." Obviously, the son didn't want her to go into all the details about how her feet were growing heavy, how horribly her shoulder blade ached, how the arrhythmia of her heart sometimes made her sit down on the closest seat at hand, on a rock, a crate, whatever, to catch her breath. The doctor in Bangwa, whom her husband had insisted she see, had told her not to drink ice-cold water, but, "What does that young doctor know?"

So she kept on drinking the forbidden water, "It calms me down"; she'd breathe in and out, her body shivering, covered in goose bumps, while her lungs gasped, valves opening as if powered by a pump. Had she started to tell him about her symptoms, he would have immediately asked if his father knew about it.

"I've had this illness for fifteen years."

"Mama, that was the car accident."

"What does that change?"

"Nothing, exactly. But after fifteen years of treating yourself, it's no surprise that things haven't changed."

"Tanou, don't forget that your father is a nurse."

If Nithap's knowledge had come up short in treating his wife's case, it wasn't because he hadn't tried. He had massaged her when she'd asked, given her shots, all the while putting up with her bad moods that were exacerbated by the pain. He had also prescribed her first rounds of antibiotics—chloramphenicol, of course—but nothing that really addressed the problems that stemmed from that car accident she'd been in. The overloaded pickup truck, swerving to avoid a car that was racing down the dirt road, had fallen into a ravine, the weight of its load causing it to roll over twice; two passengers didn't make it out alive, even though the driver came through without a scratch.

Ngountchou, happy just to have survived, had put her fate into God's hands, rather than going to the hospital in Bangwa, even though that's where her husband worked. But the body has its own ways of making its needs known, as each of us is aware. The survivor's nights soon became excruciating, she had trouble moving around. Her refrain of "Things are okay" rang hollow, with a sharp edge that hinted at a buried secret. To understand what was going on, Tanou tried to get her appointments with doctors in the capital, but she refused, once again expressing confidence in the hospital in Bangwa, and especially in her husband's care—after all, he'd been by her side her whole life, "he's really my doctor." It was a vicious cycle that not even the suggestion that she come to the United States to see a real expert had broken: in 2009 the embassy refused to grant her the visa she needed. "They knew she was going to die," Marianne would say. The son decided to get his citizenship to avoid a second refusal—"They aren't going to deny a visa to a fellow American"—but his passport had arrived too late to save his mama.

There are moments when you feel alone in the world; that's just how Bagam felt when his aunt was suddenly wracked by convulsions, "like an epileptic seizure." He saw her fall to the ground, her eyes losing focus, her tongue twisting in her mouth. By some reflex he rushed to the kitchen and came back with a wooden spoon that he put between Ngountchou's teeth, "so she wouldn't swallow her tongue." Outside, all around the house, market stands were opening for business. Some vendors had even set up a used-clothes stand in front of the home's door. That's who the young man rushed to for help. A long-standing dispute had them at odds with Mensa', who didn't want them to "flood" the front of the house and told them so, gently, each time they set up, reminding them about the rules of good neighbors, but that was just like asking the rain not to flow down the street in a storm. They called Mensa' "*nocre mamang*"* and would apologize, only to start up again the next day, for where else could they go? When Bagam called out to them, they immediately thought of her.

"*Nocre mère?*"

They carried Ngountchou in their muscular arms, stepping over the multicolored displays, and passing the frightened women who stared, hands over their mouths, crying, "Woyoooo!" or asking what had happened, "Is it the mother?" "No, it's her sister," "Her sister?" They put her in a taxi. One of them climbed in beside her, while Bagam, sitting up front, gestured wildly and shouted in panic to the other drivers to clear the way.

"Ambulance! Ambulance!"

He cried out when what he wanted was to be a siren. It was possible that Ngountchou was already dead there in the taxi. It was possible that she had actually died back in the courtyard of the house, when, as Bagam tried to put the spoon between her teeth, he heard her spit out several times a word he couldn't understand; at first he thought it was "Ngou," or "Toungou," but it might also have been "Tongolo." Once at the emergency room in the Cité Verte hospital, even if they had seen Ngountchou immediately, all they could do was pronounce her dead. When the doctor asked Bagam—who stood there, surrounded by the young men who'd tried to help, almost all about his age, some with their hair cut in bushy crests, others not even combed, wearing jeans and soccer jerseys, all with pained expressions and eyes wide open in disbelief—if the "deceased" was his mother, instead of pulling out a cigarette that he didn't have, since he wasn't a smoker, lighting it, and taking deep drags to calm

* A Camfranglais expression used by young people in the city: *nocre* instead of *notre* (our), *mamang* for *maman* (mama); other common expressions include *nor* for *non* (no), and *mouf*, for the English *move*, as well as *ashouka ngangali*, a smart aleck's expression of indifference.

his trembling hands, he had posted a message on Facebook that would, he thought, let "everyone" know, that would bring the family on the double, to put their arms around his shoulders and hug him tight in this swirling chaos. "The Mater is no more," the phrase had popped up on his uncle's screen, there in the United States, with a beep.

Bagam's phone immediately started to vibrate.

"What's going on?"

It was Tanou.

"How did you know?" the stunned young man asked.

Because he was the first to learn of his mama's death, because he had learned at almost the very moment that her soul passed, Tanou didn't have a chance to blame himself for not being there at the crucial moments that led up to this crisis, and that his cousin would go on to describe for him. Her loss had spawned in him a drive, an almost tyrannical need to know everything, to have what had happened in those final moments described down to the smallest detail, as if once he could see it perfectly, he'd be able to erase it. He was the one who'd alerted the rest of the family, even as he continued squeezing Bagam like an orange for ever more details of his mother's last moments. He'd been the one to tell Nithap, who was back in Bangwa, leaving Old Papa surprised like everyone else that he was hearing about what happened in Yaounde on a call from New York!

Let's not forget what happened with Marianne, who was in a taxi in the middle of Yaounde when she heard the news. "I was on my way to pay them a visit!"

"It happened really fast!" Tanou said, parrying the accusation that he'd kept the news from her.

When bad news hit, Marianne was just criticisms and more criticisms.

"Little Papa could *at least* have called me!"

"I'm sure he just didn't have a chance, Ma'," Tanou tried to explain. "When I called him, he was caught off guard."

"Even just a text from the hospital, if he didn't have time to call."

"How could he do that?"

"Well, he posted it to Facebook."

A guilty conscience is expressed in the strangest of ways, but who wouldn't have felt like that when faced with their mother's death? Marianne Tbongo was Tanou's cousin, his sister, the one he was closest to; they'd always been able to pick up their conversation right where they'd left it, starting back in their shared childhood, in the dust of Bangwa, where she was the one who'd transmit orders from the Pater or the Mater—Nithap could speak to his children only in orders, and he didn't hesitate to lift his switch when it came to Tanou, who'd been the most difficult of them. After the spanking, he'd send in Marianne, who was a bit older. "Go tell *your brother* that what he did wasn't right, but that he can go back out and play now." "*Mouf!*" Tanou would of course reply, when Marianne did come find him. Still, he'd head right back out to play, wiping a tear from his cheek. She was different from his brothers, who were more likely to reply with a taunt, "*Ashouka ngangali*," and that was what had cemented their complicity. They were kindred spirits in that large family, whose tentacles spread throughout Facebook's stratosphere, which is why the cousin was left speechless when he heard the real irritation coming through the voice on the other end of the line.

Three days later Tanou was back in Yaounde, standing in front of Marianne, who, there in the courtyard that had been the scene of the tragedy, was busy making all the funeral arrangements; "Her body is at the morgue," "Yes, of course!" He had forgotten that he really didn't need to rush home. "Some people won't get here until months later! Especially the ones coming from Paris." He stood before his father, who still couldn't wrap his mind around it and had sunk into a deep silence, a silence he did not yet see as an enigma, and before Mensa'. She was disconsolate at the thought that she was now truly alone.

"Who am I going to live with now?"

"We are here," his father said, "but, ah, Tanou, just try to explain that to Grandmother, whose sister was almost like her twin!" His words were meant to bring consolation, but they were comical, really, when right in front of him Tanou could see the brutal reality of the emptiness left behind in his aunt's heaving chest, in and out, in and out, straining less to release a sob than to release a poignant song: the song of filial abandonment. Tanou had come alone, without his wife and without Marie. "Why?" Marianne had asked. "Do you know I've never even seen your wife or your child?"

He didn't have the presence of mind to feel guilty about their absence, although during the funeral he realized that he, too, needed an arm to hold him up, a voice with an extra word of kindness, when he felt the full weight of his mother's death fall on his shoulders. The thumping of his heart didn't give him the time to linger beside her and catch his breath, as he saw her spread out, naked and ice-cold. Rather than falling into silence, like his father; rather than wearing himself out with funeral preparations, like his sister; dissolving into tears, like his aunt; or growing indignant, like those distant cousins who insisted on using spoons when they were mourning, because, according to Marianne, "they don't have flatware at home," and "they're going to steal everything they can afterward," he had retraced the path his mother had taken just before her death. With Bagam, he'd gone back to the hospital, to the office in front of which his mother had waited for three hours. Soon he stood before the doctor himself.

"It's about the case of Madame Nithap Margarèthe?"

The man leafed through a grimy notebook, while the television behind him played clips of women dancing suggestively, shaking their hips in obscene gyrations that clearly suggested coitus, *nyak*, *nyak*, *nyak*.*

"Wait, I'm not the one who admitted her. When did you say she died?"

"Monday."

"Ah, Monday!"

And his eyes went blank, lost in a scene that was playing on an endless loop in his mind. He asked Tanou and Bagam to wait outside, "just for a moment, gentlemen." When the two were brought back into his

* Dear reader, between you and me, does the Narrator really have to translate what is implied by this overly explicit onomatopoeia?

office fifteen minutes later, the doctor had a young man with him. "That's him," Bagam said, growing agitated, "it's him." As his cousin squared his shoulders, clenched his fists, and took on a defensive posture, the assistant's eyes narrowed, sinking back into his head. His voice trembled while he tried to put together the words they were waiting for, "Yes, I'm the one who admitted your mother."

Nothing that happened after that in the office—and strictly speaking, nothing happened at all besides attempts to cover things up and to stifle anger; there were parries on the one hand and shots that missed their mark on the other—nothing was able to convince Tanou that his mother hadn't just been simply and truly assassinated in the hospital.

"They are criminals," he'd always say afterward, "those doctors are nothing but criminals."

He had thought about filing a complaint. "Against whom?" Marianne had asked, especially since none of the doctors involved had been willing to give him their name. "Against Cameroon, if need be," he replied. "Against Biya, why not?" But the reality of what a trial would entail had dissuaded him; he'd have to stay in the country to push it through, and, despite the pleasure he found in waking up in a hotel bed, without being chased out of it by little Marie, he wasn't prepared to go through all that for Ngountchou, *bei aller Liebe*.*

* Despite all our love.

10

Had someone told Old Papa that he'd built up his funeral business just for his own wife's burial, he wouldn't have believed it. And yet his business had relieved Tanou from a task that would have been the end of him, leaving him instead just that one job that everyone around assigned to "the American": paying the bills. There was, for example, a certain Ntchankou', a distant cousin of his mother's, who had danced the *nkwa* for him, had taken him in her arms after reciting his thirty-eight *ndaps*, then intoned a praise song in honor of the legendary Mven Tchabou, and finally gestured as if to offer him her breast. She said how happy she was to see him again. He escaped after handing over a few bills. Maybe she did love him, but she had also called him "the American." Perhaps that's why, before he left the country, he let his cousin drag him back to the footpaths of the university campus, where twenty years before he had been a student. Bagam wanted to introduce him to some of his friends, the ones who worked with him to rile up the campus, the same ones who called him "Prez," and who were collectively known as the "Sinistrés," in honor of the Maquisards who fought in the civil war.

It was impossible to be unimpressed by the organizing they'd done, even if it was out of sync with the décor of the place that served as their "HQ," and here Tanou thought of his American students, who used the same term with a similar level of bombast. Tanou quickly realized that he'd gotten there too early, even if he'd arrived right at the time the Sinistrés had set. His cousin was the only one waiting in front of the bar,

L'Étudiant; Bagam seemed quite nervous, but who wouldn't have been? Still, Tanou suggested a few times that they give up on his plan.

"No," his young cousin insisted, "my friends want to hear what you have to say."

Was it true? He was already getting ready to leave when one of them finally arrived, practically sauntering in, wearing sandals and carrying a copy of *The Wretched of the Earth*.

He looked like he'd just rolled out of bed, nothing like the image Tanou had of a young man coming to the HQ to give speeches inspired by his readings. "*Each generation must, out of relative obscurity, discover its mission, fulfill or betray it . . .*" Nor did he have the face of a faithful reader of those grimy books with dog-eared pages that sat in a pile on a table in the corner, Cheikh Anta Diop, Um Nyobè, Samir Amin, Mbembe, one of which Tanou, ever the professor, had picked up out of habit. Foucault's *History of Sexuality*. He had started leafing through a book to pass the time, but also to avoid his cousin's embarrassment, as he hesitated between waiting there and going off to find his friends—to drag them out of bed, Tanou thought. Actually, he wasn't just leafing through the book, but turning quickly to the passages he knew by heart, because they provided the theoretical frame for his doctoral thesis. He began to read softly to himself, nodding his head.

"This is Comrade Émile," Bagam said to get his attention. He introduced the young man, whose features Tanou couldn't quite make out in the shadows. "He's our bookkeeper."

Émile held out his hand for Tanou to shake, and then went to sit down, his eyes buried in his own book.

"This is my big brother," Bagam continued, and Émile, either sleepy or distracted, nodded his head in acknowledgment.

"Hello, grand prof."

He turned right back to his book. Soon a snore was heard coming over the pages, and Tanou and Bagam exchanged identical smiles. *My favorite cousin*, the elder thought, and the same words certainly ran through the younger one's mind at the same time, as they both assessed the ridiculousness of the scene. Yet as Tanou was about to stand up, lively voices and laughs were heard in the hallway, and a dozen young people crowded into the room.

"Prez," one of them said, "we missed you at the meeting."

As he shook the slender hands, one after the other, Tanou heard several of them call him "grand prof."

"Don't tell me you don't have a watch," he began, but paused to take the iPad one of the students handed him. "Maybe we should start with introductions?"

"We'll get there."

The student who spoke, about twenty years old, wearing dark jeans and a checkered shirt, took the iPad from Tanou, who was a little lost in all the hubbub, and opened it up to a page with a big headline:

"Cameroonian Man Strangles His Child in Connecticut."

Tanou scanned the article quickly. The story was about a man who very well might have been one of his former classmates at the university where they now stood. He handed the device back and the student passed it along to another curious hand, one belonging to a young woman, who had called the guy with the iPad "Um." "Um, let me see, too, *nor*?" she'd said.

Many faces crowded around her.

"I've been following this story," Tanou said, his eyes pausing on the girl, on her chest. "It's awful."

Horror was written on each of their faces as they read the story, reflected in the flash of their eyes.

"*Akié*," the girl exclaimed.

"Is that what you want us to talk about?" Tanou asked, turning to his cousin, who also looked shocked, and to Um.

"Not necessarily, grand prof," the young man replied, "but it does point to *something*, doesn't it?"

"To what, do you say?"

Tanou couldn't help thinking about the line that, little by little, was coming into view, and that linked the names of each of these students in an extravagant display. They had all taken the names of leaders of the

Maquis, fighters in the resistance during the civil war. When a young man with a haircut like a cock's crest, who was practically grinding against the young woman's hips, piped up to say that he'd like to know why the United States was such a violent country and then introduced himself as "Moumié," Tanou cut him off.

"Are you joking?"

He turned toward his cousin.

"Why didn't you pick a name like your friends did?"

"What do you mean?"

"I mean . . ." He was searching for the right words, and didn't realize his gaffe until what popped into his head was out of his mouth and had made everyone there burst out laughing, including Comrade Émile, who finally put down his book and laughed heartily. "I mean, the name you chose is kind of *tribal*, no?"

This conversation was going nowhere, could lead only to more misunderstandings, the professor said to himself. He thought he should make an excuse and leave right then, say that he needed to meet Marianne, whom he hadn't yet visited, whose kids, his own nephews, he hadn't seen, except for at the funeral, because he'd been so busy.

"Sociological."

In Cameroon, rather than *tribal* people say *sociological.*

"Or cultural, you mean."

"If you prefer."

"Culture is the nexus of all politics," Bagam began, "and writing is its framework."

His uncle gently put down the copy of Foucault, lost for a moment in his own regrets: Being taught a lesson by his own junior, no less! Still, previous generations were wrong not to have understood that point.

"I know, I know," Tanou said, "I am one of your followers, after all."

He said that with a smile and nod of the head, as if trying to rebuild that false sense of solidarity he suddenly needed so badly. But why was that?

"The cultural wins out over the ideological."

"We're not going to start another generational battle." He tried to retreat.

"Of course we are," Bagam went on. "Cameroon holds the African Cup in Generational Battles! Just look at who holds power in this country, and for fifty years already!"

"In the penalty zone!" someone shouted.

The room was growing lively. Clearly, they were used to this sort of rhetorical jousting, although it was new to Tanou.

"Prez," someone else called out.

"Spit it out!"

Things had really changed; they were no longer talking about "class struggle." Tanou smiled, recalling the debates that, twenty years before, had pitted him against his comrades.

"I'll give you that."

"This country is a museum to the civil war."

Tanou also agreed with that. He thought back to his student years when, after a night of partying and heavy drinking in a club or somewhere, suddenly the classic insult would burst out from a corner of the room: "Your mother's ass, you idiot." And of course, then fists would fly, and even worse things would be said. Warrior culture has a history in Cameroon, he often said, the buried story of that long war. *Cameroonians have too many problems*, he thought, sucking his teeth, *tchip!*

"Is that why you all go by names from the Maquis?"

Silence. The young people all looked at each other, as if their elder, the "grand prof," had again said something stupid. One of those shared silences that adolescents break with a burst of laughter. But right then, it was the serious looks on all their young, beardless faces that he found amusing; Um replied in an equally serious tone.

"We have vowed not to leave the country," he said.

"And the names?"

"The names remind us of our promise."

Tanou sighed. He remembered his comrades from years past; they'd also taken on code names, spells to conjure their lack of power, absurd really, and they'd called each other "combatants." And yet they'd all left the country: one, Mao, was a banker in the United States, where Tanou was; another, el Che, was an insurance agent in France; and a third, Fanon, was also a professor, like him, but in Germany. The university in Yaounde, he realized, just kept on producing wave after wave of opposition members, but would this one at least have the courage of their convictions?

He'd find out all too soon. As he opened the door to his hotel room later that day, his phone rang, because he'd given his number and his Gmail address to the students.

"Grand prof," the voice said. "It's me, Um."

Thirty minutes later he found himself in Mvog Ada, across from the young man with the piercing gaze who'd pledged to stay and who turned out to be someone who dressed to impress. "What kind of beer do you want, 33 or Beaufort? Guigui? Cold or not cold?"

"Thank you, grand prof, but I don't drink beer. I live just over there," he said, waving his hand toward a poor neighborhood in the distance, revealing an impoverished background that Tanou hadn't suspected when watching him go on so just a while before. Now Um had come back to reality and asked if he could "find me a visa."

"I'm not the American embassy!" he snapped back, not missing a beat.

But since Tanou no longer had a home in Yaounde, he had lost the right to pass himself off as a local: the words *United States* were written right across his face.

"You see, I want to get out of this fucked-up country."

"Do your *comrades* know that?"

Tanou couldn't even imagine what Bagam would think of such a defection. He smiled at his own use of a term from his past: *comrade*. And yet soon he realized it was less a single defection than a landslide.

One by one the young people he'd met—who'd surprised him with the fire in their words, had made him dream, if truth be told, but also exasperated him—showed up at his hotel, a look of defeat in their eyes, unsteady on their feet, and with an unbelievable story on their lips. "Yes, grand prof, I was also sentenced to six months in prison, but the sentence was suspended." The most moving was the young girl who arrived, her lips bright red, blinking her heavily mascaraed eyes, in a tight outfit that wasn't bad, Tanou thought, and who minced no words with her offer. "Marthe," she said. "I'm Marthe."

"Marthe, were you also sentenced to jail?"

A hotel allows for certain liberties. Even though Marthe admitted that she was really looking for her "white man," he didn't even ask her what her name, her real name, actually was.

Playing the game, he said to himself as he massaged her small breasts, with little rings on each nipple, *They learn how to do that earlier than we did; that's what this country has come to. But who taught them to?*

His theory was that the *wataroutification** of Cameroon had begun with the local fritter seller, Mamy BH, who, already back in their day, used pages from the paper *Le Messager* to wrap up her wares. It was her fault, he told himself, not Foucault's, not Derrida's, and the thought amused him, even as he heard Marthe's sharp cries in his ears as his fingers probed deeply into her sex—what was he looking for? her intestines?—and a laugh began to form in the tunnel of her body. "Grand prof, did you find what you were looking for?" She grabbed hold of his penis and began to squeeze. She left Tanou gasping for breath on the bed. She must be an Eton girl, he thought, for it had been a long time since he'd felt such a whirlpool of sensations.

Maybe she faked her orgasm? he thought as he watched her head silently to the bathroom and heard the flush. *This country sucks the soul out of you.*

Soon she'd be back and would reach for her purse—earlier she had pulled condoms out of it; "I have some already," he'd said, opening the bedside drawer; "Don't trust the local condoms," he remembered the advice from his friends. "Over there, the girls poke holes in them with nee-

* The *watarout* is the sewer, so the *wataroutification* of Cameroon is the transformation of the country into a sewer, into a whorehouse. The year 1956 marks the beginning of this scabrous adventure, as a historian might put it, using their academic jargon, of course, but we understand.

dles." "Why?" "*Pour touabassi le mbenguetaire avec un mouna*"*—and she'd find the bills he'd put on the table, actual dollars, thirty, in fact, because he didn't have any more local money, and he wasn't about to use his Visa card for that. "Changed into CFA francs, it's a decent amount," he said, by way of excuse. "I'm leaving tomorrow." He was startled to see how easily the girl pocketed the money.

"How old are you?" He couldn't quite catch her mumbled reply. "Huh?"

"Eighteen."

"What do you want to study in the United States?"

"I don't know."

"Maybe it'd be good to know before you get there," he said, stroking her neck. "Don't you agree, my little kitten?"

The kitten smiled, touched by the false promise.

"Philosophy."

As she got dressed, he tried to worm a promise out of her—one he hoped she'd keep—that she wouldn't tell the Prez anything, but it was useless. She just burst out laughing. He didn't ask her what she found so funny, he didn't dare, just like he didn't dare ask which of the young men got to undress her. *Moumié? Maybe Comrade Émile? Are they better lays?* Then he imagined several of them undressing her together, there in the HQ, and smiled. *We used to do that when we were students.* Then his iPhone rang. It was Angela.

Call u bk in 10 mn, he typed.

Just enough time to say goodbye to the kitten and quickly make the bed, so the background would be appropriately sanitized for an intercontinental exchange with his wife and daughter. Only the sounds of the city remained in the background, once the room was straightened, because Skype doesn't transmit odors.

---

* Here are just a few ways to translate that phrase: "Lock down the Parisian with a baby," "Make the carrier pigeon land," "Box in the 'Merican." It would also be possible to bring a Baudelairean poem into play, "The Albatross," which would lead to "Clipping the seafaring animal's giant wings," and according to Cameroonian legend, only certain girls have that talent: Doualas and Etons.

"Baby," Angela's voice filled the room. "You haven't even told me when your flight arrives!"

"Papa!"

His daughter's voice.

"My little one!"

11

"Baby!" He heard the reproach in Angela's voice. "You just missed I-95."

Tanou was driving them to Fredericksburg and he was distracted, which, like always, led to disputes in the car and drove Marie to listen to music on her headset, which would soon lull her to sleep.

"You're going to get us into an accident."

"I'm following the GPS."

"You'd do better to follow your *head*!"

Angela had decided not to let her husband just do as he pleased, because she knew that Route 276 would bring them to 476, and then on to Route 78, across Harrisburg, which would add at least fifteen minutes to their trip. The conclusion was categorical.

"We will be late."

Tanou didn't give up so easily.

"That depends on *who* is driving."

"Say what?"

He really shouldn't have said that—it just sent the ball back into Angela's court. "You're not going to speed on these roads!"

Tanou smiled. *That's one love!*

"Of course not, baby."

"We really don't need to get a ticket."

The ping-pong of married life; it even bored Old Papa. He stared out at the snow-covered greenery that flew past on both sides of the road. Sometimes he looked at Marie, his little one, trying unsuccessfully to strike up a conversation, because she was wrapped up in a song that no one else could hear, but which had her tapping her fingers on the back of her mother's seat and occasionally humming along. And so, the car and its four monologues continued on into the depths of Pennsylvania.

"Not on a Saturday!"

It was an invitation from Céline to Nithap—*Saturday the 20th, historic reenactment of the Battle of Fredericksburg. Will you join us?*—that had gotten the family on the road. Angela found these stagings "stupid," but clearly Old Papa couldn't go by himself.

"We'll meet them there."

So, since Old Papa couldn't go on foot (the eighty-two miles that separated him from Fredericksburg were not exactly comparable to the few kilometers he walked in the fields around Pennington), and since Angela didn't want to have to take care of Marie all by herself for the weekend ("Not again"—after all, she wasn't a single mother, damn it!), a family outing was the only solution. To put some icing on the cake, or perhaps one could say to add some salt to the sauce, or even to calm the nerves of his wife, who was aggravated by his teasing, Tanou decided to tell her a story, a *really* Cameroonian story, and in English, of course.

"You never told me about your mother's funeral, and that was four years ago, you know?" Angela noted pointedly.

"Quite true!"

She hadn't yet realized the need for fiction, at least not in the way her husband was feeling it right then, by which I mean the need to find a story that would satisfy her, please her, while navigating three levels of censure: evading the ears of his father, hence the choice of telling his tale in English, and of Marie, who, happily, was wrapped up in her music—Tanou kept an eye on her in the rearview mirror to be sure of that—as well as sidestepping the most salacious of his Cameroonian stories, like, for instance, the one that made him chuckle each time he thought about it, the call he'd received when he was in bed with Marthe and the ten minutes he'd lived through in fast-forward, trying to create a sufficiently Skype-able backdrop.

"*Baby, I love you,*" he said in English.

Angela looked at him in surprise, then looked right, still surprised, and straight ahead again, no less surprised. She looked back at him again and shook her head, then smiled and stroked his thigh. English was the language of her heart, the one that both took his wife back to her roots in far-off Bali Nyonga and recalled all the years of their married life, which, with their many battles, their ups and downs, were so hard to capture with the word *love*.

"I love you too, babe."

With a smile he stepped on the gas and watched as the moments of their life together paraded by on the windshield, from their wedding when they were students to this very moment. *I won!*

Those who cannot speak of the past, the future, or the present are stuck in the moment.

"I love you."

"More than anything."

In an instant of silence, sons become their fathers without realizing it. Really, it's the daily repetition of this sort of moment that makes a marriage, that brought them together, there on the front seat of a Cherokee, him on the left, her on the right. "No, no," Old Papa had insisted, "I'd rather sit next to my little one," as if he wanted to showcase their marriage, as well as his own, which, after fifty years, had led him to the state he summed up with a word drawn from the depths of his silent sadness: *widower.*

That's the end of the story.

Filling up the days of a retired widower was as complicated as writing a novel, especially since Old Papa had always left it to his wife to organize his daily life. For Tanou, the idea of taking Ngountchou's place was more reassuring, provided that his father wasn't living in far-off Bangwa. That's the possibility that most frightened Angela. The sudden image of her father-in-law spending his days, even his weekends, surrounded by graves, terrified her. She knew that would mean reliving his wife's burial each week. No one wants to think about that, and she was ready to help her husband and her father-in-law out of that impasse. Old Papa wanted to be the master of his last days. But there was no reason to act as if that were a given.

"I love you, baby!"

Having children means voluntarily giving up the freedom to write the story of your life on your own. Tanou had not chosen to be born, as he had so often told his parents during his adolescence. Now that he was over forty, he had decided he wasn't going to allow his father to let himself die. The trip to the United States grew out of that logic; he'd made the decision when he was in the office of those two doctors whom he still blamed for killing his mother, and against whom he'd been able to do nothing. When Nithap had told him that he was having memory lapses, and fainting spells, and headaches, the son's decision was easily made: "Come get taken care of here."

They're not going to kill my father, too.

He had spent the intervening years—the four years since—getting ready: he'd become an American citizen, just to avoid the hassles that his mother had gone through and whose visa had been denied when her illness was at its worst. He was convinced, despite what Marianne thought—"All those superstitions people in Cameroon tell each other about American visas!"—that his mother had been kept from entering the United States only because the immigration officer who'd interviewed her had thought she was too weak for a long trip and concluded that she might well die midflight, thus sparing her from returning home feetfirst. She wouldn't be dead now if she'd been cared for anywhere else besides that "fucked-up country"—that was what he called Cameroon. Each and every time he thought about it, he was filled with rage.

Like everyone else, however, he had accepted that his mother was gone, and even more than everyone else in the sense that, since then, he'd taken on the role of bill-payer. In the end, there was just one simple question left floating before his eyes: *And Old Papa, what's going to become of him without her?*

Nithap thought he'd answered that question when, after several false starts, he'd finally found an activity that kept him really busy, so busy, in fact, that he'd hired a few people.

"Don't worry about it," he had tried to reassure his son. "I'm not my own grandson after all."

He was the only one who found that joke funny. But then, it wasn't really a question of money, because he was still drawing his pension from the hospital in Bangwa, and his funeral business made it possible for him to earn even more money by investing it, an investment so sure that he even asked Tanou to join in with him. "Believe me, death is a lucrative business these days." For several weeks he had been alone there in the big house in Bangwa, filling his days with his cadaverous activities, and his weekends coordinating the mourning for other people, "at those funerals that just never end," as Tanou put it. Yet one day, when he burned his hand in hot oil because he didn't know how to cook himself an egg—Ngountchou had always made his omelets—his cry was heard all the way in the United States and his son's reaction had been immediate: no more outrageously expensive phone calls and cheap "Things are okay." Down with Nokia!

I told you so, that's the message he sent to Marianne. *He can't live alone.*

What do you want me to do? Go live in Bangwa?

The old guy is very stubborn, as you know.

I know.

He could come live with you.

Silence.

But where? You still haven't seen where I live. There are only two rooms, you know. It's not like where you live.

Marianne, you don't know where I live.

So one day he took a tour of his house, phone in hand. He showed her their living room, their dining room, their bedrooms, all five of them—"For just three people!"—their bathrooms, of which there were three—"Do you like it now?"—and even the basement; he'd turned on the light so she could see all the details. "Are those bottles of wine?" "Don't worry about that." He'd even shown her the attic in detail: "This is where Old Papa will live, his bedroom, his living room, his bathroom. A studio apartment."

"Do you think I don't know where you live, how you live?"

Cameroon has changed! Tanou thought. The days from his childhood when he'd gone to spend vacations and relax in the compound of Pastor Elie Tbongo, his maternal grandfather, were long gone! He remembered the stories of people living abroad who would hire young people out of work to make monthly visits to their retired parents. And that hadn't always gone smoothly, for sometimes the distant sons were subjected to all sorts of blackmail. Sometimes their parents were abducted, as in that story he'd read in *The New York Times*, freed only after exorbitant ransoms were paid, "in dollars, if you please." The worst wasn't even those abductions but the fact that the person at the center of it all was usually the one who found the idea of having security guards ridiculous.

"Take care of me?" Old Papa had exclaimed. "Excuse me, my son, but I'll take care of myself!"

"Papa, the whites have a medical service for that."

The obstinacy that comes with old age just doesn't give a damn about the arguments put forward by children.

Nithap Sr.: "We're not living in the white men's land here."

Nithap Jr.: "Everything can change."

Nithap Sr.: "Forget about it."

Nithap Jr.: "Papa!"

"Listen, Tanou," the old man had said. "I started taking care of myself long before you were born. I'll take care of myself until the day I die."

End of discussion.

The memory loss proved a blessing. Tanou would have magnified it if he could: *It's the onset of Alzheimer's*, anything to convince his father. Since Ngountchou's death, the same conversation had been going on for years, an endless circle that had caused such turmoil between them that each time the son called, the father would barely respond, just repeating his "Things are okay" refrain, which obviously didn't reassure anyone.

When Old Papa began to complain about little things—although in reality it was Marianne who had described the lamentable state in which she'd found him in his room in Bangwa—a broad smile spread across his son's face, a very broad smile. It was time to put an end to this "escapade in Bangwa with his cadavers and his headaches," he told his sister. "The village isn't what it used to be."

Down with Nokia!

"Come get treated in the United States" was the perfect solution, and Marianne certainly wasn't against it.

"But there's the hospital here in Bangwa!"

"Papa!"

"You can't cure old age."

"Papa," Tanou interrupted, "let's not start with that again."

He invoked his mother's death.

"You know she would still be alive if she'd gotten the care she needed."

"Yes, I know."

He held back a tear and fell silent for a moment.

"Papa, are you there? Answer me! Do you hear me?"

To think she'd gone to Yaounde to die! All those years Nithap's hands had cared for her, had massaged her aching shoulders, given her the injections she needed; now they trembled as much from rage as impotence, and the son took advantage of that to reach the conclusion he'd been angling for.

"I have already made an airplane reservation."

"It's winter over there, isn't it?"

"It's August, Papa!"

"I've heard that the winters are cold, very cold. You know that I lived with the whites during the colonial era. Your mother did, too."

"I know, but you'll only be here for a while, and as soon as it gets cold, you'll head back to the old country."

It was an old, forgotten promise: On both sides of the road, Old Papa's eyes saw nothing but the white blanket of snow. He didn't complain about it, because he knew that his son wasn't responsible for all the twists and turns of his visit, its prolongation; no, the systematic dismantling of the frame of his mind, the systematic scattering of all the memories he'd stored away, that was what was shrouded in blame. More than the cold that spread an opaque layer over the window, it was his own body that he cursed. *Ah! Old age!*

12

Going back to the nineteenth century is amusing, but you still have to make do with sandwiches for sustenance. Tanou was taking a gulp of soda when his daughter grabbed his arm. Marie pointed at a cavalryman marching toward them with a rifle topped with a long bayonet strapped on his back. He seemed amused by the reaction his presence was getting, and had a childlike grin on his face. After all, everyone there had come to see people like him in action, especially the kids, who had worked themselves into a frenzy. The soldier was hungry, too, and soon headed off, a small packet in his hand, his head nodding left and right.

"He's a real star," Angela said.

"At least on this Saturday."

"Have you seen Céline?"

Her husband looked around him.

"How could I find her here?"

You could see the impatience on each and every face. Here and there you could see people looking for their friends, but it was mostly family groups. They stood huddled together, rubbing their hands to keep warm. Some couples, the man's arm wrapped around the woman, waved at people they recognized, neighbors bumping into each other. You could see the breath rising in clouds from some people's mouths, and most held a hot drink in their hands.

"We said we'd meet by the first stand."

Marie started to count.

"This is the first stand," Tanou said.

"Bob!" Angela waved her arm over her head as she moved forward, slipping between tightly packed people. "Bob! We're over here!"

At first Big seemed startled to see her, but then he headed toward her, cutting a path through the crowd.

"Off we go," Tanou said to Grandfather, who hurried after him, holding Marie by the hand. "Off we go."

"Hello, Sakio!" Bob said, after he'd kissed Angela on both cheeks, bent down to muss the hair on Marie's head, and shook Tanou's hand. "Céline is inside."

"Inside?"

"Yes, in the dressing room."

"She must be in her element," Tanou said, trying to start a conversation that everyone could join in on.

"Not really," Big answered. "She *hates* rifles."

"Me, too," Angela agreed.

Grandfather wasn't really following the conversation, or else he would have added that he had a rifle. But Marie didn't really give him the chance.

"Old Papa!" she cried out. "Look!"

Everyone turned to watch a column of cavalry making its way onto the plain, as the crowd applauded. There were about twenty of them. The horses were trotting together, forming a row, a line, seeming well trained, except for two who were a bit headstrong. The riders, waving their arms, tried to get them back under control, but even that didn't detract from the grace of their maneuver.

"That must be the first regiment."

That was going to be the rhythm of the day, watching the parade with ironic commentary from the poet. Angela pulled a brightly colored brochure out of her purse and began leafing through it. She stopped on one page, read, and then scanned the scene.

"I think they're just warming up."

"Do you mind if I sit down?" Bob asked.

He had grown weaker recently, "the illness" made him look gaunt. Tanou had overheard a couple of whispered conversations Angela had had on the phone; with a blank look on her face, she'd told him it was Céline. "Is something going on?" he'd asked. "Nothing." Tanou never insisted.

"Of course not."

Old Papa stayed standing.

"Sakio is still strong," the poet said, sounding a little jealous, which made the other man smile.

"Did Céline make all of their uniforms?"

"*You wish!*" said the poet in English. "Céline just designs them."

"Makes the patterns?"

"Drawings."

"That's all?"

"She also makes sure the costumes match her designs. It's not easy, because who out there still sews clothes these days? Everyone gets their clothes at the supermarket!"

To get ready for this outing, Tanou had in fact gone to Macy's with his father. They left with lots of purchases, Old Papa swathed in a puffy yellow jacket, his hands hidden in cotton gloves, his feet in boots, and his head in a blue cap. The whole getup had made him stop and smile as he looked in the mirror, while behind him his son commented that he'd look like an Eskimo from then on. When Nithap had arrived in August, he'd never imagined that things would turn out like this. It just goes to show that you can't take anything for granted when it comes to your health. Old Papa was philosophical about it, of course, but Angela was still worried; she saw tuberculosis on the horizon.

"The problem is that he just doesn't know anything about the cold we get here," she grumbled. "He just keeps on going for walks."

How to explain to Grandfather that snow is not a joke?

"He goes out without a jacket."

How to tell him he can't dress as if he were in Bangwa?

"Did you turn on the radiator in his room?"

Tanou had sworn that he wouldn't turn his wife into an American version of Ngountchou, and Angela clearly remembered what she had said that day: "I hate reminding you of the obvious!"

"They're all volunteers," Bob added.

"You mean this is where they put their money," said Tanou, "because this has to cost a lot."

"No joke!"

Angela was reading the names of the businesses that contributed to the event.

"They aren't lacking for sponsors," she said.

"You know," the poet went on, and this time he was speaking to his "friend," which was what he usually called Nithap now. "We Americans, we always take things too seriously."

"I wouldn't say that," Tanou cut in.

"No, no," the poet insisted. "This whole event, it costs thousands of dollars."

"That money could pay for a lot of things at the hospital in Bangwa," Old Papa added.

"Yep."

"And it will be spent in just one day."

"If it helps people to remember their history," Tanou said, "well, I think it's worth it."

"But each year?"

"Papa, look!"

"Yes, my dear."

"War isn't a game," whispered Nithap in Medumba; his son agreed, also in Medumba.

He saw Céline making her way through the crowd, a smile on her lips. Marie ran to give her a hug. The two came back and Céline kissed her husband on the mouth.

"Everything's ready for the historic battle?" Bob piped up.

"Oh yes! They don't need me to kill each other off."

Those two were connected by much more than love; it was friendship, partnership. It was easy to read the husband's thoughts by looking at his wife's eyes, and the reverse as well. Several times Tanou had wished for such symbiosis in his relationship with Angela, but had always run up against her snippy side, that part of her that liked to tease and that injected an extra word, a word too much, into the banter; or else it was he who contradicted Angela when he didn't need to. "Do we need to have this fight?" his wife had asked several times, and she was always right. In the end, maybe she understood that was part of his character. It reminded him of his father, and Angela pointed that out to him, too.

"That's just like you," she reminded him sometimes.

And he didn't find it funny.

"Missed chances."

Like when his father told him that Céline had invited him to the reenactment of the Battle of Fredericksburg. Of course, she'd let them know only the week before, but his answer hadn't really been helpful. "Why should we go admire other people's civil war, when ours nobody even talks about?"

"You should talk about it with your father," his wife had suggested. "He was part of the resistance, a Maquisard, wasn't he?"

"A Maquisard?" he'd repeated, looking at Old Papa, who was beginning to recognize his own traits in his son. "You never told me you were a Maquisard!"

"Maquisard, what's that?" Marie had asked.

"Soldier," her father had replied, adding "*sort of*," in English.

"Old Papa was a soldier?" Marie asked enthusiastically.

If she didn't already exist, that little one, they would have had to bring her to life right then and there! Tanou remembered the days after her birth, when he'd wake up wet from the milk flowing from his wife's breasts. He'd almost forgotten that insidious competition in the mornings, and some evenings, when he had to push the little hands away from Angela's breasts after she insisted on sleeping in the parental bed, offering up ever more implausible explanations that only Angela took seriously. "I'm afraid, Mama, afraid!" And he'd see her wink when he retreated from the blankets and pillows, their field of battle, whereas before she was born, that would have been the chance for a bit of early morning fellatio.

"Let's not exaggerate," Nithap said.

In truth, he never spoke about those years, the civil war, the Maquis, the years of "the troubles," as people said back in the country, and which had come to a bloody end before Tanou's birth. You really had to work to pull a word out of him about it, but here, Marie didn't wait for him to speak up.

"What was your job?"

"Nurse."

"Tell me, Old Papa."

"Your Old Papa has always been a nurse," Nithap explained. "At the time, people said 'native doctor.'"

He stopped there, even as all ears were tuned in to listen, mouths agape and eyes wide open. The story disappeared, slinking back into the silence that grew uncomfortable and angry. "That's all in the past, Tanou."

Just like the story about the name change.

The son had discovered by accident some old administrative documents that showed that his name hadn't always been Nithap, like his father's. On the contrary, when he was born, he was called Nyamsi. Salomon Nyamsi. Chance, or, rather, the arrogance of a bureaucrat, had put him on the trail of the twists and turns of his rewritten past. He'd gone to the local government office to get a copy of his birth certificate, so he could get his driver's permit; in the past, it was his father who'd gotten him copies. The overzealous bureaucrat, as only Cameroonian civil servants can be, had looked at his birth certificate and then spat out, staring right into his eyes, "This isn't the original."

Tanou wasn't prepared to hear such a thing.

"What do you mean?"

"This is a document from Kumba,"* he went on. "Was I there when you got forged documents?"

Tanou responded with a childlike naïveté, blurting out, "My certificate isn't forged!"

"Get out of here before I call the police. Forger!"

Whether he responded to the bureaucratic sneer with a gesture of rebellion or angry defiance, or, more likely, with a sob, it did nothing to advance his case, not even the smallest bit. Later that evening his father, whose eyes were always so calm, admitted, "Yes, we changed your name."

"Why?"

Ngountchou answered, "So that all the children in the same home would have the same name."

Tanou didn't dare ask the question that was needling him.

"What about Marianne?"

Yes, why did Marianne have the name Tbongo? And why hadn't he been given his father's name when he was born? Why hadn't he been given the same name as his brothers and sisters? And most of all, who was this Nyamsi who'd given him his name? Had he really been adopted as a baby?

"Where are you getting all these questions?"

The name change had happened before he was old enough to remember.

"You know," his mother said to him one day, "it was a mistake on your father's part to give one of his children his friend's name. For Marianne, it's okay, because Tbongo is my father's name. But that Nyamsi, he was *just* a friend of your father's. I had told him, but you know how stubborn he is. I told him that names should stay in families. He didn't want to listen to me. And, well, a few years after you were born, he decided I was right."

---

* In other words, a forged document, Kumba being a town in Anglophone Cameroon known for falsifying government documents. It's a typical Camfranglais expression, in which what is English is the negative of what is French—as in *Nigeria*, *federalism*, *Bamenda*; so the phrase insinuates, *You had these documents falsified yourself!*

"What happened?"

"Ask him. One evening he just told me that he wanted to change your name, because the memory of his friend made him sad when he saw you."

"When he saw me?"

"You know your father."

Ask him. Nithap Sr. had never been able to tell his son the story, the full story that would have quieted his imagination: the story of how he'd left the Maquis, gone back to working at the hospital in Bangwa, the story that gave the final word on his past. *Lock nshou*. There were several versions scattered around Tanou's mind. In one of them—and that was the one he buried the deepest, even though it sometimes came roaring back like a tornado—his father realized that his friend was making eyes at his wife—that's where the story stopped, because the son couldn't go past that border, that discovery, that scandal. He didn't want to imagine his mother caught up in some shameful story because, he thought, that just didn't sound like Ngountchou; but he could see the raging anger of his father, the nurse, tearing down the western hills, racing along the hedges, stumbling upon a trail of crab tracks—that was always how Tanou told himself the story—and then his father would chase his friend from the courtyard with his rifle, shouting out into the distance, "If I ever see you here again, I'll put a bullet right up your ass!"

Another version put Nyamsi in the middle of the civil war, his name figuring on the list of children whose parents had given the name of a political figure, names that filled the *Journal du Cameroun* back in those days. Tanou had once gone to the National Archives to look at the newspapers, where he'd found an article about name changes. He had scanned the list of people who changed their names from Ouandié* to other, less familiar names. That was the first time in his life he'd gone down that tunnel, breaking what was a family taboo. He had stared, rapt, at the yellowed pages of that misty past. Fear was what made him close the

* The Narrator is using the colonial spelling of the name throughout the text, because of course in Medumba, the name Ouandié is written Wandji. Name changers often just adopted the Medumba spelling.

files, and in the years that followed he had joined in his father's stony silence, sitting there and letting his eyes wander across the sky, his hands fidgeting with the letters of the alphabet, while his lips murmured the question he had never stopped asking himself: "Who was Nyamsi?"

That's all in the past, Tanou.

Nyamsi's death didn't haunt Tanou for very long, because there is nothing more reassuring than going back to your father's home. That his father had recognized his mistake was a sign of his greatness, and that's what his mother had stressed herself. "The son should carry his father's name," she'd said. "You're not a stranger." In elementary school, he'd glibly sung along with his classmates, "*You're a Bami, you are cursed, wa wa ou ha!*" But later, when he was graduating from university and had trouble passing the exam to get into the normal school, as well as the one for the school of foreign service, he remembered the pivotal change and the name that might have made things easier for him, he thought—after all, "the power in this country is in the hands of the *nkwa'*."* He didn't go so far as to reproach his father for taking away his chance to find a place for himself in this "fucked-up country" when he'd changed his name. Actually, it was Marianne who couldn't stop alluding to it: "Look," she said, her finger running along the list of those who'd passed the administrative exams, "the Betis have taken this country hostage. In the government, it's them, in all the prestigious university programs, still them. Everywhere, *it's always them*." The disdain that echoed when she said "it's always them" pointed to a much longer story. When he was faced with the failure of each of his attempts to become a civil servant, more than the grimy archives of those dark years, it was his sister's insistence on talking about those names, especially "Nyamsi," that convinced him to make it a problem, or rather, to revisit it. Except that here, instead of a scar, the erased name was a magical "Open Sesame" that had been taken from him.

Tanou's departure for the United States had erased all those suspicions, and in America, where it was common to change names, he forgot

* A term used to refer to any non-Bamileke people from the region of South Cameroon.

the vagaries of his own story, just like Old Papa forgot the zigzags of his youth when watching the spectacle of the Battle of Fredericksburg.

In the meantime, the extravagant spectacle had gotten underway.

"Do you see the one there in the front?" Bob said, his hand pointing at the cavalryman they'd seen just a short while before, and who was now leading the troops, his chest puffed out, his eyes fixed intently on the scene. "That's Colonel Adams. As history would have it, he's the one who led the Battle of Fredericksburg, and lost his life in it."

"I'm the one who designed his uniform," Céline added.

"That's what I wanted to say," the poet went on. "You did a great job with the epaulets, my dear."

"You think so?"

"Yes, of course."

"Who wants something to drink?" Tanou interrupted. "I'm going to get us some drinks. Marie, what do you want?"

"Coke."

"Of course."

13

"Listen," said Tanou. "The Americans take great pleasure in reliving their past. Look at Adams's regiment in perfect formation—you'd never think that they were volunteers. There's a bit of sadomasochism in it, if you ask me."

"Many of them were in the military," Bob replied. "Veterans. They took part in the wars in Iraq and Afghanistan. That helps them remember their roles."

"I get it now. War is playing out in two times, as tragedy and farce. This is the farce."

Tanou slapped his hand on his forehead and turned toward his father.

"Papa," he said, "did you know that the soldiers there are veterans?"

The old guy didn't understand. Just then, one of the soldiers of the past was sneaking behind him; his costume made him look like he was part of some carnival troupe. He paused in front of Marie, who gaped at him with eyes wide open, and patted her cheek.

"A beautiful child," he said to Angela.

"Thank you!"

"Yes, yes," Céline went on. "That's how it is in the United States: tragedy, then farce. You got it."

She said that with a mix of amusement and indignation, and Tanou began to wonder why she was a part of this thing.

"And in France, isn't it the same thing?" Angela asked.

"In the end, it's the same culture," Céline replied. "It's the same sort of people having fun on battlefields."

"It would seem so."

"Except that in France, there isn't that perfectionist side to the staging. Here it's like a gigantic play. Like some Hollywood film. First Vietnam and then Rambo, you see what I mean?"

Next to them, Bob wasn't paying attention. He was showing Old Papa the battle line that was taking shape on the snowy field. He told him the story of the battle, what was at stake in this civil war now playing out with camps that went up and down, repeatedly, with the boisterousness of a family weekend; you'd have called it a picnic if it weren't for the cold and the snow. The enemy wasn't yet in sight, of course, at least the spectators couldn't see them from where they were standing. But they wouldn't be hidden for long, because the plain spread out before them in rolling white hills, dotted here and there with shrubs and trees, carrying the drumbeat that set the rhythm for the enemy's advance. They could hear the crisp sound of the soldiers' feet hitting the ground as the infantry moved into place on the battle line.

"All of this is a little too cinematic, you know," Céline continued. "That's what's specific to the United States, and that you don't find in France. Here, everything is like in a film. In France, the details of the reenactments, the props, the gestures, the clothes, they're not so carefully rehearsed."

"A costume drama, right?"

"With real soldiers in disguise, yes."

And Céline went on to describe the detail and precision she had to put into the creation of the costumes, the construction of the hats, the shoes, and even the gloves.

"It's because they're at peace with their history that they can replay it without suffering," Tanou said. "That's not the case in Cameroon."

"Nor in France."

"*Bou tchoum*,* huh?" Nithap whispered to his son.

---

* In Medumba: There's a lot of them.

Hearing the word *Cameroon* had roused his attention, but he said nothing else. People of all ages, mostly families with kids, had crowded in all around.

"Where are they all coming from?"

"From all over," said Céline. "Like us."

"From other states," Angela corrected. "Look at the license plates. I even saw one family from Texas."

"All the way for this?"

A crowd of fans, regiments of semiprofessionals. An unbelievable link seemed to connect all of these people. There were men, older and with potbellies, some muscle-bound; senior citizens sitting on folding chairs, like Bob; women, standing with their feet close together, gloves on their hands; children clinging to their parents; all staring out at the field before them, as if what was going on were something more than a historical film, an eye-pleasing staged scene, the live filming of a television series, or a video game.

"There aren't many Blacks."

That was the conclusion Angela drew from the morning; a reformulation of the question she had already asked, even before they left the house: "Do Black people come to this sort of thing?" While they were on their way, it had been phrased as a doubt: "I think we'll be the only Black folks there." The unavoidable conclusion of the racial radar she trained on every event, and that Tanou would have been wise not to call into question, because all he could have done was point to his own family. "Your father doesn't count," his wife said. With his left arm he reached out and hugged her tight, squeezing her shoulders and planting a kiss on top of her head, the gesture he always made when he conceded a point to her, when he accepted her reading of things; then he waited for her to give him a tight-lipped smile.

A cannon shot was heard in the distance. "This is the perfect civil war," Tanou said to convince her, but he was also talking to his father, who was listening, too. "On the one side, there is the Union, on the other, the Confederates. No imperialists pulling strings behind the scene, arming the belligerents, in a battle they wouldn't fight themselves, as was the case back home." He looked at his father and his eyes made it clear that he wanted to add, *Right, Papa?* Nithap kept quiet. "The obvious cause of the war," he went on, "slavery, slaves, Blacks, yes, because that's something you could look for, the Blacks, and not what's hidden from view, what's buried deep underground. The last, perfect civil war, you know what I mean, because it was fought openly, face-to-face, and what's more, for the common good, for the freedom of the Blacks."

"Yet there were so many who died."

"Yes, hundreds of thousands."

"That's the problem."

"Which one?"

"Fratricide."

Accidents often happen during reenactments of historic battles. Using weapons more than a hundred years old isn't easy, not for those who've had practice, not even for soldiers. A man who has driven an assault tank with an electronic screen doesn't necessarily know what to do when he finds himself in front of a cannon and gunpowder. So most of the accidents, and the deadliest ones, occur with the cannons. Sometimes they go off too soon, breaking the arm of the anachronistic cannoneer. Sometimes it's a musket that blinds the guy who should have known better how to use it. These weapons don't come with a set of directions and warnings, and they're as fragile as the volunteers who're expected to use them. These kinds of problems actually led to unbelievable numbers of deaths in wartime, including during this civil war. But then those accidental deaths were just added into the tally of those who died in battle, attributed to the enemy forces.

After asking everyone what they wanted, Tanou was going to get drinks. For Marie, some soda, for Bob and Céline, water. Angela wanted a cup of tea. No one was hungry.

"I'm coming with you," Angela said. It was clear that Tanou wouldn't have enough hands to carry all the drinks.

Then Old Papa stepped in. "No, I'll go with him."

"Use the joint credit card, okay?" Angela added.

That made Tanou smile: his wife never failed to toss out that phrase.

Father and son went off to stand in line at the concession stand, where a heavyset woman, wearing a SUPPORT OUR TROOPS T-shirt, was deftly serving everyone with a smile and a kind word.

"Yes, my dear," she said, then quickly recited back Tanou's order; behind her, two men were busy grilling meat, which smelled delicious. "Nothing to eat?"

"No," Tanou replied. "Or maybe, yes. Just a minute. Papa, are you sure you don't want something from the grill?"

"What is there?" Old Papa asked.

"Ma'am." Tanou turned back to the vendor. "What's on the grill?"

Of all the things she listed off, the only one he caught was *lamb*.

"Is that the lamb?" he asked, pointing to the meat sizzling in the flames.

"You want some lamb?" asked the woman who, despite her plastic smile, was starting to lose patience, as the line behind Tanou grew longer.

She had already grabbed a paper bag, which she held open in front of the cook, who dropped in a piece of meat, without even waiting for the customer's reply.

"Yes, some lamb," Tanou answered, as he turned back toward his father, asking him in Medumba to head off with the drinks. "Add another two pieces, please."

When Nithap was making his way through the crowd of shoulders and raised hands, holding a bottle of soda and a paper bag, there was a second cannon blast, which made a woman nearby exclaim, "Oh wow!"

"The battle is starting," a man said.

"The battle is starting"—the phrase was carried on, repeated by mouth after mouth. The concession line was thinning out, customers turning back into spectators, when suddenly there was a third cannon blast, followed by a flash, and chaos broke out.

"Papa!" shouted Tanou.

He watched in horror as the crowd his father was trying to cut through tilted like a boat caught by a big wave on the ocean, and the roof of the shelter came crashing down on it. Soon all he could hear were shouts and sobs. Tanou would never understand why he just stood there, frozen in place, still holding on to the bag with his purchases—he'd ended up getting two sandwiches, as well, thinking that Marie would change her mind. (Marie always said no, before realizing that she'd actually like to share her father's sandwich, at least to have a few bites.) No, Tanou would never know why he just stood there in front of the concession stand, while all around him people were running left and right. He didn't know what to do; he couldn't dive into the melee and drag his father out, or run back to his child and his wife.

A young man bumped into him. That's when he came to and, by reflex, his body, arms, feet, heart, and stomach—now all in turmoil after that moment when he was frozen in place—sent him rushing ahead, the bag of food still clutched in his hands. He saw Angela.

"You're safe," she murmured when Tanou came to stop in front of her. She put her hands around his face. "You're safe."

She looked like she'd just woken from a nightmare. All around her, faces wore the same frightened expression. Tanou's eyes started searching all around.

"Where is Marie?" he asked.

"Where is Grandfather?" Angela replied.

"Where is Grandfather?"

If Einstein Were Cameroonian

1

The rhythm of a doctor's life is set by the shift schedule. And the routine of duties. That's how it was for Nithap. He had a very clear memory of that day: greeting patients in the hospital courtyard, registering them and then calling out their names, and assisting late in the day in an operation on an old man with a hernia, which meant he couldn't even take a break at midnight. Truth be told, without his work he would have known very little about the events being celebrated in Yaounde and elsewhere. In those days, Bangwa seemed cut off from the rest of the world. He was an exemplary doctor. His reputation had spread as far as the capital, and farther, even, because he was one of the rare few to receive the Colonial Medal of Merit from the minister of health, Arouna Njoya, during a ceremony the minister presided over on the national holiday, May 10, 1958. Mademoiselle Birgitte (not Brigitte) was always a bit jealous because, despite all of her efforts, she, the woman who adopted all of those children from the hospital orphanage, was never decorated.

"It's because you are *rather* Norwegian," Nithap whispered to her one day.

She had looked at him, then smiled and shrugged. He hadn't uttered the final words of his sentence . . . *and not French*. He was reassured by the woman's apparent lack of concern. In those days, people weren't always suspicious of everyone else. That came about only after the civil war, which turned everything in Bamileke land upside down.

Well before that war, it was in Mademoiselle Birgitte's courtyard that

Nithap met Ngountchou. He only learned her Christian name much later: Margarèthe. He first noticed her because of how she'd tied her headscarf, pulled behind her ears and knotted over her brow, as was typical of serious young girls back then. From her bearing, he thought she must be Bangangte and so asked what her *ndap*, or praise name, was.

Those two, who would eventually become Tanou's parents, were part of the new generation. They had grown up with white people settled nearby. Ngountchou was living with Mademoiselle Birgitte when Nithap met her. Her father, a pastor, had entrusted her to the *mekat*, the white woman, whose mission was to "raise" her.

"You're not my servant." Mademoiselle Birgitte had been insistent, repeating the phrase whenever Ngountchou's steps led toward the kitchen. "Don't become one."

Ngountchou never did. The white woman had said those words in Medumba, which she spoke quite well. Thus began a unique relationship between the two women. It was the Norwegian woman who reminded Ngountchou of the facts. "You are Bangangte. You are one of those who refused to become slaves of the Bamum. Why would you accept to be enslaved by the whites? This earth that clings to your feet is red with words of praise that the apron you're wearing cannot conceal." Ngountchou took care of the children, she was her "assistant." The word *assistant* came from Mademoiselle Birgitte; her spoken French wasn't that good, but she knew exactly what she needed there in that godforsaken corner of western Cameroon. She was the one who taught Ngountchou how to sew. She also sewed, when she wasn't on duty.

"Idle hands are the worst of all cancers," she said. "You must be very careful not to waste time twiddling your thumbs." And she organized her life by that maxim. So Ngountchou was surrounded by children when Nithap saw her, his Ngountchou, for the first time. He immediately thought of a mother hen. The children were playing all around the young girl. One of them, a toddler with a big square head and bowed legs, not yet steady on his feet but clearly determined, was leading the others on a walk along the bamboo fence. The doctor was quite amused, and then turned his eyes to Ngountchou, for whom this seemed to be a familiar routine. She was holding an infant in her arms, and the attention she was giving the baby surprised him.

"Is that your child, *menma?*"* he asked her in the local Medumba dialect, his intonation making clear it was a joke, that it seemed impossible.

His decision to speak to a young woman he didn't know in a Medumba dialect showed his unease; people usually spoke classical Medumba in and around the mission. Because that language flattened out the accents particular to each of the Bangangte groups, it was what people normally used when speaking to people they didn't know. But in daily exchanges with family and friends, dialects were the rule.

Ngountchou smiled but didn't reply. So he repeated his question, addressing her by her *ndap*, instead of as *menma*, which in the context totally transformed his question, giving it a tender, familiar note. He wondered if he'd gone too far, but was reassured when she nodded her head approvingly.

"You are Pastor Elie Tbongo's daughter?" he asked.

It was a rhetorical question, because he had recognized her. Ngountchou heard it everywhere she went, and it reflected the respect people had for her father. She smiled and bowed her head. Right then and there, seeing in her the image of the perfect mother, he decided to start a family.

That was in 1958, in June.

For him, that day would always mark the birth of his happiness. For the doctor, happiness was Ngountchou's smiling face, surrounded by toddlers, "her children." What was it that had brought him there to Mademoiselle Birgitte's courtyard? He couldn't even remember, and what did it matter, anyway? "I had come to find my Ngountchou," he always said. His War Girl.

---

* A polite but neutral Bangangte form of address, which means, tautologically, "child of your mother."

2

"You're in a good mood today, my colleague," Mademoiselle Birgitte had called out in French, when she heard him whistling as he walked down the hallway in the surgical pavilion.

"There are days like that."

They walked together between the cots where patients lay waiting in the main courtyard.

They usually met up during their cigarette break. To take advantage of those moments and not be interrupted by patients, they would hide out away from the building, on the side near the leprosy ward. Only the smokers on the staff knew about that spot.

"The Nicotine Brotherhood," as Mademoiselle Birgitte put it.

Often even Dr. Broussoux would join them in their hideout. Dr. Broussoux was the head of the station,* the chief of staff. He was the one who had banned smoking in the hospital offices. The smokers knew that he joined them more to make a show of goodwill than because he shared their vice. Sometimes Nithap would pay Mademoiselle Birgitte a visit at her home when both of them were off work, and sometimes she came to his house.

Nithap hadn't said anything to her about the happiness he'd found in her home. He preferred to keep that his secret. Not just because it was his private life, but mostly because it seemed out of place to speak of feelings

* The term, in colonial parlance, for a medical facility.

there. And then, his feelings were so new—so new, really, that to say "feelings" was certainly an exaggeration, or at least that's how he would have put it. Mademoiselle Birgitte had become close friends with one of his former classmates, Nyamsi, who was Moya,* and so a stranger in that part of the country. That relationship had strengthened the bond between her and Nithap, even if, when Nyamsi joined them, the three tended to speak in French.

"Ah yes," Birgitte continued. "You can hide the honey in a thicket, the bee will be sure to find it, isn't that so?"

Nithap smiled, realizing he'd been found out. He stammered as if he had done something wrong. But what was there for him to hide?

There was a moment of silence, a smokers' silence.

Happily, they were distracted by Tama'ntchou, the water porter, who came toward them with his two donkeys, each of which was carrying two big containers on its back. The animals were exhausted, but the man didn't seem to notice.

"Back there," Mademoiselle Birgitte said in Medumba.

Even though he came to the station twice each week to bring Dr. Broussoux drinking water, he seemed to have forgotten the way and was headed toward the leprosy ward.

"Have you become a leper, *menma*?" Nithap asked.

The porter turned toward him; at first he just stared, with a look of surprise on his face that was surely a reflection of his stupidity, but he quickly came to and gave a theatrical wave.

"No, *ndocta*," he said, then he struck his donkeys, who jumped, but refused to budge.

He looked at the two doctors, both amused by his antics, then grew embarrassed and took off his hat. He looked like he wanted to apologize for his animals. He hit them again.

---

* The Moyas are what we call the Bangangte from Down There—from Yabassi or Nten—cut off from western Cameroon since 1951, and so cut off from the Bamileke, which has only made some of them all the happier. It's not easy to know just who is Bamileke, because the administrative classifications are out of alignment with the tribal ones, but we'll figure out how to clarify things.

"I think it's your turn to carry the water now," said Mademoiselle Birgitte, trying to stifle a laugh. "They've worked hard enough. Did you look at that hill?"

She pointed at the long path sloping through landscape so green it could be found only in Cameroon.

"That is true," the man said, "very true, madam."

"They've climbed all the way to heaven, those brave animals!" she added, laughing now as her face disappeared in a cloud of smoke.

"That's true, madam, very true."

"Maybe they just need a bit of help?" Nithap added.

"*Ndocta*, that is true."

Then Dr. Broussoux came out of his office, his cap in hand. The doctors tried to pull themselves together.

"What the hell is going on here?" he said in French, his voice stern.

The porter hurried to untie the first container. When he had it balanced on his head, his donkeys suddenly started walking again. Everyone, including Nithap, burst out laughing. Dr. Broussoux headed back to his office, shaking his head.

Moments of calm like this were rare at the station, uncommon for both doctors and patients. The hospital was really isolated. With its thirty or so buildings scattered across a vast plateau, it formed a sort of parallel world, where illness was the only topic of conversation. Things that happened elsewhere were only heard about later, the delay due as much to mail delivery as to geography—the High Plateau made people move slowly, take time to catch their breath and patiently mull over any bit of news. Without anyone actually stating the rule, they knew to avoid one topic in their conversations: politics. Could that be why they seemed to be able to chat so comfortably, why the smokers were able to talk politely to each other without really being close friends?

"Doctors don't take sides." That was the rule Dr. Broussoux was always repeating.

That was the pledge that bound all of them at the station together.

Yet it would be ridiculous to say that politics first entered the hospital walls only when the minister visited in 1958. The ceremonies that marked that occasion were the first time anyone had seen Dr. Broussoux wearing a coat and tie. Nithap had two friends with whom he was "marking the day." Nyamsi was a math teacher at the Noutong Secondary School and perhaps the most talkative person around.

"Just forget about *your* Broussoux," Nyamsi said. "Your boss isn't going to stop history's advance!"

Nyamsi was known in the area for his neatly pressed trousers ("Shorts, they're for colonists," he said), and his always well-shined shoes. He'd even been dubbed "Trousers," while his bicycle was called *ben skin*,* because of how he leaned into the turns. His hair, always cut in the latest fashion—short in back, a part on the right—made it easy to spot him, even at a distance. There were a lot of stories told about his salacious adventures with his female students. He admired Nkrumah and was a fervent proponent of the domino theory that so frightened the French: After Egypt, Sudan, and Ghana, who would be next? Did he spout it out of conviction or because of the terror it traced across the faces of the colonists in the area? Either way, according to him, and he never failed to repeat it, what had happened in Accra was going to happen all over Africa, "starting with Cameroon!

"Colonialism has been sentenced to death," he hammered out, jabbing the table with his finger. "Go tell that to *your* Broussoux!"

He said "your" so aggressively, as if Nithap had anything to do with it! As if he didn't have white bosses himself! What did it matter anyway? Nyamsi had turned Broussoux into the enemy he needed in these exchanges, even though he'd never even spoken to the man. That was just how he saw the world: in black-and-white, no gray.

"Sentenced to death," he repeated, "and all the colonists along with it."

"Yes, combatant."

Nyamsi loved to be called "combatant." For him, the situation was cut-and-dried, but Nithap wasn't of the same mind. He shook his head.

---

* Here Pidgin—which already in the first part of this book Nithap tried unsuccessfully to use in front of Big—returns to the text, and for good. A *ben skin* is a sort of motorbike.

He was only two years older than Nyamsi, but he thought his friend needed to grow up. He compared him to an onion that makes everyone cry, but has a hollow center, "a little guy." But right then, something in his criticism of everything and everyone started to click.

"The worst colonialist, my dear," Nyamsi said, "is the white man who does his job well, because he's the one keeping colonialism alive."

"If that's what you say," Nithap retorted. He was laughing, clapping his hands and shaking his head. "If Einstein were Cameroonian, I swear that any old fool who is stumped by logic puzzles that a child could solve would tell him to keep his theory of relativity for the whites. Am I right?"

"Fool?"

"And how!" Nithap went on. "This is how we do it, that's the way it's done, and everyone comes up with some trick that condemns our people to failure in the name of our liberation. Isn't that how it goes?"

"What are you talking about?"

"About the teleology of failure that people like you want to sow here in the name of independence. People call it respect for our elders, but really it's just a bad attitude. Because what is wrong about doing your job, whether you're white or Black? Can you tell me that, *Mister Professor?*"

"Before independence," Nyamsi stipulated.

Nithap was always caught off guard by his friend's responses.

"Well," the combatant continued, "after independence, you'll take your rightful place, *Doctor Nithap*, and do you know why?"

"Tell me quickly, please. I have work to do."

Now Nyamsi was laughing.

"Because the good nationalist, *Doctor Nithap*, is precisely the man who does his job well after independence."

Nithap smiled. These ideas flattered him somehow. But as he listened, he always ran up against that label his friend used to describe himself, "nationalist." What about him, was he a nationalist, too?

Sakio Nithap, Doctor Nithap, a nurse by trade, was frank but reserved. Not a big talker. He'd never tell a patient blinded by a cancerous tumor that it was just an abscess. But he admired people like Nyamsi, whose profession as a teacher freed his tongue, allowed him to stand up in this living room, beat his chest, and declare himself a "nationalist," call himself a "combatant." He knew he didn't have a silver tongue—tongue-tied was more like it. And he hadn't yet gotten into the habit of writing down his thoughts in notebooks, those grimy but patiently filled notebooks that years later would help Tanou to understand him.

"I am a doctor," was what he said. "That's enough."

"A profession is not a set of beliefs," Nyamsi replied, surprised by the flaws in his logic, which he put down to bad faith.

"Being a doctor is my set of beliefs, my profession of faith."

"And my job, you think my job is just to make other people smart? You're going too far, aren't you?"

"What do you mean?"

"How can you care for the body without caring for the soul?"

"The body is already complicated enough."

"No one would ever guess you'd gone to the same school as Moumié,"* Nyamsi said with a disappointed sigh.

"Precisely," Nithap cut in. "I am not Moumié."

Nyamsi took a step back. He had put his finger on the thing that always made his friend flip out. He smiled at the anger he could read on Nithap's face. It happened every time his career was compared to that of the leader of the UPC, the Union of the Peoples of Cameroon, a pro-independence movement and political party; its three founding leaders were Ruben Um Nyobè, Félix-Roland Moumié, and Ernest Ouandié. Moumié had also been trained as a native doctor at the William Ponty Institute in Dakar. This was a conversation Nithap did not want to pursue, that he always left dangling.

You see, Nyamsi knew how to get a reaction from him! Since everyone suspected Nyamsi was sleeping with all of his students ("Bangangte women," he whispered one day to his friend, "are the most beautiful in

* A leader of the independence movement who was poisoned to death, but we haven't gotten to that point yet. His name will come up several more times in what follows.

all Cameroon, my dear; their derrieres would defrock the pope!"), Nithap always wondered why Mademoiselle Birgitte was the exception, the one to whom this serial conqueror always returned. ("It is a crime to walk by a flower and not pick it.") *It's because she's white, isn't it?* He chewed on that evil thought for a while.

"The soul," his friend began, "when you talk about the soul, it's not just about individuals!"

"Really?"

"It's really nothing personal, my dear friend."

Yes, Nyamsi certainly could exaggerate things!

"*Walaoo*," Nithap cried out. "The soul? And how does one take care of that?"

And the two of them were off again; they'd be at it all evening, while Mademoiselle Birgitte, trying not to laugh, went off to get some beer.

"Consciousness raising?"

Unbeatable, that *Trousers*!

3

Nithap could say nothing about it to his friend. But there was one thing he couldn't prevent: his maid read him like an open book, even when all he did was smile or mumble something she couldn't catch. Clara understood that the doctor was in love the very moment she heard him come into the house and casually toss his bag onto the armchair in the living room; as soon as she saw him standing in the kitchen doorway, unable to keep still, like a kid. She held her boss's soul in her hands, even if she knew her place.

"Massa has come?" she asked, using the formulaic turn of phrase.

Although they were both from Bangwa, she didn't address him using his *ndap*, but by the title that reflected his position as master of the house.

"Do you have any water?"

"Yes, massa," she said, and disappeared into a far corner of the kitchen.

The sound of a jug being closed, the scuffling of sandals across the floor—Nithap would never rid her of that habit—and there, carefully holding out a cup. She watched him swallow the water in large gulps, as if she herself were thirsty. Clara Ntchantchou was her name, her full name, but Nithap preferred to call her just Clara, and not Nsho'ntane, her *ndap*, because of her age—she was rather young. He had trouble remembering her *ndap*, it was so complicated, while her Christian name was familiar to him, Clara. He knew nothing else about her, except that she was a man's fourth wife.

"I haven't seen Tama'," said the doctor, looking at his watch.

It was the time when school was let out for the day. Tama' was his nephew and he had taken responsibility for his education. He was the son of Matutshan, his older sister who lived with her family in N'lohe, where Tama''s father was the foreman on a French plantation. He heard steps in the living room.

"*Tonton*," the young man said, addressing his uncle in French, surprised to see him there.

French was the language the doctor used with his little one, for pedagogical reasons. Because, he thought, since the child spoke with Clara only in dialectal Medumba, there was no one else around the house for him to speak French with, and that wasn't going to help his studies. But it made their conversations rather stilted, since most of what the uncle said to his nephew were orders or suggestions, like, "Tell me, what did you do in class?" or "Show me your notebooks."

It was Clara who made the boy feel like he was at home. The cook was clearly happy to mother him, since her own children never came to visit her at the house. And yet, she held her boss's soul in her hands. She smiled when she heard him whistling in the living room.

"I'll be back!" he shouted.

He took a walk every evening. When he wasn't on duty, he took his walk before nightfall, crossing the village as the shadows grew. He loved the mists in Bangwa—they were a comforting overcoat. The chill that fell at that hour let him get lost in his thoughts, coming to only when a villager recognized him and called out a greeting. Sometimes he walked all the way to Bangangte. It took three hours on foot.

Clara was right: Nithap was in love.

He had thought about marriage a few times before. In that world there was always an aunt, uncle, or grandparents who were "trying to find you a wife," but he'd never had time for it. He knew he was considered a good match, mostly because of the prestige of his profession. No one in Bangwa could understand why he was still single. Nithap remembered a conversation he'd had once with the chief, Jean Nono, who had wanted to unload one of his daughters on him.

The nurse wasn't unhappy to have escaped from the clutches of that man. Yes, he remembered their conversation: every day the chief came to the hospital to manage his epilepsy. Nono thought he'd actually been poisoned. When he spoke, he waved his arms all around, and had even scratched the doctor with his very long nails. Possessed of an oversized personality, he usually dressed in Fulani fashion, wearing a colored turban but leaving his chest bare, even when it was cold. Ever since the colonial administration had placed him on the chief's throne, he lived in constant fear. And when he was afraid, he lost his imposing demeanor and behaved like a child who'd seen a mouse. Yet the legitimate Bangwa chief had been exiled to Dschang.

"One of my wives has a grudge against me," Nono said. "I know it's the Sawa one, but she's not going to get me."

The next time he'd accuse the Moya. And that man wanted to give him one of his daughters!

Nithap still laughed about it, because as far as he was concerned, the chief of Bangwa was rather comical. "A master troublemaker," people sometimes said.

The doctor recalled the horrified expression on Clara's face when, as he was heading out one evening, he'd said he was going to the chief's compound. It was Clara's way of letting him know what the village thought about Nono.

"You don't like him, do you?" he'd snapped, in response to her icy glare.

She hadn't replied, of course, but just went back to the kitchen, wrapping herself in a silence, the meaning of which she alone understood.

What will she say about Ngountchou?

He smiled at that idea, because the person he really needed to worry about was Pastor Elie Tbongo, Ngountchou's father. The men respected each other. "He's the doctor who cares for their souls," Mademoiselle Birgitte had said about Pastor Tbongo one day when she'd seen the evangelist with his wife at the hospital. As she said that, it sounded like she was trying to get her mind off Nyamsi: that was the title he so fervently claimed for himself.

"The Cameroonian soul is a battlefield!" the teacher often said. "And education is its path."

Yes, the soul.

The pastor had come to the hospital because of high blood pressure. Dressed in a blue *ndop*, he had nothing about him of a preacher, except for his penetrating gaze, so full of conviction, which the doctor could not forget. Nithap stared for a long time at his clothes, which didn't fit his profession, since pastors usually preferred to wear a suit coat. He didn't say anything, but the patient noticed, all the same.

How can a pastor go about dressed like that? he wanted to ask.

Until then, he'd only heard the man speak from the pulpit of his church in Mfetoum, another part of Bangangte. The connection between them had been cut once the pastor was cured, when he no longer needed to come to the hospital, where a younger deacon led prayers.

What will Clara think about the pastor's daughter?

When he came back to the house, Clara had already left. On the coffee table was a sheet of yellow plastic bearing the advertising slogan of Beaufort beer—*Beaufort toujours fort*—in big green letters, and beneath it, his meal: two plates, several dishes, and an upside-down glass. He went to his bedroom and came back wearing pajama pants and scuffling his feet, which he always asked Clara not to do. He sat down in the armchair and lifted up the makeshift plate cover to find a dish of *kouakoukou*, easy to recognize because of its intense aroma, and on the plate next to it, pieces of meat. Tama' came and sat down beside him. They ate in silence: Nithap realized that evening how much he missed having a woman in his life.

"Ngountchou," he said absentmindedly, as he ate.

"What did you say, *Tonton*?" the little kid asked.

"No, nothing," he said. "Pass the water."

Nithap regularly encouraged his nephew to read, but he didn't do so very much himself. Mademoiselle Birgitte was the reader; one day she spoke to him about Ferdinand Oyono. "A young Cameroonian writer, brutalized by the police in New York." She had a copy of *La Presse du Cameroun* in her hand.

"Those racists!" she said. "They're everywhere. You should read his novel *Houseboy*."

But when he was on duty, Nithap just didn't have the time, and his days off, his evenings especially, he spent with his friends, Nyamsi mostly. Sometimes when he wasn't on duty, he paid Mademoiselle Birgitte a visit, as he had on that day when his life took a turn. She was always so busy with the children, her sewing, the hospital (how did she find time to read?), so she appreciated the chance to pause for a bit.

When Nithap retired to his room for the night, burping and cleaning his teeth with a pick, he picked up a book from the wicker shelf, *Tropical Medicine*, which Dr. Broussoux had lent him. Once in bed, he leafed through it, read one or two pages, then turned on the radio. He was at first distracted by the news from France, and then by the mosquitoes, but soon his mind began to wander. He looked at the photographs on his walls, the calendar, his portrait in black-and-white, a fly on the wall. He got up and followed it, book in hand. He swatted at it, but missed twice before finally squashing it. Despite all that, once he lay back down, it was Ngountchou's face that appeared before his eyes, that image of her that had made him decide to start a family: her, cradling an infant in her arms. He turned off the light to go to sleep. He usually relied on music to rock him to sleep, but that night he couldn't stop smiling. Such was the power of that War Girl over him.

Nithap knew that while the formal declaration of love is made on one's wedding day, the path leading up to it is difficult. Bangangte was at that time the seat of the regional administration, and the road leading there was especially busy. A borrowed pickup and porters helped him to deliver bags of *macabo*, bunches of plantains, and watermelons. Because he wanted to marry that pastor's daughter, who had become a surrogate mother because of a Norwegian woman, there was one word he forbade himself from saying too soon, out of superstition. The word was *nkoni*, love. When he headed back home from Bangangte, the doctor was often accompanied by Nyamsi, on his motorbike. His friend saw it as a good excuse to visit Mademoiselle Birgitte, as he often did, and to interrogate Nithap, who seemed to be taking things too slowly! He said he wanted to give his fiancée time to "grow up."

That made Nyamsi laugh.

"Under these conditions," he said, shaking his head in disbelief, "it's impossible to marry a Bamileke girl."

Nithap didn't let him finish the thought, which he knew by heart: *You might as well just make her your mistress.*

"Then start learning to speak Medumba," he snapped, "you Fake-Bassa." Since Nyamsi was a Moya, from Yabassi, he was considered Bassa by the administration. Nithap opted not to add that while *his* Birgitte managed the language quite well, Nyamsi, who'd been born in the country, and who proclaimed himself a "nationalist" to boot, was still using French.

A few days earlier, Mademoiselle Birgitte had actually called Nithap out about the relationship he'd started behind her back.

"I see that my colleague has fallen in love with the pastor's daughter."

"In love?"

"I hope so!" the Norwegian continued. "I am not going to give *my daughter* to the first fella who happens by!"

Nithap had to admit she'd won! *My daughter.*

"Do you have another one?"

He was asking about cigarettes. She reached her arm under her smock and pulled out two packs of Bleues, filtered cigarettes, and matches. The snap of the match filled the silence that had settled in between them. It took him three tries to get it to light, and he had to protect the flame with his hand. Then he took a long drag and stood silently, lost in his thoughts.

Mademoiselle Birgitte was nothing but happy with the news, but she was surprised by his secrecy. Yes, why had Nithap thought he could keep his heart's secrets from his friends? What was there to hide anyway, since the girl in question lived with her?

"You've made an excellent choice," Mademoiselle Birgitte said. "I hope you know that."

That's when she repeated that Ngountchou's father was the "doctor of the soul." You have to picture Pastor Tbongo: fruit of the best evangelical school, in Ndoungue, he was as adept with Bible verses as with the letters of the Bamileke alphabet, Bagam. His knowledge of both made him a virtuoso: he both officiated and translated during services. He dedicated what little free time he had to the translation of biblical passages into the local alphabet. He had launched that titanic project on behalf of the Kumzse,* and was the group's local representative. He was the only one in Bangangte or anywhere else who was really able to read that alphabet, which had become "his thing." "The only one now," the pastor said, "but not the last."

Then he'd nod and turn back to his papers, his wrinkled brow showing an anxiety that he didn't put into words; on the wall behind him, you could see the calendar with eight days each week, where he recorded the fruits of his hard work. If Nithap wasn't a great reader, he became one, thanks to his conversations with Elie Tbongo. He hadn't ever been very interested in the intellectual production of Bamileke land; it was only after all those trips back and forth to the catechist's home, with bags of *macabo* and bunches of bananas, seated on the back of his friend's Zephyr, that he discovered the Bamum pantheon, Mount Pleasant, and began to trace the genealogy whose roots extended all the way to Foumban. *Nga shun Mven Mum*, the Friend of the Bamum King, that's what the chief of Bangangte is called.

The villagers respected Nithap, seeing his white uniform as proof of a miracle. They admired his hands' mastery of the secrets of life. But as a thinker, he stuck to the middle of the road. He never did anything more than apply the treatment protocols prescribed for boils, tuberculosis, or sleeping sickness, which ravaged the area. He meticulously followed what he'd learned in his training at William Ponty, but went no further.

"Why are people so afraid of doctors?" he wondered sometimes, repeating the question asked by his white colleagues.

---

* Kumzse, a progressive Bamileke cultural organization, founded in March 1948, tightly linked to the UPC until its disbanding in 1951. Led by Mathias Djoumessi, the chief of Foréké-Dschang, it is the best-known incubator of the Bamileke anticolonial political awakening.

"How many lives would have been saved if they hadn't gone to the witch doctor first!" His own answer differed little from theirs: "Superstitions!"

The ardor, the fanaticism with which Nithap had thrown himself into the fight against superstition, and into implementing DDT detoxification campaigns, had made him the spokesperson of the Bangwa hospital. He was the one who gave a lecture in Medumba to a certain old man, obviously infected with syphilis for years, who had passed it on to all of his wives and even lost his sight as a result. It was also he who spoke to some young woman who hadn't given her baby Quinimax as she was supposed to, or who hadn't vaccinated him against all those diseases that were decimating homes in the region, and had made her baby an invalid. His shock at the suffering he saw was equaled only by the real respect he received from those men and women, whom he sometimes found naked in their villages during his campaigns against trypanosomiasis, and who afterward filled the hospital courtyard, listening with a hand clapped over their gaping mouths, or pressed to their shoulders or breasts, as he called out the names of patients on the waiting list, so amazed by his white smock and his very presence.

Nithap had grown used to that silent admiration wherever he went, and he had a very clear idea of what the villagers thought.

"I am the son of villagers!" he often said. And he told them where he'd been born. "Right here in Bangwa."

Patients came from all around the region. Many of them knew his family, and if the most elderly were the only ones who called him by his *ndap*, that's just because they had seen him running around barefoot in the dirt, chasing a wooden hoop he'd made himself. They often made fun of his Medumba, which he now spoke with a white accent; they smiled when he dropped a word of French into the middle of a sentence, and were surprised when he'd start to speak to them in classical Medumba, only to switch abruptly in the middle to the Bangwa dialect.

"Of course, we know your father," his patients would say, and he'd use that to help wear down their resistance.

"And your mother, too."

"Let me tell you. Your father sold wood at the market in Bangwa, am I right?"

"My wife went to the fields with your mother."

"I know, papa," he'd say. "I know."

Nithap only ever listened to his patients with half an ear, and only really to distract them from the medicine he administered. His own biography, like the list of his *ndaps* that some recited to him like a prayer, was no more than a diversion. While he was absentmindedly chatting with a patient, he'd tap their forearm, looking for a good vein, and suddenly say, "Voilà," in French when he found one; then he'd come back to the story that he'd barely been listening to. Sometimes, as a patient was telling him the ups and downs of a sore throat, he'd start in on his well-worn medical sermon. He wasn't even aware how condescending he was being. Those men and women with runny eyes and aching bellies, who looked to him for commiseration, were, to his mind, as much to blame for falling sick as they were stupid—they were the ones who failed to follow the advice on prophylaxis and prevention he and Dr. Broussoux gave when they went out into the field.

Nithap didn't go so far as to disdain his patients, but only because that was a privilege his white colleagues had taken away from him. Of course, he was irritated by the racist phrases he heard them say: "They'll need a hundred years to get out of their dark night!" or "How would they ever know what to do with independence? They don't even know how to make a needle!" But if he had actually tried to dig up proof that those villagers were no longer living in the heart of darkness, he would have been hard put to find any. All of which to say that, in the end, he shared the opinions of his white colleagues, even if his sense of pride made him feel mildly indignant whenever he heard such things in the middle of a conversation.

Had they said, *You know full well we're right*, he certainly would have stammered his agreement.

Or perhaps he would have just redoubled his efforts, given additional sermons to the villagers, insisted even more fervently on the lesson, because it had become a point of personal pride. But still, he wasn't the one who'd had a man who'd been walking around naked at the market thrown into jail, even though some mean-spirited gossips pointed their fingers at him. When you don't have a comfortable place to sit, pride can make for a really sore behind. You see, our doctor had grown used to knowing the community was proud of him. Dressed in his white smock, stethoscope across his chest, he'd walk through the courtyard, between the rows where patients lay, some on bamboo cots, others on woven mats, and each person, regardless of how they were suffering, would pull back their feet so he could pass. His arrival was always preceded by a characteristic hubbub—rustles and whispers—and all eyes turned to him, as if to say, *That's our son!* It wasn't so much that he was overly proud, it was really more of a defense. He was putting on an act for his white colleagues, and it was a reflection of his fears: fear of the humiliation of being taken for one of those villagers, despite the smock he wore to set himself apart; fear of being taken for one of his relatives, although his job had cut him off from them. It was out of fear of being thrown in with his patients that the doctor sometimes walked all the way back to the village still dressed in white. And proudly so.

His white outfit was a sort of shell.

So when, on one of his visits, Elie Tbongo showed him some bits of his translation of the Bible into Bagam writing, Nithap suddenly heard in his heartbeat the hymn of a pride he'd never before felt. The pastor explained to him that while the whites had helped to solidify the place of Medumba by using it in the schools, the translation of the Bible—the key to establishing a new literary culture—remained unfinished. He was working, for his part, on standardizing spelling in the Medumba alphabet, because, he added, "the Latin alphabet doesn't account for the inflexions of our local languages.

"The translation of the Bible will be incomplete without *our alphabet*."

He said "our alphabet" as if those were Nithap's words, even though Nithap had been unaware that a Bamileke alphabet even existed. Pastor Tbongo showed him the fruits of his hard work, softly reading the lines that otherwise would have remained no more than hieroglyphs, but that now revealed a paradise. The doctor would have liked to borrow those scribbled notes, to run across the hills and show them to his white colleagues, to Dr. Broussoux. But, realizing how ridiculous that impulse was, he got ahold of himself. Pride is only a poor substitute for ignorance. That's how he, who had been brought into that living room by love, became the pupil of the man he hoped would become his father-in-law, moved by nothing more than a desire to improve himself or, simply put, to strengthen his "soul."

So, his dream of marrying Ngountchou was bolstered by his will to become her father's disciple. Nithap would rush along the path to Pastor Tbongo's home with wings that only love can put on a fiancé's feet, and have the supplies and delicacies he brought carried to his mentor's back courtyard. Then he'd take his place at the feet of the man of the church, with the rabid hunger of someone who has just awoken. He was no longer only trying to wheedle his way into the man's heart so he could marry his daughter; no, he had opened his mind completely to take in the unbelievable world this man revealed to him, word by word, page by page.

4

Who in Bangangte didn't know Elie Tbongo? A big man, no mustache, but with a full beard beneath his chin, usually wearing a black *togho*, a caftan embroidered with designs in red and yellow, and strands of multicolored beads around his neck—the garb of the traditional nobility from which he was descended. Snide comments from the peasants gathered around the bar in the chief's compound were the only things that tarnished his reputation: "Alas, he only had daughters," "Just two children."

Perfidious words were sometimes whispered—"He thinks he's a white man"—because no one understood why he wasn't polygamous. Nja Yonke', his wife, would have told those men about her repeated miscarriages, about her pain for having buried five children, all who had died too soon. But, as disgustingly drunk as they were, who would have heard her voice? Sarcasm is second nature to the Bangangte. You try to explain to any of them why the joy of that woman, with overflowing breasts and strong arms, was now expressed only in the songs and dances of the Women's Chorale that she led! Who among them would have had the patience to see why that woman had finally found in the Bible the refuge that this chaotic world refused her, and why she'd shaped the intelligent young man her husband Elie Tbongo had been into the catechist he'd become? Everyone knew the pastor, but few people in Bangangte were aware of his garden of secrets.

Tanou still remembers him today, even though he knew him only through his mother's words. He had taught Bagam writing to his daughters. And it was during those years—those years when he used to spend vacations back in the village with his cousins, his aunt Mensa''s children and others—that Tanou had found that old woven raffia bag, his first *bom tcha*, which had somehow miraculously survived and in which he discovered four notebooks of lined paper. A miracle that they hadn't been destroyed! That those grimy, dog-eared documents, stinking of insecticide, had survived his move to America was a real miracle! It was those notebooks that made him the Narrator of this tale today, because he was able to flesh out what he found in the pastor's notebooks with stories, both little and big, improbable and true to life, *nou* and *tcho*, *tcho* and *toli*,* and put together his family history.

"Did he also give a bag of stories to Bagam?"

That was Angela asking.

"Impossible." Tanou added, "He never got to meet him."

"So how did he learn the writing, then?"

"Our Little Papa is amazing!" His cousin was lost for a moment in his thoughts, then added, "We should bring him over here."

The house in Bangangte hasn't changed at all, just like most of the other houses in the West, really, it remains swathed in that eternal blanket of dust, that laterite that at once pulls it out of time and preserves it. Today, like yesterday, the house remains imposing, bearing witness to a colonial architecture that used local materials, mud bricks strengthened with straw, but a white man's design. The veranda, protected by a hedge of *nfekang*,† opens up onto a kitchen garden, planted with cinchona, for quinine, but also the tobacco that filled Elie Tbongo's pipe, and beyond that, onto the crossroads by the market, to the pulse of the village, to the greetings, in turn respectful and sly, of those passing by who, either way, never forgot the salute owed to the *Passitou*, as they called him, and who bowed to the ground when they saw *ndocta* sitting beside him. Because that veranda was where the pastor would read each afternoon, sitting in his bamboo armchair. That's where he worked, surrounded by people,

---

* *Nou* is History; *toli*, a story; and *tcho*, the tales we tell.

† *Nfekang*, or peace tree, is a symbol of peace for the Bamilekes.

and also where—with the dog Kouandiang sitting at his feet, licking himself to chase away the flies, and scratching his reddened ears—he welcomed Nithap, the hungry visitor at his door. The two men would go inside to eat only when Mensa' called them to the table, followed by the mutt.

"Maman is calling you," the young girl would say, before disappearing. "The food is ready."

Sometimes, however, they would linger on the veranda, and Mensa' would come back to clear the table later, after they'd eaten.

The pastor's reputation in this region, scarred by centuries of war against the Bamum and by the Church's paternalism, was really due to his preaching. When he interpreted the priest's sermons, a white man's sermons, he added the eloquent flourish of Medumba, rhetorical turns of phrase that made more than one person pause to consider the power of his words, then shake his head and smile. Rather than echoing through the church, his raspy voice sounded like your neighbor in the village. His sentences were longer than those he translated from the French, because he added layers of nuance and his own personal touch. This didn't displease the priest, who listened to Tbongo just as carefully as if he were delivering a parallel sermon. For soon his voice would be carried on the lips of each of the villagers sitting in the parish church, who recognized themselves so clearly in his words that after each sentence they'd look at each other and say, "*Ne ne ne*," "Yes, so true."

Mensa' was the younger of Elie Tbongo's children and seventeen at the time. She was the one who, as people used to say, was "still in the house." Tanou would never be able to figure out just how much education his two mothers had received—as they aged, he thought of them as twins—nor even if they'd ever actually gone to school. Toward the end of her life, Ngountchou had a shop in the Bangwa market, spending her time there as people do to while away the days of retirement. That's where Tanou had grown up, among the displays of yams and *macabo*, bunches of bananas and multicolored parasols, and where he'd gotten an education from the lively exchanges among the market women. Ngountchou was a wholesaler, regularly going to Bazou to replenish her stores;

it was on one of those trips, which she usually made before dawn in an *opep*, a pickup truck, that she had the accident that changed her life. That accident had, little by little, led to her death, as Tanou would later say. His first memory of her was sitting there in her well-stocked shop, surrounded by women, lively *bayamsallams* with acid tongues, pagnes tied tightly around their hips, scarves around their heads, and a change purse tucked between their breasts, each pointing out the goods they wanted to buy.

Pastor Tbongo hadn't wanted that kind of shopkeeper's life for his daughter, quite the contrary. When he'd entrusted her to the wisdom of Mademoiselle Birgitte, he'd summed up his dreams, the future he envisioned for her, in one sentence: "I'm giving you my daughter so you can raise her." So the Norwegian woman's home had become the place of Ngountchou's apprenticeship, and the children were her masters, if you'll permit the expression. Spending time with them was the most agreeable—and also the most exhausting—of tasks. You see, although Mademoiselle Birgitte wasn't married and had no children of her own, her heart was as big as those of the mothers in our legends. It was simply impossible for her to see a child orphaned in the hospital and not feel responsible. Where did all those children come from? In a society where girls were supposed to be virgins on the day they were married, in a village where women were seen as valuable only if they were wives, "mistakes" were a source of personal shame you could see written on the faces of the children in the orphanage.

Maybe it's because she spent her days surrounded by children who'd been given up, some by girls her own age so they could finagle a legitimate marriage in the future, that Ngountchou stayed chaste during her long engagement. She never suspected that her father had sent her to live in the middle of all those abandoned children to make her aware of the consequences of an immoral life. Her headscarf always neatly tied, her eyes downcast, she had the habits of a well-brought-up girl, one on a straight and narrow path—which was what every parent hoped for. The doctor's visits did nothing to call that future into question; on the contrary, they were its crowning glory. When she decided on her own that she'd become a seamstress, Pastor Elie Tbongo acquiesced with regret.

"My daughter is intelligent," he'd say later to Nithap, with not a hint of doubt in his voice. "She can do better."

Nithap didn't reply, *With six children?* Yet the couple would eventually have six children. Tanou, born in 1972, would be the next-to-youngest.

"She can aim higher."

"And who will take care of *our children*, then?"

If the description of hell is always a catechist's best pedagogical weapon, Mademoiselle Birgitte's home offered the promise of paradise. At least, it was that image of paradise that stuck in Nithap's mind when he saw the woman who would soon become his wife. He could never imagine her differently than that first time he'd seen her, an overly young mother surrounded by children. Yes, she awoke in the morning to cries and tears, and that was just the start of a day that would only really end once the last of the tots had worn themselves out and fallen asleep; yes, the assistant was exhausted at the end of each day. But when she woke up in the morning already on the verge of exasperation, she'd pause and consider that she was not so much fulfilling her father's dream as that of the man who had looked at her and seen the future mother of his children.

Soon she was *waiting* for his visits.

It's impossible to say it was love at first sight. *Waiting* is the right word, because, yes, she waited for her fiancé's visits, growing ever more distracted, her eyes trained on the bamboo fence. The days when Nithap wasn't on duty, his visits to Mademoiselle Birgitte's allowed him to pursue his suit. The children were an escape for the young lovers. Nithap could always take one of them into his arms and speak to Ngountchou about the child, as if he were their own.

And you could count on Nyamsi to give a name to the desire Nithap felt for that young girl—which kept him from sleeping, kept him marching along the trails around Bangwa, tracing differential equations with each step, and made him walk with one hand in his pocket to keep his *bangala* in line. All of that because she was nothing like the girls at the Noutong school. "Typical Bamileke," Nyamsi said. "You, so educated, you can only choose for a wife a girl who hasn't gone to school."

He didn't go so far as to say that Ngountchou was a *mboutoukou*, not very smart and illiterate, but it was just as if. Besides, that was only because Nyamsi's girlfriend didn't give him the chance to.

"Don't insult the training it takes to keep a home," said Mademoiselle Birgitte.

"I know, I know," he'd say, raising his hands in the air. "It's clear you just want to marry your own mother, Oedipus."

Nithap would laugh, as much because he'd been caught out as because he was proud of the unquestionable clarity of his feelings. He didn't know that Nyamsi, whose particular talent was to see clearly into everyone else's character, had already written the scenario for his friend's wife's future. She'd never leave the nursery; she'd never lose that insistent smell of dried milk stains on a mother's bra. Every two years she'd have a sleeping child tied on her back, or another bawling child holding on to a corner of her *kaba ngondo*; and step-by-step, meticulously and inexorably, she'd go through the stages of her life as if she were playing a role written out in advance by two men who were joined, ever more tightly, by their mutual admiration for each other.

"That's enough," cut in the woman who was friends with both of them.

And she was right.

Nyamsi knew how to respect the limits of friendship. What Nithap didn't tell his companions was that his feelings dictated his behavior. If he wanted to start a family with Ngountchou, *waiting* was what he had to do. *Waiting*, yes, that's the word, by which I mean waiting for each of the parties involved to get used to things, waiting for all the details to come into focus, for the terms of analysis to be clearly defined, and the interlocking traditions to fall into place.

"*Your fiancé* is here," Mademoiselle Birgitte would say at each of those visits, visits that used to have an entirely different purpose.

Ngountchou would appear, free for the moment from the children. She'd greet her "fiancé" with that ever-enigmatic smile on her face. She'd mumble one or two words, brief answers to questions, really, replies rather than things she wanted to add to the conversation herself, and then she'd disappear.

"The Bamilekes are complicated, huh?" Nyamsi would murmur. "Why this game of hide-and-seek?"

He wouldn't go any further than that, though, shot through by his girlfriend's glare. There in the living room, in the cocoon of that benevolent friendship, Ngountchou could observe the man who would become her husband. She observed and knew she was being observed, as well. She observed, knowing that here she couldn't even sit down next to that man who desired her so, because etiquette imposed a certain distance. The engagement period is one of the most political moments of life for the Medumbas! It is an exercise in patience, but also helps to develop in each of the parties a talent for calculated observation, so that it is as much a game of chess as a play, a hesitant bit of choreography on the edge of a precipice, where each one needs to have nerves of steel.

Mademoiselle Birgitte said she could see the reasons for her own decision to stay single playing out in front of her, while Nyamsi, for his part, saw in it the reasons why he preferred the excitement of illicit affairs. You could tell that neither of them was Bangangte. You see, the controlled transformation of the future bride's impatience into deep care for the man who desires her, and of the inquisitive gaze of the man into a clear plan of action, well, that sums up what was really at stake in this staged sentimental drama. It might one day lead to love, but for the moment it was focused on the coming proposal.

For Nithap, these ritual repetitions—the visits, the winks, the silent pauses, even the children—didn't just let them get to know each other, they created a craving, a need, connection. Because, of course, if Nithap hadn't noticed Ngountchou, then she would have looked upon him with the same indifference she had for other visitors, or she'd have glanced at him with only the half-hearted curiosity a young girl has about any man. But he had been able to pique her interest, which was most clearly seen in her nervousness—the nervousness that made her hold on to the hem of her dress whenever she spoke to her fiancé.

Ngountchou didn't look Nithap in the eyes, because she was trying to hide the trembling of her hands, which made her lose the self-assurance she showed when he wasn't there. That nervousness made her feel vulnerable, irritable, plunged her into a whirlwind of emotions that was betrayed by her embarrassment and sealed her lips tight. *How to get a word out of her? How to make her say something?* That was what Nithap asked himself, because her vulnerability made her all the more appealing in his eyes.

But vulnerability doesn't turn a fiancée into a wife, that goes without saying. Nithap began to bring her clothes. There were no limits to what he would do—not to how much he would spend or the time it would take. Soon he was no longer talking to the girl in an apron that he'd seen surrounded by toddlers, but to a woman in a flowing, flowery dress. Each one of her transformations stoked his desire, turning him into the ideal fiancé. Because that's really what this was about, letting desire build slowly, as each learned to keep their feelings in check; that's how love is traditionally cultivated.

Ngountchou often wondered if the mothers whose children she cared for had felt love grow, step-by-step, as she had, or if it had come upon them in a sudden rush—but she'd sweep those thoughts out of her mind. She'd watch them coming down the Bangwa hills, racing off to meet their fiancé in a thicket, and that just made her feel all the more embarrassed. There, on the hilltop where the station sat, cut off from her childhood friends, and even from Mensa', she held, you could say, her love in her own hands. Were it not for the notes and letters she wrote to her sister, there'd be no record of this slow blossoming of love in her heart, because she lived through the start of her marriage in solitude, enthralled by the brilliance of her passion.

5

And then there was the question of the dowry. For Nithap, there was only one person who could serve as his witness during the ceremonies. That's why he was on his way to visit Nyamsi. His friend lived in a bachelor's apartment—not even the pines and bougainvilleas around the veranda could make it look any less spartan. His landlady greeted Nithap in the courtyard, where she was sitting, shelling pistachios.* "Yes, the teacher is there," she said, spitting on the ground. Nithap knocked on the door several times before realizing it was unlocked. Nyamsi was shaving. He was naked from the waist up, holding a mirror in one hand and whistling a popular tune by Joseph Kabasele. *Table ronde, indépendance, table ronde, indépendance.* When he saw the enamored doctor, though, he started the conversation out on a very different note.

"Bangangte is the only place these days," he said, without even greeting his friend, "where one can support the UPC and still live in peace."

Ah yes, that's Nyamsi for you. He didn't even give his friend a chance to sit down, much less tell him the reason for his visit.

"Is that why you don't bother locking your door?" Nithap tossed out.

"Look around a bit," Nyamsi went on, coming into the living room

---

* Francophone Cameroonians call "pistachios" what the Anglophones and others in Africa call *egusi*. They're a delicacy—but the word is also a reference to female genitalia. (Remember that for later.)

and gesturing to his friend, while his blood-shot eyes scanned all around. "Here, everything is calm and peaceful."

Then he started whistling Kabasele again.

"Bangangte has always been calm," Nithap interjected, starting to get worked up. "Are you just figuring that out now?"

"And how!" Nyamsi jumped in. "There's a reason why the largest group of migrants in Cameroon comes from Bangangte. Who protested when the Germans were filling Mbanga and Nkongsamba, N'lohe, Melong, and Bali with people from Bangangte?"

"Here, diaspora is part of the culture," Nyamsi concluded. Nithap knew that his friend was parodying him.

"Well, that's what I say," Nyamsi added. "Don't get angry, my brother, but you are cowards. You run away instead of . . ."

"Fighting?"

"Yes, here that's true. But not in Mungo."

"Those who refused to become slaves, have you forgotten?" Nithap interrupted.

"But that was against the Bamum," Nyamsi said. "I know *your* history. 1890. Ngantue." Then he started to mimic Nithap: "The dynamism of the Bamilekes is a reaction against the Bamum conquest . . . It's a reflex born of resistance . . . Cameroon has a Bamileke problem because the Bamilekes have a Bamum problem . . ." He held out his open hands and shook his head. "But just look at today . . ."

"Are you forgetting Daniel Kemajou?"*

"Yes, I know, his last hurrah protesting the state of emergency in Yaounde, after he'd gone to New York to contradict Um Nyobè, and had gotten everyone here to vote for Ahidjo's constitution. We know he was trying to fix his reputation."

"Fix it in whose eyes?"

---

* A Bangangte traditional chief and politician, Kemajou was president of the Legislative Assembly, ALCAM, at a time of great consequence for Cameroon's constitution today. The pivotal moment came when Ahmadou Ahidjo, then prime minister, was given "full authority" to combat the UPC rebellion. The speech Kemajou gave on October 29, 1959, against the state of emergency and the descent of the country into tyranny was historic. The country still has not emerged from that crisis.

"Drop it! After he gave his speech, he fled and sought refuge with the Anglophones, right or wrong?"

That's how Nyamsi was! He couldn't accept defeat in arguments, was quick to lay down ultimatums, to draw battle lines. He headed back to the rear of the apartment. Nithap sat down and started counting the holes in the couch. He was tempted to shout out, *What about Ntchantchou Zacharie?* but thought better of it. He already knew his friend would reply, *One more who voted for the state of emergency!*

Instead he said, "Ouandié Ernest," and stuck a finger into one of the holes, as if trying to make it bigger. That was his wild card.

He was expecting his friend to say, *Ouandié is Bangou*, and then to give him a lesson on the kinship between Bamileke and Bangangte, between Bangangte and Bangou. *Do you even know that* you *yourself are Bangangte?* he wanted to ask. But Nyamsi wasn't listening, the sound of running water made it clear what he was doing. *What has gotten into him?* the doctor wondered, baffled by so much aggression.

"What Cameroon needs," Nyamsi began, coming back to the living room, his face fresh and bright, "is a large people's party." As he spoke, he applied aftershave to his cheeks. "A party that would bring us all together, you and me, the Bamilekes, the Bassas, the Betis, the Northerners, and transform our friendship into a *political project*."

Ahh! thought Nithap, his hand now fiddling with the doily. *This must be about a girl.*

"*Political ambition*, you mean, but that makes it a crime."

"A party with the courage to represent all of our greatest aspirations," his friend plowed ahead, like the train from Nkongsamba. "A party that would take the voices of the city folk into account, and the villagers, too, men and women alike." Nyamsi held his razor up in front of his face.

Hmm, this is getting serious, Nithap thought. *Who could it be? He must not be getting laid.*

Nyamsi's voice echoed in the freshly perfumed living room.

"That party already exists, and it's the UPC, but alas! *They* are destroying it as we speak. *They* won't compromise, because their goal is the total destruction of the enemy."

Nithap had never seen him so worked up. If Nyamsi had given him the chance to get in even one word, he would have asked, *Just who are* they? and then continued, *You need the colonists to bring the people together.* He might even have gone on ironically, *Is that why you're sleeping with Mademoiselle Birgitte? To humiliate her, am I right?* He knew that Nyamsi would reply, like always, *My dear, God created woman, and nuns the diaphragm.*

Instead he said, "Tell the truth. The real tragedy, according to you, is that Cameroon is already independent. By throwing the country into independence, the French cut you off from the enemy you need to unite the Cameroonian people. So just what do you mean when you say 'they,' my dear?"

Nyamsi didn't let him go any further.

"The Cameroonian people," he cut in, "that's their enemy. *They* declared war against the Cameroonian people. My brother, the civil war has already begun, and right now, here in Bangangte, life goes on as if nothing has happened. Calm and peaceful. *Nda' nda', nda' nda'*, gently, gently."

He said those words in Medumba with a smile, that satyr with the cutting words.

"And you, you're putting on perfume."

But Nyamsi wasn't listening to him.

"War," he went on, suddenly lowering the hand that was still clutching the razor. "Sometimes I want to just give everything up and join the *Maquis*."

When he said *Maquis* he emphasized the *i*, like the Bassas do. A silence fell over the living room and came between the two men, a very long silence during which Nyamsi meticulously, almost methodically, examined himself in the mirror, twisting his lips and stretching out his features, as if trying to confirm that it was really he who'd just formulated that thought. It was as if, knowing he had an audience, he took some pride in the word he'd dared to say. He was basking in the silent applause. A sly smile spread across his lips, lighting up his face, which already looked much younger, thanks to the shave, returned to a more childlike, oval shape. Two light taps on his cheeks, and he started whistling "Table ronde" again.

"So," he said, "am I handsome now, Mister Fiancé?"

As if the one who asked that question hadn't just declared himself a Maquisard. He didn't even wait for an answer but disappeared into his bedroom. Nithap sat back down in the living room. There was a stack of books on a shelf next to him, alongside some political brochures, one of which, *Le Patriote kamerunais* (with *Cameroon* spelled with a *k*, German-style) caught his attention. He leafed through it, pausing on the photo of Ernest Ouandié and Abel Kengne,* then noticed a revised version of the national anthem. *How does he manage to get these things in Bangangte?* There were also some French fashion magazines that he leafed through, stopping here and there and wondering if any of the outfits could work for his future plans, but still mulling over his friend's words, which were at odds with the reason why he had come to see him. A jacket in the catalog from the French store La Redoute caught his eye, then he turned quickly to another. "Not bad."

When Nyamsi came back out of his bedroom, the question his friend had on his lips left him perplexed. "Will you come with me to Ngountchou's?"

"If it's for *that*," Nyamsi said, his voice taking a teacher's objective tone, "the black jacket won't do."

"Yes, combatant."

"Unless you're already planning to bury the Sinistrés!"†

The two friends smiled, because obviously neither of them wanted that.

* Ernest Ouandié and Abel Kengne (alias Abel Kingué), independence leaders; we'll talk more about them later. Please be patient. —The Narrator.

† *Sinistrés* (or victims) and *tsuitsuis* are both local terms and synonyms for members of the Sinistre de la Défense Nationale du Kamerun, SDNK, during the civil war. The members are also called Maquisards (or resistance fighters), as well as "terrorists" by the powers fighting against them, and "nationalists" by their supporters.

For Nithap that day had been a marathon. Pastor Tbongo had asked him to come to Bangangte. He said he needed his learned advice. The doctor of souls wanted to hire someone to manage a building project, a new house; he hoped Nithap could come with him. So, before he'd gotten to Nyamsi's, Nithap had already spent the morning with the pastor. They'd gone together to Bangoulap, the neighboring town, and knocked on the door of a house built in the traditional style, with a roof of woven raffia, mud walls, and low windows; ducks and hens were wandering around the courtyard. A scrawny man dressed in the traditional *tayangam* and *touma'** had come out from the smoky house, a broad smile on his face, and knelt before them, with his palms outstretched, as if he were greeting a chief. His wife, whom he'd beckoned from the back of the house, soon appeared, wearing just a branch of *nfekang*, peace tree leaves, in lieu of a loincloth; she bowed in the same way and then ran back, disappearing in the shadows of the house, only to reappear, now with an orange-flowered pagne tied around her hips and holding a calabash filled with water.

"I was waiting for you, *Passitou*," the man said; then he turned toward Nithap and, bowing even lower than the first time, added, "My *ndap* is Tankongan."†

Nithap told him his, while the pastor helped him up.

"*Ndocta*"—the man's use of that title showed his respect for Nithap's position—"I am happy to welcome such *eminent people* to my home."

His emphasis on *eminent people* was matched by his own self-effacement, as evident in the dialectal intonation of his words.‡ He had a deformity, a clubfoot, which made it hard for him to move about, but on top of that, his movements reflected a subservient politeness. His enigmatic phrasing struck Nithap. *Here's a real Bangoulap*,§ the doctor thought

---

* *Tayangam*, a sort of trouser worn by the Bamilekes, made of a piece of cloth wrapped between the legs; *touma'*, a Bamileke shirt.

† Tankongan, a Bangoulap *ndap*, or praise name, means seller of munitions, bullets.

‡ For example, pronouncing *p* instead of *b*, saying *pôn* instead of *bôn*, the word for couscous.

§ Since Bangoulap and Bangwa are neighboring villages, like so many other *ntang la'*, they are linked by a number of stories, myths, and stereotypes.

with a smile. Tankongan led his two guests to the rear of the house, toward a display of bricks beneath a canopy of woven banana leaves. They passed another woman, naked as well, who was kneeling in the shade of a rack for drying corn and grinding spices on a stone, the rhythm of her work marked by the swinging of her breasts. Pastor Tbongo greeted her with her *ndap*, "Ntchankou, o," then bent down to pick up one of the bricks pointed out by her husband and looked at it intently. He broke off a chip and passed it to Nithap, asking his opinion.

The woman rose and disappeared into the smoky kitchen. The chickens and ducks rushed to the spot she'd left.

This was the first time the doctor had been consulted about a building project; he took it as a sign of confidence from the man he hoped to make his father-in-law.

"I don't know what to say," he began honestly, because he was actually wondering why the man hadn't used his bricks to build his own house. During the discussion that followed, he stayed silent.

"The brickmakers are all ready, *Passitou*," the builder began. "If I understand correctly, we'll need hundreds of bricks."

"Yes, several hundred."

He stuck his right hand into his *tayangam* and scratched his testicles.

"For five bedrooms and two living rooms?"

"Yes, precisely, to begin with."

"I see."

The men spent the rest of the time looking over the plans that the pastor had spread out before them. They went over all the details, considering the placement of the rooms, their layout.

"That's the family crypt," said the pastor.

"There is still more usable space," Tankongan added. "This is a large piece of land. Even a duck couldn't fill the courtyard with shit."

"That's where my family will be buried."

Nithap turned to consider the man, both taciturn and determined. *He only has daughters*, he thought. *So why is he building such a large crypt?* Never had the idealism of his future father-in-law appeared to him so clearly as in that moment of resistance against a fate that had already marked him as defeated. "Ngountchou will be my wife," he whispered, and that sentence echoed in his mind like a private act of dissidence, a gesture of refusal, a mark of his own *Tchunda*,* as opposed to the one that was taking shape in front of him, and which seemed to him condemned by biology to remain just a dream. *This man doesn't want his daughter to marry*, he thought, and the building, the plans of which were sketched before his eyes, appeared as the temple of his fiancée's silence.

Soon the pastor and his interlocutor moved on to the choice of masons, coming up with a list of names.

"I know them all, *Passitou*," Tankongan said. "They're the ones who built the palace of the Bangwa chief."

"Nono's† palace?"

The phrasing was carefully calculated. Pastor Tbongo said "Nono," without any title or term of respect, just his *fit*, or patronym, which amounted to an insult.

"Yes, *Passitou*," Tankongan replied, choosing his words carefully; for the first time a certain agitation could be heard in his voice, "but they did it in honor of Chief No Tchoutouo."

Imposed by the French after they'd exiled the legitimate heir to the Bangwa throne, Jean Nono—whom people around here still called *nshun mekat*‡ and who had learned the art of intrigue from his experience as a trader in Douala—hadn't dared to move into the legendary palace. Even presumption has its limits. The high commissioner had awarded him the Colonial Medal of Merit, but that didn't mean he could do just

* *Tchunda*, a derivative of *tchun*, which means buttocks or sex, and *nda*, home: the buttocks of the home, or its foundation, but figuratively the family—or lineage, more precisely.

† Even today, mentioning the name of this Bangwa chief causes trouble; so, dear reader, please do not do it, especially not in front of a Bangwa, unless you're trying to provoke him.

‡ *Nshun mekat*: the white man's friend, very pejorative in this context. He earned this name for, among other things, his actions in support of France in 1940, when he was part of JEUCAFRA, the Jeunesse camerounaise française, or Franco-Cameroonian Youth Association, the antecedent of the political party that is still in power in Cameroon.

anything. In any event, his epilepsy* already condemned him to living a reclusive life. The breaking of the line of succession, however, had covered the whole region with shame, and this builder in particular. Despite the dignity of his art, Tankongan had had to take the money and build the palace the new leader demanded.

Nono had come to the Bangoulaps looking for artisans, because none of the Bangwas wanted to work on his "cursed palace." The Bangoulap chief himself was forced to intervene to convince Tankongan to do it. It was the largest project he'd completed to date. Yet the builder wasn't proud of it because the corruption was contrary to his principles and everything he'd been taught. The artisan in him couldn't help but mention his masterpiece, however, especially since it was the first time he'd used bricks, after he'd received his diploma from the art school in Foumban.

The mention of the name Nono embarrassed him and then made him bitter. His shame was all the more apparent because he was talking to a pastor. You'd have thought he suddenly wanted to burn down the palace he'd built himself! And now he needed to set a price for the bricks and, what's worse: haggle. Talking about money, that's torture for the Bangangtes!

"Give me what you want," he said quietly, obviously mortified. "I'll do a good job for you."

"In any event, we'll first have to get Nono's authorization to build the house," the pastor cut in.

"Even in Toungou?"

"You know how he can cause trouble, don't you?" With that, Elie Tbongo revealed his pragmatism and, in the same stroke, his tactical skills. "But I won't pay him for it."

The man, who remembered quite clearly how he'd been persecuted by the chief back when he was locked in a struggle for power with the Kumzse, was drawing a clear line in the sand. He was also clear that he didn't need to hand out money to mobilize an army of Christians, as

* Epilepsy remains a bone of contention between the Bangwas and the Bangangtes, the latter accusing the former of maliciously causing the spread of the disease through their territory.

he often did to cultivate his own fields. Now everything in the chief's domain had a price. The resentment that had spread over the region came from that extraordinary shift: the replacement of an age-old, dignified tradition of gift-giving by commercial transactions. Once, a wise noble had termed it the "sowing of misery." "Even in a hundred years, we'll never grow rich with such a system," a man had said—a man who will soon make his entrance into this story under a different name: the Extraordinary Villager. For Tankongan, a man too honest, the real breaking point had come when the title of Manveun* had been bought by a woman he called "the prostitute from Njombe who works for the white planters." The builder and the pastor looked at each other, realizing how they were caught up in a system they'd be hard put to escape.

On the way back, Nithap, who was from Bangwa, felt he needed to say something.

"What happened in Bangwa isn't unique," he said.

The doctor began to list off the names of chiefs who'd been imprisoned, removed from power by the colonial authorities, or sent into exile because they had refused to serve the regime.

"Campo," the pastor added, "Douala, Dschang . . ."

The two men stopped listing the many places where chiefs had been imprisoned. A silence fell over them, a clear sign of their growing complicity. Much later, an order from the Bamileke prefect would allow Pastor Elie Tbongo to build his *Tchunda* in the forest of Toungou, near Bazou, in the village where he was born.

"This land is grumbling," Nithap said.

"But who will listen?"

Suddenly the doctor realized how protected they had been till then from the upheavals that were shaking Cameroon. There was that story of usurpation in Baham that had turned the chief's compound into a powder keg. They said the rebellion that was born after the legitimate chief had been deposed had spread through the region of Bafoussam,

* Manveun: Mother of the Chief. This is both a title and a position. The position is, obviously, biological, but the title . . .

throughout all the West, really. They said that the dissidents had formed a rebel army and called themselves the Sinistrés. They talked about a leader named Wandji: Earnest Ouandié.*

But Nithap was really thinking about the deputy Samuel Wanko,† the deputy from Bafoussam who'd been assassinated in 1957 in awful circumstances, after having been forced to march through the city in his underpants, with a sock stuck on his head; he thought of the brouhaha caused by that episode, which even made its way to the hospital. That was the reason why the minister of health had visited and distributed all those medals, "To calm things down." "To bring peace." The minister had later appeared at a reception at the chief's compound, *nfekang* in hand, but still surrounded by his bodyguards. That's certainly why later that day, when Nyamsi exploded with anger and accused the Bangangtes of cowardice, Nithap mentioned the name Kemajou, the paramount chief from Bazou and president of the Territorial Assembly, who'd opposed the imposition of martial law, which gave unlimited power to the president of the republic. He was living in exile in Nkongsamba.

"Who will listen to the grumbling of the land?" Nithap repeated. He was thinking of the High Plateau.

The pastor didn't reply.

---

* A very common name in the region of Bangangte where the patronym, the *fit*, can be either inherited or given. As noted above, the different spelling here is just a reflection of transliteration.

† A deputy in the National Assembly, which was granted no parliamentary immunity from the prime minister's powers under the state of emergency, and so provided no protection for its members, who were caught between the hammer and the anvil.

6

Two days after settling Ngountchou's dowry, Nithap was abducted. He had left the hospital late that night. The ceremonies hadn't upset his work schedule. He spent the final days of his single life planning their honeymoon. He had thought about a trip to N'lohe, to see his older sister, then to Kumba, where his other siblings and cousins lived. Although his family was from Bangwa, they'd been scattered along the coast after the dispute over naming a new chief. Thousands of people had left Bangwa and some of his brothers had become Anglophone. He didn't see them often. In fact, they now lived in another country, Nigeria.

When he found the door to his house open, his first reflex was to imagine he was already married.

Ngountchou must have forgotten to close the door, he said to himself.

He went through the door and a violent blow to the head made him lose consciousness. When he opened his eyes, he was in a bamboo hut. The cooing of weaver birds and the cry of a rooster in the distance told him it was morning, and the scent of fresh earth that he was in the bush. Because of the mist, he knew he was in the highlands. An awful headache kept him from moving. He wanted to cry out, but stopped short when he saw Clara Ntchantchou come through the door. His face lit up.

"Clara," he exclaimed, practically shouting as he tried to get up. "Clara, why am I here?"

She hurried over and held him down.

"Don't move," she said. "Massa, don't move, I'm here."

Nithap was shivering. He grabbed hold of her hand, while she tried with all her might to keep him lying down. Clara was wearing a dress that he had bought for his fiancée's dowry.

"Where is Ngountchou?" he asked.

"Massa," Clara insisted, "do not move, *ne tchou'*, please."

Nithap was so confused and distressed that, as he looked into the face of the woman who had taken care of him and even lived under his roof, all the questions swirling around in his mind came down to one simple cry: "Help!"

"Massa," she whispered as she held him down, "nothing is going to happen to you here. Nothing *can* happen to you."

With those words, and her intonation, she was trying to apologize. She saw the fear in the doctor's face.

"Clara," Nithap asked, "is that you? Is it really you?"

"Yes, massa."

"Why am I here?"

"Nothing can happen to you, massa," Clara insisted, as she turned toward the door. "We are here."

Right then a man came into the hut.

"My husband," she said, as she stood back up. "You know each other."

And in fact Nithap did recognize the man, dressed in *tayangam* and *touma'*, who leaned toward him and took off his hat. He had seen him several times before, first at the hospital, when the man had come to be treated for a snakebite. His foot had been bandaged and Clara was holding his hand, while his three other wives, who were a bit older, sat beside him, each with ankles crossed and one hand pressed against her temple, as if they were already in mourning. The snakebite he'd needed treatment for was quite common.

Rather than coming back to the hospital for a follow-up, he'd shown up in Nithap's courtyard, accompanied then by only one of his wives, Clara. Nithap told him that he didn't treat patients at his house, but the man replied that he'd come looking for work for his wife. He pulled a chicken out of his bag and showed it to the doctor.

"Are you trying to bribe me?" Nithap had shouted.

The man had taken the puffy hat off his head, politely offering repeated apologies; then he put the chicken back in the bag, grasped his wife's hand, and pulled her away. Moving awkwardly, mechanically, he put the cap back on his head as he went. Nithap watched him go, limping and lecturing his wife, who was lagging behind and seemed to be complaining under her breath. Nithap had thought for a moment and then called them back. *That woman can take care of my nephew*, he'd thought. He was struck by the husband's over-the-top routine, just as he'd been amused by his hat, which suggested noble origins, but clashed with his funny gestures. *The Extraordinary Villager*, he'd dubbed him. *He thinks he's a* tchinda, *the chief's adviser, when actually he's a clown.*

That was how he'd come to hire Clara, but he hadn't taken her husband's chicken.

So Nithap found himself in a hut in the bush, once again facing the Extraordinary Villager, who was now holding his hat in his hands, although his gestures were still just as mechanical. This time it was he, the doctor, who was at the other's mercy.

"*Doctor*," said the man, crumpling his hat in his hands, and pronouncing the word in an accent no Bangangte peasant had. "Don't be afraid, you are my friend."

"Your friend?"

"You gave us food when you hired Clara to work at your house," he said. "You did us an immense service. We'll never forget that. We are friends."

"We?"

Nithap still didn't understand.

"We are friends," Clara repeated, nodding.

Her husband encouraged her to go on.

"We are *all* Sinistrés," she went on.

She looked at the Extraordinary Villager, as if hoping for a sign of approval, which he gave, then she looked back at the doctor.

"Sinistrés?"

When Nithap met the commander Singap Martin, the man had nothing but curses in his mouth. As if each of his sentences, in order to really be complete, needed to be peppered with curse words. Besides his liberal use of *lackeys* and *puppets* whenever he was talking about his enemies, he had developed an extensive vocabulary of dirty words that he spewed out at anyone who crossed him, whose face he couldn't stand, or whom he just wanted to go away immediately.

"*Ènè fumigène ndocta man wé di bring am soso?*"* he asked his soldiers in Pidgin when Nithap came up to him.

Pidgin was the language of the Maquis. Singap stared at the doctor, looking him over from head to toe; his words had made the doctor jump. Any doctor knows how to recognize the strategies that patients develop to contain their fear of death. For this man—an uncouth man with a childlike face, who wore his hair combed into a crest, Ghanaian-style—that strategy came down to dousing everyone around him with insults, forcing them to endure an endless shower of nauseating spite. And his disgust overflowed when Nithap, who had only just come out of his own stupor, was brought before him.

Singap, bedridden by a bullet, was chewing tobacco to control the pain. He pointed at his chest, where seeping blood had formed a large round black splotch. At the doctor's request, he shifted his body slightly.

"*Wéti you môsi catch din laquais so?*" Why are you watching this colonial lackey? he spat out as a challenge, though it made him cough. "*Lèf am so, hi fit go wôsi, he?*" Leave him, he's not going anywhere, is he?

They all looked at each other and then, except for Clara and the Extraordinary Villager, left the room. The doctor leaned down over the wounded man.

"Ow, Doctor! Be careful!"

The doctor smiled at him.

Nithap knew how to convince his patients to comply, even the most difficult ones. When faced with a problem he hadn't anticipated, he had a

* Now we're back to Pidgin, the Camtok style of Pidgin used in the Maquis, in contrast to Camfranglais, which is urban. This could be translated as, "So this is some unlicensed doctor you've brought me?"

habit of linking his fingers and cracking his knuckles loudly, as if trying to loosen himself up. That's what he did when Commander Singap opened his shirt and showed him the large wound on his left side, covered by a bloody bandage. Nithap turned immediately to Clara, speaking in the dialectal Bangwa he usually used with her.

"You'll bring me clean water and a knife?"

"Yes, massa," she replied.

She came back quickly.

"*Matériel na wôsi?*" Singap suddenly asked for the supplies.

Soon a man came in with a medical kit. Nithap recognized the symbol on its side: it was from the Bangwa hospital. He looked at the commander and his men.

"If you need supplies, you have to go get them," Singap spat out.

The doctor bent down and dug around in the kit.

"A cloth," he ordered the Extraordinary Villager.

"You are lucky," he said to Singap. "The bullet went straight through and didn't hit your lungs."

Martin Singap sighed, which led to more coughing.

"Gently," said the doctor, as he washed the wound. "You're not out of the woods yet."

Nithap would have to operate with the help of only two people. He spoke in Pidgin, and only to Clara.

"Take this," he said, handing her the knife, without a glance in her direction. "*Molo molo*, gently, huh?"

Clara took the bloody cloths as the doctor held them out.

Never had any village woman better filled the shoes of the nurses who usually assisted in operations at the Bangwa hospital! Only later did he realize how surprising that was, and a warm feeling flooded his heart, joy at having found such pure, raw talent. She was his left hand, his most courageous assistant, the most irreplaceable. He recognized in her a woman he'd never imagined back in his living room or in his kitchen, when he watched her shelling pistachios with her teeth.

7

Commandant we bi sign fô sonja wôk
*We bi sign to wôk sonja fô our heart!**

The next day Nithap woke up to a song. When he came out of his hut, he felt the slap of an icy breeze. He saw men and women singing and clapping in time, standing in a circle around a man playing a lute. This was how the combatants kept warm. One of them turned toward Nithap and pointed to another hut.

"*Commandant go si you fô ya.*" The Commander will see you there.

Singap Martin!

Who hadn't heard about him? Nithap said "Singap Martin," because that's how people referred to him, and also how it was written in the government newspapers that were delivered to the hospital, and where his name was always preceded by the phrase: "the terrorist." Two days after the operation, the doctor went to see his patient. *The Terrorist Singap Martin.* He recognized the jeep parked in front of the door to the hut as Dr. Broussoux's 2CV.

---

* This song should be easy to understand, so let's take it as an exercise in how to read Camtok, the first in the history of Cameroon. Let's translate it together, so we're prepared for what's coming next: *Commandant*, that's easy, in both French and English, *we* using the English pronoun instead of the French *nous*, *bi* is a particle, commonly added, *sign* again the English, which is like the French *signer*, *fô* based on the English, instead of the French *pour*, and *sonja wôk*, for the soldier's work, which means war. Translation of the first verse: "Commander, we are signed up for war." Can you translate the second?

Singap was sitting on the bamboo bed. Slowly chewing his tobacco, he carefully looked over the man who'd relieved his chest of the pain caused by the bullet, then leaned forward and, with a thoughtful look on his face, scratched his neck.

"Sit down," he ordered.

The doctor sat on the nearest chair, also made of bamboo. An uproar ensued: that was the commander's chair. Those who were singing outside came in, scandalized. A wave from Singap, and the hut was calm again.

"*You di sauver ma laf*," he murmured. You saved my life.

A smile lit up his face.

Nithap quickly recognized how childlike his features were, as if he'd never really grown up.

"I can kill this traitor," he said suddenly, pointing at Nithap, still smiling all the while.

Traitor? No one had ever called Nithap that before: *fingwong*. But Singap wanted to frighten him. He liked to frighten people. *He wants to establish his authority over his men, just like a child*, Nithap said to himself.

"I don't kill, I take care of people."

Nithap thought about the reputation of that man. *A killer*, according to the press. *A slaughterer*. And what else? *An extremist*. *So, this is the rebel*, thought Nithap. *Really!* Almost certainly because of the newspapers, he had imagined him a bit stouter, but mostly less verbose, less arrogant. He stood up. The Sinistrés again came running, and again, Singap told them to let him be.

"*Long crayons na emmerdeurs*," he said. Intellectuals are pains in the ass.

Nithap bowed and left the hut. Outside, wind was rustling through the trees. A man was pissing into a clump of reeds, his weapon on his back.

"*Ndocta*," he said, hurrying to zip up his pants. "*Ndocta*."

He didn't finish his sentence. Nithap wasn't paying attention, he was distracted by a little boy, naked, playing in the distance.

Later, much later, during the Trial of the Angels, in January 1971, at the end of the civil war, people talked about the Salvation Army that tried to mount a coup against President Ahidjo; a lot of Cameroonians interviewed on the radio would say that their battle was a spiritual one, that they relied on the arms of faith to free the country from the dictator. Singap Martin's army, the SDNK (Sinistre de la Défense Nationale du Kamerun, which he founded on October 10, 1957, in Baham, proclaiming himself the movement's military leader), would not be mentioned. As a result, they would be condemned to remain forever underground, although they were actually who Nithap met back then. And even at that point, the army had a long and storied history: it had set the West aflame and embroiled Bamileke land in the civil war!

"We are all Sinistrés," that's how Clara had welcomed Nithap into Singap's camp.

He thought of all that this army had accomplished: the attacks on chiefs' compounds, first in Baham, then Bacham and Balessing. Schools and churches set on fire. And then attacks on police stations, military camps, munitions depots, guard posts.

Nithap's heart was racing. This was before the SDNK had transformed into the ALNK, or Kamerun National Liberation Army, so before 1960; before another bullet, shot from a gun in a place the doctor visited only much later, would pierce Commander Singap's chest and turn him into the hero who, according to rumor, "even Semengue's bullets can't kill."

"The bullet came in the front," people would say, pointing to their chests, "and went out the back."

"He turned invisible."

No one said anything about the doctor who saved him.

There are several versions of every story, several different realities. Nyamsi never told his version. But that's not entirely his fault. He no longer remembered just who had told him about his friend's abduction. Was it Ngountchou? He couldn't say. Had he been at home or at school when he'd heard? He didn't even remember. What he did remember was how quickly he raced across Bangangte on his bike, heading toward Bangwa and skidding down the hills as if a furious, roaring lion were on his heels; how he seemed to charge headlong into his destiny and its rain of devilish blows.

"Who's there?" Mademoiselle Birgitte asked when she heard the knocking at her door.

She opened it to find Nyamsi, panting and out of breath, even though he hadn't been running.

"It's me," he said. "It's me, Bir."

There were two white men sitting in the living room. He recognized them as colleagues from the hospital, one of whom, with a large belly and Alsatian-style mustache twirled at the ends, was smoking. He didn't rise but held out his hand, with a smile that showed all his teeth.

"Jacques," he said.

"Nyamsi."

Nyamsi always introduced himself that way, with his family name. The other man, a bit older, had a very firm handshake. When he shook Nyamsi's hand, he looked him straight in the eyes, as if he were trying to discover a secret truth hidden within. Unlike Jacques, his lips were pressed tight, which seemed to erase his mouth altogether.

"Théophile," he said. "But you can call me the Burgundian, its better."

Nyamsi already knew his story, although they'd never met. He was called the Burgundian because he was the only one to ever have contradicted Dr. Broussoux, who came from Bordeaux.

"He works in the emergency clinic," Mademoiselle Birgitte added.

"We'll be needing you, then," Nyamsi began, unsure of what to say. "Given how things are these days."

Then he repeated the man's nickname.

"But I see I am interrupting a conversation," the teacher continued.

"Oh no," Mademoiselle Birgitte answered. "Not at all." Turning toward her colleagues, who'd fallen silent, she added, "Dieudonné is a friend of Sakio's. We are among friends and colleagues here."

The Burgundian, who had gotten to his feet, did not sit back down. He walked toward the window and looked outside.

"I feel well protected," said Mademoiselle Birgitte.

"Really?" asked Nyamsi.

There is no more unsettling question than that one. It wasn't the woman who replied. Rather, it was Jacques, who gave him all the details about the "rebel raid," leaving Nyamsi stunned, his eyes wide open and his mouth gaping more with each word. Nyamsi was shaken to the core and began to recognize the fear that had taken hold of the two men.

"They're all asleep," said Mademoiselle Birgitte, as she came back from the room where the orphans slept. "Children are like that."

"Angels," replied the emergency room doctor. After a moment he added, "I'm going to go. Jacques can stay."

But the commissary officer didn't stay. When he rose, Nyamsi saw he had a hunting rifle with him. Mademoiselle Birgitte didn't want him to stay.

"Nyamsi is here," she said. "He'll stay."

It was difficult to contradict her, even if, in this dire situation, any decision taken would necessarily be rash.

Nyamsi did stay.

"They sent out a search party," Mademoiselle Birgitte said, as she closed the door behind the two Frenchmen. "Sakio is nowhere to be found."

Nyamsi just listened.

"Abducted!" Mademoiselle blurted out suddenly. "Do you realize? Just like that!" The fragility of her own life was revealed in her trembling words. "I am happy that you came. You know Ngountchou left for Bangangte."

She picked up a pack of cigarettes.

"Do you want one?"

They stayed there, facing each other, chatting for hours, breaking down bit by bit the world that, in the darkness of the night, could be summed up in a series of owl cries, the meaning of which escaped them. Nyamsi needed many words to convince his friend that he didn't know where Nithap had gone. She listened as he explained the details of the political "situation," laying out the various possibilities before them. As he spoke, he tapped his cigarette on the ashtray sitting in the middle of the table. He spoke, but the words themselves didn't matter; they were just a balm for her soul.

Nyamsi fell asleep on the sofa where he'd been sitting. He slept, his feet poking out from beneath the too-small green sheet that Mademoiselle Birgitte had brought him. He'd lain there for a while, his eyes open in the dark, then got up to get a book that had been left on the side table. It was *Mission to Kala*, by Mongo Beti. He leafed through it, rather than reading it, but soon fell asleep, the book by his side. Before turning off the kerosene lamp, he looked at the door to the bedroom, which was still open, and smiled, thinking about how Nithap might imagine his relationship with Birgitte. This was actually the first time he was spending the night.

But what did Nithap know? All he knew about Nyamsi was his penchant for words; he knew only the theoretician, the teacher. What he didn't know was how seriously he was courting Mademoiselle Birgitte, how he raced up and down the hills, gasping on his bike. When Nyamsi felt the touch of a thin hand on his now-cold foot, his first reflex was to pull back. Then he grasped the hand and pulled it toward him, and along with it, the body of Mademoiselle Birgitte, who had crept over to the sofa while he slept.

"Will you come?" asked Mademoiselle Birgitte.

A meaningless question. But it was only the next morning that they made love under the mosquito netting, in her bedroom, on the bed. That night, the sofa was enough; then later they lay down on the bare floor, on top of the green sheet. Nyamsi never let go of the hand that had woken him up, and held tightly to his girlfriend's body. In the dark he had looked for and found her breasts, then her lips, and her tongue. He felt her sex close in around his, while her breath and her voice whispered in his ear words that could only be Norwegian, but that their embrace translated so well. The pack of cigarettes was still on the table. Later, Mademoiselle Birgitte found it, lit a cigarette, and took a puff; her face momentarily lit up, then there was just a spot of red in the dark. She passed the cigarette to Nyamsi, who smoked and smiled in the shadows.

8

Sitting in the back of the jeep, Nithap was driven away from the Sinistrés' camp. A thick sock had been pulled down over his head so he wouldn't recognize the place where he'd been held. Strangely, he wasn't afraid. He hadn't ever really been afraid during all those days. Was it the presence of people close to him—he was thinking of Clara—that gave him such courage? He'd never really know. He felt lighthearted, relaxed, and started to nod off.

He thought about death, but not the one he'd faced many times in the hospital operating room. His own death. He was that cadaver over which doctors leaned. It was as if his body were floating, light as a feather, as if he were a branch of mimosa startled by the wind's song. Around him, Singap's men were silent. They were munching on guavas and spitting the seeds out along the road. They gnawed on sugarcane. The one who was driving was smoking *mbanga*,* turning the inside of the car into a suffocating cage.

Soon the car stopped and the space around Nithap emptied out.

He struggled to get out. Someone pulled the sock off his head. He opened his eyes and saw only darkness all around.

"*Waka*," said a threatening voice behind him.

He jumped.

---

* The connection between marijuana and the town of Mbanga, stronghold of the Sinistrés, is not random. Fabricating courage is really quite simple.

"*Waka*," repeated the voice.

He felt the muzzle of a rifle on his neck and walked forward. He quickly realized he was heading off alone. He didn't turn around but continued on, into the shadows. The mist was so thick that he couldn't see where he was putting his feet. He stumbled. In his heart, the feeling of lightheartedness that had possessed him transformed into a prayer, a song that seemed to reverberate across the universe, in time with each of his steps.

"I don't kill, I take care of people," he murmured.

He followed the Sinistré's order and kept walking ahead. Soon, without realizing it, he began to hurry, and then to run. He stopped to catch his breath and, when he turned around, saw no one behind him. He thought once more about his death, and then set off running again. He ran through the heart of the night, through the endless expanse. Suddenly, in the deep darkness that spread out before him, he could make out a shape ahead. He stopped to see what it was. The shape came closer. It was a villager, riding on a donkey with bamboo baskets strapped on its back.

He waved and the man stopped.

"I'm lost," he said.

The man got down off the animal's back and, initially fearful, came closer.

"Oh," he gasped, bringing his hand to his mouth. "You're the doctor!"

He was so overcome that he jostled his donkey, who reared up.

"You saved my wife," he went on. "I'm sure you don't remember."

"Where am I?" Nithap asked.

The villager looked at him in surprise.

"In Bangwa, Doctor," he said. "Have you forgotten the way?"

That's when the doctor recognized the hills around him. The strength that had carried him that far suddenly gave way and he collapsed at the feet of the villager, who cried out.

He woke up in a hospital bed.

He turned his head left and right, looking for a familiar face. He saw Ngountchou and gasped loudly. She was there, surrounded by doctors. He called to her. She hurried over and threw herself at him. He felt her chest rising and falling gently as she cried.

"I imagined the worst, we all imagined the worst! Two weeks!"

"Madam . . ." he heard someone say.

The voice spoke with authority. Nithap tried to get up. A hand held him back—that's when he recognized Mademoiselle Birgitte.

"He fainted," came a monotone voice from behind his head, "but his pulse rate is normal. Nothing's broken. No concussion, he just fainted."

It was Dr. Broussoux.

"Where am I?" he asked again.

"In the emergency room," Mademoiselle Birgitte replied. "You're a *patient*." Nithap tried again to get up, but his colleague's hand held him back on the bed, and a friendly voice reassured him, "Nothing serious, there's nothing really wrong."

Nithap saw the silhouette of a man he didn't recognize, dressed in green, wearing loose shorts that showed his muscular legs. He looked at him cautiously. Suddenly there was a commotion.

"Can we begin the interrogation?" asked a voice.

"Of course," said the doctor. "Do your work."

After clasping Nithap's hand, Mademoiselle Birgitte stood up to leave. The door to the room opened and then was pulled closed by the military officer, who took a quick step forward and leaned over the doctor.

"Where is Ngountchou?" Nithap asked.

"She can stay," said the officer. "I'm Bayiga Sadrack, police commissioner, Bangangte Subdivision."

Ngountchou came over and sat down beside the bed.

"Where is Tama'?" he asked her.

"At the house," she said, gently wiping his brow. "Nothing happened to him."

"Thank god."

He fell back on the bed, out of breath, but calmer. Then he turned toward the officer.

It was April 1960. The Bangwa hospital was occupied by the military. The Sinistrés' raid had had consequences. The Maquisards had broken down the door to the pharmacy and emptied its stores. The door had been repaired in the meantime, but you could still see signs of the violent attack.

The pharmacist, a redheaded woman with an accent from Marseille, still couldn't believe she'd survived—even though the attack took place at night, when her office was closed. She was terrified and wandered along her shelves, shaking her head.

"They took everything," she said to her clients with a sigh. "Even the Mercurochrome!"

Later, when he went back to work, Nithap realized how life in the hospital had been upended. The station was surrounded by men in uniform, their weapons slung over their shoulders. There was always a guard at the gate. The patients, and those who accompanied them, were searched before they could sign in. Access to the station was limited.

Only Mademoiselle Birgitte came to join him during their cigarette breaks. But even she didn't linger like she used to. One sign of her anxiety: she tried several times but couldn't light her cigarette. In the end, Nithap helped her.

It hadn't been easy for the doctor to start back to work. He'd had to go through some twenty interrogations, the most stressful being when Dr. Broussoux called him into his office. The station chief had his reasons. His car had been stolen and his medical kit taken. He couldn't get over it.

"It's the water porter," he said. "I'm sure it was him. He's the one who opened the office door for *them*. No surprise that he hasn't been back since!"

As Dr. Broussoux said *them*, he tried to catch his assistant's eyes. His tone shifted.

"You really don't know where they took you?" he asked.

"I was blindfolded."

"The whole time?"

"I was unconscious."

"Unconscious?"

"I'd fainted."

"I see."

"I told you already."

"I know, I know." Dr. Broussoux sighed. "But what can we do?"

He held his fist up to his mouth and stared pensively. Someone behind him said, "They are everywhere!" He stared blankly. Two orderlies who were going by, carrying a patient lying in a hammock, suddenly stopped. Dr. Broussoux waved them away. The telephone rang. He went to his desk, picked up the phone, and started to pace as he spoke, holding the cord with his other hand.

"Not now, *Jean*," he said. "We'll talk about it again tomorrow. Tomorrow."

Like the pharmacy, the doctor's office still bore traces of the violent attack.

"Two weeks," he spat out as he hung up the phone. "And you don't think you could recognize their hideout?"

"I've already told everything to the police."

The chief of staff continued pacing. He paused again in front of the window and looked out at the courtyard.

"Did it take long to get there?"

"How can I know?" Nithap replied. "I was blindfolded, I was unconscious."

"An hour by car?" Dr. Broussoux pushed on. "Two hours?"

"They are everywhere!" came a voice from the corridor.

"But who are they?"

The attacks on the Bangwa hospital and on Nithap's home had been coordinated. The medical staff still wondered how the Maquisards had been able to move so quickly. Until then, the region had stayed on the sidelines of the violence that was shaking up other parts of Bamileke land. Maybe it was partly because of the personalities of the local leaders. That's what Nyamsi would say. The campaigns of Daniel Kemajou, like those of all the other Bangangte dignitaries in the region, had had some effect. People just couldn't understand what was happening in Bafoussam, Baham, Mbouda, and elsewhere in the West.

That extraordinary peace was broken the night of the abduction. The confusion evident on the faces of the white staff at the Bangwa hospital reflected the fact that suddenly they also needed to think of their workplace as part of a battlefield; they knew they were in danger. That's why the deputy from Bangangte paid them a visit.

Nithap remembered the uproar the deputy's arrival had caused at the hospital, and the chills that ran over his body when the official who had accompanied him appeared at his bedside.

"The Honorable Ntchantchou Zacharie," said the deputy with a smile, holding out his hand.

He was light-skinned and frail, with a long face and a mustache that curled up under his nose like two commas, as was the style then, and his piercing eyes scanned the bedridden man for a long moment. Nithap didn't really listen to what the politician said. But he noted how he stressed that he, too, came from Bangwa, which meant that they were brothers and needed to "join forces against the bandits." Nithap recalled only one phrase from the representative's speech, a phrase the man had repeated several times, in both Medumba and in French, while staring intently into his eyes: "*A mvelou ke nzui ou*. It's your brother who kills you."

The doctor was thinking only of his maid, and there was one question torturing him: *Where is Clara Ntchantchou?*

Dr. Broussoux's daily interrogations were just the start of what Nithap had to live through from then on. Now his white colleagues no longer spoke to him only during the breaks. In the middle of an operation, conversation would turn to "the rebellion." A nurse who had never given anything more than a tepid response to his greetings now stopped when she saw him coming down the hall, to speak to him about the "terrorists." Sweepers, porters, mechanics—all the subaltern hospital staff now stared at him curiously; sometimes he saw a spark in their eyes, maybe a question, maybe a reproach. He wanted to tell everyone there: *I am not the rebel spokesman!* But he knew it would be futile.

The role of hospital spokesman that he'd held until then was taken away from him without explanation. He realized the day after he'd started back to work that a young Frenchman was now doing that job. *Things had to keep going in my absence*, he told himself, and he didn't protest when Dr. Broussoux said that very same thing to him. "I understand." It took Nithap some time to realize he'd been placed into a sort of quarantine.

The doctor first complained about this to the pastor. *Complained* is too strong a word—it was more like a confession. Yet, as he told his tale, he couldn't avoid expressing a certain surprise, or making an accusation: you see, he hadn't done anything wrong, and he saw himself as a victim both of the abduction and of how he'd been treated since.

Ngountchou listened to him. She was still reliving the trauma of the night of the attack. On her face Nithap could read the same confusion he saw in Dr. Broussoux's. Mensa' seemed caught up in a panic. Standing next to the dining room table, Nithap's mother-in-law, just as upset, stifled a cry. Kouandiang, the only one indifferent to the tale, jumped around, licking hands and feet and barking happily. The animal's joy was in stark contrast to the somber looks on the faces all around. The dog raced about, out into the courtyard and back, yipping.

Pastor Elie Tbongo had taken in Tama'. Nja Yonke' had insisted. "They might come back," she'd said; she encouraged Nithap to come stay at the house as well. But the doctor mentioned his night shifts at the hospital. These days, it practically seemed he was living there.

"What I just can't understand," Nithap said, his voice expressing a wail he could not release, "is why they let me live."

"Did you want them to kill you?"

"No, but there are nurses they have abducted and assassinated."

Elie Tbongo grasped his hand and looked him straight in the eyes.

"You don't know the circumstances surrounding their deaths," he said, "so you shouldn't talk about it."

"All the same."

"You cannot judge."

Nithap realized that the pastor spoke of the Sinistrés with a certain sympathy, something he hadn't noticed before. When anyone else interrogated him, he could sense their condemnation. Here, for the first time, he heard something different. Suspicion: that was what had made the hospital unlivable for him, and made him linger in this living room.

"Yet people judge and condemn every day," he said. "You just have to read the newspapers. I myself could have been tried, convicted, and put to death for treason back there. *Fingwong*. Treachery. Abetting the rebellion, threatening the internal security of the state, engagement in subversive activities."

"I know," said the pastor in response to each thing he said. "I know."

"So then?"

"That doesn't mean it's right."

Nithap was reassured that the pastor didn't just fall back on religion. Although, really, it didn't surprise him.

"What is right, then?" he cried.

"If I understand," the pastor went on, "they needed you. Someone was wounded."

"Yes. The minister of heath had ordered that we report any gunshot wounds."

"So how could they treat their wounded?"

"By abducting doctors, obviously. So they needed me."

"As a doctor."

"As a doctor."

"And doctors don't take sides."

That phrase—for Nithap, it was Dr. Broussoux's refrain. He saw again the panic in his boss's eyes. He saw him pacing back and forth, looking out the window of his office, judging the patients and all the local staff from afar with one repeated phrase: "They are everywhere!" That state of siege, the doctor knew it well. He lived through it every day at work.

"Yes," he repeated, "doctors don't take sides."

"So what do you blame yourself for?"

"Nothing—nothing at all," Nithap admitted. "It just seems like *everyone else* blames me for something."

"For what, exactly?"

"Having done my job!"

He had stressed "everyone else" on purpose, wanting to see the pastor's reaction.

"I don't blame you for anything," he said. "After all, I wouldn't have wanted my daughter to be a *widow* right after receiving her dowry."

Nithap hadn't thought of that.

"That wouldn't have been right!"

The pastor agreed.

But then Elie Tbongo seemed to want to take it back, as if he regretted expressing an idea too close to his own interests. He waved his hand.

"What I really mean," he said, trying to correct himself, "is that you don't change people by pointing a gun at them, but by education."

He spoke as if he were giving a sermon, carefully weighing each word.

"The bravado of a man who dives into the water to save a child, forgetting that he doesn't know how to swim, amounts to suicide, because it just leads to his own destruction," he began, fixing Nithap with a stern gaze. "That's what this is really about. We're given an impossible choice, and we're asked to die for one or the other. What intelligent being can say that making a choice in this situation is the right thing to do? We haven't even learned who we are and already we want to die to defend what we should become. We don't know the meaning of the symbols we use, but we're trying to read our future into each of them. It's absurd!"

Elie Tbongo continued speaking, and it was as if he were addressing all the thatch-roofed houses around, all those newly built walls of red mud bricks, those ceilings with visible cracks, those triangular doorways: the whole country silently drank up his words. You see, the pastor had chosen the metaphor of the drowning man on purpose. Nithap saw the ruins and the shipwrecks that suddenly became insults, curses, gobs of spit. He wondered if there was still a place for metaphysics in this world.

He thought about Singap and his vocabulary made up of nothing but insults, about his childlike face; about the man who'd had to abduct a doctor who worked for the system he detested, which he put his life on the line to combat, just to save his own life. Comparing the Medumba of Pastor Tbongo and the Pidgin that created an odd community among the insurgents, Nithap saw his own doubts reflected in the disgusting figure the pastor described. "Absurd," he said. But he also seemed to recognize those the Sinistrés referred to as "puppets."

"Am I a puppet?"

It was Ngountchou who roused the men from their silence.

"Lunch," said the woman who'd become a daughter once more.

9

Nyamsi also questioned his friend about the consequences of the abduction. Did he support the rebellion or no? Sitting in an armchair in the living room, he imagined a fictional battlefield laid out before him, while his fingers, hands, body, his whole body traced the contours of the conflict. His fiery gaze saw battalions where there were chairs and tables, soldiers where there were books.

"Put yourself in my shoes," said the doctor.

But Nyamsi was not in the habit of putting himself in anyone else's shoes. His own he filled with intensity, and his pride didn't allow him to think otherwise. Was it jealousy? Or that tendency—all too common in Cameroon—to make facile extrapolations—something he himself referred to as "me-tooism"? He was the one who, not so long ago, had thought about joining the Maquis! That he had been bested in that race seemed to have left him disoriented, because suddenly his arguments didn't hold up, his passion bordered on hysteria, and several times his friend had to ask him to lower his voice.

"That's how *Cameroonians* are," he went on. "Unable to ever give a simple answer to a question."

He shook his head and started off again. Was he going to launch into his general theory of Cameroonianness, which, according to him, didn't line up with the rather European distinction between reason and passion, but was more like a fork that separated egoism from generosity and had laid the cultural foundation he called the ABBAs of change?* "Nationalism takes roots among generous people," or so he thought. "It's not for nothing that the Bassas and the Bamilekes got fired up, whereas the Northerners and the Betis . . ."

He knew what he was talking about, or so he said.

"They're watching us, you know," Nithap whispered to him.

"I always told you so," he continued. "We are at war. A civil war. Brother against brother, father against son, son against father, daughter against mother. And all of that under the aegis of the French, who, like Pontius Pilate, pull the strings and keep their hands clean. It's impossible not to choose sides, impossible to remain neutral when you see your brothers being massacred. Taking their side, that's a show of generosity, and so, of nationalism. You see, *the Bamilekes are the avant-garde of the Cameroonian revolution*. In other words, my dear friend, we are all Bamileke! You went straight into the lair of the nationalists, you stayed there with them, you even took care of Singap Martin, and now you come back and tell me you've maintained your neutrality like Ngountchou her virginity?"

"What are you talking about?"

Nyamsi burst out laughing. He'd scored a point.

"Because you think you're a saint, don't you?"

"A saint?"

"Only *Doctor* Nithap could think so!"

As he said "Doctor Nithap," you could see the sarcasm in his eyes: he looked possessed. Nithap knew that because he was Moya, Nyamsi had some leeway there in the West that the Bamilekes did not. Besides, he often said, he'd been posted there to cut him off from the Bassas. He was *a fish out of water* and so able to say what he thought because, as far as the government was concerned, his words had no weight. But this time he'd gone too far.

"Then tell me you weren't there in the camp with Ernest Ouandié," the teacher spat out suddenly.

---

* ABBA, or Alliance Bassa-Bamileke, was seen as the basis of revolutionary activity, the avant-garde, the engine of the Cameroonian revolution; the name distills the war down to a tribal alphabet so the idea can take root.

"You're off the rails," Nithap shot back, "off the rails."

He got up to leave and tipped over his chair. He put it back upright.

"But you, you are blind," Nyamsi retorted. "Blind. Just ask anyone. Whether you like it or not, *you are a* tsuitsui, *a Maquisard*."

In the end, it seemed like he was no longer talking to his friend, but rather turning him over to Ahidjo's thousand spies who were waiting for him in the street.

"You are crazy."

Nithap was already at the door. Rain was falling, marking a beat on Nyamsi's roof, and then bouncing down to an overflowing bucket. The water spilled out of the bucket, tracing a streambed across the courtyard. He breathed in the scent of the earth. The word *tsuitsui*, even more than *Maquisard*, or *Sinistré*, or even *terrorist*, reverberated in his mind like a grenade. The courtyard was revealing nature's violence to him. The wind had risen, shaking the trees this way and that. Leaves were flying. Nithap retreated back to the shelter of Nyamsi's living room. His friend was waiting for him. He hadn't moved from his armchair.

"How many times are you going to run away from your own destiny?" he spat out at Nithap. "How long are you going to wait for destiny to knock on your door and forcibly carry you off? How long are you going to claim that you've been spared? Coquetry dictates your life more than it does any woman's! But I know what makes you shiver. You're afraid of the truth."

"What truth?" Nithap shook his head, regretting already having said anything.

"Are you Bamileke, yes or no?"

That time the doctor really did leave, slamming the door behind him. He ran into Magni Sa, Nyamsi's landlady—people said she was a hundred years old. She greeted him with a gesture, holding her palms open before her. The rain no longer made him pause. He ran, slipped, and almost lost his balance, but caught himself at the last minute.

"He's going to get me arrested," he mumbled as he walked on. "He is crazy!"

The soldiers had taken him all around the region of Bangwa, looking for the hill on which he'd been held, searching in the bushes he pointed out. The Bamileke countryside had shown him its limitless beauty. Sometimes, between clumps of reeds, the soldiers found ashes from a fire, tracks left behind as a group had moved through, the remains of a bivouac; but they could have been made by farmers. Nithap told no one, other than Nyamsi, the name of the person he'd met in the Maquis. Mentioning Clara and the Extraordinary Villager would have compromised him. Made him seem complicit in his abduction, because Clara had worked in his home for more than a year, and he was the one who'd hired her. Without knowing it, Nyamsi had put his finger on the essential point: yes, he was cornered.

The papers were talking a lot about Paul Momo, whose influence they saw everywhere, and about Tankeu Noë, both lieutenants in the SDNK. They also said that Ernest Ouandié had come back to the country. Even Nyamsi had fallen into that trap. Yet the government newspapers believed that Singap Martin was dead. But Nithap had met him—that was what had his friend raving.

Nithap had promised the soldiers, his bosses, everyone, that he'd be vigilant. He had accepted that guards be posted in front of his house. "In case they come back." Nyamsi's anger could only make his situation more complicated, because Nithap knew that he was being followed. So, when he came out of his friend's apartment, Bangangte suddenly felt unfamiliar, like a place he did not know at all. It was as if the trees over his head, swaying in the wind, were conspiring together to make him talk.

The rain heightened his sense of solitude. For the first few days after his release from the hospital, he'd stayed with Mademoiselle Birgitte, sleeping on her sofa. That was where he realized just how far he'd come. He'd felt the freest when he was at Nyamsi's. But now something between them had broken, and that's why he was running through the rain. He saw a hangar and hurried over to take shelter, alongside peasant women with *sha*, woven baskets, on their backs, who recognized him and greeted him happily. Once the rain calmed down, he continued on his way.

Staying with Mademoiselle Birgitte for those days had brought him closer to Ngountchou. One morning when he was taking a bath, the door opened. There standing before him was his fiancée. The two just stood there silently: he naked, a dipper of water in his hand, she frozen in place, both equally shocked into silence.

"I'm sorry," Ngountchou apologized. "I didn't know . . ."

Then she shut the door. Nithap heard her steps moving away, but didn't call her back. Several minutes later the door to the bathroom opened again. This time he took hold of her arm, pulled her close, and, with his foot, shut the door behind her. He took off all her clothes. He spread her legs and, lifting her up in his strong hands, he thrust into her, right there, leaning against the wall, while she clung to his neck, smiling and moaning. Afterward, he crouched down and washed the blood from her pubis with several dippers full of water. He used his foot to push the purple water toward the drain; to Ngountchou, it looked like a flood.

"I'm afraid," she said.

He would never know if it was love that had brought her back to him.

Was Nithap afraid as well? Of whom? She didn't want to have waited in vain.

"*They* could have killed you," Ngountchou went on.

"I'm here now. And now, *you are my wife*," he replied, buoyed up by the euphoric beating of his own blood.

When he went back to his own house, he felt overwhelmed by everything that had happened. He couldn't stop thinking about the doctors who'd been abducted and killed. *Why kill them?* The reason for his own survival wasn't clear to him. It was Clara who had let the Sinistrés into his home, she who had told them where he would be and when. How had she mistaken the salary he'd given her for a contribution to the "war effort"? Nithap changed the lock on his door, but it did no good; his living room was still possessed by ghosts. He let it be known around Bangwa that he was looking for a new house. "Near the hospital." It was the right thing to do. Even empty, the house where he'd been kidnapped was haunted by the spirit of his Maquisard-maid. He saw her everywhere he looked.

She appeared to him, her hair braided in the "three hills" style, which he'd only ever seen before on his own mother, her eyebrows plucked bare, as always. Her calm confidence made a strong impression on him. Her face provided answers to all the questions his abduction raised in his mind. When Nithap was hungry, hers was the name that always popped up on his lips; sometimes he even walked over to the kitchen, convinced he'd see her there. He'd open the different baskets lined up, the bowls and containers where food was stored, and he'd take out the meal that had been left for him. He'd unwrap the *koki* that Ngountchou had made, but as he ate, he thought of Clara. She was the fiancée he dreamed of.

He spoke to Clara, asking her why she had saved his life. He asked her many other questions. He'd see her husband, the Extraordinary Villager. He'd relive the scene when they came looking for work. He watched the man put the chicken—the one he'd refused to take—back into the sack and wondered if his soul hadn't taken the bird's place, captured by that false noble who had turned out to be a real Maquisard.

"It was just a trap," he cried. "I was bewitched."

Then he laughed at his own superstition.

And yet he'd wake up with an erection, because he'd felt Clara's body wrapped around his own, her breasts rubbing against his chest. He'd open his eyes and once again see Clara during the operation, wearing Ngountchou's dress, following each and every one of his orders like no nursing assistant ever had. The familiar ease with which he spoke to her in dialectal Medumba, there surrounded by all the Sinistrés, the frankness of her replies, was a balm for his heart. He'd close his eyes and see her standing naked in front of him, her breasts hanging down on her stomach, covered with tattoos of symbols and signs. In that world where everything was foreign to him, surrounded by that blinding mist, it was as if the two of them were joined in a pact, one that excluded even her husband. He saw again Singap Martin's bloody bandages, his hand as he passed them, one by one, to Clara, after washing the commander's wound. He remembered the chill he'd felt the day when Deputy Ntchantchou Zacharie had paid him a visit at the hospital.

Betraying her would have meant turning himself in.

A mvelou ke nzui ou. "It's your brother who kills you."

After his argument with Nyamsi, he saw a woman carrying a conical basket strapped on her back. He thought he recognized Clara, and so followed her, called to her. The woman turned around, offering up the spectacle of her smile, her filed-down teeth, her unfamiliar face.

"Excuse me," he stammered. "I made a mistake."

He couldn't see through all the rain.

"They're making me lose my mind," he said to himself, shaking his head.

Clara became the central knot of his secret.

10

Tama' had been welcomed into the pastor's home after Nithap's abduction. The kid had been happy to find new grandparents, as well as an older sister in Mensa'. He'd also been given a new chore: taking care of Kouandiang. Elie Tbongo had had no trouble enrolling him in the primary school in Bangangte. One day, shortly after he'd left the house to go to school, he came hurrying home, waving his arms.

"Come to the parade grounds!" he said. "The parade grounds!"

"What?" Mensa' shouted, her hand clutching at her heart.

Nja Yonke' came running. Mother and daughter paused for a moment on the veranda, anxiously scanning the horizon. People were running toward the square. Others, women with infants, ran in the opposite direction, back to their homes, jostling the children on their backs. Mensa' went down the porch steps. Waving her arms, she tried to find out what was going on from the other onlookers, whose eyes were filled with concern.

"The parade grounds!" Tama' said. "It's about to blow up."

She was carried along with the crowd.

Four severed heads were exposed on the steps of the prefecture, right beneath the flag. Their eyes were still open, and two of them had a cigarette between their lips. Next to them, two severed breasts were lying in a pool of blood. A soldier was standing beside this terrifying display, his weapon in full sight. He seemed to enjoy the fear this spectacle cast over the faces all around, and he stared at the men and women who stood with hands clapped over their mouths or arms clutching their shoulders.

Women were gasping in panic, covering their children's faces with their hands. Mensa' turned and headed back to Bangwa with Tama'.

"They cut off their heads!" she said, turning first to her sister and then to Nithap, while Tama' went to his room to put his things away. "It's horrible!"

"Who?" Nithap asked. "What?"

"They cut off their heads, too!"

"Who cut off their heads?" Ngountchou insisted.

"They had tribal scars on their cheeks."

"Tribal scars?"

"Yes. As black as the bottom of a pot. With long scars on their cheeks, like scratches. *Bou nkoua ngueu'*. Tribal scars."

"So they were *mafis*?"*

"Military officers were there," the child piped up, as he came out of the house. "They were watching."

"They were watching what?"

"They were watching us."

"They were watching you?"

"I don't want to stay in Bangangte anymore," Tama' announced.

Soon the commotion reached the hospital. Not just because some of the whites who worked there had joined in the search. Nithap learned that one of the severed heads belonged to Tama'ntchou, the water porter. He had disappeared after the raid on the hospital and the police had been looking for him ever since. His name had come up several times when Nithap was interrogated by the military.

Nithap didn't tell Ngountchou that he recognized one of the men who'd been beheaded. But he knew one thing for sure: with Tama'ntchou's decapitation, the Bangwa hospital had gotten the revenge it needed. And yet, that revenge didn't have the effect people had hoped for. On the con-

---

**Mafis*: the nickname given by southerners to soldiers from Chad or, by extension, soldiers from the North (Mudang Gizigas, Tupuris, people from Yagoua, Mokolo, Kousseri), or the Cameroonian army in general, because they didn't speak French and always answered any question they were asked with, "*Mafi*," which means no in the Chadian dialect of Arabic.

trary, it only made them more suspicious. Because the murder made one thing clear: civil war had come to the hospital and it was there to stay. Everybody had their own version of things, and they didn't agree on all points. But one word kept coming back again and again: *spy*. Everyone was stunned by the guy's excessive discretion—someone used the term *sneakiness*.

"He was here all the time!"

"And how!"

"With his donkey!"

"I remember his face so clearly."

"You can't tell a rebel by the uniform."

"Uniform?"

That was the pharmacist who asked that, her face distraught. She had misheard: *You can tell a rebel by the uniform*. She sighed loudly when the phrase was repeated for her and then her face lit up.

"But how do you recognize them?"

"That, madam, is the question!"

"They are everywhere!"

This was the end of the Nicotine Brotherhood. *It's unbelievable how violence brings out the worst in people*, Nithap thought, when he ran into a colleague in the hall who said something he'd never forget: "You want to see force, well you'll get it!" *You?* Just who was he talking about? It was a mild-mannered man who worked as an accountant in the hospital. His glasses and nearsightedness made him look like a bee. Nithap still remembered the gift the man had given him for his engagement, a beautiful little children's book, with an inscription: *for your future children, this tale from Languedoc*. *We're only just getting engaged*, Nithap had thought. *A little soon to be talking about kids*.

Things were really falling apart.

One morning Nithap saw Jacques take his hunting rifle with him into the commissary, after he'd walked across the courtyard with the weapon strapped on his back for all to see. He was known for his hunting. How he'd bragged one day, telling everyone that he'd killed a panther with one shot, yes, the Bangangte totem, *Nzui Manto*! Who could ever forget that? And he just kept on telling that story, so often that he soon earned the nickname "the Panther."

That's where things were when Lieutenant Colonel Semengue arrived at the hospital. His jeep pulled into the station unannounced—they'd always had advance notice when other dignitaries visited. Nithap wouldn't have known it was him except for the whispers that flew all around. He was a little man who was always smiling, and his demeanor was in stark contrast to the anxiety on everyone else's face. Semengue greeted the personnel, then went to Dr. Broussoux's office and stayed there for almost an hour.

When he came out, all eyes were on him. Dr. Broussoux walked alongside him, shooing away the staff and patients with quick waves of his hand. He showed him the damage left by the attack.

"Here," he said. "They certainly came in through the window." He was talking about the pharmacy.

When Semengue went into the surgical building, the staff all rose to their feet. He stared straight into their eyes, one after the other. He stopped in front of Nithap when he was introduced.

"So it was *you*?"

His voice had the rhythm and intonations of people from the South, his accent very affected.

"He's the one I told you about," Dr. Broussoux added. "He's the one they kidnapped."

A smile appeared on Semengue's face.

"Sakio Nithap, native doctor," Broussoux continued. "An excellent surgeon."

"It's no surprise, then, that *the rebels* took him hostage," Semengue replied.

He stared at Nithap for a long moment, as if to assess the effect of those words on him.

"Not at all," continued Dr. Broussoux. "He's a local boy, trained in Dakar. William Ponty Institute."

Semengue cocked his head.

"Really?" he said. "Cameroon needs doctors."

He didn't say that Moumié had been trained at the same school, but you could see that he was making that subversive connection, because he stared again at Nithap. Then he moved on. All Nithap had said to him was, "Hello, sir," so you couldn't really call it an exchange. But the insistence with which the man who was the head of the armed forces had stared at him made it clear that he'd heard all the details of Nithap's story.

Since the start of the civil war—so, since 1956—many doctors had been abducted, and there'd been many assassinations of medical personnel, too. What happened here wasn't unique. What was extraordinary was the slow transformation of the station into a place of violence. Nithap paused for a moment in the hallway to collect his thoughts and watched the people hurrying around the courtyard behind the lieutenant colonel. Mostly whites, but also some soldiers. He heard the name of the French military academy several times, Saint-Cyr, and then a question: "And should we really trust him to protect us?"

It was obvious: Something was broken and beyond repair. Everyone in the hospital went to the training sessions organized by the soldiers. The room was full, the white personnel sitting in the front, the Blacks in the back. Clearly, that was the way it would be from then on. Panic could be read on all the faces in the front of the room, which contrasted with the calm of those in the back as they listened to the presentations.

"How do you recognize a rebel?"

That was the question that had everyone on edge. Especially the pharmacist. That her little office had been attacked seemed to have devastated her. She looked like she was suffering from a fever—one all the more contagious because in order to be really heard, she stood up and waved her arms, pointing at the hospital courtyard, the sky above, and the earth below.

"Precisely, madam," said the instructor, a Frenchman with a short brush cut. "That's what has us worried."

"So you admit it!"

The soldier realized his gaffe. He was there to reassure people, and had just done the opposite.

"Don't worry," he said, lifting up the cane he'd been using to point at symbols on the blackboard. "They are easy to recognize."

"Really," said the pharmacist, still on her feet, and now addressing everyone gathered there. "Now we're all quite reassured!"

"Please listen, madam," said the soldier. "We're not going to be intimidated by a few bandits, are we?"

That line got a response from the crowd.

"Please sit down, madam, will you?"

He came up to her, as if to help her to her seat. Grumbling, she sat down.

"Well," the instructor continued. "How to recognize a *rebel*?"

That time everyone listened quietly.

Several days later, Mensa' noticed a crowd gathering at the market in Banga-ngte. Deputy Ntchantchou Zacharie, dressed in a blue gandoura, with a black chechia on his head, was showing the crowd a group of about twenty men, rifles on their shoulders or lying at their feet. They were all dressed in green jackets and shorts; some of them also wore wide beige hunting hats. One of them was chewing on a matchstick, staring blankly at the crowd, or sometimes at the sky overhead. The men were surrounded by a large group of *mafis* armed with bayonets, glaring menacingly and pushing back the curious onlookers.

"Who are they?" a voice in the crowd called out to a soldier.

"*Mafi*," the soldier replied.

"Rebels!" another voice piped up. "Maquisards!"

The villagers stared, curious about the men displayed there. The honorable official, flanked by two of his colleagues, had a hard time hiding his pride at their catch. He gave orders right and left, full of confidence.

His men moved around busily.

"They've rallied to whom?" someone in the crowd asked.

"The government," said one man. "They've changed sides."

"Since when are the Maquisards *congolibong*?" a voice whispered; people edged away. "Look carefully under their hunting hats. They're just policemen."

"They're gendarmes."

"Bandits, I'd say."

One of the deputy's assistants was taking photos of the Maquisards. The crowd retreated when he wanted to take a photo of those who were gathered; people used their shirts or hats to hide their faces.

"Don't be stupid," said the deputy. "Help the government! Can you see here what the forces of order were able to round up in our region?"

He was shouting over everyone's head, waving his arms wildly.

"You see these bastards," he continued, his eyes scanning left and right. "They were creating disorder, keeping you from going out at night, destroying your homes. Now, thanks to the government's persuasive arguments, to the magnanimity of His Excellency the President of the Republic, and to my own efforts—me, your humble servant, your honorable representative in Yaounde—they have now decided to give up their weapons. Isn't that right?"

He said "Isn't that right?" while fixing a menacing eye on the Maquisards. They all nodded.

"Isn't that right?"

"Yes, sir!" said the men, suddenly jumping to attention.

He pointed to the plastic bags at their feet, filled with this and that, and at the piles of machetes, axes, and shovels, as well as a few new rifles.

"Don't forget what I always tell you," the deputy said, turning to the gathered crowd. "It is your own brothers who are killing you. Here they are, right in front of you." He paused, then called out, "Photographer!"

The photographer came running. With wrinkled shorts and bare feet, his colonial cap covered with red dust, he held his camera with both hands and stared at the representative as if he were his slave.

"Take the pictures!"

The photographer jumped, and his hat did as well. Propelled by the order, he picked out one of the Maquisards and ordered him to pose in front of the pile of weapons on the ground.

"Not that one," said the deputy. "Pick him."

The Maquisard indicated by the deputy stepped forward, trembling.

"He's the leader of the Maquisards," said the deputy. "Nkuindji, you all know who he is."

The photographer positioned him next to the weapons. He took many pictures, each time asking him to shift his stance, or to pick up one of the weapons. The man was blinded by the camera's repeated flashes.

"Now come here," said the deputy once the pictures were done. "Come here."

Then he posed in front of the Maquisards with his chest puffed out, and asked the photographer to take a few more shots.

"There you go," said the deputy, rubbing his hands. "That's good. I'll make sure you're rewarded!"

Turning back to the crowed, he ordered everyone to leave. Grumbling, they dispersed. Some of the villagers discreetly shook their heads. Mensa' moved away with the crowd. When Ngountchou told Nithap what her sister had seen, he had only one thing to say: *they* are capable of anything.

A few days later, *La Presse du Cameroun*, the government newspaper, printed a photo showing the deputy standing in front of a group of men holding weapons and wearing hunting hats. The title, all in capital letters, read:

MAQUISARDS RALLY TO THE REPUBLIC

"There they are," said one of Nithap's colleagues, holding up the newspaper. "There they are."

He rushed across the courtyard, the pages of the paper rustling in the wind, and burst into Dr. Broussoux's office.

"Who is it?" he asked.

"The rebels!"

11

*Ceremonies at the chief's compound offered a welcome break for everyone. Es*pecially Dr. Broussoux, whose responsibilities at the Bangwa station had kept him on edge since Nithap's abduction. So when Jean Nono called on the phone to let him know there would be a celebration at the compound, he didn't hesitate. Chief Nono was a friend, and on good terms with the French as well. That quality had become all too rare in Bamileke land, much to the doctor's chagrin. Not that he was for colonialism, even if Nyamsi was convinced he was. The doctor finally had an occasion to get dressed up—and he was always happy when he could wear his best beige shirt, buttoned up to his neck, but without a tie (an "orphaned neck," as people said), with matching shorts, brown socks, and a khaki hat.

Before independence, he had kept a calendar of the festivals held in each of the chiefdoms, and he always made an appearance, his camera, a Zeiss Ikon, slung over his shoulder, taking pictures of all the extraordinary sights the occasions offered. He had come to Cameroon to get away from his native Bordeaux ("as you can hear," he always quipped when introducing himself), and had discovered in the country a rich culture that had become his passion. He had been there for five years already, serving the past two as head of the hospital, a post he'd inherited when his predecessor had suddenly announced his own departure, saying, "Things are going to blow up in this shithole country, and I don't want to be here when it happens." That was in 1959. The attacks that had since shaken up Bamileke land, as well as in Mungo, Douala, and many other towns, had made many of the whites lose their heads; they started seeing drawings of hammers and boots—the symbols the *tsuitsuis* used to claim responsibility for an attack—everywhere.

Dr. Broussoux wasn't one of them. He was a bit rough around the edges, and the difficulties only made him more determined. So, unlike the others, he had decided to stay put. Didn't he hear that song in Pidgin, carried down on the winds from the High Plateau, whistling in his ear?

Frenchman, Frenchman
Frenchman you must go
You give we double sofa
So Frenchman you must go!

Well, yes, he did, but he didn't think it was directed at him.

"I'm staying at my post," he had declared. And that's just what he'd done.

He'd refused to be transferred to another location, and hired new colleagues to replace those who'd left: people from Holland and Switzerland, and also one Norwegian woman, Mademoiselle Birgitte. The French who'd stayed were of a different sort. They didn't have the easy-going demeanor of those who'd come during the colonial period to do good works and find themselves. They were mostly hardened souls, "coconuts" he called them, still believing in a cause that kept reinventing itself, putting on a different face. Sometimes their methods were harsh—as was the case for that Alsatian shopkeeper who had planted the heads of Maquisards on pikes around his courtyard, as a means of revenge. Or that other one, who'd left the bodies of assailants he'd killed scattered around his courtyard for days. Dr. Broussoux, for his part, insisted that his patients needed care and that doctors don't take sides, and also that the Bamileke region, so endearing, had become his home; that Cameroon was his country. He sometimes added, "Bamileke languages are well suited to the natural sciences, because they are deeply conceptual." That made people laugh. "The way they combine words makes the language a sort of playground for all the Bamilekes," he said. At the beginning, he'd always been thrilled when he learned that a good employee was Bamileke. "One more!" he'd exclaim. Sometimes, too, he'd add that it was because Bamileke masks were the most beautiful specimens of art he'd ever seen. He had quite a collection of them; his office was filled with prize examples. Whenever he traveled back to France, his bags were always filled with works of art to show all of his friends, who now called him "the Cameroonian."

And that flattered the Cameroonian. But his explanations always skirted around the essential, which he had trouble explaining: his love for the Bamilekes. That's why he'd taken Sakio Nithap under his wing. Except for the names—so hard to choke out—and especially the system of *ndaps* that still had him baffled, he felt a deep connection to the soul of this country, where everyone, it seemed, offered his daughter to him in marriage.

Starting with Chief Nono.

The celebration at the chief's compound gave him a goal, became a symbol for all the reasons why he had stayed in Cameroon. Among his collections, there were many photographs taken at chiefs' compounds, of the walls around the properties, of people building houses, as well as masks, of course, and articles of clothing. He'd developed the photographs himself, some of which he'd framed, including the one hanging behind his desk. Of course the official portrait of Ahmadou Ahidjo, which was on display on walls throughout the administration, had pride of place in the middle, but what was most dear to his heart was the mask with round eyes that he'd been given at a funeral ceremony in Batie, and that he'd hung to the right of the photograph of the president. For him, that mask summed up Cameroon. He saw in it the complexity and the spiritual depth of a country that he understood to be enigmatic. He didn't talk about it often, but just walking into his office and seeing that mask—no, that face!—had a profound effect on his days, especially during the troubles. But like any collector, he felt there was still something missing from his collections.

The chief's compound in Bangwa wasn't far from the hospital, although those three kilometers were long enough to make the doctor's soul sing even as the road's red dust made him cough and filled his eyes with tears. There were peasants, with a machete in one hand and bunch of bananas balanced on their heads, who stopped along the track when they heard the sound of his motor and who looked at him with smiling faces, happy when they recognized him; *malafoutiers* wearing only a *chiche bila*, a loincloth, perched high in the palm trees they tapped, their gourds and their testicles swinging in the breeze; and especially those children who started to jump up and down at the sound of the car's horn, and who followed him a little ways down the road, running and shouting to announce the white man's arrival, "*Mekat! Mekat! Mekat!*" Sometimes Dr. Broussoux would stop and give them a franc or a cookie. This time, however, he didn't want to run afoul of the security measures put into place in those anxious days. He had arranged to be escorted by two soldiers—both Tupuris—whom he'd seated in the back of the hospital's new car, an old purple Land Rover that he used since his 2CV had been stolen. In the West, and also throughout Cameroon, really, a white man didn't usually chauffeur around Cameroonians. That's probably why a wry smile greeted him as he came through the gate around the chief's compound. The chief's servants were rather surprised, and the soldiers who were sitting where the boss was supposed to sit were trying to keep a serious face. That unusual aspect of the convoy just burnished Dr. Broussoux's reputation all the more; when the women saw him, they greeted him with a chorus of ululations. He nodded this way and that, to express his thanks, and stepped on the brakes to greet and shake the hand of a notable who was hurrying toward him, arms outstretched. He stopped and then edged the car forward again, after mumbling the usual formulas. Of course, he didn't really speak Medumba, but he knew how to greet people politely. Sometimes, out of habit, he said hello to people in French, but that didn't bother anyone, because everyone there addressed him in his native language.

"*Bonjour, monsieur! Bonjour, monsieur!*"

"*Bonjour, Docteur!*"

"*Bonjour! Bonjour!*"

He parked his car in front of the entrance to the chief's home. In a break with protocol, it was the chief himself who came out to welcome him. Nono was dressed in his usual way, in Peul garb, with a blue turban on his head. The two men embraced like the old friends they'd been since they'd met in Ndikinimeki, where Dr. Broussoux had held his first medical post, and where the chief had worked as a trader for the Compagnie Soudanaise.

Nithap hadn't gone to the celebration at the chief's compound, although everyone else who worked at the Bangwa hospital was there. He was on duty that day, and so his conscience was clear. But when he was walking in front of the administrative building, already closed for the night, he heard the sound of machine gun fire in the distance. A number of doctors came running out into the courtyard to see what was happening. He joined the group. Mademoiselle Birgitte hurried over to him. She was pale.

The ambush into which Dr. Broussoux had fallen had been planned well ahead. Only later did anyone realize how lucky Nithap had been. His shift had saved him. A leaflet found at the end of a trail in Bangangte named him as a *fingwong*, and accused him of betraying his comrades, who'd "fallen under the treacherous bullets of the lackeys of colonialism and their conspirators." The reference to the water porter was explicit; his name was mentioned. This was news to the doctor, but what did that matter: it was he—so the leaflet said—who had *delivered the SDNK spy to the enemy*. Nithap found himself in the sights of the Sinistrés, but in a very different position than that which had cost his boss his life.

The road that led from the Bangwa hospital to the chief's compound was straight, with no detours or obstacles. Because of the curfew that had weighed over the western part of the country since the start of the siege, since the imposition of martial law—so, since 1956—and that spread all the way to Bangwa after the abduction, Dr. Broussoux had needed to head back to the hospital before the end of the celebration. Night hadn't quite fallen when he got into his car, happy images dancing in his head, relaxed after this break from what he called "the stress" of his job. A straight road, yes, but that didn't take into account the herd that blocked his way at the start of the hill leading from the market up to the hospital. A dozen cows were apparently moseying along at their own pace, followed by a debonair cowherd. The doctor knew the place well, and he knew that there was nothing for him to do but hit the brakes.

"That's how things are in the village," he said to the soldiers who were serving as his bodyguard. "Everything moves slowly here."

Still, he honked and slowly tried to maneuver through the animals. Two herders, holding banana leaves over their heads like parasols, were leading the cows. They waved their sticks and the animals started to move, some going left, others right. It wasn't clear if the herders' brusque gestures were moving them off the path, or maybe steering them back toward the middle of it.

"That's our *Bororos* for you," said Dr. Broussoux with a laugh, using a pejorative term for pastoralists. He was speaking as much to himself as to his bodyguards, who were Northerners.

"Don't get out of the car," he cautioned one of them, who started to open the door. "They know what they're doing."

So they waited for a moment, surrounded by the herd, but soon Dr. Broussoux grew impatient and honked again.

"*Nyako*, my friend," he said. "We're not going to spend the whole night here, come on!"

That's when another herder popped up in the middle of the cows, threw his disguise on the ground, jumped in front of the car, machine gun in hand, and started firing, and firing. The whole scene unfolded so quickly that Dr. Broussoux only had time to drive the car into a ditch, crash into a tree, and shout, "Shit!"

When the soldiers from the Bangwa hospital arrived at the scene of the murder, they could only attest to the disaster. The chief doctor and his guards hadn't even gotten out of their seats. The white man was riddled with bullets. The soldiers each had one big hole in the middle of his face.

The cows were found scattered in the bush, and that's how they were able to put together the circumstances that led to the men's deaths. Searching the area gave them no leads, because most of the houses there, behind the leprosy ward, had been abandoned. Those that were not had been emptied when the soldiers went searching door-to-door after the abduction, when heightened security measures were put in place around the hospital.

When the bodies were brought through the hospital gate, chaos broke out unlike anything seen there before. People had held on to hope that, just maybe, Dr. Broussoux had survived, that even his bodyguards hadn't died, that each of them had managed to escape alive. The doctors rushed to try to save their boss.

"Stay with us!" said the Burgundian. "Stay with us!"

"Stay with us, Gérôme!" said the pharmacist.

Without realizing it, she was using his first name, which no one there had ever used.

"Don't give up on us," they said.

A thousand words filled the courtyard. There were cries and exclamations, there were prayers. Had anyone listened carefully, they would have heard a woman, a Black nursing assistant, crying, but no one there had ears to listen anymore.

"It's no use," one doctor said.

"Stay with us!" the emergency doctor kept repeating.

"Don't give up, Broussoux!" a woman said.

"The killers!" said another.

"Stay with us!" the pharmacist cried. "Stay with us!"

"He's dead," someone answered. "It's too late. He's dead!"

The commissary officer needed to be dragged away forcibly; held in his colleague's arms, he let out a cry so deep that it echoed through the whole hospital.

"They killed him!" he said, his face and hands covered in blood. "They killed him!" he kept repeating. "They killed him!"

Looking all around, his eyes were filled with rage, with hatred in search of a victim, in search of a target.

In that chaotic moment, a wave of insanity flooded through that place, now emptied of its patients to make room for this dead man who'd been its chief.

"Assassins!" said one doctor. "The assassins!"

"The killers!" said a woman.

Like the eruption of an anger that had been boiling too long in the belly, chest, veins, and heart of this building, it flowed out into the courtyard. The soldiers had to intervene to keep this convulsing sob from turning into a disaster.

"Clear the courtyard!" they ordered, for no good reason, waving their rifles. "Clear the courtyard!"

There was nothing to do but obey the order. Everyone knew that when things were bordering so closely on hysteria, it was imperative to retreat as quickly as possible; to pull back from the precipice so as not to fall in. But how? The lights in the hospital windows spoke of their pain, and also of their anger, which wasn't just going to disappear; it might be locked away in a drawer, but just one little turn of a key would release it. Each of the employees hunkered down in their own rage, their own hatred. At the center of all that resentment, there was one cadaver—because no one mentioned the bodyguards, even though they, too, had lost their lives. One name made the people pound on their chests; that name, that incandescent name, was Dr. Broussoux.

Nithap understood well that pain, that rage; he didn't need to witness it himself. He understood that what he really needed to do, for his own good, was put himself and all his family someplace safe. Because he knew that, while Mademoiselle Birgitte's testimony had saved him the first time, and even though she'd been with him when the murder had taken place, he'd need to defend himself from accusations that he was a Maquisard. But all common sense had deserted the station. He knew that. He had seen the community come apart at the seams. He had lived through its transformation into a harbor of suspicion, and now, watching its center explode, he knew that nothing, really nothing at all could keep his colleagues from seeing him as something he was not: *a rebel.* That's when Nyamsi's words came flooding back to him, and he saw his friend's face. He saw his certainty, and how it had laid his soul bare. Nyamsi's words were still echoing in his mind when he quickly dressed in his wife's clothes and escaped through the back door.

"Go to your father's," he'd told Ngountchou when he woke her up as she slept, surrounded by the children in the orphanage. "Go to your father's."

She didn't ask him why. Fear had sewn her lips shut, because she, too, had heard the machine gun fire. Because Mademoiselle Birgitte's house was within the hospital walls, she was inside danger's perimeter. Ngountchou tried to hold on to Nithap, because the night all around was so uncertain, because she was trembling at the thought of being left there in that house surrounded by chaos. He clasped her hands.

"I promise," he said, his mind already leagues away. "I'll come back to find you there."

12

The tragedy faced by colonists is that no one will ever understand the feeling that links them to a land that is not their own; and that lack of understanding mutes their pain, because it is sunk in the context of a much greater pain, that of the dispossessed and of colonization's victims. Dr. Broussoux was, in his heart, Cameroonian; it wasn't only his friends in France who called him that, but all those who filled the hospital courtyard for his funeral. His assassination had shaken the country. The official press had done what it could to rile people up. Arouna Njoya, who had come to the hospital several years before when he was minister of health and had signed several orders warning the nurses not to provide any aid to the Maquisards, was there again, this time as minister of the interior. Along with him were the minister of the armed forces and, of course, Lieutenant Colonel Semengue, and the French ambassador. They were accompanied by public figures from Bamileke land and the surrounding areas, deputies like Ntchantchou Zacharie, obviously, as well as mayors and prefects, who filled the main courtyard of the Bangwa hospital with their sullen faces, mumbling the lyrics of the national anthem sung by a choir of children:

Ô Cameroun, berceau de nos ancêtres,
Autrefois tu vécus dans la barbarie,

Comme un soleil, tu commences à paraître,
*Peu à peu, tu sors de ta sauvagerie.**

A white man was filming the event, sometimes leaning to the left, sometimes to the right, and grimacing. Three coffins, the middle one, Dr. Broussoux's, covered with a French flag, the ones flanking it with Cameroonian flags, added an air of solemnity to the ceremony unlike any other that had previously taken place in Cameroon. For even the ceremonies that had marked the burial of Deputy Wanko, and which had everyone talking back then, paled in comparison to such pageantry, and couldn't be compared to what took place in the courtyard of the Bangwa hospital. It was impossible not to emphasize Dr. Broussoux's love for his patients, for the hospital: he had sacrificed his life for them. Minister Arouna Njoya said he was a national hero.

Standing in front of the coffin, other men spoke of the family he'd never had, "Because his family was Cameroon!" "Because Cameroon was his country!" Some speakers underscored his love for Bamileke culture, and even made light of the kilometers he traveled throughout western Cameroon, just to photograph a mask. The man who said that then paused, his disbelief bursting through the stranglehold of his pain: "A mask!"

It was decided that the surgery building would bear his name, even though one voice called out, "No! The whole hospital!"

"The hospital!" everyone cried out. "The hospital!"

People clapped, overcome with emotion for a man who—each recalled, each had seen for themself—expressed his feelings through his work, with his hands.

"He loved his work!"

---

* These verses are from the original French lyrics, used as the national anthem until 1970; the lyrics of the English version are markedly different and do not reproduce these lines. Here is a literal translation of the French: "Oh, Cameroon, Cradle of our Ancestors / Once you lived in barbary / Like a sun, you begin to rise / Little by little, you emerge from your savagery."

"A model doctor!"

"A master!"

"He trained so many Cameroonians!"

"He left behind many disciples!"

That's when somebody thought of Nithap, the one who'd been closest to him, whom he'd trained as a surgeon, the one who, encouraged by the doctor and thanks to his letter of recommendation, had been admitted to the William Ponty Institute in Dakar, the one everyone had always assumed would succeed him.

"But where is Nithap?"

Silence muffled the scandal, because no one—really no one—could imagine this answer: "In the 'maquis.'"

"In the Maquis?"

"That's a really bad joke."

"Why be surprised?" a nursing assistant piped up.

"They are all like that," another nurse mused.

"I told you so," mumbled the pharmacist. "*They are everywhere!*"

She looked around, surprised that everyone seemed to agree with her statement.

"Staff doctor, Maquisard at heart."

"Good God!"

"Tell me it's a lie!"

"Slander!"

"A Maquisard right here among us!"

"A traitor!"

"Oh, the Bamilekes!"

"Masters of treachery!"

"To think of all we did for him!"

"To think that without us, he'd be nothing at all!"

"Without Dr. Broussoux!"

"He'd just be an animal!"

"A pig!"

There in the midst of those exchanges, in the belly of propaganda, surrounded by the sparkle of suit coats, cars, and official gestures, a sense of doubt was worming its way into people's minds; they discovered a silence that forced the most incredulous among them to look at one another, suddenly aware that civil war had planted its roots in the Bangwa hospital.

Just who is Marthe, asshole?

1

The friendship between Céline and Nithap grew closer in the hospital. Maybe fueled by a guilty conscience? Still, Tanou refrained from reading everything Céline did for his father as an expression of her guilt for that handwritten note: *Saturday the 20th, historic reenactment of the Battle of Fredericksburg. Will you join us?*

The day Nithap was admitted to the hospital, Céline was at his side the whole time, just as shaken up by the drama as his family. Old Papa had woken up surrounded by worried faces and bouquets of flowers, one of which, chrysanthemums, she had arranged herself. The committee that had organized the reenactment, of course, also made a show of their concern. One of their members came by.

"I'm a mechanic," he said, then brought up the question of insurance. "We are so sorry for the accident."

"He could have been killed!" Angela cried. "Do you even realize?"

The *Fredericksburg Sentinel* wrote several articles about the accident, with many pictures, including one of Nithap lying in his hospital bed, surrounded by his family. Marie's face beamed for the camera; she'd made a real impression on the photographer that day. In the text, several paragraphs were dedicated to Robert Adams, "the famous poet, author of many collections of poetry, recipient of multiple prizes, and a pacifist, who was attending the event"; but the part about Grandfather said he was "a veteran of the Vietnam War." That really irritated Tanou.

"Journalists always write just whatever they want," Bob said.

Angela chuckled at the thought that the Old Man had been taken for an African-American and kept shaking her head.

"He's not Obama," she said.

Still, she cut out the article and posted it on the refrigerator, next to the magnet that read BARACK OBAMA FOR CHANGE '08.

"It's hard to believe he made that mistake," Tanou said.

He later crowed, however, when the reporter who'd written the article called him. You'd have thought it was he, and not his father, who'd been hurt. He put on his best suit coat and tie, and was waiting impatiently in front of Old Papa's bed when a young man in jeans and shirtsleeves came into the room and introduced himself, a polite smile on his lips.

"I'm a reporter," he said, "for the *Fredericksburg Sentinel.*"

The idea, he said, was to write an article about Old Papa's experience in the Vietnam War. Tanou burst out laughing; clearly, the joke had gone on too long.

"He only speaks French," he told the confused young man.

"What do you mean?"

Tanou still laughed each time he told the story, remembering the look on the journalist's face. "French?" "Yes, it's a world language." He never figured out where the confusion had started. But it was Bob, not wanting to be the center of attention, who had mentioned that the wounded man was a veteran: "He's the one who actually fought in a war." After Old Papa had started stopping by his house to visit, the poet had gotten a much clearer sense of Nithap's past than Tanou ever had. Old Papa had told him his story, with details the son hadn't heard. He'd talked about the attack on the Bangwa hospital, something he'd never told his son about. The real warrior there wasn't the poet—the journalist had figured that out, even if it never occurred to him that they might be talking about a different war. How typically American—Tanou made that point clear.

"They're so ignorant about the world," he said.

Céline had brought a copy of *Le Monde diplomatique*, which was lying on the bedside table, as well as several magazines. Old Papa dived right in, poking his head up every now and again to see what was going on, while Tanou unleashed his sarcasm on the young reporter.

"I'm so sorry," said the reporter. "There's been some sort of mix-up."

There would be no article, but there was a poem Bob wrote, "The Fields of Honor," which Tanou set on the armchair in the living room without reading it. One day, Marie surprised everyone by reciting it. Another day, Marie recited a poem of her own, written in English. She'd gotten the idea, she said, from seeing Big write.

Snow Snow Snow!
It's snowing like flow
If you can see it's
Only follow me!
I don't know but it snowed
And my feelings must be bold!
So get out there and
Just say Snow!

The little girl held out her arms like a ballerina, puffing out her chest to pronounce each word carefully. In her gestures, her posture, her theatricality, Tanou seemed to recognize his father. She raised her arms, her face lit up.

Those sublime moments were brought to an abrupt end by the death of the poet. What struck Tanou that day was the silence that greeted him when he opened the door of number 26—it was unlocked. He'd gone to check on them the day before, in part because he hadn't seen her and in part because of the mix of surprise and fright in Angela's voice when she'd asked in the evening, "Have you seen Céline?" But Céline hadn't come to the door then, despite his repeated knocks. Since the rooms were dark, Tanou left it at that and headed back home. The next morning, Angela asked Tanou to stop by again before he dropped Marie off at school. They'd been dreading for some time, without ever really talking about it, the day they'd hear of Big's death. The immortality of the Poet may well be a prevalent literary theme; each poet meets death one day.

Céline seemed to have just woken from a deep sleep. She was rubbing her eyes, still confused and shaky on her feet. She let Tanou into the living room, where he was met by the image of the silenced Word: The poet lying stretched out in his bed.

"I fell asleep," Céline said, and then she repeated herself, or rather said something else. "I was so tired."

From behind him, Tanou heard a noise, like the drone of a basso continuo: it was his father, his wavering voice intoning a mourning song. But the son cut him off.

"Papa," he said in Medumba, "I'll see you back at the house."

Nithap didn't insist, but retreated furtively from number 26, making room for Angela, who arrived a few minutes later. She hadn't gone to the office, as Tanou had thought. She'd had a premonition, "a sixth sense," she'd say; an unease, a suspicion, a feeling in her gut about what had happened—only women feel death in their gut.

"When did he die?" Tanou asked.

Angela leaned down over the body, took hold of his hands, and gently rubbed them. Those heavily veined hands had composed poems—poems each person there had heard read.

"I don't know," said Céline, as she opened the curtains. "I really don't know."

The daylight revealed a tragic scene, but also the peace on Bob's face—he'd suffered so from his illness. Tanou had sensed it. The last time, the very last time he'd seen him, the poet had invited them over, no doubt in order to say goodbye. They'd talked about poetry—what else was there? And, grasping his hand as he often did to drive home an argument, the poet had left him with one final word—a word that was not up for debate, because it was his last word: "Walt Whitman is the best poet." That was the conclusion of the debate that had long had them on opposite sides, he the disciple of Césaire, versus the poet, who'd written several books on Whitman.

Tanou had smiled. He thought back to all the many discussions they'd had there, because that living room had always been a space of exchanges, debates, and even confrontations—like, for example, that day when the poet (who always introduced himself, with a smile, as "born too late to take part in the Korean War and too soon for the one in Vietnam") had asked him why he didn't write about the Maquis.

"You know," Tanou had confessed, "I'd really like to."

"So . . . ?"

"It's just, my father never talks about it."

Bob hadn't yet told him that he and Nithap had spoken about the war on multiple occasions, about the war that the doctor had fought. The poet hadn't yet told him that whenever his father came to visit he opened up his heart in that very living room, or that he sensed that there was still more to the story, which was why Big had suggested Tanou write a book about it. Tanou smiled at the unbelievable situation that had led his father to trust his story to someone other than him; to "a stranger," he thought, but then was ashamed, knowing that word was unfair. The story was written in his veins, in his body, in his genealogy. But he also knew that for his father's voice to come into its own, it would need crutches, stairwells, someone to lend him words—things that had easily been found in this French living room among friends his own age.

"At home," Tanou went on, his heart growing heavy, "fathers and sons don't really talk to each other."

The next day in his office, he'd typed *Robert Adams* into Google and the poet's face had popped up, when he was young and not yet sick. First alongside an article from *The New York Times* about his life, and then in a number of YouTube links. He had listened to him read a poem. He didn't want to share that memory, because he knew the effect it would have on Angela, on Marie.

It would be as if he weren't really dead, he thought.

Then Tanou remembered another day—it was back when Old Papa was in the hospital, after the accident in Fredericksburg—he'd come into the room, where his father was sleeping. The son was trying to shield himself from Marianne's shouts and hurtful words, worse yet Mensa''s, not to mention Angela's: words and shouts that were almost hysterical, accusing him of having killed his father. He'd sat down on his father's bed, thinking, *Surprise! He's still alive!* And in fact, the doctor would later tell him, "It really is a miracle that he made it out alive when the roof collapsed! A real miracle!" But then and there, at his father's bedside, he saw the books.

The man who only ever read one book is changing, he thought, because there next to the Bible was a collection of Bob's poetry, translated into French, and also *The Poor Christ of Bomba*, by Mongo Beti. Tanou didn't remember giving that book to his father. It's true that Nithap often had the house to himself, which meant he had his son's bookshelves when everyone else was out. And what else was there for him to do in that house except pick up the mail the postman delivered, mostly catalogs bearing a stamp: *PRSRT STD U.S. Postage Paid*, the meaning of which escaped him. Tanou had already told him that he didn't need to answer the phone, since his friends only ever called on his cell.

Some time later, when they were at the mall, Nithap had asked his son what he thought about Mongo Beti. The question had come out of the blue, and the son had turned around to get a good look at the person who'd asked it, to make sure it really was his father.

"Mongo Beti?"

No one was left unchanged by conversations with the poet.

"Now you're reading Mongo Beti?"

"Why not?"

Tanou recognized that habit of his father's, of always answering questions with questions, which made it impossible for them to actually have a real conversation! Now the son smiled when he thought back to that surprising exchange. He saw Old Papa's face light up.

"It's true that the priests also went a bit too far."

Then they talked about the *sixa*.*

They actually started to talk. To talk to each other.

About their surprise that there would be no funeral for Bob.

He was Jewish, Tanou said.

---

* A residence for young Catholic girls before they marry.

"And Jews don't have funerals?"

"He was cremated."

Old Papa was horrified to learn that. Tanou remembered seeing Céline walking Sahara, and asking her about plans for the funeral; he remembered her tearful sadness and how stunned she seemed.

He was Jewish. Tanou never would have known that, except for one day he and Big had talked about the diaspora. Tanou thought that the African diaspora had everything to learn from the Jewish diaspora. But he hadn't shared what he really thought, that the Bamilekes needed to learn everything from the Jews. He was convinced of it, truth be told, having come to that conclusion during his years spent far away from his country; of course, his father didn't share his conviction, since he'd never met any Jews, except for those in his One Book, from which he'd gleaned a certain apprehension that the son still didn't want to name.

"We're not organized," Tanou said.

"What do you mean?"

"Dispersed," he explained, "scattered, but not organized."

He thought about his own life, there in the New Jersey suburbs, lost in the forests of Pennington, as disconnected from the country as he was from other Cameroonians in the US—he knew, hoped, guessed there were many like him, who were just as cut off from their compatriots as he was, and who occasionally popped up on his news feed, on WhatsApp, or some other platform. "This country is huge, so huge!" He spread out his hands to show how profoundly alone he felt in this immense expanse, but struggled to find the right words to express it. "Jewish," that was the word he came up with to explain what he couldn't quite grasp, what "the Bamilekes can't grasp."

"I am Jewish," Bob had said. "And I can tell you that you are romanticizing things."

"What do you mean?"

"About being organized."

And the poet confessed that he had only ever believed in the power of poetry, of solitude. Tanou was speechless.

"And, of course, in gestures of tenderness."

As Bob said that, he caressed Céline's head. Realizing that no one understood him, Tanou fell silent.

One day—the last Saturday of the month—he'd taken Nithap to the Mandjo Bangangte in New York. A long trip that had thrown them into the warm embrace of about twenty Cameroonians, crammed into a small living room, and that had made Nithap happier than his son imagined possible.

There were several faces Tanou recognized from the weekly soccer game that brought them together "in the summer," but also women and children, and the aroma of traditional foods. When they came in, the topic of the day was how to sign up for or renew a health insurance policy, mostly for those who didn't have papers. Sitting behind a table, the man leading the meeting paused to welcome Tanou and his father.

They had exchanged many text messages—*address?*; *what street? You forgot to tell me the street!*; *and at what time?*; *Yes, I'm on my way*; *I'll be there with the old guy, of course*—and the man greeted both father and son happily.

"Family!" Old Papa exclaimed, when it was his turn to talk. He stood up before beginning to speak: "Family-ooo!"

"Oh-hohhh!"

"*Tchunda!*"

"Oh-ho!"

Even there on the tenth floor of a high-rise in the Bronx, they hadn't lost their village reflexes; you could see the joy on their faces as they heard the assorted tones of different Medumba dialects. Someone standing behind Tanou was speaking to a child in Bazou.

"Don't put too much on your plate."

"I am so deeply moved to see all of you gathered here like family," Nithap gushed, a large smile on his face. "Really, I'm immensely happy."

"That's enough, now go sit down," the parent continued.

"*Menma'*," a woman interrupted. "Let the child eat, as long as it's not McDonald's."

"Where is your wife?" asked the president of the Mandjo, speaking loudly with his eyes on Tanou, his intonation suggesting a friendly reproach that, in this setting, was really an invitation.

"And the kids?"

"Next time," Tanou conceded, imagining Marie there, learning Medumba.

"Next time?"

"Sir, if you come back without them," the treasurer chided, "you'll be fined."

He opened up his account book.

"How much?" a woman chimed in.

"That's twenty dollars, Tong Ngoulap," the treasurer said, rousing the room with a sharp whistle blow.

"And do you usually bring *your* wife?"

Tong Ngoulap paid no mind to the man who was carefully writing something down in his account book.

"Make it a hundred," she grumbled.

"Really, I promise to make sure *my whole family* comes next time," said Nithap, his eyes on Tanou, who, as he headed toward the buffet table, was already imagining how it would go if he tried to convince Angela to come with him to the Mandjo.

That was what brought them all together, the exclusion of Cameroonian reality from their day-to-day; as his wife often said when he dragged her to some Cameroonian gathering, "Why didn't you just marry a woman from Bangwa? She'd know how to make *nkui* for you."

"My whole family," Nithap continued. "*My children*, there is nothing better than being united, than being organized. Especially when you're abroad, it's your duty to be organized."

"We gather at one person's home and then at another's," said a voice. "Maybe next time we'll be at Tanou's!"

"Next time, yes," said Tanou.

The man in the back who'd been speaking to the child in Bazou stared at Tanou as he filled his plate. Tanou was already thinking about that next time, since the promise his father had made in public was one he'd have to keep. He was thinking about the things that made Angela smile whenever he talked about the Cameroonian community, "big cars, dark suits, bad red wine, plastic flowers." Just then, the man asked him if they hadn't met back in the country, listing off a few possible places. "It was in Tsinga, no, in Mvog Ada, or maybe the central market.

"What neighborhood did you grow up in?"

"Actually, I grew up in Bangwa."

The man, holding his index finger to his lips, didn't give up.

"And you didn't live in Yaounde?"

"I did," Tanou admitted, "but not for long."

"That's what I thought!"

"Four years."

"What neighborhood?"

"I was a student. I lived with my aunt."

"Where?"

"In Melen."

"Aha!"

The man was lost in his thoughts—retracing Yaounde's meandering paths, the crossroads tucked away between houses, back behind noisy, dusty courtyards, and in front of lopsided windows—trying to work out that intercontinental equation that links a neighborhood in Yaounde, "a Bamileke neighborhood," to the Bronx.

"What was the *ndap* of that aunt of yours?"

"Mensa'."

"The one who had a bar on the Montée de bois?"

"Yes, that's the one."

With his hands outstretched, the man traced the imaginary contours of breasts and hips. "Nice and round, like that? . . . Her husband had a hardware shop?"

"That's it."

The same joy of a neighborhood reunion transported all the way to the United States. "The world is small," Tanou said, while he hugged this unexpected brother with one arm, the other still holding his overloaded plate. Their joy illustrated what Old Papa had said in his little speech.

"Do you realize!" There the man paused, his hand covering his lips, his eyes sparking with happiness, overcome by the memories that came flooding back. From across the crowded room—where Nithap was wearing a suit coat, although many others, notably the man leading the meeting, were dressed traditionally in brightly colored *ndops*—another voice reminded everyone that "the visitor from back home" had been a *médecin infirmier*, a native doctor, and was now retired.

"That's what he said."

"In Bangwa?" someone asked.

"Just stay united," Nithap went on. "Like one big family."

There in the living room where so many reunions were taking place, Nithap brought his hands together to form the symbol of family, a *Tchunda*.

"Please, you must have some more," a woman said to Tanou, pointing at the buffet. "*Ndolè*. Fritters. There are drinks, too. You can't just chat. You have to eat, too."

"There's even Beaufort!" a man said, waving toward the beer. "Don't tell me you only drink Coca-Cola now, like the Americans."

Those around Tanou burst out laughing. "Me, I drink Pepsi-o," piped up the woman who was proving to be the family clown.

"A Beaufort, then," said Tanou.

"That's more like it."

"*Envoyez!*" someone said in French. "Open'a beer, hey."

"I get this shipped from the country," the man said, while the other one, who'd recognized him from Melen, went to tell his wife and their neighbors, who couldn't believe it.

"Yes, yes," he said, "we were neighbors."

Later Tanou would give a little speech, too, stumbling over the Medumba words he'd forgotten, holding a full plate in his hand, and hearing people behind him making excuses for him. "He's a professor." "What university?"

On their way home he explained to his father that he didn't go to the Mandjo regularly, because too often the gatherings ended with fights.

"So they've exported bad behavior, too," said Old Papa. "Even back in the country, that's how it is."

"Well, yes," Tanou continued. "Sometimes scuffles erupt over nothing."

"Usually it's about money," Nithap added.

"Or a woman," Tanou continued. "But sometimes politics, too, because some of the folks who move here, they take advantage of the freedom they have in the United States to support the dictatorship back home."

"People from the embassy?"

"No-o," Tanou explained. "Just compatriots. Sometimes they don't even have enough to eat or a place to live, but they're the ones who voice their support for the dictatorship."

"Are they paid to do that?"

"Most certainly."

Nithap couldn't believe his ears.

"So that's where Biya is spending the country's money."

"Ne ne ne."

"To divide us."

Tanou decided it was best not to tell him about that time, either the first or second time he'd ever gone to a *tontine*. It was in Washington. Everyone was enjoying themselves when suddenly from the back came a shout: "Your mother's ass!" Then, "Your father's *bangala*!" And it had degenerated into a brawl. Chairs went flying. To make it worse, he'd run into one of his old friends from high school, someone he hadn't seen in years, who people said had gone "off on an adventure." When he recognized him, the guy was taking off his jacket and asking people to hold him back, "Stop me, or I'm gonna smash his face!" People did hold him back, pleading with him.

Instead, Tanou spoke about *fingwongs*, traitors.

"That's all they do," he said. "Just like in the past."

"How do you know?" Old Papa asked.

The son didn't answer. A little later, Nithap admitted that he was amused by those stories about money, because for him, money was nothing more than a "stand-in for action."

"It's like a hen's pregnancy," he added. "You can't see it, which is the big difference between a hen and a goat or a cow or any other animal. You don't know anything about it until you find eggs in your henhouse."

When Nithap mentioned that Ouandié was the one who'd taught him that, Tanou realized that was the first time he'd gotten his father to talk about *the events*.

"You knew Ouandié?"

2

The manhunt for Nithap was organized at the hospital for which he had long been the spokesman. The commissary officer was put in charge, and he made it his personal business. It was as if that task had suddenly awoken a centuries-old hatred in the Panther. Even the soldiers needed to put the brakes on his impulses, or else he would have ransacked everywhere. The death of Dr. Broussoux had brought the French army into the dance. They were the ones who did most of the work, of course, but to make it easier for themselves, they relied on the help of people who knew the region well. The hospital's white personnel all rallied to support the army, which had set up camp in the station's courtyard, now emptied of patients.

Conflict always reveals the animal in men.

"Our role," the officer in charge of operations said, "is to protect French citizens!"

Saying that, he looked around at the whites he'd gathered in Dr. Broussoux's now-empty office. The chief's absence was signaled by the boxes lying here and there on the floor. The one mask still on the wall was hanging crooked, but now that the spirit that collected all those objects had been snuffed out, no one seemed to notice.

"What we must do is take the battle to the terrorists," said the Panther, "so that they don't keep bringing it to us."

He was sitting on a box and, as he spoke, he leaned forward, his hands on his knees.

"Offense," he said, "offense."

Each of the men there was given a weapon—yes, the women were excluded, especially since the pharmacist had had a panic attack when she'd seen a cleaner—someone she actually knew—in the darkened hallway of the surgical building.

"Don't hurt me!" she cried, and then ran off, terrified. "Don't hurt me!"

"Madam," the man beseeched. "It's me!"

"He wants to kill me!" she raved in the courtyard, an accusing finger pointed at the man holding a broom. "He wants to kill me!"

"It's her nerves," the military officer had concluded. "Nerves are the most important weapon in the battle against terrorism. You have to have nerves of steel in a situation like this."

The nerves of what would from then on be called "the white community" were not soothed by the arrival of Semengue. For the colonists, it seemed, he was no different than those they were hunting for, those who had killed Dr. Broussoux. His reassuring words did nothing. His task was all the more thankless since he wanted to arrange for "the evacuation of the European medical personnel." To say that the men laughed right in his face is a euphemism. "We didn't come here just to run away!" the commissary officer responded.

"The problem," several animated voices chimed in, "is that the region hasn't been secured."

"The country isn't secured!"

"They are everywhere!"

"The station has become our last stand."

"But no one can protect us!"

"No one!"

And those people, who were holding rifles in their hands, glared at the Cameroonian Army's chief of staff, who had, in turn, pivoted toward the French army officer there with him. "So what are we going to do?" Only women went to take their places in the military truck that was waiting in the courtyard. The pharmacist was the first to take a seat, her hair a mess, her clothes wrinkled. To everyone's surprise, Mademoiselle

Birgitte refused to leave. She gave the excuse that she couldn't leave her children; after a protracted exchange, during which the phrase "skeleton medical staff" was repeated several times, she was allowed to stay.

"And besides," she added, "I'm not French."

Those who stayed regained their calm only after Colonel Lamberton arrived. Everyone knew his name and what he'd done in Bassa land. He was the one who'd been responsible for the pacification of that zone, and according to most people, he'd done it with such enthusiasm—by which I mean, such violence—that "never again would a Bassa even think about joining the UPC."

A well-built man, with a broad chest and solid calves, he strode across the courtyard of the hospital as if he already knew the place well, strutting down the hallway with the white community trailing behind. With a glance he recognized the Panther's skill as a hunter and, in a wink, he gave him the job of finding Nithap.

"Capture him," he said, "but I need him alive."

"I'll get him to come out of his hole," the hunter swore.

"I repeat," the colonel insisted, "take care that he comes back in one piece."

Lamberton was also convinced that they needed to take the war to enemy territory. He was the one who organized the searches. Some evenings military trucks would return to the hospital filled with battered, raggedy men. They'd be rolled off the sides of the truck, there in the courtyard, where they fell with a thud of flesh and bone. After having "been to the pool"—by which I mean being ordered by a *mafi* wielding a bayonet to roll around in the muddy ditch that was dug for that purpose in the hospital courtyard—they were dragged off by soldiers into rooms that used to be wards for patients, some dragged by the foot, others by the collar of their shirt.

One day the hospital's van, which served as an ambulance, arrived, filled with cadavers arrayed like so many bunches of bananas.

"There's no more morgue here," Colonel Lamberton told the driver.

It was Lamberton who transformed the Bangwa hospital into a military camp, replacing the medical personnel with a police interrogation infrastructure, because what they needed, he said, was to wrest out of those men in chains, who'd taken the place of the patients, the information they needed to make even more arrests. There were huge raids that once swooped up a groom at his own wedding, depositing him in the hospital courtyard still wearing his tuxedo, while his bride, sobbing in her white gown, led a parade of crying women.

"Search them out!" he ordered. "Bring them all in!"

The fact that Pastor Tbongo had only daughters protected him from that war. Yet several times the military paid him a visit.

"I know nothing at all about this business," Mensa' said.

"After the war," a soldier told her, "I'll come back to marry you."

He said that with a laugh, his eyes on her father.

"Isn't that right, old man?"

"You'll be my third wife," another said to Ngountchou, as she glared back, her eyes ablaze. "You're a stubborn one, aren't you?"

Tama' had come back to Bangangte, opening a new chapter in a life full of migrations, an experience shared by so many children his age during those years.

"He's just a child," the pastor said to the soldiers who showed up at his door the day after Nithap's disappearance. "He's my child. He's only eleven!"

"That's not going to keep me from giving him a taste of the whip," said the soldier. "Future terrorist!"

And the little kid trembled, trembled; never before had he seen the somber eye of a rifle staring at him.

"He's a schoolboy," the old man insisted.

They searched the house thoroughly, but came up with nothing about where the doctor was hiding. It's impossible to get a confession from someone who really knows nothing. In the end, the soldiers who came one after the other—who stood in front of Pastor Tbongo and asked the same question, "Where is Nithap?"—had to accept the truth. The pastor wasn't tortured as others were, because there are things that even civil war doesn't permit, especially since Elie Tbongo always greeted them Bible in hand.

"Where is Nithap?" each of the uniformed men asked him, again and again. "Where is Nithap?"

"We don't know."

Nja Yonke' never failed to open up both her henhouse and her storeroom to the soldiers, because it was only once they had their hands on her bunches of plantains, her bags of corn, or her hens, wings flapping in their firm grasp, that they'd leave the courtyard, laughing and making crude jokes about the pastor's two daughters. Peace was restored to the house until the next search, the next raid, the next theft by Semengue's soldiers or the French army.

3

Nyamsi's erasure came about after he'd abandoned his post. That was how the administration handled the scandal of the disappearance of the doctor and his friend, which had shaken up Bangangte, transformed the Bangwa hospital into a fortified camp, and sent soldiers into courtyards. Their photographs were displayed at the entrance to the market with the words THESE MEN ARE DANGEROUS written beneath, but that didn't really have much of an effect on anyone. The feeling of dread would come only later, when a squadron seeking revenge came in the middle of the night and dumped a bag full of heads and severed breasts at the crossroads. No one ever knew it was the Panther who was behind that.

That was the price for bringing some peace back to the Bangwa hospital, as the Burgundian admitted later to his colleagues, with a sigh, for, he said, "*They* will now just keep on fighting among themselves."

When Nyamsi was accused of raping a woman from the village, they were trying to replace one atrocity with another: no one believed it. The night of Dr. Broussoux's assassination, Nyamsi had been woken up by gentle—but repeated and insistent—knocks on his window. He jumped out of bed.

"Who's there?" he asked. Once Nithap answered, he opened the window.

At first he hadn't recognized his friend, who was dressed as a woman, but then he burst out laughing.

"So, you've *finally* chosen sides?" he said.

It was almost as if Nyamsi'd been waiting for something like this to happen. He hopped around, crisscrossing the living room several times, looking for things he didn't need. Then he went into his bedroom and came out, patting his friend's shoulder and saying, with a smile, "Now, my dear, I will marry you."

"I know the trails," Nithap answered.

"All the better."

Nithap was sitting on the back of his friend's bike, his scarf and dress floating in the night's breeze. They made their way through villages, using paths only a doctor would know, discovering trails familiar only to local kids, and following red laterite tracks through the bush that were only ever used by men who'd grown up there. Nithap realized how well his friend knew all the UPC networks in the area. Nyamsi left him with a villager who proudly displayed the *tsangan** and chanted incantations. After that, the doctor slept in the homes of families whose living rooms served as meeting places for the local committees of the UPC, and he was transported in the vehicles of pastors who, when push came to shove, supported the nationalist cause and who spoke with him about *kiakde*, independence, with the same passion found in their sermons. One of them identified himself as Ngrafi at a police checkpoint, then sniggered as he told Nithap how stupid the *mafi* were.

"Those Chadians!" he said, shaking his head, his chest full of laughter. "They don't even know that the Ngrafis are Bamilekes!"

When they got to Nkongsamba, Nithap hid for a while in the Sixth Quarter, then he was put on a cargo train. Lying on top of bags of coffee, surrounded by their suffocating, heady scent, he let his mind wander. Sometimes when the train stopped, he'd lift his head to read the signs: NDOUNGUE, MANENGOLE, MANJO, NGOTENG—so many dark and unfamiliar train stations along the way. It was a bumpy ride, but focusing his mind on the rhythm of his body, his breathing, renewed his sense of hope, which he so greatly needed. When he'd fled the hospital, he'd

* A symbol used by the Sinistrés to recognize each other.

made fear his enemy. He kept it at bay by controlling his breathing, but he also inhaled the scent of coffee. Floating on a high from that *mbanga*, he closed his eyes, and for the first time he felt that his fate was tied to that of this place. Each time he'd come to visit his sister Matutshan before, he'd felt that the coffee that controlled these towns was like a drug. His brother-in-law, Tama''s father, worked right next to the train station for Sergef, the largest coffee plantation in town; coffee was both giver and taker of life in the region.

When the train's tracks squealed and he saw N'LOHE written on the sign, he jumped for joy. He rushed out of the car, realizing only when his feet hit the ground that he could barely walk. His body was racked by excruciating cramps.

"At least I'm not dead," he said, startled at the thought.

N'lohe wouldn't have existed were it not for the coffee plantations, and the forced labor of the colonial regime. The Loum train station was the heart of the town; it hadn't been built to transport passengers, but slaves. Its run-down appearance served as a warning. N'lohe was also one of the many Bamileke outposts, a transit point for the migrations that sent the inhabitants of the High Plateau to cities all over Cameroon, across Africa, and then around the world! The cargo cars that brought those condemned to forced labor on the plantations up and down the banks of the Mungo River were filled with Bamilekes! No surprise that they settled into a tight-knit community, as was their custom.

Tashu', Matutshan's husband, was Bamena and lived in the Bamileke neighborhood. He was a descendant of that first migration in 1910; his father had been brought there when the Germans were building the train line, although he also claimed Mbo roots, as his mother's family was native to the area. He proudly displayed his father's tax stub; and it was he who, by waxing nostalgically about the German Road that crossed the area, had traced out the path for Nithap's honeymoon, which became the path of his exile. Barrel-chested and muscular, with big strong arms, even though he'd put on weight over the years—"Your sister feeds me well"—he was the kind of man made to give orders, and not really to take them. When he came home from work and saw his brother-in-law sitting on the woven raffia couch in the living room, he opened his arms wide and greeted him happily.

"Where is Ngountchou?" he asked. "Where is my beauty?"

"How is Tama'?" That was Matutshan.

The question was only a formality, because she hadn't given her son to her brother in order to take him back. She was also thinking about the promised honeymoon, her mind filled with trivial matters. Like many people in N'lohe, the couple turned a blind eye to what was going on around them, and their questions reflected what they wanted to see. They'd heard about his engagement. And yet, when Tashu' learned Nithap's story, he wasn't surprised.

The truth was glaring: N'lohe had become a transit point for the Sinistrés. Because of its location, at the foot of Mount Kupe, the town was unavoidable for those from the West who wanted to reach Tombel, on the other side, in Southwest Cameroon (or really, what was then Nigeria). Hence its attraction for the *tsuitsuis*. Nithap had had to leave Bangwa quickly. Reaching his sister seemed like a good idea. He didn't know if he could stay there, but the town's location near the Nigerian border was reassuring, because he could no longer live in Cameroon. He knew that he was—that he needed to be—a fugitive.

"Let him rest a bit first," Tashu' said.

That's how Nithap settled in N'lohe, with one eye already looking toward his next destination. But provisional was the way things were there; he was struck by the decrepit architecture of the houses built of *caraboat*, wooden slats, and by the poverty. The coffee plantations ripped the soul right out of the environment, and the people had accepted the precariousness of life as both a motto and the way they made do. They all dreamed of one thing: cocoa.*

Thinking of Ngountchou depressed him. He wondered if she was safe at her father's. Once Tashu' had asked "Where is my beauty?" he couldn't stop thinking about his deferred nuptials. He saw the question

* N'lohe did eventually shift to cocoa production, but not until . . . 1985!

hanging there in his brother-in-law's eyes; Tashu' responded to Nithap's stuttering with an "I understand," but didn't really listen to his story.

Nithap had no idea that so many refugees were making their way to N'lohe, whether they had stories similar to his own or were just fleeing the "troubles in Bamileke land." Carrying all their worldly possessions balanced on their heads and dragging along their wives and children, they would come to stay with an aunt or an uncle because their home had been burned to the ground, or because they'd seen a member of their family decapitated. He wondered what his colleagues were saying about his absence, his disappearance. He imagined the hateful words that spilled out each time his name was mentioned at the hospital, and could hear the judgment levied against him. *You are a tsuitsui.*

Nithap's story was all too common, although the doctor didn't realize that until the day at the market when he suddenly bumped into Clara.

"*Massa?*"

She recognized him despite his scruffy outfit. His patched trousers and makeshift plastic shoes—*dschangtchouss*—made him look like any other worker from the coffee fields.

"You don't recognize me anymore, massa?" she said, in dialectal Bangwa.

The woman who spoke to him was dressed like a local field hand.

"Clara! It's me, Clara."

Only then did he rouse from his torpor, because, with a machete in his hand, he, too, looked like all the other peasants trudging along around them, heading down the German Road on their way to the plantations.

"Clara Ntchantchou?"

The strap around her forehead, which held a woven basket filled with a giant bunch of bananas on her back, made her almost unrecognizable. There, in the middle of the street, in the middle of the crowd, the doctor and his maid embraced as they never had before.

"Where is your husband?" he suddenly asked.

Why that question? It came straight from Nithap's gut, from his heart, from his past, from everything that had happened to him, and all he'd dreamed of. Because several times during his escape, he'd dreamed of Clara. When he was lying on sacks of coffee in the cramped space of the freight car, it wasn't Ngountchou's face but rather Clara's that appeared before him. He saw her so clearly, because he could still remember the words she'd said there, on the High Plateau, when she'd revealed herself to him: "We are all Sinistrés." That simple phrase had proved true, and Nithap had realized to what extent that woman, who'd brought such life into his home, was actually the mistress of his life; she could see into his soul, read the lines of his future, take control of his dreams.

"What are you doing here?" she asked.

"Nothing at all."

Then he said that he was going to undress her, relieve her not only of her burden, but of her peasant garb, and that they would lie together. He described for her his one and only dream, of them joined together in a sweaty, intimate embrace.

"Since my abduction."

She allowed herself to be carried away by his desire, but pulled back right when he was about to take her.

"I'm bleeding," she'd said.

She had to add, "I have my period," before he understood the taboo that denied him his pleasure. That whole night, their embrace would be a long dance of feints. She devoured his lips, running her tongue all around inside his mouth, then climbed on top of him and massaged his penis, but she wouldn't give herself to him. Long afterward, he could still feel her rough tongue on his gums, her bosom beneath his fingers, the sweat of her skin on his hands, her strong legs around his hips. He remembered how her body trembled when he'd played with her breasts, and he felt her weight, as if she were still there. Yet he hadn't taken her. In his dreams, he would see her coming toward him. Once she was dressed in a *lela* with strings of multicolored beads, which she took off before nestling in his arms. Another time he'd seen her with tattoos on her belly, the top of her head shaved bare. Each time she had a different appearance. He who'd tried in vain to escape his fate, who held so tightly to the future promised by his profession, now held in his arms the woman of a thousand faces. He caressed Clara's neck and imagined her serving him each evening the rebels' staple meal of *kouakoukou*.

"My husband?" she asked, finally coming back to his first question.

"The Extraordinary Villager!"

Clara burst out laughing. "Is that what you call him?"

"What do you call him?"

"He has a thousand names."

And what about her? Ah, Clara Ntchantchou! Clara! Did Nithap really even know her at all? He knew one thing, he loved to run his hand over her head, to feel her hair smooth beneath his palm, her head, which she covered with a brightly colored scarf. Sometimes he wondered when he'd started to see her as something other than his servant, and every time one image came to mind: Clara, sitting in the kitchen, the mortar and pestle between her splayed legs, her *sandja* hiked up to her hips, revealing her generous thighs. She was grinding corn to make *bôn* for his dinner, or maybe she was turning the pestle as women do when they're grinding taro, her whole body swaying with the repeated motion. That image of her, covered in sweat, was always fleeting. Whenever he'd go to the back of his house to get a drink of water, Nithap would pause awkwardly at the sight of Clara in the shadows of the stifling kitchen, her breasts bared. Then he'd ask Tama', who'd be sitting in the doorway, helping Clara with the dishes, a meaningless question: Where's the cup?

"Give some water to your father," the cook would say, understanding what he really wanted.

But more than this motherly mask, it was that thrilling image of her as a fighter that he sought to recall, and that haunted him even in the darkest shadows of the bush. Years earlier, in 1956, when the UPC met in Kumba, during that legendary gathering that led to the creation of Singap Martin's army, Clara had surprised everyone there by pulling out of her corsage—from between her magnificent, famous breasts—a purse full of bills: the contributions of the women of Bangangte, which she gave to Ouandié. There were several thousand francs. It was one of the largest donations made by any of the groups of village women who'd organized themselves into a network of *tontines*. Nithap would wonder if that bounty included the two hundred francs he gave her as wages at the end of each week. That was who Clara Ntchantchou was: a farmer with a thousand faces, a woman of action, whose husband had given her to him as a *ngkap*, as currency in a trade.

4

Nithap burst out laughing when Clara told him she was "working as a peasant," because her metamorphoses were as familiar to him as her cooking. Sitting down to a dish of *nkeleng nkeleng* after living on guava, licking the *nkui* off his fingers after a month of raw potatoes, tasting her *kondre* after weeks of manioc root—he really needed no more to make him cry tears of joy, and to turn him into that woman's husband. And yet it wasn't her spiciness, it was the tale she told him that kept him from dozing off. After he'd healed, Martin Singap had decided to make an incursion into the Bamum kingdom. He was fulfilling a promise he'd made to Moumié when they'd been in exile in Conakry. "My husband can explain that better to you," she said. For Moumié, Foumban wasn't just the capital of the Bamum kingdom, it was the natural capital of all Cameroon. History's vagaries had resulted in political decisions that gave Douala, Buea, and finally Yaounde, in turn, the honor of being named the capital. Yet Foumban was really the heart of Cameroon. That town was the alpha and omega of the national struggle.

If they could take Foumban, they would strike a blow at the very heart of Cameroon and make the whole country fall. Moumié took it personally that Minister Arouna Njoya had done all he could to make that plan impossible. He had smiled when the French colonial authorities had promised to restore the sultan's throne—which had been in a precarious position since the death of the legendary Sultan Njoya in exile in Yaounde—and to make the Bamum kingdom a principality within the republic. The battle over the succession to Njoya's throne had gone on until 1948, with the French administration trying until the bitter end to impose their docile lackey, Mose Yeyap, in his place. The French promise to return a legitimate heir to power, in exchange for help squelching the rebellion, was what motivated the man who'd in the meantime become minister of the interior. He used his police and all the resources of the state to wipe out the Maquisards in the Bamum region. When Moumié had met Martin Singap in Conakry, he'd pronounced the phrase the commander had kept repeating ever since: "Foumban is our Bastille."

"Our Bastille," Nithap echoed, unable to believe his ears.

"Yes," Clara replied, "from a military point of view."

The battle for Bamum land was thus the first and the only real battle that Martin Singap wanted to wage when he returned from Conakry in 1959. The commander didn't want to die before winning it. Nithap's abduction was a necessary step toward reaching that goal. The doctor had saved his life, and he spent his convalescence, there on the hill where Nithap had cared for him, preparing for that battle. He spent his nights studying maps, having discussions with his soldiers, including the Extraordinary Villager, his most trusted lieutenant. "The mother of all battles," he called it. All the resources collected by the Sinistrés were mobilized for the march on Foumban; the first step was Foumbot, which would open the door to Bamendjing and Bamileke land.

That's how Nithap learned that he'd taken care of Martin Singap on Bamendjing hill. Would he have stayed to live through "the mother of all battles" had he known? There in Bamendjing, several hundred Sinistrés prepared for battle, sharpening their courage and their weapons; then, in the dark of night, they launched their raid on the opposite shore of the river.

"I wasn't with them when they attacked," Clara said. "I stayed behind, waiting in the village."

"The Bamum have always waged war against the Bamileke," said the commander. "This will be the last battle." When they took Foumbot, there were no casualties, because the Sinistrés found the town deserted.

They set fire to houses, took some goods they found, and left. The next day, the Bamum sultan had mobilized his army, which he'd hidden in the bush when the Maquisards had moved in, and his militia. Along with reinforcements from Semengue's troops, they'd crossed the river. Finally, Minister Arouna Njoya could fulfill the promise he'd made to the Ahidjo government: to wipe out the Maquisards in Bamum land "once and for all." He just let it play out. The sultan's soldiers had moved into Bamendjing, sounding a centuries-old battle cry; everywhere, there was nothing but flames and blood. There were hundreds of dead. "The sultan's soldiers brought him severed heads as a tribute," Clara said.

Nithap jumped.

"Severed heads?"

"Yes. Then he used the jawbones of those his soldiers had killed to decorate his gourd of raffia wine."

"You're lying."

"How could I lie after what I've seen? Because I saw the sultan's men shove banana stalks into the vaginas of pregnant women. I saw groups of four men gang-rape women, and after they raped them, run their sabers through their vaginas and sever their breasts. I saw men grab infants by their feet and smash them against walls; rush into houses with their sabers outstretched and come back out holding the heads of small children, dripping with blood. I saw pregnant women disemboweled, their unborn children hacked to pieces and tossed in the courtyard. I saw men hanged from the roofs of houses. The cruelty of the Bamum is unequaled. It seems they still cook up the bones of those they've vanquished, after eating their flesh. They use bones instead of wood. Semengue's soldiers didn't need to wage war themselves. They just watched, moving in only to stop people from escaping into the forest. And then there's the French. There was a helicopter circling above, spitting fire. The gates to the town were shut. Someone must have given the order to kill everyone, and that's what the sultan's soldiers set out to do. They were the killers. They burned everything down."

It had taken days to fish all the bodies out of the river, and to "figure out who'd disappeared and who'd been killed, to separate the men from the animals. They even killed the dogs!" Clara said that masked men had come through the neighborhoods, picking up the dead.

"The survivors were endlessly searching for their lost relatives, calling for their family members across the plantations, shouting out names throughout the night and into the forest. For weeks, for months, Bamendjing echoed with the sounds of their voices, and all of Bamileke land was in despair, because Semengue's soldiers put up barricades to keep the Bamileke from organizing and seeking revenge. Their trucks and police cars took over the region. They set up checkpoints everywhere, declared a curfew. They searched everyone; they even kept the village men from going to work in the fields with their machetes, and the women with their hoes. People were arrested and convicted, even though no one arrested or convicted any of the sultan's soldiers. They are still doing war dances, rifles in hand. The palace militia trains out in the open, for everyone to see; the whites even come to take photographs of their training sessions, pictures they then print in their books, saying how beautiful these traditional festivals and masks are. There's nothing left of Bamendjing, nothing at all. Just a couple of shacks."

Clara had managed to escape from the massacre.

"It was my period that saved me," she said, with a loud laugh. "Otherwise they'd have . . ."

"Killed you?" Nithap finished her sentence in disbelief. "What happened?"

Suddenly the woman stopped laughing; you see, she explained, that night she'd woken up in a sea of blood and thought she'd died.

"But it was just my period."

"Your period?"

"They killed everyone. No exceptions."

Nithap put his hand to his chin, both confused and terrified by the tale of his maid, saved by her own bloody body.

After that disaster, Singap Martin had retreated to Tombel, to the safety of British Cameroon, to bandage his wounds and prepare for another attack.

"That's why we're here," Clara concluded. "My husband is with him."

"And you, you're in N'lohe," Nithap added.

"I'm working as a peasant," she clarified, quite seriously. "The Mbo are kind. When they saw me arrive here from Bamendjing with nothing, they gave me a bit of land in Kupe-N'lohe. Just on the other side of the mountain. I work in the field every day. I'm growing peanuts and plantains. You'll come see. I'm sowing and waiting for the harvest. I sell what I grow at the market. I live in the Bamileke quarter, like you."

Nithap burst out laughing, because now he understood. Right there in N'lohe, she was organizing a network of women to provide supplies to the *tsuitsuis* hiding in the grottoes up in the mountains. He started to look more carefully at the peasant women who headed up Mount Kupe at dawn, with woven baskets on their backs, only returning at nightfall. He didn't mention Ngountchou or his aborted marriage.

*Ernest Ouandié was in Nigeria in 1961. He didn't come back across the Cam*eroonian border; the borders shifted to take him in. The country changed shape right beneath his feet, and its history swallowed him up. He had no choice but to return. News didn't circulate then like it does today. Now Tanou could read about what was happening every hour on his news feed; he looked at his nephew's posts every day, and Skyped with his family every weekend. Then, Fenkam Fermeté, the courier with the "freshest news," who worked as a wholesaler in Douala in his daily life, had been the point of connection for those living in exile; he made it to Ghana, where Ouandié had been staying, only twice in two years. *Twice in two years*—yes, you read that correctly, you, sons and daughters of your parents, now struck with *connectivitis*! There's a moment in every battle where even the most enthusiastic of propagandists recognizes the hollowness of his own slogans. Complaining ceases to be an option and the situation on the ground sets the terms of engagement.

In Tombel, Singap met Ouandié with news of the defeat. Each of the men had been transformed by his experiences, one by the constant proximity of death, the other by the asphyxiating expanse of exile. The easy bond between them was evident, however, in how sarcastically each man responded to the front-page headline of the newspaper Ouandié held in his hands: "Conference in Foumban." The leader's despair was all the greater because he had worked closely with the men behind that conference, and knew their dirty tricks by heart.

"They're all just like Charles Assalé,"* he said. "Give them a ministerial position and they'll sell you their mama!"

"*Bougres, dêm,*" said Singap. "*Na akwarar fô sondja. Dan pipi no get respect fô nathin.*"†

Ouandié shook his head.

"A Bamileke can't accept such disorder."

Vexed, Singap spat on the ground. The more they talked, the clearer it was that they had to do something, whatever the cost. But what? For Singap, it was obvious; that conference was a slap in the face of the Maquis. Foumban had been chosen to put a political stamp on the military victory that had pushed back their forces and resulted in the pogrom in Bamendjing. He immediately saw the implications of holding the conference in Foumban in purely military terms. For Ouandié, however, Foumban was the heart of the country, the only place where the reunification of eastern and western Cameroon made any sense, because its history had been in turn German, English, and French. In his mind, Foumban was the political equivalent of Mount Kupe in terms of geography: sitting astride the Anglophone and Francophone parts of the country.

"It's not so much the Mungo River," Moumié would say, "but the Noun that keeps us out of paradise."

"Tombel," said Ouandié.

He placed his right hand on a corner of the table where he was sitting, and then added, "N'lohe," as he put his left hand on the opposite

---

* A founding member of the UPC, but whose political carreer played out mostly on the opposing side.

† "Those buggers! Those soldiers are just whores. They've got no respect for anything."

corner. Then he paused, quietly, thoughtfully. He stayed there, his arms stretching across both sides of the table, marking the two poles, connected by a line. Then he quietly drew his hands together, clasped as if in prayer. Singap nodded and stood up. That's when the Extraordinary Villager came in to announce the arrival of the doctor from Bangwa.

"*Ndocta!*" the commander exclaimed, recognizing the peasant, holding a machete, who was standing in the courtyard. His childlike face lit up. "*Dis man na ndocta. He di sauvé ma laf!*" That man saved my life.

He headed toward the courtyard, his arms outstretched.

Nithap was standing behind Clara, feeling lost in his disguise. Ouandié also rose and walked to the door. That was the only time he'd seen Singap express such pure joy, and Ouandié stared at the man whose appearance had so suddenly shifted Singap's mood.

"*Na ndocta wé*," Singap said, slapping his shoulder, "Dr. Nithap."

"You are from Bangwa?" Ouandié asked him, in dialectical Medumba, once they'd been introduced.

Clara had stopped in front of the jukebox, staring at it with all the curiosity of the villager she was, her woven basket at her feet. Her husband came and put a coin in the machine, which swallowed it down with a clank. Soon music filled the space, and the Extraordinary Villager took his wife by the hand and, whistling all the while, led her in an unexpected dance.

Nithap watched the actions of the man he'd always considered the *tangkap** of that woman he now knew so intimately. Nithap's relationship with Clara lasted throughout their stay there. N'lohe became their own personal Maquis, their retreat in the bush where together they found succor and warmth. Suddenly Clara's cramps seemed like an omen to him. Massacres covered Bamileke land in blood. Clara's period foretold the tragedies that befell the thousand villages of the West. Soon all he needed was to hear her moan and he knew that somewhere people were being killed. The doctor never swore an oath of allegiance, but he

* According to the Bangwa matrimonial practice, the *tangkap* is a man who has authority over a woman—including that of giving her in marriage and receiving her dowry in the place of her father. Usually the *tangkap* is a woman's uncle.

was accepted into the inner circle of the Sinistrés. Because he had cared for the commander in that most critical moment, he was welcomed into the very heart of their camp.

Ouandié's reserve melted away as he heard the tinkling sounds of his mother tongue. Nithap had already spent several months in N'lohe, which was near the coast—in what was then called Cameroun Oriental—and had earned everyone's trust, even in Tombel. The reunion became even more friendly when, as he introduced himself, he mentioned the marriage that hadn't taken place. Ouandié's face lit up.

"The daughter of Pastor Elie Tbongo?"

"That's my father-in-law," said Nithap, pride brightening his face. He took Clara as his witness.

"*Ne ne ne.*" That can't be.

"I swear it's so."

"Pastor Tbongo," Ouandié said, "was my teacher." Adding for everyone else, "His father-in-law taught me philosophy."

Singap shook his head and gestured to the serving woman.

"*Dan long crayons*," he said. Those intellectuals.

Ouandié scratched his beard. He cocked his head and added, as if he were talking to each of them, "You see, we're one big family."

The music stopped. What was bothering Nithap, and what had brought him there, was that in Bangangte, "the village where my in-laws live," he'd been named in leaflets distributed by the Sinistrés as a traitor, accused of betraying the water porter. He'd been given a death sentence.

"That's why he came here," Clara added, her eyes downcast. "He wants to clear things up."

"So," Singap asked Ouandié, as he took a seat in front of the doctor, trying to meet his eyes, "our doctor is not a traitor?"

"I am not a *fingwong*," Nithap insisted.

It was only when he saw the men laugh as they whispered to each other, "This man is dangerous," repeating "dan-ger-ous," to taste the full sense of the word, that he understood that that accusation had been a way for the Maquisards to protect him publicly. They needed a full-time doctor in their ranks, and that's how they'd recruited him.

"That's all?" Ouandié asked him.

Nithap wanted nothing more: he understood that from then on, he was a *tsuitsui*.

He saw the pistols on the table, but didn't touch them.

5

Protected by the ferocious regiments of gnats that came down from the mountain each evening, and by a suffocating cloud of dust throughout the day, Tombel remained the nationalist citadel it had become in 1955, when the first wave of Sinistrés arrived. The town had grown, of course, spread out, but it was still just as dynamic. The Bamileke communities came back to life with the arrival of Martin Singap and Ernest Ouandié. Several of the original members of the UPC, chased out of Douala, stopped by to pay their respects to "the President," whom they all knew since the days back in New Bell. Each visit brought its own tale, although they all led up to a story that began with Ouandié: the campaign that he orchestrated for the active boycott of the 1956 elections. Ouandié firmly believed that the end of their pain was near, that the whole world knew of their suffering and their hope.

But Ouandié didn't speak about what was happening in Sudan to a wholesale dealer from New Bell—a Bamileke who had escaped from the flames and arrows at the Congo market; nor did he talk about Guinea, because, between you and me, what did Conakry really matter when there before him was a refugee from Bafoussam who told of losing all of his brothers in just one day? He didn't speak about Ghana, either, because doing so would have been self-indulgent when the child before him had taken a torturous path to escape from the carnage at Kekem. As for Cairo, what could he say about it when he saw before him the somber eyes of that couple from Bamena who had somehow managed to find each other as they wandered along the pathways of misery after they'd been chased from Ebolowa wearing nothing more than their underclothes? And what really did his trips to China matter when the woman from Dschang who stood before him clasped her breasts still heavy with milk, although she'd lost her child to the heinous plot launched by the Betis in Sangmelima? And Nithap couldn't even tell him how he'd had to abandon his fiancée, because his tale paled in comparison with those of the Anglophone Bawoks who'd been sent "back home" to Bamileke land, even though they'd told the *balafrés*—soldiers with tribal scars on their cheeks—that they were Ngrafis! Or what about that young man from Baham whose whole family thought he was dead—they'd mourned him and even buried the trunk of a banana tree in his stead—and who one day came home from the forest, safe and sound. And then there was that "Bafang from Bakondji"—that's how he introduced himself—who insisted on meeting him; his name was Penté Jean, and he was the owner of the Tchango Bar,* there at the Two Churches Corner in Akwa, where an explosion on June 6, 1958, had brought the civil war to Douala. By then, Ouandié had already left Cameroon!

"It was a Bamileke bar!"

"From then on, all the dead have been Bamileke."

In Tombel, the leader realized that he had crossed back into the perimeter of misfortune, and that misfortune had become the lot of the Bamilekes.†

Really, that's what Martin Singap was telling him in his own words when he stressed—in a whisper, of course, and tapping his finger on the table—that the combatants were Bamilekes. When he accused the Bassas of having betrayed him, of playing dirty politics and, what's worse, having put down their weapons, he was making it clear that for him the battle was no longer national: "*Bassa man na fingwong*," all Bassas are traitors.

* Whether a coincidence or bit of historical irony, in Medumba, *tchango* means the people's business.

† And all around him a rumor was slowly taking shape, one that would result in the schoolyard taunt his son's classmates would later chant: "You're a Bami! You are cursed! Wa wa ou ha! Wa ou ha!"

Ernest Ouandié always flinched when he heard such declarations from the man who had created a Bamileke dissident army right under Um Nyobè's nose, because, after all, Ouandié's wife Marthe was actually Bassa—did that mean she was a traitor now? When the fight for freedom becomes a civil war, it narrows in scope, and when it becomes a tribal war, it's on a first-name basis with defeat. When military goals dominate the political field, it's over. So, when he looked into Singap's eyes, he saw the mother of defeat, even as the commander was looking for his approval, hoping to find in him an ally for his *flawed* analysis.

"The Bamilekes can't liberate the country on their own," Ouandié insisted, a smile lighting up his face, because what he really wanted to say was this: *My dear friend, keep going on like that and Ahidjo will be able to sleep in peace, no worries.*

"*Mi no bi mbout man*," Singap replied. "Combatants *fô dis fêt na Bamileke pipô. Make you git sense. Mayi Matip . . .*"*

Ouandié didn't let him continue. He knew that the name Mayi Matip was explosive—and that Singap mentioned it for just that reason—and an explosion was precisely what Ouandié wanted to avoid.

"Whoever hasn't already understood that the struggle for power in this country is tribal can say all he wants about Cameroon, he still hasn't understood anything about Cameroonians!" That's the refrain that was spinning around in his head, making him trace circles on the table with his palm even as he spoke. Ernest Ouandié was beginning to understand why so many of those who came to meet him wanted more from him than just hope—they wanted *real leadership*.

"Without an idea worth fighting for, any battle is just fratricide . . . That's the danger that lurks behind civil war . . . Does Singap know that? . . .

---

* The history of Cameroonian nationalism includes several traitors, one of whom, Théodore Mayi Matip, was a police officer recruited by Um Nyobè; although the two became quite close and Mayi Matip barely escaped death when the secretary general of the UPC lost his life, he later led the wave of UPC supporters who rallied to the government, rejecting the "Bamileke-UPC." He subsequently became vice president of the Cameroonian National Assembly.

"The *long crayons* he so despises are the ones who could give a *national significance* back to the battle. Otherwise, why put your life on the line? A bandit risks as much when he steals a bag as does a man who wants to liberate a country! *Neither the bandit nor the liberator wants to live as slaves.* But without the intellectuals, there is only carnage, butchery, theft, pillaging": that's what Ouandié told himself. What he saw in the eyes of those who came to see him was the will to find a shared purpose after all the suffering they'd endured; a purpose for which they were willing to suffer still more. They were simply looking for the right words to sum that up.

"*Kiakde*," he finally said. "Yes, liberty." But then, how could he explain that they needed to fight for freedom when the country was already independent? How could he explain that they were taking up arms for the unification of Cameroon when, not long before, the Foumban conference had sanctioned the return of the Anglophone part of Cameroon, which had been Nigerian until then? He needed to find the words to tell those people that there were good reasons, *several good reasons*, why they needed to continue the fight for freedom although on the first of October there were people—even right there in the dance halls of Tombel, where they were, and especially among the Bakossis—who celebrated the independence and reunification of the country!

So just what was the meaning of that *kiakde* that, according to Singap, now roused only the Bamileke neighborhoods? Now more than ever, Ouandié needed to become *Comrade Émile*, because even his most effective lieutenant, the Sinistrés' military leader, was turning the national problem into a tribal affair, limiting the scope of the conflict. At the same time, the news was saying that the Bassas were rallying under Mayi Matip's banner, stressing the peace that reigned in Bassa land, in contrast to the war raging in Bamileke land. That *tribal division* didn't seem to pose any crisis of conscience for Singap, who talked about his soldiers, Bamilekes for the most part, and suggested that this battle was theirs alone, even though it wasn't and had never really been.

"War is won with the army you have," he said. "But it's not your soldiers who determine who your enemy is."

"*Bamileke fachin fô Bamileke fêt*,"* Singap cut in.

His pronouncement imposed silence all around. Had Ouandié publicly contradicted him, the commander would have said that just showed the difference between the ease of exile and the reality of life in the bush, between Ghana's luxury and the harsh conditions of life for those fighting in the Maquis, between the naïve ideas of the "*long crayons*," who'd grown used to muddy theories because they'd lived "warm and snug in Europe," and the pragmatic action of the Sinistrés.

What could Ouandié say to that? Most of all, he knew he needed to avoid another conflict among the leadership, because he knew that in the heat of battle, nerves wear thin, and the least bit of dissension becomes a river that divides people of goodwill. He didn't want the Western Front—because that was what they called the war in Bamileke land—to become a separate battle. "A United Front": that was his vision, and that was what was running through his head as he walked along the twisting paths of Mount Kupe behind Singap. A man in front was cutting the tall grass with a *tsangan*.

Invisible, Dr. Nithap was part of the troop following behind.

It's freezing at the top of Mount Kupe, even if there is no snow. The forest around Kupe-Tombel is as thick as the jungle, but then fades into coffee plantations and, finally, into houses with damp, grassy courtyards. The town wakes up to an orchestra of roosters, and falls asleep to another of crickets. The mountain itself—which is a refuge for weaver birds, sparrows, village weavers, and shrikes—rises lazily in the afternoon, swathed in clouds of mist. In those years, it was also the refuge of the *tsuitsuis*, but not everyone knew that, because they were active only at night. The town didn't yet have electricity, so she kept her eyes closed as they marched through. Only nocturnal animals disturbed the calm of the reeds as the *tsuitsuis* went back and forth along the paths they'd cleared. Sometimes monkeys gamboled alongside them, jumping from

* "A Bamileke war is fought Bamileke-style."

branch to branch, and there were also crows, whose haphazard flights made the superstitious troops shudder. Sometimes they'd hear a noise in the distance. Those marching would pause to listen for the echo. Soon an owl would open its eyes and then cut through the air as it gracefully took flight.

"*Na balock i dé*," one of them murmured. That's bad luck.

Several times the *tsuitsuis* had to gather branches to rebuild an abandoned bridge. They covered their tracks once they'd passed. The closer they got to the summit, the quieter they grew, because they were confronted by the immensity, by the monumental significance, of the freedom they'd chosen. They walked single file, with porters bringing up the rear. Only their breathing, the crunching of grass, and the soft sound of their steps gave away their presence. At several crossroads, they met sentinels who cleared the way, quickly waving them on. They were young boys whose eyes had been open all night. They stood tall when they saw their leaders. Singap gave them an encouraging pat on the back. He seemed inured to fatigue, despite the steep incline and the slippery terrain.

"*Assiah!*" he called out to them. Courage!

"*Wi dé!*" was the response he heard. We're here!

They arrived in a clearing in front of a series of gigantic boulders, which turned out to be entrances to grottoes. Suddenly the grottoes came alive with noise, and men came running out.

"Commander," they said. "Commander!"

The Sinistrés were dressed in an odd assortment of mismatched clothes. Each one had his own particular style, but most wore shorts and had homemade plastic sandals, *dschangtchouss*, on their feet. Some had on shirts with buttons, which made it easy to recognize the lieutenants. No one wore a hat, though some had a gourd or even a cooking pot on their heads, and bags tied around their hips; those with a real sense of humor protected their heads with a cracked chamber pot. Some had ammunition belts. Most had wooden rifles, or else the machetes typically carried by the peasants they seemed to be. There were several hundred of the fellows; with their bright eyes piercing through the shadows and their shoulders squared, they were an imposing sight. Looking more closely, Nithap noticed several women among them, but there was nothing that set them apart. As for the traditional healers, their picturesque accoutrements made them stand out.

Then Singap strode toward the pole on which waved the red flag with a black crab in the middle;* he cleared his throat, getting ready to speak.

"*Assiah!*" he said.

"*Wi dé!*"

"*Today na lucky day*," he said, turning left and right, "*for big general fô révolution na comôt fô ana si am. Camarade Émile you na di ya di comôt for dé to si am.*"

He gestured to Ernest Ouandié, who was standing next to him and nodding his head.

"*Hi di go fô Franci, fô Cairo, bicôs révolution di call he sèp. A mitam fô Guinée dan dé a di gô fô waka. A di tell hi wôk we di do fôr ya. Good wôk wi di do plenti, hi sé, di make pipô tok. Pipô di tok for Ghana fô wôk wi di do fôr ya. Nkrumah di put mof fô wôk wi di do fôr ya. Nasser di put mof fô wôk we di do fôr ya. Sekou Touré di support wôk we di do fôr ya. Mao Tse Toung di support wôk we di do fôr ya. He no sabe sondja wé dé fit defit am, hi di sé. A bi tell hi sé bi sinistrés di win dan fêt. He sé hi nô sinistrés gô win 'caus wé di fêt fô truth.* Today is a lucky day, because our great revolutionary general has come to visit us. Comrade Émile has come to visit us. He who has gone to France, to Cairo, to answer the call of the revolution. I met him in Guinea when I was traveling there and I spoke to him of the work we are doing here. He said that we are doing good work, and that people everywhere are talking about it. That people talk about it in Ghana, and that even Nkrumah supports the work we are doing here. Nasser supports the work we're doing here. Sékou Touré supports the work we are doing here. Mao Tse-tung supports the work we are doing here. He doesn't know any soldiers who can beat us. That the Sinistrés are going

* This was Cameroon's first flag; as a result of the events we're discussing, it became the emblem of just the UPC, of the independence party.

to win this war. He said that he knows the Sinistrés are going to win because we are fighting for truth."

Then he paused again, weighing the effect of his words on everyone around him. "*We di fêt fô kiakde. We go win, he say, 'caus we di fêt fô countri we, no be so?* We will win the war of independence because we are fighting for our country, am I right?"

"*Na so i day!*" cried the Sinistrés. Let it be so!

"*Laquais for Ahidjo no fit nak sondja wé,*" he continued, "*no be so?* Ahidjo's lackeys can't beat us, am I right?"

"*Na so i day!*"

"*Fantoches sondja for Semengue no fit nak sondja wé, no be so?*" Semengue's puppet soldiers can't beat us, am I right?

"*Na so i day!*"

"*Whiteman no fit comot for contri wé, and nak wé, no be so?*" The white man can't come to our country and beat us, am I right?

"*Na so i day!*"

His speech captivated everyone. The soldiers began to sing the refrain, "*Na so i day!*" and to dance, pretending to shoot rifles and fight. Spreading out across the courtyard, they began to look like young people celebrating, even as they summoned their shared courage, the courage that let them throw themselves in front of Semengue's bullets armed with only hot pepper cartridges, and come together here, singing the age-old hymn of soldiers of the red earth, of the incandescent forest. As they danced, they were transformed into members of secret societies, dancing in the heart of the night as if they were possessed, waking everyone all around as they roared like animals and swayed like *njunjus*.*

When Ouandié began to speak, they had fallen back into neat lines, but the leader had nothing to add to what Singap had already said. His words were just a formality, really, because his very presence said it all. It was the beginning of this battle's United Front. So he just raised his rifle, and the soldiers did the same with their bits of wood, their joy so great it would have lifted up the whole mountain had he just given the word.

* Traditional Bamileke masked dancers.

"*Assiah!*" he said.
"*Wé day!*"
"*Wé go win dis fêt!*"
"*No so i day!*"
"*Wé go kiakde dis contri wé!*"
Soldiers of the revolution!
We are here!
We will win this war!
Let it be so!
We will be independent!

*On that day, on the top of Mount Kupe, they celebrated their renewed commit*ment to the fight that quickly grew and spread through all the Maquis in Bamileke land, all the way to Douala! It was August 1961. That's surely why those months have found their place in the collective memory of the civil war as the time of Ouandié's return, because the momentum rushed down that mountain and took hold of the *tsuitsuis*, who headed into the bush with a renewed sense of courage. The different rebel groups, with code names like "Dakar," "Moscow," "Nanga Eboko," "Accra," and many others, quickly learned that Ouandié had returned from exile, that Comrade Émile was back. His name was passed along from cave to cave. Never since the beginning of the civil war had such a healthy dose of courage infused the ranks of the fighters, all now on alert, awaiting his orders or even a visit. The thousand rebels coalesced around him, like the trees that ring Mount Kupe; the country came together around the mountain, a valley of lush green spreading out all around. Hope has a thousand faces, but in the minds of those men and women—who for several years had done little more than count the growing number of cadavers fallen from their ranks, mounting only sporadic raids—it now had just one: the face of Comrade Émile. From the mountaintop, Ouandié gave the battle cry once more, and he did it by saying to all those fighters just one magic word, which is still used as a greeting in Mungo today: *Assiah!*

Nithap stood silently at the leader's side, as if he were being reborn.

6

It was Nyamsi who had shown Nithap the flyer that named him as a traitor. He'd also taken him on his bike to the border of Bangangte. When he got back, he didn't even have a chance to go tell Ngountchou that her fiancé was safe. A thin cord stretched across the road at the edge of town brought him to a stop. When he was blinded by a flashlight coming from a scrubby stand of eucalyptus and Banenkanen sisal, he understood that he'd reached the end of his path.

The sharp bark of a voice brought him to attention, and he found himself standing at the end of a bayonet.

"Your travel permit, sir."

From the accent he knew it was a *mafi*. He reached into his shirt pocket—nothing. Then searched his pants pockets, nothing.

"My papers?" he asked, buying time.

"Your travel permit."

Nyamsi had his business card in his pocket. The soldier didn't give a damn; there in the dark, he just kept chewing loudly on a kola nut and spitting on the ground.

"Where are you coming from?"

"Bafoussam."

Nyamsi's voice suggested he'd made a longer, bumpier trip; his strained breathing made him sound like a man who knows he's been caught. The soldier noticed this and asked another question.

"You went to Bafoussam to do what?"

The man had certainly asked everyone who passed by during the night that question. The tribal scars on his cheeks showed he was from Chad, making Nyamsi think: *Yes, he's a* tirailleur. *A Sara.*

"*Chef, a bi nkwa',*"* he said, but that did not impress the soldier.

"Follow me to the station."

Standing in front of the officer in charge, Nyamsi answered the same questions, in the same monotone he'd used the first time. He answered them again as he stood in front of the commissioner at the Bangwa hospital, in the room that had formerly been the pharmacy, even though that was after he'd been taken to his home in handcuffs to "look for the travel permit." His house was ransacked, and the soldiers gleefully showed him their explosive finds. They couldn't get over it themselves. No need to stick their bayonets under the bed or to cut holes in the ceiling. They'd pinched themselves, trying to convince themselves that a teacher could be such an idiot and keep such compromising documents in his house. "Subversion," they said when they found the typed pages of the speech Um Nyobè gave to the UN in 1952; "Subversion" at a handwritten letter from Ouandié to a French girlfriend; "Subversion" at a text by Osendé Afana, "For the end of the Kamerunian crisis": subversion, subversion, subversion.

"And what about this one, boss?"

"What?"

"By Jean-Paul Sartre, *Dirty Hands.*"

"Do you have to ask? Put that bullshit here!"

"Subversion."

In the Bangwa hospital, exhaustion, as well as the certainty that nothing he said would let him avoid the sentence reserved for "subversion," suddenly made the captive lose his cool. Of course, it didn't help that when he'd been thrown into the truck that transported him there, hands and feet bound, he'd fallen and wrenched his shoulder.

The federal inspector for the West region came to see him in his cell

---

* *Nkwa'* is the term used to indentify anyone who is not Bamileke. "*A bi nkwa',*" a phrase in Pidgin, is the shibboleth used by anyone who wasn't Bamileke to get through military checkpoints.

that afternoon. Enoch Nkwayim stood silently. He kept his hands clasped behind his back and only once did his gaze meet Nyamsi's.

"You thought you were smarter than who? You're gonna tell us who sent you here."

He left shaking his head.

"What do you want from me?" the prisoner shouted later at the police commissioner who was sitting behind his desk, scribbling away in a notepad, underlining certain words with a ruler. "What do you want from me?"

"I'm the one who gets to ask the questions here, *Mister Teacher*."

The commissioner was a Bassa with a very strong accent; his words flowed out like a winding river and he pointed with his thumb and index finger to emphasize his points. He stood up and began pacing the length of his office, then went to the window, his posture reflecting his impatience.

A Frenchman came in. Nyamsi recognized him, but he didn't even glance his way. It was the commissary officer. Jacques pulled a pack of cigarettes from his shirt pocket and lit one. He turned a chair around and sat astride it, his arms crossed on the back.

"I also used to be a member of the UPC," said the commissioner, lighting a cigarette from the one held by the Frenchman, "but I *rallied* to the government."

He smiled. Nyamsi looked at Jacques, who was waiting to hear a word that would not come.

"You say you don't know where Nithap is?" the commissioner continued.

"No."

"That you aren't a member of the UPC?"

"I'm more of a nationalist."

He was speaking to the commissary officer, digging down deep within himself for the strength to fight for his life.

"Which means?"

"I defend the Cameroonian nation."

The commissioner smiled, walked back toward the prisoner, and patted him on his aching shoulder.

"Me, too, since I'm a civil servant," he said. Then he turned to the commissary officer, who was gently tapping his cigarette and scattering ashes on the floor at his feet. "We all defend the Cameroonian nation."

A smile appeared on his lips.

"You, you're from Yabassi," he continued suddenly, "and me, I'm Bassa. We're both on the same side, against the Bamileke rebellion, am I right?"

Nyamsi knew there was nothing more brutal than the treatment a former UPC member who has rallied to the government reserves for someone who's still faithful to the UPC. Later, when four policemen attached his hands and legs to a metal bar suspended between two tables and asked him to sing some UPC songs, he didn't protest, he just sang: "*Enfants du terroir, specimens d'antan.*" Knowing he was caught, he let his passion take control of his body, and from deep within he sang, "*Soldats du Cameroun, vous qui peuplez le pays, venez . . .*" When he got a word wrong, an electric shock ran through him, and the commissioner shouted the forgotten word in his ears. When he stumbled over another, blows rained down, reminding him of the rhythm: "I'm a member of the UPC, I told you that."

Nyamsi thought of Nithap. He could see him—stethoscope around his neck, making his way among the wounded and saving lives—right there in this room where he was now being tortured. He could see him coming into this office—the cell where he was now tied—and, leaning over the table, scribbling a prescription on a scrap of paper. He could see him smiling at Jacques. And he saw himself at Mademoiselle Birgitte's that evening when the Frenchman was there, standing in another's shadow. If Nyamsi could have told the Nicotine Brotherhood that he'd been tortured in their offices in the Bangwa hospital, Nithap certainly wouldn't have believed it. Birgitte wouldn't have believed it. Who could ever have believed what happened in Bamileke land during those bloody years? When he was served his "black coffee," he mumbled: "Raise the standard of life of the population." That was the first lesson his instructor had written on the chalkboard, as he said, "More than independence or the reunification of Cameroon, this is the real goal of our battle." The second time, he didn't think of anything at all. He soon lost consciousness, abandoning his body to the "cement bucket" treatment. He was scrawny, and his weakness was what saved him, because he passed out. The commissioner stood up, covered in sweat.

"Stop," said Jacques. He picked up a bottle of Beaufort and dropped his cigarette butt in it. "Bring him here. Lay him out on the table. Like this."

The man spread his legs to show the position he wanted.

"Hold his hands."

It was done.

"Pull down his pants."

Nyamsi woke up in a windowless cell. He let loose an unending wail. Soon the depth of his pain called forth a song. This time, from the dark, several timid voices joined in the chorus.

Venez vous joindre à nous
Pour la libération du Cameroun
Singap et Ouandié ont parlé!

That was how the teacher realized the cell was filled with others as wretched as he. Trying to move his feet, he kicked someone's head, eliciting a groan of protest.

"I'm not dead," he said aloud.

"What's really true, my brother," a voice replied from somewhere in the locked cell, "is that we are in the hospital. This is a place where people can also heal."

Nyamsi tried to make out the face of the man who'd spoken, but soon everything went black again.

The next day, he was displayed at the Bangwa market, alongside three other fellows pulled out of the same pitch-black cell, and whom he was able to see for the first time. They were each holding signs; on his, beneath his name and age, it was written: RAPE OF VILLAGE WOMEN. The crackling flashbulbs nearly blinded him, but he recognized Enoch Nkwayim standing there. There were other officials as well, all dressed in suit coats, and, of course, a group of about thirty police officers and soldiers. Several Frenchmen were there, too. Nyamsi looked at all those people, and a faint smile appeared on his lips.

"Here is the gang that was raping women in this village," said Commissioner Bayiga. "They took advantage of the disorder to commit crimes all over the region. But they didn't count on our guardians of the peace, on our national guard and the commandos.* My great thanks to our armed forces."

People applauded. Journalists scribbled down notes.

"We have arrested the sorcerer's apprentices who were ruining your daughters here in the village, as well as their leader, whom you all know—the teacher Nyamsi Dieudonné, from the secondary school in Noutong. His own students have testified about his misdeeds."

He paused.

"About his room, too," he added with a smile.

Nyamsi heard the description of the awful man they introduced to the journalists and who bore his name. He could see the reporters' pens racing back and forth across their notepads. A few times he caught one of them smiling. *That one there, he knows this is all a farce*, he said to himself. He watched the man continue to take notes, then glance back at him again, still smiling. He wanted to shout out that the commissioner was lying. But he knew that his word was worth nothing compared to that of his jailer, who was rubbing his hands together as he spoke; that his word was worth nothing when the somber-faced prefect stood there with his hands clasped behind his back. Nothing he could say would make it into the article about his arrest, and which was sure to appear on the front page of *La Presse du Cameroun* the next day. A man in civilian clothes was taking pictures of the journalists.

Nyamsi was condemned to seven years in prison.

He was never heard from again.

---

* Local militia groups.

7

*Sometimes Singap Martin would venture down into the liberated villages** and, standing on the back of his car, speak to the crowds. Dressed scout-style, as was his wont, but in UPC colors. He wore sunglasses to make an impression. Sometimes, too, accompanied by his four Amazons, he'd go into the neighborhoods and oversee the judging of the *fingwongs*. His Amazons were women he'd assigned to his service and who, it was said, made sure that when his sentence came down—and it always came down—it was carried out, whether they used their machetes and cut down the condemned right in their homes at night, or whether they took them out in the bush and split their heads open. They were feared much more than the commander himself, because of their ferocious reputation. In Mombo, people still recall when they cut off and ate a man's testicles. Singap trusted no one but them, because they were his "sisters"—meaning that they weren't just Bamileke but, like him, from Bandenkop. They were also the ones who sent him to seventh heaven. At least that's what people whispered. While their leader had a shaved head, they each had tattoos of animals on their bellies, like the Bamileke women warriors of the past. Those women were Singap's "things," and everyone imagined what would happen when an aspiring lover undid the shirt of one of

* By which I mean villages where, for pragmatic purposes, he'd established a supply network based in the Bamileke neighborhoods and in the *tontines* or, in the best case, the Mandjos.

those women: they'd freeze at the sight of the tattoos, make some apology, and then run for it, disappearing into the forest.

Ouandié's arrival in Singap's camp hadn't changed the routine. The leader let the commander do what he would have done without him there. The most Ouandié did during those days, really, was start recruiting his team. He devoted his time to questioning the fighters, which allowed him to identify those he wanted close by his side. The task wasn't easy, because the Sinistrés came from such varied backgrounds. Some were dedicated UPC faithful, but there were also local chiefs who had refused to become lackeys for the colonists, people motivated by a desire for revenge and who were quite open about it. There were some who had been unemployed or disinherited, and even children kidnapped from their families. He listened patiently to these people living in the bush and took notes.

"*You bi menusier?*" You're a carpenter?

"*Na so*, Comrade Émile. That is so." Ouandié wrote it down.

"Why did you join the Sinistrés?"

"My boss had a thing for my wife. I said that he wasn't going to beat me, so I joined the Sinistrés."

Ouandié's left hand scribbled on his notepad: *revenge*. He looked at the man, who puffed out his chest; just holding a wooden rifle—a placeholder for the weapons promised by Czechoslovakia—had transformed him.

"*Patron sèp, na wôsi?*" he asked. Where is that boss now?

"Nko."

He meant Nkongsamba, and started to weave a tale about "cocoa" that ended up losing the leader.

"What's your wife's name?"

"Marthe."

Ouandié stopped and stared at the man, shriveled, but with a fighter's profile, who wanted to avenge his Marthe. He thought about his own wife, also named Marthe, who was in Ghana.

"*Make you go!* Move!" he said.

As the man limped away, thoughts of his personal mission stiffened his back and strengthened his step.

Next came a young man who also had the swagger of an armed fighter, thanks to his wooden rifle.

"Mathieu Njassep," he said, without waiting to be asked.

Ouandié let him continue, because words were clearly burning on his lips, eager to tell a much longer story.

"Alias Ben Bella."

"Why did you take Ben Bella as your nom de guerre?"

"*A fit do fô Cameroun wôsi Ben Bella wé di do fô Algeria.*" Because I can do for Cameroon what Ben Bella did for Algeria.

The leader looked at him and smiled.

"Go on! I want to see what you'll do for Cameroon."

He put down his name in the notebook and beside it wrote, *Ben Bella*. The man became his secretary.

A very different scene was playing out, however, in N'lohe, down in the valley. Singap was presiding over an improvised revolutionary tribunal in the Baham community center.* Sitting on a chair, his Amazons by his side, he listened to the charges brought against a haggard man. He was a kola vendor from the North; people accused him of being a *fingwong*. The man was wearing a tattered gandoura, and his face was bruised. His eyes expressed a silent plea, while anger twisted the faces all around.

"*Com fôr ya, fantoche*," said Singap. "*Tel me sé you no be fingwong.*" Puppet, come here! Tell me that you're not a traitor!

Suddenly there was a commotion in the back, voices whispering.

"*Mafis!*"

The warning raced through the crowd. First, everyone froze, then panic set in. But it was too late: Military jeeps roared down the streets of the neighborhood and soldiers started shooting. Chased by commandos, people climbed over the fences around houses, tried to hide in living rooms. Some women even jumped into wells. The sound of gunfire

* In every city in Cameroon where they've settled, the Bamilekes set up tribal meeting houses: Bangou, Baham, Bafoussam, Bangangte, etc., built by the community. They are gathering places for the folks who live in the neighborhood; monthly meetings of *tontines* and other sorts of activities are held there.

rhythmed their flight, as the cries of the dying and the wounded punctuated the scene.

The attack was bloody. Even dogs and ducks lay sprawled across the courtyards. Several Sinistrés were able to escape, Singap among them. He had blended into the crowd and found his way back to the forest. This wasn't the first time he'd had a close call. He ran methodically, guided by several other Sinistrés, including the Extraordinary Villager, who led him back to the German water tower and provided him with cover at the same time. He ran toward that refuge, the only place where, because of the rock wall surrounding it, he knew he'd be safe. A gunshot rang out, coming from a stand of porcupine grass. One of his lieutenants fell. Singap stopped running and turned back, checking the man's pulse. He was still breathing. Singap tried to help him to his feet.

"Go!" said the dying man, one hand on his belly. "*Make you go!*"

Singap stood up.

"*Assiah, o!*" he said. "*Assiah!*"

The Extraordinary Villager opened fire several times, shooting in the direction the shot had come from. A salvo raised a cloud of dust in the forest. Singap took off running again, cutting between the trees, seemingly unaware of the steep terrain. Ahead of him, one of his Amazons was hit. She collapsed into a thicket of brambles. A bullet flew by his left ear. Right then, a third rifle shot rang out, this time coming from the sky above. He was hit in the back and fell, his hands outspread, on top of the Amazon lying in the ravine. His mouth was spitting blood, or maybe words, as frightened dragonflies and butterflies took flight. But who was listening? All around him, it was each man for himself.

The next morning, peasants found the path that goes from N'lohe to the water tower lined with severed heads. Enoch Nkwayim later expressed regret, however, that Singap's body hadn't been displayed at the crossroads along the main East-West road, so as to "take advantage of the psychological shock that his death would have had on the broader Bamileke population"; but that's just because the police learned only much later, when they read the notebook that the Extraordinary Villager left behind at the scene of another attack, that they had shot down the

Maquis's greatest tactician that day. At the bottom of the page, the federal inspector of the West added a note of his own: "a dissident notable from the Bangwa chiefdom," a clear reference to the Extraordinary Villager, one that only added to his reputation. On that same day, Ouandié began to have hemorrhoids. He blamed it on the stress of that armed confrontation, and thought no more about it.

As for Clara, well, let's not talk about her.

The man Singap wanted to judge didn't escape from his sentence, however, despite the commander's death. On November 23, 1961, while he was praying in his courtyard, he lifted his head and saw the flash of a machete wielded by a farmer: with one blow, she split his head like a coconut.*

"*Fingwong*," said the Amazon before spitting on the ground.

The man she'd just killed made no sound. He was still splayed out, soaking in his own blood, when his wife came back from the market. She saw her man there, surrounded by a pool of blood. On the ground, next to his prayer beads, a hammer and boot were drawn. She let loose a cry

* Every story about the Maquis has several versions. Here's a second: A man from the North, a kola vendor, had decided at the end of a rewarding day of work to relax with his friends with a game of *ndjambo*, or *trikat*, or some other game of chance. Things didn't work out well for him, though, because his opponent, a Bamileke with better luck, relieved him of all of his cash. Anger is not a good adviser. The Northerner struck the Bamileke, who, unfortunately, was also the stronger of the two. A knife was pulled, which changed the balance of power, leaving the Bamileke sprawled out dead on the ground. The Bamileke community started to think about revenge: What? A Maguida slits the throat of a Bamileke and we do nothing? *Yehmaleh*, a *Wadjax* who wipes his *bangala* before eating kills our brother and we do nothing? *Wombo, oooo*, a Nkassa who sits down to take a piss is too much for us? We do nothing? They turn him into a sacrifice, a *nzolo*, and we do nothing? What followed was a ping-pong of cadavers that roused the Northerners in the neighborhood; they attacked any- and everything Bamileke, setting fires and killing indiscriminately.

According to the third version of this incident, an order came from on high, from President Ahidjo, a Northerner himself, to set an example in N'lohe, to make the town a martyr, a sort of Cameroonian Sodom: to make the town pay the price for becoming the supply center for the Maquisards based on Mount Kupe. For how else can we explain, the locals wondered, even now, and the Mbos especially, that a town so prosperous in 1960 became so destitute that trains no longer stop there, and that even those who were born there and managed to strike it rich still refuse to invest in it? That they don't even want to hear N'lohe mentioned? Better yet: that they speed up, even if they have a flat tire, when they have to go through N'lohe on their way to the West?

that woke up the entire Muslim neighborhood. All the Northerners in the town flew out of their houses, their kitchens, their bedrooms, or the mosque and ran to the victim's home, where they found him splayed out on his prayer mat, lying in his own blood. *Walaï!*

"Who did this?" a voice asked. "Who?"

Rage was boiling up in people's bellies, and a desire for revenge made them clench their fists, beat on their chests.

"Who killed him?"

"It's the Maquisards!"

The sentence that had been hanging over the town came down hard again.

"The Maquisards?"

"*They* dared to do this?"

"*They* are going to hear from us!"

"*They*'ll hear about this!"

Hatred spiraled out of control, even though it was directed at an undefined and undefinable "they," because in this town—where Bamilekes and Northerners had settled at about the same time, where, since both groups were traders, they met at the market, the Northerners selling cloth, and the Bamilekes foodstuffs, some selling retail, others wholesale—nothing really set them apart, other than presumed political allegiances. As a result, all too often the Northerners were called "Ahidjos" and then were treated like government collaborators, while the Bamilekes were called "Maquisards" and were seen as the torchbearers for that movement. An exchange of names and epithets that tied everyone to the conflict.

"*They* will pay for this!"

The flames lit at the first house in the Bamileke neighborhood were like a guided missile: they had a specific goal, just like the arrow that flew into the eye of the man who came rushing out of the house. His family jumped out the back window. Because they had a horde of Northerners on their heels, they ran and threw themselves in the Dibombe River from the top of the German railroad bridge, where the water twists and turns between boulders. Before they'd gone to the house targeted for reprisal, the Northerners had prepared for things to go from bad to worse, "*ça gate, ça gate.*"* They'd gathered bows and arrows, cutlasses, an entire arsenal of the things that everyone in this town of peasants, traders, and hunters used for work. Then they set up at street corners and waited for the residents to come home from the fields, arrows nocked and ready to fly. One man hid in his ceiling. His home was set on fire, while his pregnant wife, who'd been unable to climb up with him and instead hid under the bed, was disemboweled: she and her baby were thrown into the stone-filled drainage ditch. Revenge glowed red like the flames that spread from one house to the next, engulfing the entire Bamileke neighborhood. The *caraboat*, those dry wooden slats used to build the houses, served as kindling. All you needed to do was light the straw roof. Soon even the neighboring areas were in flames, the entire town lit up by the deadly fury that had taken hold. Everyone, whether Mbo or from another tribe, tried to save their life by answering, *A bi nkwa'*, when asked the deadly question: *You bi bami?*

The firemen didn't come. Later, the mayor of Manjo, the next town over, will say that the trucks, which were usually used to water the coffee plantations, were all empty. The soldiers watched the carnage unperturbed, happy, no doubt, that the locals were taking charge of cleaning up the region—a task that the government had given to the French army and to tirailleurs from Chad. Defenseless before the flames and the arrows, the Bamilekes sought refuge in the river, hiding beneath the daisies and the reeds, waiting for daybreak. The next morning, they left N'lohe by following its banks—an extraordinary exodus of haggard folks, stripped of all their belongings and covered in blood. They shivered in the trucks of the local police, even thanked the patrols of commandos who stopped them at their usual checkpoints; their neighbors' deadly violence had thrown them into the arms of the very forces that were the source of their misfortune.

When, some time before these events, Nithap had pointed at Mount

* It is said that a wise Northerner tried to make them listen to reason and was almost lynched by the crowd, thirsty for Bamileke blood. The man managed to save his life only because he fled in a car: he had wheels.

Kupe, lost in the clouds, and told his sister that he wanted to climb it, he asked her if she knew a good guide. Her husband had warned him against it.

"It's volcanic," he'd said.

"Volcanic?"

"You don't know? It's where the *Maquisards* hide," Tashu' explained; he said the word *Maquisards* as if it were an insult, something you'd say about bad people. Then he added, "I heard that even *the chief of the Maquisards* is there."

Ouandié, no less.

"Whether we want to be or not," Nithap had replied, patting him on the shoulder, "we are *all* Maquisards."

What he meant was, *We, the Bamilekes.*

Soon after, Nithap had left for the mountain, with Clara leading the way, Clara whose womanly body unsettled him. He had gone to Ouandié, answering the call he'd heard in Bangangte and that had led him there. That decision had saved his life, and cost Tashu' and Matutshan theirs. As Bamilekes, they had paid the price for the misty mountain's rage. They were among the hundred or so unidentified bodies whose heads had split open on the rocks of the Dibombe. They were among the charred bodies found in the ruins of the *caraboat* houses, among the cadavers thrown into latrines and wells, among the severed heads displayed along the roadside. Those who survived left N'lohe, stepping over the cadavers of their own relatives, their own neighbors. They built the town of Mbete. Clara became their prize jewel when she came down from the mountain, her basket filled with two bunches of bananas, and made her home in Tombel. When she set up her home in the Bamileke neighborhood, she became their guardian angel, so she could nourish with her breasts the hope of the English town, still quaking with fear from the echo of distant gunfire. A woman-witness, a visionary. People lined up before her stand in the town's market to hear her apocalyptic visions, their mouths agape, hoping that one day she'd know how to make Mount Kupe and its valleys rise up to avenge their brothers and sisters who'd died on "the other side of Cameroon." But they all disappeared on the

Bloody New Year of 1966, when the town that had been their refuge—Tombel! Tombel!—was also caught up in the anger of the misty mountain. Bakossi commandos attacked Quarter #5, where she lived, over some vague land dispute, planting pickets all along the German Road, all the way to Nyasoso, pickets adorned with the severed heads of the town's inhabitants. Including hers.

Clara, the *Megni Nsi.**

Nithap would learn all of this only after the war. Tama', too, learned only later that he'd been orphaned. He grew up in his improvised adoptive family. With Nithap gone, he discovered the authority of Pastor Elie Tbongo, whom he always called Grandfather. He found a place for himself in that home, which had been missing a boy. The situation worked out well all around, especially since he was only a few years younger than Mensa'. He became her "little brother," and that's what she would always call him. He would become an uncle for Tanou—that's how Tanou always saw him, because he was the father of Léonard, our "Bagam." It's quite difficult—impossible, even today—to tell that Léonard's not actually Mensa''s son. But what does that matter to Tanou, who always thought of him as such? Tama' calls Mensa' "*nzam,*" which means "my elder."

The fact that Mensa' was the youngest of the pastor's family had buffered her for a long time from the general unrest. In Tama' she found the companion she needed. A visible complicity—built of teasing and enigmatic silences—still unites them today. Sometimes when they're talking, Mensa' will laugh at something from their shared childhood. Tama' was a timid child and doesn't like to be reminded of it, especially not in front of his son.

---

* She was a seer, yes, for this people—the Bamilekes—for whom the future is always miraculous. Soon another seer would be found in Douala, a Bazou baker known as Mven Tchabou, the bread distributor.

"Do you still remember the day when *they* attacked?"

That day, at the Bangangte market, gunfire was heard in the distance, followed by the sound of helicopters. A chorus of ululations shook the village.

"You were supposed to protect me."

After all, Tama' was the boy. Traditionally, only a man can cut off a chicken's head. But in their house, it was Mensa' who did it. The village, the whole village, started to run. People dashed back to their houses, women hid under their beds, hens in their coops, and the whole universe exploded in never-ending ululations.

That's when Mensa''s voice burst out in the living room.

"*Tama' ya?*"

An especially troubling question, since, just a bit before, he'd been in the house with the dog.

"Where is Tama'?"

Wasn't he just in the kitchen, warming up leftovers from dinner the night before to have for a snack?

And that's when the family of Pastor Elie Tbongo rushed out into the street, while everyone else was rushing away from it. Mensa''s blank stare met the gazes of those women and men who'd been transformed by their fear. Not even the pastor could hide his emotion, his eyes searching left and right, because he was sure he'd seen Tama' just a bit ago, giving sweet potatoes to the dog! But shouting out his name, as they usually did, would just drive home the danger swirling all around them!

"*Okolooooo!*" Nja Yonke' bellowed out nevertheless, trying to stifle the cry in her belly.

"*Oukoulou!*" came the response from outside.

"Have you seen Tama'?"

Imagine the anguish: a village under assault, whose fleeing inhabitants were each stopped, one by one, by a mother, by the pastor's family.

"I saw him headed this way."

And Mensa' rushed off to the left.

"No, it was the other way."

Mensa' rushed off to the right.

"He was headed to the pond."

"The pond . . . ?"

They imagined that they'd see Tama' coming toward them with Kouandiang gamboling ahead, like a peasant heading to the fields with his dog, whistling as if the sky above the hills weren't already on fire. He'd be remarkably calm, as if he were just out for a walk; his demeanor would make the panicked group fall silent. Fear often morphs into anger, but here it would turn into tears, bursts of joy, hugs, and greetings; the coming together of a family reborn in troubled times.

"Where is Tama'?" Mensa' would often ask, trying to find the echo of that terrifying day, for when fear lifts, it becomes a farce. Pain can be chewed like a kola nut to release its sugary juice.

"Tama'?"

It was Mensa' who finally found him.

"He's under his bed," she said, "*a baa tchun la kounda.*"

Everyone laughed and the mood lifted. "He's under his bed." There are actions that stay engraved in one's mind because they are what bind us together, and the thought of that one never failed to bring back to Mensa' the relief she felt when, looking under the bed, she saw Tama''s "two big eyes," as she always said, staring at her, "just like the dog's."

Every family is a sum of memories. Bagam's father felt a wave of shame each time that story was told, because in the end it was just a false alert that had sent all of Bangangte into a terrified flight.

Bang! Bang! Bang! In the heart of the night, however, around midnight, everyone woke to the sound of machine gun fire. And this time it was Elie Tbongo himself who ran through the darkened house, into the living room, bumping into chairs, the table, and ordering his family to get out. Outside, the whole universe had gone mad; they heard a rhythmic rush of wind above the roof, as if a giant blade were slicing through the sky, and then suddenly the whistle of bullets.

Bang! Bang! Bang!

"*A baa ke?*" Nja Yonke''s voice cried out. "What's that?"

The suffocating air signaled a nearby fire, and yet the pastor's voice was firm, authoritative. He went from bedroom to bedroom.

"Already outside!" said Tama', "*me baa nshounda!*"

Bangbangbangbang!

"Mensa' ya?"

"I'm outside, too."

It was important not to stay in the house. Everyone had to sidle along the wall and hide in the bushes. They spent the whole night in a field.

How long did the attack last? In the morning, Bangangte awoke to find its houses in ruins, just a few corner posts standing, burning embers where there used to be whole neighborhoods. Total devastation. Was it joy at having survived the attack that made Nja Yonke''s heart race? That sent her husband, the pastor, rushing outside? Running left and right, the dog rediscovered the universe of his barking. As for Ngountchou, she carefully tightened her pagne beneath her arms before coming out to join them.

It was Kouandiang who found a body—a charred body—amid the still-burning rubble of a house. It was Nyamsi's house. The dog led everyone to the pile of debris. In the middle of the ruins, he started to dig, moving bricks and bits of bamboo with his teeth, jumping left and right, both afraid of the embers and anxious. Soon he uncovered a human form, charred and as black as the bricks.

"The dog is eating a person!" a voice cried out.

But Kouandiang was really just licking; he licked the incinerated skull that poked out of the ruins. A tossed stone sent him scurrying away.

"It's Magni Sa!" howled a mournful voice. "That's our grandmother, don't you recognize her?"

"Yes, it's Magni Sa!"

"The teacher's landlady."

"What teacher?"

"The one who used to teach at Nountong."

"The one who was arrested?"

Everyone could imagine the woman, her flattened breasts hanging down like cloths over her belly, sitting in her courtyard, shelling pistachios, lifting up her joined palms when passersby greeted her, and immediately, reflexively, spitting on the ground.

"Magni Sa, o!"

Led by Nja Yonke', the tearful chorus of women repeatedly called out her *ndaps*, their voices rising up in a mourning song as their left hands pounded their chests, their wails echoing the hymn of a terrified Bangangte heard in the distance.

"O, Magni Sa, o!"

Digging in the place from which they'd chased away the dog, a woman lifted a brick here, a container there, and then sat down on the ground, with her feet stretched out before her, her body swaying in a dance for the dead. Soon she had a pile of bones next to her, as well as blackened remains. Her hands gestured to what had been Magni Sa, and her voice split the sky, remembering how she'd called to her to come out into the night. But the grandmother had preferred to stay in her house. The old woman had refused to flee. She had chosen to die in her home.

"Why are old people so stubborn?" the woman asked, as she lined up the bones in a container. "Why did Magni Sa do this to me?"

Beside her, another woman was sobbing, rolling on the ground.

The army had set fire to all the homes, had purposely burned down the shacks. It wanted to run the Maquisards out of their shelters, out of the bush, and fire was the tool it used. The blazing passage of the soldiers was a warning—the old woman knew that quite clearly, for she had already survived the German conquest.

"She just stayed in her bed!"

"O, Magni Sa, o!"

"She was burned with her bed!"

"With her house!"

"They want to burn us all alive, us, too," a voice said. "They want to kill us all."

That's the day the pastor's two daughters decided to leave Bangangte.

8

The back door of the house opened and in came Sahara. Marie's face grew pale. She yelped.

"Don't be afraid," Céline said, hurrying over and grabbing the dog by the collar. "Don't be afraid."

But Sahara wrestled free of his owner's hand and scurried under the table, wagging his tail while the adults passed around Marie's poem, another one she'd written, and gushed over the drawing that accompanied it.

"I'm not afraid," said the little one, "I'm not afraid."

But she was frozen still and staring at Tanou, who picked her up and put her on his shoulders, as Sahara kept barking.

"Shhh!" said Céline.

Sahara wouldn't quiet down. On the contrary, he was running all around the living room and sniffing the furniture, although he was quite familiar with it already. Then he came back into the kitchen and barked loudly.

"Sahara, sit!" said Céline. "*Sit!*" she repeated in English. "He's just happy to see us."

But the dog got up again.

"Sit!"

Sahara went over to Tanou, who stood up. Marie's head was almost at the ceiling. Clutching onto her father as if he were a palm tree, she stared down below.

"He hasn't been out all day," Céline said.

"I'll take him for a walk," Grandfather offered.

He rose and quickly grabbed Sahara's leash. That got Marie's attention.

"Can I come?"

Everyone looked at each other in surprise.

"Please," she pleaded, adding another "please," this time in English.

She put on her most beseeching face, holding her hands together like she was praying. How could they say no, especially when she added, "I'm not afraid." She said it mostly to convince herself. She was still trembling when Tanou set her down. "I'm not afraid."

"Well, come along, then," said Old Papa. "Let's go."

"Are you sure, baby?" Tanou asked.

"I'm sure, Papa," Marie insisted. "I'm sure."

In the kitchen, Céline smiled as she listened to this exchange among the three generations of Nithaps gathered around her dog. But she stayed out of it, focusing instead on making coffee.

"I think I'll head off, too," Tanou said.

Sahara barked. Marie clambered back up the tree that was her father, and Grandfather set off.

"I'll go with him," Tanou said.

"Maybe you should buy her a small pet," said Céline. "It would help her get over her fears."

Wiping her hands on a dish towel, she followed the family out. She spoke about her own children, one of whom was extremely afraid of cats.

"We tried everything," she said. "But all it took was showing him a picture of a cat, a lion, a panther, a tiger, and he'd panic. He'd get all red and shout. He said it was the cat's eyes that frightened him the most. The eyes, can you imagine?"

"But I'm not afraid," Marie piped up. Everyone burst out laughing, which she didn't find funny.

"We bought him a hamster to start."

Marie really didn't like having everyone laugh at her. A grimace spread across her face and she glared, her lips pinched tight, her arms crossed. "I don't like it when people make fun of me."

"But no one is making fun of you, my dear," someone said. "Not me!" "Not me!" "Not me!" each adult added in turn. Then off she went, following her grandfather, who'd started walking, holding Sahara on his leash.

"That's children for you."

Tanou watched Grandfather and Marie walk away, with Sahara in front and Marie bringing up the rear. He remembered the switch his father had always kept beside him at mealtime, and which he used when his son wouldn't eat, especially okra stew, which he really didn't like as a child. Now he watched his father cajole Marie, who had a similar aversion to vegetables. Old Papa walked on, looking back over his shoulder because he didn't want to lose sight of the little girl, who'd gotten distracted by a flower and then stopped to pick up a stick on the sidewalk. Tanou remembered taking walks with his father. He could still hear their conversations. When he was little, he used to read aloud everything written that he saw along their path. His father would correct his pronunciation: "boutique," "printing shop." Standing beside him, Céline was also watching the trio's advance. Tanou's father shook his head and crossed the street, then stopped and turned back to look again. Tanou had an answer on his lips for the question Angela was about to ask: "Marie has taken Sahara for a walk, do you believe it?"

"Where is Marie?"

He also remembered, although he hadn't told anyone before, that he had also been very afraid of dogs when he was little. And there were always folks who'd let their mutts wander all over. Even when he was a student in Yaounde, he remembered their neighbors in Melen who had no pity for the passersby and just unleashed their brutes to snap at their calves. "He won't bite," they'd say with a snigger. "He's had his shots." But as soon as he came close, the dog jumped on him! Tanou wondered if his father had also been afraid of dogs. Maybe, though, it was a fear he'd inherited from his mother, from Ngountchou? He remembered that his grandfather the pastor had a dog. "Maybe they'd gotten it to help cure his mother's phobia?" He hadn't known the dog, but everyone talked about him gingerly, calling him the "cannibal."

"He had a taste for human flesh," they said.

It was with that story in mind that he went back into the living room, where Angela, still dressed in her workout clothes, was watching television.

"I can't believe Obama's second term is almost over."

He didn't tell her about his own fear, nor of its possible roots in far-off Bangangte. He knew that she'd find it funny. His father had never brought it up, and he was grateful for Old Papa's silence.

"Honey," he said instead, "what would you say about a little *massage?*"

Angela looked at him, her eyes saying clearly, *This is not the time*, while her voice said, "Do you realize *he's* winning now?"

He meant Trump. The images on the TV screen focused on his oily face, his puckered mouth, while with his left hand, palm open, fingers spread, the candidate traced endless circles next to his shoulder, circles, circles, circles, and more circles. "It makes you dizzy," Angela said, her eyes glued to the circles.

"He's hypnotized you," Tanou'd said one day.

"He's hypnotized the whole country," she'd replied, "with those hands of his."

"What about a *massage?*"

The same eyes that had said, *This is not the time*, flicked back to the TV screen. Angela had muted it.

"I just can't hear his voice," she said. "Do you realize what Marie asked me the other day? 'Is Trump going to start a war?'"

"A war?"

"That's what she asked. She looked so frightened. Is Trump going to start a war? Disgusting!"

Tanou went into the kitchen.

"Do you want any coffee?"

"Did you read his last tweet?"

An hour later, an ecstatic Marie opened the door of the house. She saw her parents sitting on the couch, Tanou rubbing Angela's shoulders, and said, "I want a dog!" She came and sat next to her father, her hands clasped like she was praying. "Please, please, please, Dad," she said in English, as he turned his astonished eyes to his own father, who, with a broad smile on his face, was closing the door behind him.

"What sort of pill did you give her?"

Obviously, Old Papa didn't answer.

"Please, please, please, Dad?" she repeated, still in English.

Angela had retreated to the kitchen; they heard the sounds of cupboard doors, of pots and plates and knives, and the refrigerator closing.

"What is she making?"

"Have you done your homework?" Tanou asked his daughter.

"We don't have any homework."

"How's that?"

"Dad!" she said, again in English.

Blackmail as a parenting strategy against a child's tyranny. Negotiating the outermost reaches of power, even Foucault couldn't have thought of this—there were no children in the paradise he'd imagined for himself. Tanou wasn't ready to give up the TV screen yet. He picked up the remote, the field of so many family battles. He switched from station to station: CNN, where he cut off the long tirades; Fox News, only the starts of sentences; MSNBC and its interviews. Even Marie's reasoning had no effect: "Papa, I don't have any homework today. Papa, today is Friday." Yet he hadn't counted on what he considered Angela's "betrayal": "gender politics." She let him know he should come help in the kitchen. "I'm not going to make dinner all by myself."

Using the child as a bulletproof shield in the early evening's defensive war:

"You get started, baby. I'll be right there."

"Yeah, and who's gonna chop the onions?"

Old Papa headed in to help.

"Just five minutes."

Should they just have pizza every night to keep the peace? *Hooray!* Marie would shout, like a victorious general.

"Baby." He heard her voice in the living room, over the tinkling sounds of cartoons. "You're not going to let *your father* do the cooking, are you?"

Tanou couldn't even use the excuse that he needed to prepare his classes, since he was clearly just watching TV.

And there was nothing about the history of the civil war on the television.

9

After his trip back to Cameroon for his mother's burial, Tanou opened his Facebook page and found a slew of messages he hadn't had a chance to read. He also found a number of friend requests—more than he'd ever had before. "I must have won the lottery," he muttered, convinced there was some sort of glitch. It took him a minute to realize that it wasn't a joke: there was a whole list of friend requests, made almost all at the same time, from the leadership of the UPC.

Um Nyobè.

Félix Moumié.

Singap Martin.

Comrade Émile.

Not to mention *Commander Kissamba*, and *Osendé Afana*, or the several "Frantz Fanons" and "Ben Bellas."

It was when Tanou saw the name *Marthe* that he remembered the Sinistrés—the young people his nephew had introduced him to at the University of Yaounde, who had all taken on the names of Maquisards—because the shape of the young woman, as well as the timbre of her voice, suddenly came back to him.

He smiled and looked over the list again, stopping on each name, starting with *Um Nyobè*.

That guy, he said to himself, *is taking this all too seriously; both his little mustache and the part in his hair seemed ridiculous and repugnant. Sorry.* He deleted his request, as well as the one from Ouandié, even if he hesitated for a minute about that one. *Tut mir leid, I'm sorry, comrade. That little guy might get some ideas*, he thought, after opening the young man's page and looking through his album. *Ciao*. He did the same thing with Moumié, although his pictures showed him to be a studious young man, very studious, and the album was punctuated by a series of Bible verses, a veritable library of received ideas. "Sorcerer," he said, as they do back in the country, "be gone!"

Tanou scanned over each of the requests, less out of diligence—since he really only used his Facebook page so he could see Bagam's posts, and get news from the country—than because he was putting off getting to Marthe. In fact, he would have jumped straight to the girl's page if he hadn't felt that he was crossing some line, or rather—let's be frank—if the memory of allowing himself to cross that line hadn't suddenly come flooding back. He ended up shutting down his computer without accepting her friend request.

It wasn't until the next day, when he was on his phone, that he accepted it. Immediately a message popped up: it was her. *hi prof.*

Tanou didn't answer then because he was driving. That gave him the time to think, should he say *hi* or maybe *hello*, or *hello Marthe*. He wondered whether it was a mistake to answer at all, and then he saw her on his hotel bed, the little rings on the ends of her nipples; should he really answer, answer her? Was it worth the trouble, and most of all, what should he say? Back in the day, one might have written, *good day or good evening, depending on when you are reading this letter*, but here, what should he say after such a long silence? He tapped his fingers on the steering wheel of his car, rather than on the keypad of his phone, and whistled; words and gestures were forming in his head, shapes were traced out, as well as letters, M-a-r-t-h-e. And then, suddenly, he wondered what her name—her real name—actually was. "I could ask her that now."

What is your name?

???

Your real name?

She immediately replied, without missing a beat: Mfoumou Bella Anasthasie Yolande Pascaline. And so it was he, Tanou, who cut it short. *I'll just call you Marthe. Like your friends.*

He was turned on by this immediate intimacy, and surprised by his own modesty. He tried for a moment to write in the same tone she was using, but quickly gave up. Girls always feel entitled to take liberties once they've seen a man without his underwear. He wanted to regain the upper hand.

Yet he still wanted to read her messages word by word, sentence by sentence, just like he'd wanted to explore her body that day. But he needed to take his time now, show how patient he was. In other words, he needed to show her the paths of his desire, without putting her off. He realized that they'd never really gotten out of the bed where he'd led her. And he wanted her there still, wrapped in sheets; he imagined her wet, sucking her fingers before she typed each letter.

After his return from Yaounde, Tanou kept ending up in front of his computer in the middle of the night, exchanging messages with his virtual girlfriend. Then the pleasure he found in her esoteric turns of phrase ran dry. She tried to reach him on Messenger. He waited, then turned down the volume, and sent her a quick message, *driving*.

Tanou was going through a very lonely period in his life. The death of his mother. Now Old Papa had taken over the attic, the tower where he used to write. Little Marie was occupying more and more space in the home, had taken over the conjugal bed and kicked him out. He spent his nights on the sofa, watching television. The few times he insisted, egged on by a remaining shard of self-respect, on sleeping in *his* room, in *his* bed, Marie just cried. Angela said nothing, except, "She'll grow up."

And Tanou was horrified to remember that he, too, had forced his parents to sleep in separate beds. *Revenge is a dish best served cold.* Now Old Papa just laughed about it.

"She's not so different from you, huh."

He still remembered Ngountchou's bed, which meant he'd stopped sleeping there when he was ten or twelve years old. The idea of spending the next few years sleeping on the couch, only able to control the remote after his child had fallen asleep, combined with what he termed a "lack of understanding" on the part of both his father and Angela—that's what had sunk him into a depression, or rather thrown him in front of his computer. Obviously, he didn't say any of this to Marthe, who certainly wouldn't have understood. How could he tell her that his house felt like a hotel room where he was no longer welcome; how could he tell her that his home had become the theater of a civil war? Because that's how he saw it: *This is war!*

The battlefields were numerous: the TV remote from 6:00 a.m. to 8:00 p.m., and the sofa after 10:00 p.m. Before ten, he had to cede the sofa to the family, and to Angela in particular, who wouldn't have been happy—that's for sure—without Rachel Maddow's diatribes. ("Without her," Angela said, "I don't know how I would have made it through all this.") And then after 10:00 p.m., there was the choice of a movie they'd both watch on Netflix or Amazon.

"I have to prepare my classes," he'd say after that, which usually meant going on Facebook and reading messages from Marthe.

Hi prof. Im in bed.

The virtual bed made up for the exile from his real one. That far-off bed, he knew it well. He had seen pictures of Marthe lying on it; thanks to the pictures, he actually knew all the corners of her room. He had seen her in jeans (*not bad*), wearing a *kaba ngondo*, back in the village, with a bunch of bananas balanced on her head, and with her girlfriends at the university, laughing in a selfie, in several selfies. *She loves her body, that's good.* He had read the short captions introducing each of the photos, amused by her nonchalance. Her posts, he'd read them, too, exchanges with girlfriends—several of whom had outrageous names. Her rushed replies—for example, to *the Ongola fairy*—made him laugh, yes, that was her style. *Just quick shots.* He knew her, and at the same time, he recognized her type. He texted back, asking her to switch to live chat. He accepted her call, happy at the sight of shapes that, not long ago, had filled the palms of his hands—but only the shapes, and the shine of her eyes and teeth.

"Eneo," said Marthe, referring to the electric company. "The power's out."

He could hear her chuckle. Tanou was amused by that, and suddenly a wave of nostalgia overcame him, enveloping his body like a steam bath. He stuck a hand into his pocket, and used the other to lower the volume with the mouse. The sound of Marthe's breathing soon took over the space—and his voice.

I can't talk, he typed quickly.

"It's hot here," she said.

Take of your shirt, dion.

He was having fun, so much fun that he didn't think twice about sending her some cash, some *$$*, as she said. She knew the easiest way to send money back to the country, Western Union, she explained. He sent her some and, at the same time, some to Mensa', as well as to several of his brothers and sisters in need. That's what he did to clear his conscience of living "in dollars," and he grumbled a little less each time about how the diaspora had become "the mother's breast of the whole country because of Biya." Marthe clearly had something to do with it if he was in a good mood when he stood at the kiosk, filling out wire transfers alongside all the Haitians and Mexicans playing the lottery. Sometimes he even traded a few jokes with the Indian woman who told him to ask everyone he was sending money to come work here.

"They're all in prison," he said. "The country is held captive."

"In prison?"

Tanou wanted to tell her about daily life under a tyrant, but he hesitated, trying to find the right words to explain it to the Indian woman, who clearly only understood how to ring up sales on the cash register; with a shrug, she replied, "I'm from Bengal."

He heard "*bangala*."

So he could send the money, Marthe had given him her full name, as well as her national identity number and her phone numbers (she had two on different networks, MTN and Orange). *Thanks, prof.*

He still didn't think he was obsessed with her. Even when he jumped at the sound of a message when he was driving, flipping through the notifications on his iPhone to find Marthe's quick *hi prof*, and then rushing to his computer as soon as he got home. Once, even, when he was giving a lecture, a message popped up on the top right of his laptop's screen: *hi prof.* Not to mention that time when he forgot to close his Facebook page and an incoming call suddenly popped up on his computer screen, projected on the board for the whole class. But those were just accidents. He apologized, "*Cameroon calling*," and then continued his talk, his mind already elsewhere, focused on the image of Marthe in her bed, Marthe hot and heavy, Marthe undoing her bra, undressing bit by bit. And just maybe he'd had to put his hand into his pocket to control his erection.

"So who is Marthe?"

When Angela asked that question on the phone, he came to, like someone who had almost drowned.

"What?"

"You heard me."

He almost caused an accident, because he was barreling down the highway, whistling along to an old song by Whitney Houston, "So Emotional," when she asked that question.

"Angela, I'm driving."

He was trying to stall for time.

"Just who is Marthe, *asshole?*"—she cursed in English.

"Wait, let me explain," he began.

But the line went dead. A song by Bruno Mars blared out. He bit his lower lip and pounded on the steering wheel with his fists. "Shit! Shit! Shit!" He hit it so hard he set off the horn. That made him jump. The driver on his left stared at him in surprise. He smiled back.

"Let's just calm down," he said to himself. "Nothing's broken."

And Bruno sang, *You deserve it, baby! You deserve it all!*

10

A minefield. That's what Tanou thought of when he opened the door, crossed the living room, and saw Angela and Old Papa sitting in front of the television with Marie, who was watching cartoons. Only one voice answered when he said hello, his father's. Mother and daughter didn't even turn around. Their eyes were fixed on the screen, on Bugs Bunny's antics. Tanou had prepared several answers, which he'd rehearsed like an actor, trying to find the right tone, but the only thing in his mind right then was the question and insult from his wife: "Just who is Marthe, *asshole*?" How did she find out?

"You had a good day?"

Again, only Grandfather answered.

"Fairly good," he said. "How was the drive?"

"Traffic jams," Tanou said, taking off his overcoat. "Never-ending traffic jams."

Angela stood up abruptly and headed upstairs. He followed her into his office. She was holding several pages from the printer in her hands. Her face was contorted by anger.

"Did you fuck her?"

Tanou was taken aback by the blunt question in English. He shut the office door and quickly realized he'd trapped himself with a fury. He tried to reopen the door, but Angela stopped him. Violently. With her whole body.

"Angela, please don't yell," he begged.

She opened his computer screen and a photo of Marthe appeared—sitting on her bed, naked, feet crossed and smiling.

"Did you fuck this girl?"

Marthe had sent him, after he'd asked, several pictures of herself, taken on that bed that fueled his fantasies. He had told her what positions he wanted: standing, sitting, from behind, full frontal, lying down, her legs slightly parted. He had promised that the pictures would remain private; *they won't leave my computer*, he'd written. He'd kept his word. Those were the pictures Angela was flipping through, one after the other.

"Did you?"

"They'll hear us downstairs," Tanou continued.

"I don't give a damn," his wife spat back, "whether they hear or not. My question is really simple and you still haven't answered. Did you sleep with this slut, yes or no?"

"I did not have sexual relations with that woman," the husband replied, knowing he'd been caught, but emphasizing each word and even raising his left hand. "Mademoiselle Marthe."

"So you think this is funny?" Angela exploded. "I really hope you at least used a condom."

Tanou recalled how he'd left his office that morning, late because he'd answered a message from Marthe and then she'd answered back, which had meant he'd needed to reply again, then going back to his office because he'd forgotten a book he needed to discuss in class; he remembered that he hadn't shut his Facebook page, that he'd left it open to that last exchange where he commented on Marthe's pictures. He was responding to her caprices, because she had asked him to describe her poses, to tell her—*honestly, I really mean it, prof*—what was missing, what he couldn't see, what she needed to do; and he had described her body, part by part, from her hair to her toes, from front to back, from her breasts to her vagina, her neck to her knees. It was those descriptions—texts written with one hand, texts in which Tanou had deployed his incandescent vocabulary, masturbating all the while—those pages that Angela held in her hands. There was a whole novel there, even if Angela was waving only three leprous pages at him, her mouth twisted in disgust and anger.

Tanou had discovered he was a writer while gazing on Marthe's body. He had never before imagined that pictures could stimulate his imagination that much, that they could set his body aboil. At one point, he'd actually laughed at what he was writing, burst out laughing. Then, just as he was orgasming, he concluded that he was a novelist. "I'm writing a novel," he'd said to Marthe. He had read her the passage describing her nose, she'd smiled and said, "That's all?" He'd read her the passage describing her lips: "That's all?" He'd read the one describing her breasts: "That's all?" So he continued, describing every bit of hair on her pubis, then her lips and her vagina, first working from memory, but then she'd corrected him, showed them to him, shifting in front of the camera, bending her body like a crab, spreading her legs, asking him to describe her most intimate parts: "Good." As he described her fingers, they started to tremble. She stuck her index finger inside and rubbed her clitoris. He came. He stopped writing so he could go find a towel.

"You are sick!" Angela spat out, holding the pages of his prose between her thumb and index finger. "Sick!"

That's when they heard noises in the hallway, Marie's voice calling for her mother to come back to the television.

"You should go see a shrink!"

The door slammed, leaving the husband to his solitude.

Hi prof, r u thr?

A message from Marthe.

Tanou shut down the computer. When he went down to the living room, he saw his father sitting alone in front of the screen.

"What's going on?" Old Papa asked. At his age, he'd learned to recognize the face of despair.

"Nothing," his son replied. "*Nothing.*"

Tanou found mother and daughter in the bedroom, in bed.

"*Dad*, what did you do to Mama?"

"I don't know": a classic lie.

Marie pronounced the verdict.

"*Dad*, she says she doesn't want to see you anymore."

The little girl hadn't even gotten up. He kept trying; he crouched down to speak to her, trying to start a sentence, to stammer out a useless lie.

"I don't want to see you anymore!" he heard from the shadows. "I don't want to see you anymore!"

"Dad!"

"Don't touch me!"

"Angela!"

"Get out!"

He spent the night at Céline's, in the poet's home, on his couch. The messages on his iPhone told him where his absence was most keenly felt. Messages from Marthe kept lining up on his phone, but there was not one call from the only woman he wanted to hear from. He picked it up and checked—eighteen messages, which he didn't read. He closed his eyes, but only to see Marthe's image.

In the morning, Tanou woke up with the sun in his eyes. He'd spent the last few nights on a couch, but this time his body seemed to rebel against it. The birdsong roused him from his sleep, and for a moment he was relieved that he didn't have to suffer through the violence of Marie's sobs. He jumped when he felt Sahara at his feet. He had taken the dog's spot and now the dog was telling him to get up. He'd spent the night in the poet's office.

He looked at the books on the worktable and got up. He ran his hand over the desk blotter that had seen the birth of so many words, so many stories. He turned around and met the gaze of the dog who, now lying on the sofa, was watching him.

Go on, Sahara seemed to say. *Go on, write.*

The smell of coffee signaled life in the kitchen below. He paused, stretched, and, dragging Sahara with him, went to find Céline. She seemed to be trying to tell him, *You know, I don't judge*. She had cleared the table of the newspapers that were usually piled all around and set out breakfast: brioches, madeleines, jams. The computer open on the side table was playing classical music, Mozart. In a quick wave of the hand, she picked *The New York Times* up off a chair. Tanou sat down in silence.

"I don't judge," was in fact what Céline said. "I listen."

Soon it was clear she could do more than that.

That morning, Marie overcame her fear of Sahara to find her father. There was a knock on the front door. In she ran, straight into her father's arms.

"*Daddy*," she said, through her sobs, "why don't you come home?"

The father took his little girl into his arms, wiped her tears, and stammered, "But I never left!"

Coughing as tears flowed down her cheeks, the little girl was inconsolable. She wouldn't calm down until Angela came to get her. There in that living room, her parents' faces revealed the devastation wrought by a night spent in a silent standoff. The woman's tears had turned into a stoic chill, while Tanou had covered his face with a mask of pride.

"Good morning," Céline said. "Do you want some coffee?"

"We should leave," Angela replied. "Marie has to go to school."

"Is Papa coming with us?"

Her mother bent down.

"Ma," she said, "you have to go to school."

"No," Marie protested.

"Ma!"

"No!"

The little girl pulled away from her father's embrace and ran, her voice flying across the living room in one long sob. "No! No! *I want my daddy!*" she wailed in English.

Angela and Tanou looked at each other for a moment, each with an identical reproach in their glare: "Do you see what you are doing?" The woman turned and almost bumped into Old Papa, who was coming into the living room, holding Marie's hand as the girl stomped her feet and hammered out her refrain: "I want my father!"

Tanou had to speak with Marie, use his most tender words, and lead her to his wife's car, making a thousand and one promises before she'd agree to leave.

"I'll come back to the house," he told her.

"Promise?"

"Promise!"

Angela didn't say a thing. The car roared off, leaving him and his father, who each knew that the really difficult part was yet to come.

"Children," said Céline.

She wanted to break the silence imposed by the quarrel. Sahara rubbed up against her feet, then headed off to the kitchen, only to return, wagging and yipping loudly.

"I'd really like a cup of coffee," Tanou said.

"Milk and sugar?"

He was stunned by what was happening, weakened by another night of tossing and turning. Céline had to repeat her question.

"Black," he finally said, sitting down in the kitchen, facing his father.

Sahara came to lie down at his feet, under the table.

"It's a little strong," Céline began, giving him a gentle pat on the shoulder.

She was talking about the coffee, of course, but Tanou understood it differently.

"I'm really sorry," he said, stirring his coffee with a spoon. "My heartfelt apologies."

"Now is not the time for that," said Céline. "Some coffee for you?"

She was speaking to Old Papa. He said no with a wave of his hand, looking down. It was clear that what was happening brought up a long and complicated story for him. Father and son sat quietly for a moment, mulling over so many thoughts, unable to come up with the words to express them. Tanou pulled his phone out of his pocket, a recent habit born of his affair, and opened Marthe's Facebook page; then, "before witnesses," as he'd later say to his wife, he clicked on the "block" button.

"Who is *that girl*?" Céline asked abruptly.

Tanou jumped: Marthe . . .

Her profile picture showed her smiling; it was a new photo, probably one of the pictures he'd had her take. There were twenty-six likes and lots of comments: *so beautiful*, *my sweet*, *hubba hubba*, *smooch*, *call me*, *love you*, and Marthe's responses. A window popped up asking him to *confirm that you want to block*, and he did. *We blocked Marthe. We apologize for the inconvenience.* He pressed "OK" and smiled, his thoughts far away. He put his phone down on the *Times*, then picked up the spoon and stirred his coffee again, before taking a sip.

"Marthe," he said, putting down his cup and then wrapping his two hands around it. "She's Ouandié's wife . . ."

He took a deep breath, weighing the silence that fell around the table following his revelation—and especially its impact on his father's face.

"Um Nyobè's wife . . ."

As he looked at Céline's face, he finally put the story together.

"Moumié's wife."

Then he picked up a madeleine and ate it slowly.

*"Piang."**

He didn't know that his answer, which he'd intended as a witty way out of a tight spot, and which he'd formulated in order to buy time, would awaken his father's memory and untie his tongue. As they sat around that table, the two men moved from one echo to the next, from Marthe to Clara, trying to express a similar obsession, an identical wild passion. It was there, in the poet's kitchen, in front of Céline—and in some sense, first for Céline—that father and son told their stories. It was there in the

---

* The end, period. Tanou could have continued on, adding what he'd learned in his research into the etymology of the name Marthe, because his obsession had gone far beyond the pictures of that girl's private parts; he'd delved into the triptych of women who shared a name, and then he went even further down that virtual rabbit hole, trying to get to the bottom of it. He'd discovered that Marthe came from the Amharic מרתא ; it was the feminine version of מר (mar), or master—mistress. Had he leafed through the New Testament and found her biblical story, he might have found a way out, but in the end, the story that satisfied his curiosity had been posted in a comment on his nephew Bagam's Facebook page. (How ironic is that?) Um Nyobè, Moumié, and Ouandié, it said, were all linked by a pact made by their mothers, that each would marry a woman named Marthe, a pact sealed in blood, if ever there was one. Still, there were those with forked tongues who said that story was ridiculous, that it was just a coincidence: that, whatever their powers, there is no way that the mythical leaders of the UPC could have named each of their wives at the moment they were born—that would have meant traveling back in time, retracing a genealogy, and imposing a fatal destiny on the past.

scent of coffee that Tanou found his voice, which he had buried under the multiple layers of his shame.

"So who is Ouandié?" Céline asked.

Tanou looked at his father.

"Papa, can you answer that?"

The next morning Tanou woke up, his face drawn and his mind still under the sway of that distant girl, of the sensation of her body around his. Then he took a shower, opened his eyes, and cried for love. Later, returning to Big's office—because it would still be several days before Angela would come to terms with his betrayal—he sat in Bob's empty chair, wrapping himself in the mantle of the departed, even if it was too big for him, and picked up some blank paper Bob had left behind. One sentence after another, one word after another, he wrote the beginning of a story that was as much about him as it was about his father: it was his father's story and his daughter's, his aunt's and his mother's, his wife's and his mistress's. And so, moving from chapter to chapter, until it was a book, he wrote the chronicle of his own birth as a novelist: *This must be what death is like, what else could it be? Waking up groggy on a day when the sun is slow to rise . . .*

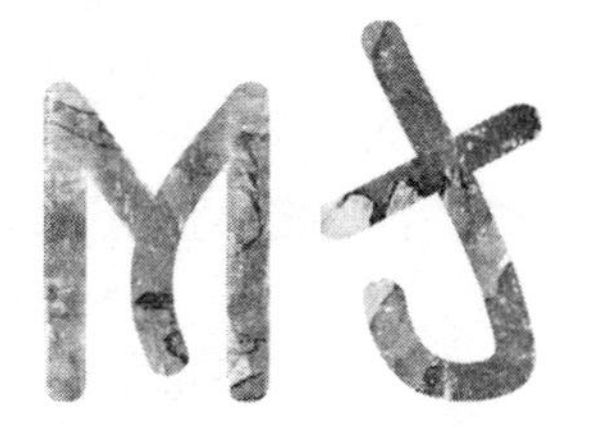

Black as a Mafi!

1

Because of her sheltered upbringing in Bangangte, Mensa' wasn't used to the ways of the world. Yaounde's high society—composed of a handful of Cameroonians and many more French—had been invited to the Presidential Palace for the Reunification Ball. It was barely a month after her marriage to Deputy Ntchantchou Zacharie, and she wasn't even pregnant with her first child yet. The young woman was getting to know her husband, whom she'd met in town. Her wedding had put an end to her dream of attending the Noutong school. The grandeur of the ball at the palace, its magnificence, made her feel like this event was a second wedding, especially since it was an occasion—a greater, more sumptuous occasion—to be introduced to the closed circle of people in power.

She followed her husband, who was used to such events. He saw many people he knew. He bowed his head to greet a white couple, clasping his hands together and saying, "Hello, *Monsieur l'Ambassadeur*!"

The ambassador kissed the young wife's hand, which she offered nonchalantly. Turning to his spouse, the deputy added, with a broad smile on his face, that this was the French ambassador. And then her husband greeted another white man, who, recognizing the deputy, held his hands out open before him.

"Ah, Monsieur Tchatchou!" he said, pronouncing his name with a strong French accent.

"*Ou yun mekat-la, gi?*" Ntchantchou Zacharie whispered to his wife. "*A hi ben kii Consitution Cameroun.*"*

She scanned the room.

"The one over there in the three-piece suit," he added. "A bald head." Then he repeated, "He's the one who wrote the Constitution."

The man was already heading toward them. Ntchantchou Zacharie exclaimed, "Monsieur Rousseau! I didn't think you were still in Cameroon!"

"But yes, of course. Madam?"

Mensa' gave her hand to M. Rousseau, who had a long head, like a horse. She and her husband looked at the author of the Cameroonian Constitution. A strange man; everyone suspected—and it was the whites who said it out loud—that he'd also written Um Nyobè's speech at the UN.

"I heard M. Debré is here, but I haven't seen him yet," Ntchantchou Zacharie said. "I did see Minister Murville."

Mensa' didn't know either of those men.

"Hello, Colonel Lamberton!" he said to a man with a boxer's build. "You've come back to town!"

Mensa' recognized that man.

"You, too," he shot back.

Mensa' had practiced back at the house, in front of the mirror. She had repeated the gesture of offering her hand to a man, to a dignitary, as her husband put it. He had shown her how it was done. She was wearing a form-fitting suit in a dark greenish blue, made from cloth he'd purchased at a store in Paris—a wedding gift. Her sister, Ngountchou, had made it for her, since Mademoiselle Birgitte had just bought her a Singer sewing machine. For a long time, Mensa' had stood nervously in front of the mirror, staring at herself. Her neighbor, Marie-Irène Ngapeth, who was a few years older, had tried to reassure her. She was so lucky to live next door to that lady; the life she led and the amazing stories she told left Mensa' breathless.

---

* "Did you see the white man over there? He's the one who wrote the Cameroonian Constitution."

She'd been the first to come knock on their door.

"So, this is *Madam Deputy*," she'd said.

Mensa' tried to speak to her in Medumba, because of her name, but she'd bristled.

"I'm Bassa," she clarified. "But my husband, you'll meet him, he's from Bangangte."

Still, she always told Mensa', "You are my little sister."

Mensa' told herself that Yaounde would have been a very sad place for her without "the Amazing Mme Ngapeth." She often shared with Mensa' stories of her adventures in Douala's neighborhoods, "after May 1955," and how she'd crossed the Wouri River at night, during the "troubles"; then her eyes would light up and her voice would take on a conspiratorial tone.

"I was carrying my last-born in my arms!" she said. "I went to Bonamoussadi in a canoe and stayed there, at an old man's house, for a whole month."

She'd stare her interlocutor in the eyes, trying to recollect the face of that old man who had saved her life. "He gave me advice, explained how the world works."

She also talked about her trip to New York.

"This is our party!" she said, speaking of the reunification.

And yet she also said, in the most casual way, "Don't believe that truth is always on the side of the poor, because no one has a monopoly on wisdom." She told how Soppo Priso, the incredibly wealthy man who was then in power, had taken care of her children when she was in danger, "me, a *UPC supporter*!" One day she whispered to Mensa', "Above all, don't believe that people only have one face." The deputy's young wife would often think back to that first lesson: "Truth is, all adults lie. And let's not even talk about politicians, because everything they do is political!" Why had she rallied to the government? "Because the poor man will give everything he has to the rich, but not to another man as poor as himself. You know why?" Then, with a laugh, she answered her own question. "Because he's afraid his brother will become rich at his expense!"

How haughty she could be!

"The legendary kindness and natural solidarity of those in need," she concluded, "I just don't believe in it anymore! Among themselves, the poor are like crabs in a cook pot. They each pull the other down so they all end up cooked. I know what I'm talking about. I lived in exile, too, in Nigeria, where my husband and I, we lived disguised as Yoruba traders. I know what need and poverty are like. I practically ate stones to survive. Need doesn't transform the riffraff into leaders, and exile is no cure for a bad heart.

"So why did I rally to the government? Because it costs too much to be poor! The cost of suffering is too high! Misery doesn't lift you up, it destroys you! A poor man's paradise is still hell!"

She waved her hand to dismiss all that.

Later Mensa' would wonder if her husband was lying when he talked about the hundreds of UPC members in Bangangte who'd switched sides. Weren't they just Bassas like Mme Ngapeth?

"The UPC's mistake," she whispered, "is that they chose *the crab* as their party emblem! The ant, that's what I would have said, or termites, even. But the crab! The most egotistical of all animals! You'd have to be an idiot to choose it as your symbol."

Mensa' preferred to shut her ears when Mme Ngapeth started talking about what she called "Um Nyobè's idiocy."

Ntchantchou Zacharie was sporting his finest suit coat. She had adjusted his tie, as she often did for her father, the pastor. There are things about which men are unsure, whether pastor or deputy, father or husband.

"It's an honor to be invited," Ntchantchou Zacharie said.

He couldn't get over it himself. A deputy from a small village, he knew that his fiefdom was "in the bush."

"Good day, Colonel Lamberton," Mensa' said, giving a slight curtsy, as she'd practiced. The colonel didn't recognize the young woman he'd interrogated back in Bangangte, when they were searching for, and trying to capture, Nithap. There was a real beauty standing before him, and Mensa' was no longer afraid.

"We'll see each other tomorrow, right?" the man whispered to her husband, and the deputy's face stiffened. "Tomorrow."

The colonel disappeared into the crowd. Never had Mensa' seen so many white people. Clearly, this was well before her trip to Paris: "the high point of my life." Never before had she danced with one, either. These people were not like Mademoiselle Birgitte or any of the others she knew in Bangangte and who'd come to her wedding (the pastor at the mission, for example). These people were sophisticated. Her husband had warned her. He'd asked her not to be too impressed. But how could she not be? He was, too. He had a broad smile plastered on his face and was weaving through the people, who all turned in wonder when they saw her.

"Madam," said a man with a wide part on his head, "I'm so happy to meet you."

The flash of a camera blinded her for a moment. The man with the part asked the photographer to come back.

"Please take another beautiful picture for me with Madam," he said.

"That's the minister of foreign relations," Ntchantchou Zacharie whispered to his wife as they moved away.

"The president's secretary general."

"The minister of health."

Next to him, a voice was saying, "The Bamileke rebellion has no chance." It was a white man speaking. "The Bamilekes need to understand that they're not acting in their own best interest."

"You try and explain to a Bamileke what's in their interest."

"So hardheaded, those people."

"Getting them to talk is a real challenge!"

"They're no worse than the Fellaghas!"

"Do you recognize that man over there?" the deputy asked his wife. "Let's go say hello."

A voice interrupted them.

"Your Honor!"

It was the minister Arouna Njoya, a broad smile on his lips.

"I am happy to make the acquaintance of your *charming* wife." His eyes sparkled as he stared into Mensa''s eyes.

He stressed the word *charming*, touched his lips to the back of her hand, but didn't seem to hear her say, "Congratulations on your nomination."

"Madam," he said. "You must pay us a visit. Those of us from the West must support each other here in Ongola."

He locked eyes with Ntchantchou Zacharie.

"I'll come by," said Ntchantchou Zacharie, "I'll come by."

"With your *charming* wife," the minister insisted.

After they'd moved away, Ntchantchou Zacharie pulled Mensa' close and whispered, "He was a senator *in France*." Mensa' turned back and saw the man bow to a white woman and then kiss her hand. She heard his voice.

"I am so happy to make the acquaintance of your *ravishing* wife, *Monsieur l'Ambassadeur*."

"He thinks he's white," Ntchantchou Zacharie whispered. " 'You *must* pay us a visit.' "

Mensa' looked at her husband. "Must." He rarely spoke so openly to her. They really didn't talk to each other much at all, because he was so busy with work. That was the first time she'd heard a certain complicity in his voice. She leaned in closer to him when a voice piped up behind them, greeting her husband in Medumba: "*Tcho fia?*"

Ntchantchou Zacharie turned around.

"Joseph!" he exclaimed loudly, holding his arms wide open. "I didn't know you'd be here today!"

"You thought you were the only one invited, is that it?"

The two men burst out laughing, grabbing ahold of each other like two lost souls who'd found each other in the middle of the forest. Mensa' didn't offer her hand to Joseph Mbeng but her cheeks, both sides. He asked for two more kisses, "as is our custom." She laughed and again offered her cheeks.

"Your Medumba isn't bad," Ntchantchou Zacharie said to him. "I almost mistook you for Enoch."

Mbeng smiled. He wasn't Bamileke and knew the effect that his greeting in Medumba always had on the native speakers.

"About that," Ntchantchou Zacharie continued. "Enoch, have you seen him?"

"He's in the garden with his wife."

Mbeng had been at their wedding. He'd come with Enoch Nkwayim, who'd introduced him, saying, "Here's the prefect from my village." The presence of this familiar face at the ball put Mensa' at ease. It was as if she'd found her footing; so she let her husband move on without her toward a young man whom he greeted effusively. Ntchantchou Zacharie introduced his wife while she was still talking to the subprefect.

"Paul Biya," he said. "He's just joined the service and already the president has adopted him."

"Let's not exaggerate," said the man.

She chatted with him for a bit, but later went out and joined Mbeng on the terrace.

"Mensa'," he said suddenly, his eyes lighting up as if he'd found his lost sister in the middle of the desert. "You are resplendent!"

He asked her what had become of her father's translations.

"You don't know my father," she said with a smile. "Otherwise you wouldn't have asked that question."

"Pastor Tbongo!"

Their conversation was interrupted by a brouhaha and a voice that announced, "The President of the Republic and his wife!"

Mensa' stood up on her tiptoes: the President of the Republic was smaller than the rest of the crowd. She had never seen Ahidjo or his wife Germaine, who was known far and wide for her beauty. Of the President's speech, all that she remembered was the sentence, "Total calm will return to the troubled region." Perhaps because the word *calm* contrasted with the jitters she was feeling, it echoed in her mind for some time. She kept repeating it to herself, pressing her clenched fist into her breast: "Calm down, Mensa', calm down, Mensa'."

The reception hall in the Presidential Palace is big, very big, and that day it was packed. Music filled the room, signaling the start of the dance. Mensa' had never heard anything like it before. It was as if each instrument in the band were pulling at her heartstrings. Back in Bangangte, the love songs young people whistled and that they copied down in their private diaries had prepared her for this. Sometimes she'd been carried away by singers, because when women sing in Medumba, the tremolo of their voices can crush your soul. She'd been so enchanted by their voices that tears would flow from her eyes. Only Congolese music could move her in the same way. Even if she didn't speak the same language as those singers, she still knew their tunes by heart, listening to them over and over again on the turntable Pastor Tbongo had received from the Norwegian Mission. When the band's guitar player launched into a solo, she began to bob her head, and then to tap her hand on her thigh, as she did when she was dancing by herself. Ntchantchou Zacharie didn't notice his wife's enthusiasm, because he didn't like dancing, at least not to white people's music. He knew he wasn't a good dancer and there was no way he would dare to dance at such a fancy soirée. But Mensa' had other worries on her mind. She was in awe of the outfits worn by the other women. Ngountchou had put all of her talent into making the suit she was wearing, which she'd copied from an image in a department store catalog, La Redoute. But here, her talent couldn't compete with the latest designs by Coco Chanel and other famous Parisian labels. At the start of the evening, Mensa' had noticed, or sensed, a hint of condescension in the eyes of other women when they complimented her. In other words, let's say, a certain irony.

Bangangte can't compete with Paris, you know! was what the women seemed to be saying. *Let's not even mention Bangwa!* She saw her sister at her sewing machine. She knew she was talented, but Parisian haute couture was something else. It was the smiles on all those women's faces, their cruel smiles, that had frustrated her and kept her in her husband's shadow.

"Beauty must not be hidden." That's what a man, a young Frenchman, said to draw her out of hiding.

"Monsieur Dupuis, a technical adviser to the minister of territorial administration," her husband had said when introducing the man, who seemed barely out of puberty.

"I'm not hiding," she replied; later her husband would tell her that he was the brains behind Enoch Nkwayim.

"May I?" he'd gone on, this time addressing the deputy, who nodded his assent.

And that's how Mensa' found herself on the dance floor, where M. Dupuis's shortcomings were soon revealed. For him, dancing was a form of exercise, while for his partner, it was an art.

"Forgive my feet," he said when, in the middle of a merengue, he stepped on Mensa''s toes.

There was no shortage of occasions to dance in Yaounde; many dances were organized by the Frenchmen who were leaving the country in droves. Mensa' had never gone to dances in Bangangte, but there are things that our bodies want and know how to do; her dance steps, how she moved her feet, revealed an innate talent that was not matched by her partner. Joseph Mbeng looked on, scandalized to see such ineptitude.

"May I?" he said to M. Dupuis, adding, "You're not tired, I hope," to Mensa'.

"No, no."

The band started in on "Les Jeunes de Beguen," by Tchadé, one of the songs she'd copied down in her diary: *Ecoutez ce tango, qui vous fait tourner autour des femmes! Le monde se demande qui la chante . . . Et pourtant sur la montagne habitée par les ancêtres qui prient pour les jeunes de Beguen . . .* She couldn't contain herself and started singing along as she swayed her hips to the music. At first Mbeng was surprised to hear her voice, but he was soon captivated by the sound of her abandon. With one finger and then another, starting quite gently, he tapped out on his partner's back each of the notes of that refrain—*yaiyaya!*—that made her bob her head and sing as she danced. She smiled and looked at him, her face lighting up.

"You're not going to sing anymore?" he asked.

Their eyes met. They didn't say another word during the rest of the dance, and yet it was quite clear that something had happened that set them apart there on that crowded dance floor where everyone was thinking of something else, and where everyone was uncomfortably aware of their own steps and gestures. In that ballroom in Yaounde, Mensa' was finally seen for who she was: she had revealed something that only Ngountchou had known before, a secret passion that until then had only been expressed in her parents' living room. Mbeng knew that he had caught a moment of grace midflight. He knew it instinctively, just as he'd been able to recognize, amid the hundred other dancers there, the wasted potential of the deputy's wife.

"You dance quite well," he told her.

Later, when Ntchantchou Zacharie said the same thing, Mensa' was convinced. And the soirée was just beginning.

2

Throughout the evening, Mensa' danced with many partners. She danced, of course, with Enoch, whose wife also danced with Mbeng, who danced with a good dozen women in the room. Even Mme Ngapeth held out her hands to Enoch.

"Won't you dance with me?" she said. "Me, your *sister by marriage?*"

He would have preferred to avoid doing so, but said yes. In this Cameroon, there wasn't yet any equivalent of *People* magazine. But he could still see what the caption beneath the photo of them on the dance floor would have been: *Minister Dances with UPC Supporter.* Ow! Foolishness like that could sink a career in a split second, he thought. He remembered a conversation he'd had with a group of students in Paris: "Yes, I'm on the right," he'd said; his face was a stony mask and he spoke with a precise accent he'd acquired in Germany and of which he was quite proud. "You may laugh, but the only thing that matters to me is my career."

He was the first student from Bangangte to write a graduate thesis and, back then, the oldest of the students who'd received scholarships.

"When you get into power," he added, "you'll find you need qualified jurists, too."

Then, turning to the young UNEK* members who were booing him, he spat out, "A good player will always find a spot on a team."

---

* The UNEK (*Union nationale des étudiants du Kamerun*), or National Union of Kamerunian Students, was a student group aligned with the UPC that had affiliates on college campuses in France.

Monsieur Ngapeth joined the group. He introduced himself to Mensa' and her husband in French, even though all three were from Bangangte.

"Life and its surprises," Mbeng said, looking at the couple dancing. "Those two are now allies."

"Who isn't friends with Mme Ngapeth?" Ntchantchou Zacharie said significantly. Then he looked at his wife and, speaking in Medumba and using her *ndap*, offered her a drink: "Mensa' *ou koo ndjou' gi?*"

Mensa' smiled, even as the thought popped into her head that her husband was happy to escape from M. Ngapeth.

"Waiter!" he called, and a man approached. Then, with his eyes still following Mme Ngapeth, he switched into French: "All by herself, she rallied all of Sanaga-Maritime to the government, not to mention her husband!"

The waiter held out a tray. He took a glass of champagne and offered it to her.

"She should come and help me in Bangangte," he said with a smile. Then, turning back to M. Ngapeth, he added in Medumba, "*Me jou' mbe ou tche-a ʒe Bassa ndonni ndje.*"*

"Please speak French," protested Eva, the German wife of Minister Nkwayim, who didn't speak Medumba. "In French!"

"I'm just teasing him," Ntchantchou Zacharie replied.

"And what number will this one be?" M. Ngapeth asked her, having realized she was pregnant.

"The third."

"You're a real African," he said.

Eva blushed.

"After this one," she said, "I'll give it a rest."

Her husband came back.

"Who's arresting people?" he asked.

"*Monsieur le Ministre*," Mbeng said to him, "no one but you."

---

* "You're from Bangangte, and you're under the spell of your Bassa wife"; a devious way of suggesting, *You've become a UPC supporter.*

"I hope you'll have a boy, sir," Ntchantchou Zacharie said to Nkwayim, before turning to Eva. "Am I right, madam?"

"Another daughter would be fine by me," she said, as she led the two other women away. "But after this, I'm done."

"The repose of the Woman Warrior," Enoch added suggestively.

The men burst out laughing.

"So, do you still like my village?" Enoch Nkwayim asked Mbeng.

"And how! I've already learned Medumba."

"*A yi la, me tasa'tchang!* That's it!" Ntchantchou Zacharie agreed, using his *ndap*.

Enoch Nkwayim didn't test him, but rather continued in French.

"I hope you are taking good care of my mama," he said.

And that's how their conversations went. Mbeng's professional situation was rather complicated, since he was working in his boss's hometown. But that's really all they had in common. Sometimes, as a result, their exchanges got heated. While the music kept drawing couples onto the dance floor, they kept talking about the High Plateau, chatting about what was going on and the advantages of the *cadi*.* "The Bamilekes aren't like the Bassas. Without the *cadi*, do you think even one of them would rally to the government?"

They didn't even notice as the women, who were also engaged in a lively conversation, headed off with Mme Ngapeth. She'd turn her head left, toward Mensa', and then right, toward Eva, sometimes stopping midsentence, effusively greeting someone she knew, and introducing them to her two allies for the evening. She seemed to know everyone there.

"You are still talking about Bangangte," said Mme Ngapeth, "or am I mistaken?"

The three men jumped, their faces lighting up as they realized they'd been caught. They hadn't even noticed that the women had come back.

"*Schatz*," Eva said, "*gehen wir?*"

"*Gleich*."

* A public confession; a Bamileke tradition that was used strategically during the civil war. We'll come back to this later.

You could hear the exasperation in his voice. He realized that and started again.

"*Noch fünf Minuten, ja?*" he asked her.

"*Nimm deine Zeit.*"*

"The language of Goethe," said Mbeng wistfully, then his eyes caught Mensa''s. "I studied Spanish in school instead. *Hola!*"

She smiled in amusement.

Mensa' saw Mbeng the next day as she was coming out of the main post office. Or rather, he saw her.

"Now, that's a coincidence," he said. "What is Mme Ntchantchou doing *alone* in the city?"

"Hello, *Monsieur le Sous-Préfet*!"

Mensa' noticed that he had a much more pronounced Beti accent then than when they were dancing.

"In fact, I'm here because I got a telegram from Bangangte," she said quickly.

"Your father, how is he?"

"Nothing's wrong," she answered; that was her way of saying she'd rather change topics.

Mbeng took note.

"Here, I am in *my village*," he said, stressing *my village* with a broad smile on his lips as he gestured toward the main post office, the intersection crowded with cars, and the other stone buildings in Yaounde.

"Ah," Mensa' exclaimed in surprise. "Are you from Yaounde?"

"Ewondo, through and through," he said, his face suddenly lighting up. "My family comes from Ongola. We're the ones who gave the Cameroonian capital to the whites, and ultimately to all Cameroonians. It was Charles Atangana, the paramount chief of the Ewondos, and the Banes who invited the Bamilekes, the Northerners, and everyone else to move here—starting with Njoya. He's the one who gave land to all the other tribal groups, so he's the one who founded Yaounde."

---

* "My dear, shall we go?"
"Sure . . . just five more minutes, all right?"
"Take your time."

"I didn't know that," Mensa' said.

Like any Good Cameroonian, his village—even if, in this case, that meant the capital—was Mbeng's favorite subject; he was thrilled to talk about it.

"Charles Atangana Mballa," he said. "*You* must have heard of him?"

Mensa' didn't notice that he'd shifted to using the informal French *tu*. She just said no.

"The patriarch, the one who worked for the Germans, and the French, and who recruited my father to fight to liberate France. The Man of Three Countries, the *Tripolitan*. My father is a veteran. He crossed the desert and went all the way to Paris. We call him Champs-Élysées. A tirailleur. You should meet him. A living legend."

He waved his hands as he spoke. They'd made their way back to Mensa''s car and the chauffeur opened the door for her. But she had to promise Mbeng that she would meet his father. He insisted.

"As soon as possible."

"Since Yaounde is *your* village," she said; her expression was formal, using the French *vous*, but a smile spread across her face.

"True. Have *you* already visited the Bamileke neighborhoods?" he asked, insisting on the *tu*. "Excuse me," he added quickly, with feigned embarrassment, "we were using *tu* yesterday, weren't we?"

"Yes," Mensa' replied. "But I still have to get used to that."

"To being on familiar terms with me?"

"Yes."

"It'll come," he said with a laugh. "*Tu tu tu*."

Mensa' hadn't yet visited the Bamileke neighborhoods, even though, like everyone from the West, she had family living there, distant aunts and other relatives. She got into the car. Mbeng kept talking.

"Mokolo, Nkomkana, Obala," he said happily, holding the door open. "You should go to the Mokolo market. It's the biggest one in Yaounde. The best prices, too," he continued, sure of himself. "I know about the Bamileke and *affaire ngkap*."*

---

* Money matters.

"The Bangangte are the exception," she said, trying to sound haughty. "You know that."

Obviously, he didn't.

"There's a Bangangte neighborhood, too."

Mensa' started to shut the door.

"My father will talk to you about Yaounde," he said, backing up, now speaking through the door's lowered window. "You won't forget, will you?"

Mensa' promised she'd meet his father the next time. His voice was ringing in her ears as she watched him walk away, crossing the traffic circle in front of the post office, weaving through the cars, and then hurrying on his way. Then his lanky silhouette blended into the crowd.

Mensa' hadn't been able to talk to her father. The connection had been bad and communication difficult. Several times she had to shout instead of just talking, and on the other end the pastor just kept repeating, "Nothing's wrong."

"Take me to the central market," she said to the chauffeur.

Opening the car door, she almost hit a man on a bicycle, who stopped, ready to unleash a mouthful of curses, but then went on his way when he saw a woman getting out of the car; he could tell by Mensa''s face that she was one of those women—the sort referred to as a "My Husband Is Capable"—that you did not give any trouble. For a brief moment, that encounter distracted Mensa' from her worries—her father back in the village, the villages set on fire by the army, fire as a tool of war. And the pastor still didn't want to leave Bangangte. He was living in denial.

When the car drove past the Printania department store, Mensa' had seen Mbeng going in. Now the two buildings of the central market were there in front of her. She was wondering which one to go into when the chauffeur parked at the main entrance. Women passed by, some in floral dresses with scarves on their heads, others barefoot. Images and sounds from the Reunification Ball the night before came rushing back to her. She remembered how the women had been dressed. She called to a vendor, a woman with a basket balanced on her head.

"Where are the cloth sellers?"

The woman pointed to the building on the left. Mensa' told the chauffeur to wait.

"I'll be back."

In front of her there was a sign for a store, Champs-Élysées, and suddenly she thought of Mbeng. Who would have thought that they'd just met at the Presidential Palace the night before? She remembered the first time she'd seen him, in Bangangte. He was wearing his official uniform, a kepi on his head. The second time he was in a tuxedo. And just now in a suit coat, dressed for the city. It was as if each time she met him, he'd put on a different face.

She went into Champs-Élysées, her mind filled with all of these thoughts, but also determined that the women in the capital would never again look down on her or dismiss her as a woman from the village: "I am not a *villaps*."

The owner stood up when he saw her come through the door. He was a Frenchman, impeccably dressed in a suit coat, like she'd seen at the ball. When she came out of his boutique, a boy followed behind carrying various outfits with a now-well-known three-letter monogram. She pointed out the car to him and then went into the boutique of a Hausa man, who was wearing a flowing blue gandoura and chewing on a bit of root. He pushed back the long sleeves of his robe and gestured for Mensa' to sit down beside him. Before she even told him what she wanted, he seemed to understand just by the way she was looking at the pagnes he had on display. He picked up each piece of cloth on which her eyes had lingered, and spread them out before her.

"Dutch wax," he said. "Less expensive than you'll find in Briqueterie."

Three pagnes, one red, one blue, and one green. He spread out the red one, showing her the motifs of the design. Then he opened the blue and, in turn, the green. His gestures were automatic, and with twinkling eyes he undressed Mensa'. You'd have thought he was trying to make her his wife, instead of a customer.

"The red one, here, this is what women really like."

He wrapped the cloth around himself.

"Look."

He minced about like a woman.

"It's perfect for dresses, but also for outfits."

When Mensa' went in the shoe shop, she was holding the green pagne. The shopkeeper's trousers were held up with brightly colored suspenders. He looked at her and, again, it was as if he were taking her apart, piece by piece, rifling around inside her purse, counting the money and licking his chops.

"My beautiful lady," he said. "Here, I will create you."

Mensa' burst out laughing.

"These are Italian pumps," he said. "The best."

Then he showed her another pair.

"These are French, very stylish. Do you know your size?"

He looked at Mensa''s foot.

"I'd say thirty-seven."

He was right. He waved quickly to his assistant, who was observing the exchange with the eyes of a hungry dog watching a man eat. The boy jumped, ran outside, and came back with four pairs of shoes that he set down in front of Mensa'.

"This is your size, thirty-seven," said the salesman, picking up the Italian ones first.

When she left the shop, she was wearing the French pair. She held the shoes she'd gone in with in her hands, wrapped in a new plastic bag.

"Hello, my *mamy nyanga*," said the jeweler.

He was a Moor, and his eyes moved methodically over Mensa''s neck. He spoke to her, but his eyes never left her neck.

"You have a beautiful neck," he told her. "I will decorate it *for monsieur*."

"Don't be so sure of that," she said.

"Madam," he said, "if monsieur doesn't like it, you come back here and I'll marry you. *Walaï!*"

"And what if Madam doesn't like it?"

He smiled.

"Do you want some kola?"

Mensa' said no. He bit into a piece of nut, chewed, and then opened the glass case where bracelets were displayed. The same routine played out with the Fulani perfume seller. The same self-confidence as he chewed the kola, after first offering some to Mensa', which she again declined.

"Coco Chanel here," he said. "Dior. That's what women like."

"Oh really?" said Mensa'.

They were clearly knockoffs.

"Women in Yaounde have good taste."

Mensa' jumped. She was outraged. That man seemed to have seen the villager within her. *I am not a villaps.*

"I'm going to spoil you."

"Oh, these are too expensive," she said as she left.

That was just a pretext.

"You'll be back," the man shouted after her as she walked down the corridor between the shops.

Mensa' did come back.

"I told you so."

"You give me that price," Mensa' said, "but show me the *real ones.*"

The man smiled, revealing a gold tooth.

"Madam, I've already lowered the price for you," he said, looking with pleading eyes at the bottle she'd selected. "*Walaï!* I'm already losing money at that price."

Mensa' stopped listening.

The transformation of the deputy's wife was a collective endeavor. Mme Ngapeth showed her how to put together all her purchases to make a stylish outfit, and how to transform herself into a woman of the capital, of high society. Mensa' joined her at the *tontine* the Capable Wives. On that day it was meeting in her neighbor's living room; of the twenty or so women there, Mensa' recognized many she'd seen at the presidential ball. And with her plunging neckline, the new arrival got her revenge on those grand ladies. As she introduced the women, Mme Ngapeth always underscored their husbands' positions. The wives of the most powerful men in Cameroon were all there, because, as Mensa' realized, name by name, the country was led by a small handful of people who all knew each other.

"We get together each month," said the hostess of the day, adding, "You'll get your turn, but next time we'll be meeting at the home of Madam, the wife of *Prefect* Sabal Lecco."

The woman smiled.

"It will be a pleasure."

Another woman arrived, the scent of her perfume filling the air.

"Capable Women!" she called out.

That was their rallying cry.

"*Actons!*" all the women replied in chorus, using their Camfranglais slogan, "Let's take action!"

The woman took her place in a chair Mme Ngapeth showed her.

"You have already met the wife of *Deputy* Ntchantchou," she said, looking at Mensa'. "She will be joining our group, but today she is here as a guest, am I right, Mme Ntchantchou?"

Mensa' said yes.

"She lives in Etoa Meki and Bangangte, and so we will be very helpful to her," she added. "After all, so much of our action will be focused on Bamileke land. Who else has a *second home* in the West?"

The way she said *second home* made Mensa' jump; she thought of her father.

"Besides madam the wife of *Prefect* Keutcha, of course," Mme Ngapeth added. And she said *Keutcha* with a French accent, rather than the Medumba pronunciation, *Nki'tcha*.

"Madam Deputy . . ."

"The pleasure is mine . . ."

Mme Ngapeth looked at the woman who'd interrupted her, and then continued.

"The first woman deputy from Africa," and that phrase lit up the faces all around with pride, especially Mme Nki'tcha's.

"She's the one who convinced Djoumessi* to rally," whispered a woman sitting next to Mensa'. "Do you know what she told him?"

No one knew.

"She told him, 'Drop the Kumzse, and I'll make you a minister in the government.' She kept her word."

"Who is Djoumessi?" asked another woman, who looked to be about thirty years old.

"Well, I offer a toast to you," Mme Ngapeth cut in, taking control of the floor again. "Yes, yes, *as a member of the UPC*, it was an honor to see our struggle rewarded in that way."

As she said "as a member of the UPC," she struck her hand on her chest. She was scanning the room, judging everyone there.

"I will give you the floor in just a moment, Madame *Keutcha*. We will all listen to what you have to say today. But now we were speaking about second homes in the West."

"In New Bell–Kassalafam," one woman piped up.

"Douala doesn't count," Mme Ngapeth replied.

"How so? It's a Bamileke neighborhood."

There was a rustling among the women.

"It's still not the West," Mme Ngapeth cut in. "Besides, everyone here has a pied-à-terre in Douala, am I right?"

"There are pied-à-terre and pied-à-terre!" insisted another woman, whose wide headscarf, tied in Yoruba fashion, made her stand out.

"Madam, wife of the *President of the Assembly*, you are not going to argue the point with me!"

Having been called out like that, Mayi Matip's wife lifted her hands in defeat.

"Let's get back to our agenda, shall we?" Mme Ngapeth went on. "In just a moment I'll give the floor to Mme *Keutcha*, because she's the one who introduced us to the ritual of the *cadi*. She'll explain how it works and just what it means for the Bamilekes. The reintegration of fighters is a problem, especially for their families. If it is possible to provide for

* A Bamileke traditional chief, and first president of the UPC.

their children, and to get their wives involved, we will have already done much to resolve the problem. Because *even when they're in the Maquis, men are loafers.*"

That caused a bit of an uproar among the women.

"I know what I'm talking about," Mme Ngapeth insisted.

Her words quieted the room. Mensa' realized just how much her neighbor was respected by everyone there. Another woman arrived.

"Capable Women!"

"*Actons!*"

"Madam, wife of *Inspector* Dibongue," Mme Ngapeth scolded, "you are late."

"We were looking for the house," said the woman, by way of excuse; she was wearing a red turtleneck and a gold necklace that hung down across her chest. "The chauffeur kept driving around in circles without finding it."

"Ah," Mme Ngapeth exclaimed, "the house certainly isn't hidden. "You make a left turn at Le Restaurant africain."

"And then a right, but we couldn't find it."

Mensa' looked around the room. She felt queasy. If Mme Ngapeth hadn't been holding her hand, she would have been really intimidated. And yet the familiar comfort of the living room was reassuring. She'd been there before, and she suspected most of the other women seated in armchairs had as well. When she rose to go to the bathroom, she didn't need to ask her way, even if Mme Ngapeth's eyes pointed her in the right direction. Mensa' stood in front of the mirror for a few moments, repeating to herself, "I am in Yaounde!" Then she touched up her eyebrows, her mascara, wig, and lipstick, flushed the toilet, and went back to the living room.

When she took her seat again, Mme Nki'tcha was talking. Her hands were clasped, as people do in the West when they're speaking to a group. Mensa' had met only her husband before; he was also from Bangangte. She promised to introduce herself to Mme Nki'tcha after the meeting, but didn't get a chance to—Mme Ngapeth was one step ahead.

"She married one of your brothers," she said to Mensa', "like I did."

"We are all implicated in this business," Mme Nki'tcha was saying, her eyes moving from one woman to the next around the room. "Mme Ngapeth can attest to it. My own little brother, who'd gotten a scholarship from the Union Française to study in France, was caught up in the circle of UPC supporters over there, and suddenly I no longer recognized him. He only ever talked about nationalism and revolution. And then I asked him if he wanted to wage revolution against his big sister, because I'm the one who raised him. He grew up in my home. Or if he was rebelling against his papa, because we come from a line of chiefs. When I saw that he just kept getting angrier and angrier, instead of calming down—he even called me, his sister, a puppet! Well, I had him repatriated. Madam, wife of *Minister* Eteki, helped me, she can attest to that. Where is she?" She scanned the room and saw her sitting on the couch, nodding. "He came back in handcuffs. And once back in the country, he went straight to the Maquis, rather than taking up the job we'd gone to great trouble to find for him. We are all together in *this war*."

As she said "this war," her tone grew practically maternal. She was about thirty, but she looked a good ten years older.

"She saved her brother from *the firing squad*," whispered a woman next to Mensa'. She gazed admiringly at Mme Nki'tcha as she spoke about her little brother who preferred the mosquitoes in the bush to an office in the capital.

"The civil guards arrested him in Tombel during the massacres," the woman continued in a soft voice. "He said he was on his way to Mount Kupe!"

She paused.

"When everyone else was fleeing the volcano," she added, to emphasize the extent of his folly, "he . . . he wanted to go to Mount Kupe.

"I just don't know what bug bit him in France," the disconsolate Mme Nki'tcha continued, as she pulled a handkerchief from her bag and wiped a tear on her right cheek.

"He was going to join *the Maquisards*?" one woman asked loudly.

None of those women ever mentioned the name Ouandié Ernest; they just said "the Maquisards."

"What *folly* has taken over our children in France," said another woman. "It must be the books they read over there."

"And we thought the most dangerous thing was losing their head over white women!" added a third.

She looked around for everyone's approval.

"He wanted to kill himself," said Mme Nki'tcha, wiping another tear, this time from her left cheek. "But death refused him."

And yet, years later, another of her little brothers, whom they called the "Beautiful Kid," and who'd become pro-Chinese when he was in Paris (soon they'd say he was Maoist!),* would lose his head when he was part of Osendé's Maquis:† it was displayed along the road in Ebolowa, for all the villagers to see.

* Maoist, which means someone who carefully reads only one book, the *Little Red Book*, the collected *Quotations from Chairman Mao Tse-tung*, bought in a used bookstore on the rue des Écoles, in Paris.

† A short-lived group of Maquisards organized in the south of Cameroon by Osendé Afana, the first doctor of economics in Cameroon; he was killed there, too.

3

The meeting Mensa''s husband had attended the day before at the ministry was very different. Mbeng was there, too. The continuation of the secretive discussion begun at the Reunification Ball took place in Enoch Nkwayim's office. There were whites there, of course, including Colonel Lamberton, who signaled to Ntchantchou Zacharie from the other end of the table. Ngapeth had been called to the meeting as well, along with a man Nkwayim introduced as "Minister Arouna Njoya's right-hand man."

"Fochivé,"* said Enoch Nkwayim, greeting the man who was sitting in a corner of the room. "As you can see, this is not a *Bamileke plot*."

Nkwayim had a habit of taking the bull by the horns, which made people smirk. It was how he usually expressed his innermost thoughts. Now he looked around the room, an evil joy traced across his lips.

"Why don't you talk about the Littoral Region that's giving me such a hard time?" said Fochivé. "Certainly, Minister Arouna Njoya is not going to disagree with me."

"Go on," said the man he'd called out, who that day was wearing a suit coat and a fancy bow tie, as if he were attending another big party. "Go on, I'm listening."

"The situation in Bangangte is troubling," Nkwayim interrupted, now looking right at Ntchantchou Zacharie. "Rebel actions are intensify-

---

* Jean Fochivé, the legendary chief of the political police, and so of the secret service, under both Ahidjo and Biya.

ing, according to our security report." As he said that, he turned toward Fochivé, who nodded, but didn't add anything. "*Monsieur l'Inspecteur*, is it confirmed that Ouandié has set up his headquarters there?"

"Affirmative," said Fochivé.

"Surprising," Ntchantchou Zacharie added, "because he's from Bangwa."

"*You* mean from Bangou," Enoch Nkwayim interrupted.

His use of the informal *tu* escaped no one.

"Yes, from Bangou, of course," added Ngapeth. "Badoumla."

"What difference does it make," Semengue's voice cut in, "since they're all Bamis?"

That phrase left an uncomfortable silence in its wake. The Bamilekes in the room avoided catching each other's eyes. Even Nkwayim stammered, because he knew he was walking on eggshells.

"In terms of police investigations, it does matter," he said. You could see in his eyes that he was waiting for Fochivé to offer some support, but he didn't.

"The origins of the *terrorist* are not the question," Semengue continued. "Rather, it's where *terrorist* activity is taking place that is the problem."

He had a particular way of pronouncing the word *terrorist*, overemphasizing the *r*'s, which gave the word the dry click of machine gun fire. As he spoke, he looked at the white man sitting next to him. The man, rather old, nodded.

"That's precisely why I called this private meeting," said Nkwayim. "It's not easy to get all of us together in Yaounde, and I'm particularly happy that the subprefect from Bazou has joined us."

He scanned the faces in the room.

"Monsieur Joseph Mbeng." Then he added, in a lighthearted way that broke the tension in the room, "I've entrusted him personally with the protection of my dear old mama."

"And your mama is doing quite well," Mbeng added, "for her age . . ."

"She refuses to leave Bazou," Nkwayim added.

"That's our mamas!" someone said with a sigh.

"Bangangte," Nkwayim cut in. "We were talking about Bangangte."

"Yes, *Monsieur le Ministre*," Ntchantchou Zacharie spoke up, his eyes focused on Semengue. "The colonel has been conducting raids for two years, well before the assassination of Dr. Broussoux made front-page news. The curfew is strict. The public confessions, impressive. *Nyamsi.*" Pronouncing that name, Nyamsi, he looked first at Semengue and then at Fochivé. "There is not one village that the soldiers haven't combed through carefully."

"The problem is the people," Semengue added, turning again to the white man sitting beside him. "The people," he repeated, "not an individual."

"The problem is the Bamilekes," Lamberton interrupted.

Everyone was silent.

"Let's try not to go off on a tangent," Enoch Nkwayim began again, still walking on eggshells. He didn't add *tribalist.*

He knew Colonel Lamberton's positions.

"We've been able to get many groups of *people* to rally to the government," Ngapeth added, without clarifying just whom he meant by *people.* He was really speaking to Lamberton and calling on the other Bamilekes in the room as his witnesses. "Mme Nki'tcha and Mme Ngapeth"—that's how he referred to his own wife, as if he weren't saying his own name—"are very active on the issue. Deputy Ntchantchou, who is here, also presided over the rallying ceremony last week, during a *cadi* at the party headquarters."

He placed a copy of *La Presse du Cameroun* on the table, so people could see the photos. He pointed to one, his eyes again scanning the room.

MAQUISARDS RALLY TO THE REPUBLIC

"You are confusing psychological action with military action," Semengue interrupted; a broad smile spread across his face as he held the pages of the paper open in front of himself, "because if we need to start discussing *Deputy Ntchantchou's fake Maquisards . . .*"

A wave of commotion spread through the room. Ntchantchou Zacharie was more than embarrassed. The phrase "Deputy Ntchantchou's fake Maquisards" really irked him. *That guy's so full of himself*, he thought. And then, really, *Who is wasting whose time here?* If Semengue hadn't been the army chief of staff, Ntchantchou certainly would have lost his cool and challenged him—especially since he was taller by two heads. He'd have said, *You've made your choice*, mbap.* Instead, he just focused on swallowing his spit, breathing in and out, and carefully choosing his words.

"It seems to me, Colonel, that the two are connected."

"Precisely," Semengue interrupted. He again looked at the white man sitting beside him. "It's the difference between upstream and downstream. Here we're talking about upstream; and Bangangte has become a terrorist stronghold in Cameroon."

"It's no longer Mount Kupe?"

"It's no longer Mount Kupe."

The white man put a leaflet into Semengue's outstretched hand.

"Besides, Ouandié has already declared that Bangangte—your constituency, *Monsieur le Député*—is *liberated territory*."

He passed around the tract, coated in red dust. Each person looked it over in turn and nodded. On it was plainly written, "Bangangte, liberated territory, signed ALNK," the Kamerun National Liberation Army.

You're the soldier! Ntchantchou Zacharie wanted to say, but he kept quiet.

"In sum, the front line has come to Bangangte," Arouna Njoya said emphatically, tilting his head to stretch his neck and then folding his hands on the table. "It's in the bush between Bazou and Moya."

Semengue looked again at the white man and then folded his hands as well. He looked satisfied, because the conclusion he would have drawn at the end of his comments had been expressed by someone else in the room.

"There you have it," he concluded.

"So, what do we do about it?" Arouna Njoya asked.

**Mbap* = meat. An insult in Medumba, a symbolic act of cannibalism.

"Solve the problem," Enoch Nkwayim replied. "But how?"

"You already know my position," grumbled Colonel Lamberton, still sitting off in a corner.

His position was, in fact, well-known to everyone there—too well-known, really, since he circulated it in jargon-filled articles published in French military journals: "*Every war is an opportunity. As for the war in Bamileke land, it provides the chance to establish the French presence in Cameroon, by multiplying our forces on the ground and militarizing the region. Rather than just putting an end to the rebellion, we must, on the contrary, let the situation decay even more, for another four or five years. Ouandié is a formidable alibi.*"

"Quite true," said the minister of the territorial administration, "who doesn't know your position?" He looked at Semengue, and then at the white man beside him. "The recolonization of Cameroon, that's what you want, right?" He didn't add, *you idiot!* but that's just what he was thinking.

"In Bazou," Mbeng began, "we will need more forces to contain the rebellion, and to keep it from spreading."

"Our esteemed subprefect is a worthy replacement for Daniel Kemajou in my hometown," Enoch Nkwayim interjected; his eyes met Fochivé's amused gaze. "He's doing an excellent job."

"The rebellion comes down from *on high*," said Fochivé.

His eyes sparkled with a gruesome glee as he spoke, his eyes searching out those of the Bamilekes in the room.

"Once more," Semengue interjected, "the people are the problem, because they have been contaminated, but"—again, he looked at the white man beside him—"General Dio* has a suggestion for us."

Finally, General Dio took the floor.

"It's simple," he said, "they must be put in camps."

"Camps?"

---

* A French military adviser to the Cameroonian National Army, one of the first Gaullists, he formed the very first regiment that, in response to the call from London in September 1940, aligned behind Philippe Leclerc, began the rallying of Central Africa, and took up arms to fight for the liberation of occupied France.

Enoch Nkwayim was the one who reacted. The general's long years in Africa, as well as his experience in World War II, gave his words a weight no one could contest. Of course, in the comfort of his home, Enoch could not say to Eva, *Auch wir haben unsere KZs.** Did she, who was Jewish, ever know?

Not long after, people chuckled as they told each other how Enoch Nkwayim had barely escaped being taken hostage by the *tsuitsuis* when he'd been on his way to Bangangte to inspect the sites where the resettlement camps were being constructed. He was able to get away, it was said, only because he'd left as soon as he'd heard gunfire in the distance. He fled, people murmured, too. Otherwise, he'd have been captured *by his brothers*. You can imagine what the minister of territorial administration thought about such blatherers and those out to ruin reputations: *Those schouains!* Clara hadn't escaped from her second pogrom, but Nithap would only learn that later. He had kept on dreaming of her. "I'm bleeding": he heard that phrase whispered in his ears when he was lying in his bed of brambles, he could feel her breasts in his hands, and her nipples between his lips. She was in Tombel when the Northerners attacked the Bamileke neighborhood. She lived through the fall and the devastation of the coffee city. But had her gut warned her about the attack of the Bakossis? That, he could only hope. He often thought about her and her husband. And mostly, he thought about Tama'. Once he dreamed of a teenager who was disappearing, swallowed up by the flames, and of his final cry, a man's cry that shook the universe. He woke up trembling, out of breath. In his horror, he had screamed out into the night.

He was nothing if not pleased that Ouandié had chosen to set up his headquarters in Bangangte. It allowed the doctor to rebuild his scattered family life. For the leader, Bangangte was the goal—it always had been. Even when he was in Accra, he lumbered on, like a sleepwalker, weighed

* We also have our concentration camps.

down by thoughts of that town. He hadn't said anything to anyone, but his return to Cameroon was his answer to the call of that community. He hadn't been born there, but it's where he spent much of his time when he was young.

So, when Ouandié knocked on Pastor Tbongo's door one night, he knew he was repeating the gestures of the child he once was, whose teacher had taught him the principles of Cartesian logic. The town still didn't have electricity, unlike Nkongsamba. It was Kouandiang's barking that gave the first sign of their presence. There was a moment of uncertain silence, then a man's voice asking, "Who's there?"

"It's me," Nithap said.

"Nithap?"

Elie Tbongo's eyes discovered two men. Nithap saw the fear in those eyes he knew so well. The pastor needed some time to realize that one of the men was his son-in-law. Nithap had to say it again, "It's me, Nithap." The pastor wrapped his arms around him. He looked at him as if he were a ghost, and pulled him in tight against his heart once more. Only then did his eyes fall on the man accompanying Nithap.

"Papa," Nithap said, "this is President Ouandié Ernest."

"Hello, papa," said Ouandié. "Can we come in?"

Pastor Tbongo hesitated.

"Yes, of course."

He was stunned. It was as if he'd seen an apparition, the presence of a spirit in his living room.

"We thought you were dead," he said suddenly to Nithap, staring right into his eyes. "Three years without any news from you!"

"I hope you didn't replace me," the doctor replied; he was trying to be ironic, but sounded brusque—the pastor didn't seem to notice.

"Replace you?"

The joke was in bad taste.

"Ngountchou is in Yaounde," the pastor went on, as if he hadn't heard Nithap. "She has suffered a lot, but now she's with Mensa' in Yaounde. There is danger everywhere. They burned down the whole village. People don't know whom to fear more." Then he changed the topic. "I'm alone here with my wife," and, turning to Ouandié, "but we won't leave."

"Don't you remember me anymore?" Ouandié asked. "You were *my schoolteacher.*"

"Your schoolteacher?"

Elie Tbongo tried to make the connections between that living room and many other places, between this present moment and many times from the past, to recall the leader when he was a child, an adolescent, and maybe a young man, in a classroom, surrounded by a dozen other students.

"Dschang."

"Of course I remember you," the pastor cut him off. "Of course, I have always remembered you, everyone here remembers you. How could I have forgotten? Dschang."

And the years of his own intellectual quest came flooding back to him, when he'd joined the Kumzse, the stormy meetings in Chief Mathias Djoumessi's residence, debates about the politics of Bamileke culture. In 1951, the year of the ideological realignment of the UPC. That's why he'd ended up not joining the UPC. Dschang. Everything was coming back, although Ouandié had started talking to him about his younger years. Then suddenly, as if he turned a page, he spoke, his words clipped and brusque, revealing his rage. "What are you doing to this country?"

"*Passitou*," Ouandié said, "what is this country doing to us all?"

"That's your question?"

"That's *the* question."

"Why did you come here?" the pastor suddenly asked Nithap. "You're putting us all in danger."

"That's not my intent."

"Ngountchou," the father said suddenly. "She's not here anymore."

"Ngountchou."

"We can't stay here," Elie Tbongo said suddenly, when he noticed the leader's rifle. "My wife is sleeping."

"*A wou?*" Just then they heard Nja Yonke''s voice asking who was there, and the light of an Aida oil lamp signaled her arrival.

"*Sam mentchun*," he answered. No one.

He led the night's visitors outside. There they found two other men, whom Ouandié introduced as his secretaries.

"Ben Bella," said one of them.

Soon the group headed toward the *Tchunda*.

"It's really taken shape."

His arms pointed to the shadowy shape of the building, scaffolding tracing its profile along the horizon.

He remembered the steps, the furrows, the drawings, the calendar, the cellar, the idea at the start of it all, his first lesson from the pastor. He didn't say how he'd put it to use.

A point in time is an opening into eternity.

4

Deep in the heart of the Toungou woods, the Tchunda rose before them: its construction was now on hold, but its contours held the promise of a gigantic home. "Like the annex to a chief's residence," which was what the pastor wanted. It wasn't until the following day that Nithap was able to see how much work had been done since his departure. It was just him, the pastor, and Ouandié. Comrade Émile was clearly impressed by this work of genius taking shape in this remote village, in the depths of the forest. It was easy to recognize the pre–Njoya Bamum architectural style—Bamileke, really.

"This is the family crypt," the pastor explained to Ouandié.

Nithap didn't say anything.

The pastor led them into a room. The shadows soon lifted, revealing a window and, in the sky above, the moon.

"Of course, that hinges on the family returning," Nithap said. "For now, we're leaving, all of us are leaving."

"Even Njoya died in exile."

Ouandié pronounced it as you do in Medumba, "*Ngue'ya*," instead of Njoya. The pastor noticed and smiled.

"The Bamilekes are chased away everywhere they go," Nithap interjected, finally expressing the conclusions drawn from what he'd seen in N'lohe, in Tombel. "Soon there will be more in the diaspora than still living here."

"Well, maybe history will learn from its mistakes. We'll see, because we're living under its protection."

"History's?"

"Our one and only mistress."

"Don't you mean under those who are in power?"

"They are just its *instruments*. That's the irony of it all." Then the pastor paused, before changing the topic. "Here you will be safe. No one will come to *chase you away*." Then he turned back toward Ouandié once more, staring at him intently. "What is this country doing to us?"

"It's turned us into Sinistrés, into victims instead of citizens. You wouldn't think we were independent. Here, everything has gone up in flames. Elsewhere people celebrate their independence, but we, we act like we've just lived through a huge defeat."

"The events of May 1955?"

"Yes, but more than that. Colonialism. Slavery. Forced labor. We are the Sinistrés born of a very long catastrophe. History was wrested from our hands long ago. It's up to us to put it back together, to take control of all of its links, to shape it."

"By killing?"

"They're killing us."

"By doing what, then?"

"By winning!"

Ouandié was practically shouting, a heartfelt cry. He rested his rifle between his legs before going on. It was a machine gun, a tommy gun that he usually had slung over his shoulders. He waved his hands in the gathering darkness.

"Let's not confuse things," he said. "We're the ones who were chased away. We're the ones who are hunted down across the land. We're the ones who are assassinated. Each time the reactionaries plan and set a plot in motion, they hold the victims responsible for it. Now it's up to us to teach our people how to succeed."

"Succeed," a voice echoed behind him—it was his secretary.

"It's 1964 now. A lot of water has flowed under the bridge. A lot of blood, too."

The pastor didn't recite a list of the assassinations blamed on the UPC, but his words imposed silence all around. Had he seen Ouandié's face, he would have noticed a moment of hesitation, because there was no way around the truth.

"The situation hasn't changed," the leader said.

"Which one?"

"The impasse."

"You have a lot of courage and will, but that's not enough to bring about a revolution. A child may throw himself into the flames, but that doesn't mean it's a wise thing to do. Our shared suffering gives us no rights, even if it imposes duties upon us. What good does it do to divide the people into reactionaries on one side and nationalists on the other? What good does that division do? Politics are not the foundation of life, nor of our future, even if they're the field on which we are all forced to fight."

"*Passitou*," Ouandié interrupted. "Everything is politics."

He had grabbed hold of the pastor's hand, as if to give even more weight to his words.

"No, that would be too easy. Can the rope bridge over the Noun tell us what really connects both sides of the river? Will the Ngatuè—those Bangangte who live among the Bamum—just cease to exist? During the troubles of these past years, the French did everything they could to show us how different the Bamilekes are from the Bamum. You see all the meaningless deaths in Bamendjing and Foumbot. That's what human stupidity creates and tries to pass off as politics. But the family trees of our people go back to one common source. The title of the chief of the Bangangte isn't *Nga shun Mven Mum* for nothing. But is there anyone who still wonders why the chief of the Bangangte is proud to be called 'the friend of the Bamum chief'? People just react to how the breeze blows, and that breeze is what passes for politics!"

Ouandié thought this was a reference to Moumié, but he kept quiet. This time the pastor was no longer drawing signs on the ground, but in the air.

"So, start with the Bangangte, and move back from there. You'll always still arrive at our common ancestor, Ngan-Ha. Now, it depends on what sorts of combinations you want to make, but you will always be able to find a path that connects Bamenda and Bangwa, Bamum and Bangangte, Kumbo and Bafoussam. So, why do some of them speak English and others French? Why do the Bangangtes from Bali speak English? That's because of politics. But if you base your judgment on just that one factor, then you'll fail to understand the deeper connections between them, you'll fail to grasp the *Tchunda*." He paused, his eyes scanning the darkness all around. "You'll miss the entire country, *ziar*." He paused again. "That's the *konsen*," he said, "as Ngue'ya taught it to us."*

"*Konsen*," echoed Ouandié, who hadn't dared interrupt him; then he smiled, having understood the game. "You mean the crab."

"Yes, the crab that you UPC supporters are always talking about," the pastor went on. "And yet you still need to talk to the Bamendas and the Bangwas about it; you need to talk to the Hausas and the Doualas. Um Nyobè's mistake was believing that Cameroon already had a soul. But that's really what we need to create for this country. That's the only task for our era. Because without a soul, a country, like a body, is inert. For our own survival, we have to teach Cameroonians what unites us; we have to give some substance to this country that is self-destructing. That's what I'm trying to do here."

"And me in politics!"

"Can a Bamileke be communist?" the pastor asked.

"Be what, now?"

The two men looked at each other and smiled.

"To think that the French accuse me of being communist, just because I went to China," he said suddenly, shaking his head. "That shows how little they understand the Bamilekes!"

"So true," the pastor agreed. "A people who have always known to mark the border of its *Tchunda* with a gate, but who are always so toler-

---

* *Ziar* and *konsen* are words in Shumum, the language Njoya invented in the nineteenth century, a sort of pidgin based on Bamum languages and others from the region.

ant and welcoming to the foreigner that they offer him land and a wife, who say that the foreigner belongs to everyone, is the people's property, they can't be communist. *Ghe ngoh*."*

"*Ghe ngoh*," Ouandié echoed. "The French have confused respect for the stranger with submission. Because the Bamilekes did not submit."

"Oh no, certainly not," Pastor Tbongo agreed. "The Bamilekes did not submit. After all," he continued, "when I was growing up, people still walked around carrying cutlasses here." He pointed at his hip. "And then, the names white men give us are insulting, because for us, Bamileke autonomy is a given."

He again paused.

"The problem is that the Bamilekes take things too seriously," he said, coughing into his hand. "*Gründlich*, as the Germans say, *sehr gründlich*—very deep. Look, it was the Bassas who started the UPC, but now the Bamilekes have joined, and they act like it's their thing."

Ouandié burst out laughing. When he laughed, it was as if the whole universe were celebrating, especially since his laugh was so contagious, quickly cascading along to his followers, an expression of joy that shook up the world around: *ha ha ha*. He was laughing because he remembered that story Elie Tbongo had told him the day after their reunion, as he was showing him the construction site in the forest, a story that, he was quite sure, had cemented their friendship.

"Yesterday you talked about the great defeat," the pastor had said, "but you see, we're not beaten. It's high time that we start to fight for ourselves. Until 1884, we were protected by a gnat. America had been entirely colonized, the Indians exterminated since 1700, but where we lived, even during the slaving era, the whites hadn't been able to reach us. They couldn't overcome us even though we were neighbors, because we fought with everything we had, with the sky, the earth, the pebbles, the bush, the rivers, with the birds in the sky and the animals on earth. With everything that was deep inside us and with the whole of our universe, we resisted. So, they all stayed on the coast, using *fingwongs* among us to

* Quite literally, the word for foreigner means property of the country, of the people.

compromise us, because the forest was our impenetrable line of defense. Even today, all our capitals are on the coast, because our heart remains impenetrable! Our king was a small little animal, nothing much at all, but he fought more ferociously than any soldier, and quietly defeated the French, as well as the English and the Germans and the Portuguese, simply by making them fall asleep. The tsetse fly. Since 1884, however, Africa has been an open battlefield, and it's our turn to take up arms because our universe has fallen silent. The whites found a remedy for malaria, but you took up arms to continue the resistance. The forest remains our collective home. I understand your plan. We have to replace the tsetse fly with the crab, and reignite the long African battle against slavery."

"Speaking of that, what is your ndap*?" Ouandié asked out of the blue.*

"Talun," the pastor replied.

"Tamnet," Ouandié went on, quickly listing one after the other, as the old man nodded happily, thrilled to hear the infinite list of his praise names. "Yanjo. Nka' nku. Nzi Yabmi."

Pastor Tbongo was in heaven. But Ouandié also knew that a Bangangte can refuse nothing to someone who knows how to recite his *ndaps*; even so, he jumped when the prelate suddenly said, "Let us pray."

An unexpected request, if ever there was one. The man adjusted the hat on his head, and pushed up the sleeves of his *togho* before crossing himself.

For a long time, Nithap would sleep in this secret forest citadel, which in the past had helped him to understand Bamileke philosophy. Now tucked away in the temple, in the heart of that overgrown thicket, the man who had come to measure time's passing solely by adapting the agricultural calendar that Elie Tbongo had taught him to keep track of Clara's menstrual cycle—"I'm bleeding," she'd told him during their first embrace, which had coincided with a pogrom, had signaled the alarm—redefined his life once more.

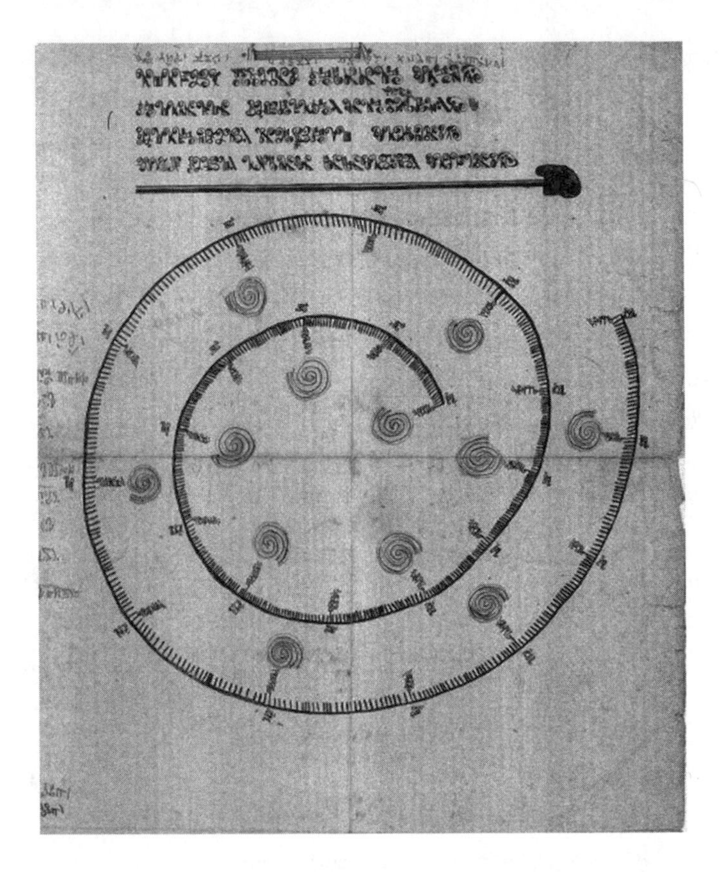

The numeral in Bagam script marked the date of the start of Clara's period.

The serpentine designs, each with a name written beneath, recorded the succession of massacres.

The frequency of the swirls signaled the implacable logic of the series.

Ouandié set up camp in Toungou, there in the Tchunda, *and breathed new* life into the Maquis. But really, he'd retreated. Since the failed attack on Foumbot, the ALNK had kept on losing ground. In Douala, Tankeu Noë, who was patrolling the city, was arrested and executed right there in the market. And then, of course, the army set houses and whole neighborhoods on fire. These setbacks forced Ouandié to rethink his plans. At night, the pastor would join him and they'd pick up their conversation. He came when the moon was at its highest in the sky. The Sinistrés would sit around them, like pupils. After a while, Ouandié would stand and lead him outside. Nithap would follow along. Sometimes his secretary, Ben Bella, would join them as well, although he never spoke during these nighttime meetings.

One evening, Ouandié leaned toward the pastor.

"*Passitou*," he said, "you're not going to convert me, and you know that quite well, because I was always your most recalcitrant student. But now I'm asking you to leave."

He locked eyes with Nithap.

"Take your son-in-law with you."

Then he turned away, gazing out into the distance.

"Happiness awaits you in Yaounde," he said. He was speaking to Nithap now. "A wife. A home." Then, to the pastor, "Your family is in Yaounde. What are you still doing here in Bangangte, where your own son-in-law is letting whole villages go up in flames and putting everyone in camps?"

"You came back, too, *Comrade Émile*."

Pastor Tbongo said "Comrade Émile" to show how irritated he was, and also to let his interlocutor know that he was familiar with the UPC ways. "Not everyone can leave. I am old, my wife is, too. I'm entitled to happiness, but the young people are even more so, because I've already had my turn. This house is my life, my family, my existence. I built it to stay here, and to give all those who, like me, have stayed behind reasons to live." He spread out his hands. "Just imagine if my children came here and learned that I had fled."

"No one is talking about fleeing."

This time, as Ouandié answered, he avoided looking at him.

"Not so fast," Nithap interrupted—it was the first time during the exchange that he'd spoken. "I know that I can leave whenever I want, because you told me so. But I'm the one who decided to join you. It took some time, but now my decision is made. I have chosen sides."

Even he felt the cruel weight of his words, because the man standing before him was Ngountchou's father. Perhaps that's why he spoke in a rush. He was upset, and his hands shook as his words flew out.

"I miss Ngountchou every day. But I would miss the Sinistrés even more if I were in Yaounde." He paused, but no one interrupted. "I don't think I could be happy all alone in the capital. When I worked at the hospital, I missed my patients in the same way."

"And yet you no longer work at the hospital," the pastor said.

"On the contrary, it's as if I still do."

"Dr. Nithap is my personal physician," Ouandié cut in.

A silence fell over them.

"What's waiting for me in Yaounde," he added, "is a death sentence."

"Is that why you don't want others to be happy?" Pastor Tbongo asked him. "Forgive me for being so direct. But hear me well."

Ouandié recoiled at such an accusation.

"Yes," he said, his chest puffing up as he stifled a laugh. "You see where the education we give our children leads. I was your best philosophy student, and I've become the *chief of the Maquisards*.

If anyone could have seen in the darkness, they would have known he was amused by this—he always found some humor in life's tragic moments. Ouandié turned to face the pastor.

"*Passitou*," he continued, bending down and picking up a bit of stone. "Our cause is just. We are in the right. Anyone with any intelligence understands the reasons why we've taken up arms and is on our side. I know that you are worried, but I share your concerns. No family has escaped unscathed from the catastrophe that has befallen our country, because we are united in this war. Civil war hits families first, scattering them. Family is its first battlefield."

"That's not the question."

"And yet . . ."

Ouandié walked toward the courtyard, still playing with the stone. It fell, sending some sentinel weaver birds flying. Along the horizon, a yellow field of grass stretched out as far as eyes could see, and in the rising mists, like letters written on the surface of the universe, three women were walking toward them, each with a bundle of wood on her head and a baby strapped onto her back.

"And yet?"

"This is our land. Mine and yours." He again paused, before continuing in his professorial voice. "Look at the beauty of this country. It's breathtaking. A wonder. A treasure that belongs to those who live here. The grandeur of our culture. The beauty of our civilization. But how have we gotten to the point where our three sisters there cross through this beauty, this wonder, this treasure, without seeing any of it, totally unaware? That's the crux of it all. This country no longer belongs to us, and it has made us into slaves right in the shadow of our ancestors' palaces. That's the real problem. We are no longer 'natives.' We need to learn again how to be human beings. We need to learn again how to dream."

He turned back. The half-finished *Tchunda* rose up before him. The pastor was listening to him.

"What is a world with no utopia worth?" he said.

5

Mbeng knew that a married woman is only conquered by surprise. Mensa' was surprised when the Tupuri doorman at her home in Etoa Meki announced that a man was at her door.

"The subprefect from Bazou," he said.

"My husband isn't here," Mensa' said to Mbeng when she greeted him, standing at the door to the house, which was covered in gold pollen after the rains the day before.

"I know," he answered. "Champs-Élysées, do you remember?"

Mensa' first thought of the store.

"My father is at my house," Mbeng went on. "You wanted to meet him, didn't you?"

"Your father?" Her thoughts quickly turned to her own.

"He'd really love to meet the people who have taken away his son from him," he added. "For the past two years, you know, I've been posted in Bamileke land."

It was difficult for Mensa' to get out of this invitation. When she'd seen Mbeng, her heart had started racing. This time she didn't ask her chauffeur to accompany her.

"I'll be right back," she called out to Ngountchou as she closed the door behind her.

"This will make my father happy," Mbeng said. He had thought this conquest would be more difficult.

Champs-Élysées was sitting in a bamboo armchair on the porch of the house, his feet crossed in front of him. He held a flyswatter in one hand and waved happily to welcome the couple.

"Mbeng," he shouted, speaking in French, "for once you bring me a beautiful woman." He looked at her intently. "I hope this isn't *somebody else's woman?*"

Mensa' smiled, embarrassed as much by the "for once" as by the "somebody else's woman." Mbeng said a couple of things to the old man in their own language; all she caught was the word *Bazou*. Champs-Élysées wasn't much of a listener, but his mouth had things to say.

"*Dzon esse mbeng mbeng*,"* he suddenly hummed, giving Mensa''s hand a hard squeeze. "My daughter, do you know what that means? It means that everything is marvelous!"

His eyes took in the young woman, then switched back to his son.

"That's how he is," Mbeng whispered to Mensa'.

"Oh, my old bones!" the father continued. "My son Mbeng, standing there before you, was born just after I'd left for Paris, *nnam dzom esse ine mbeng mbeng*![†] His mother thought I was going to die among the white men, that I'd never come back. That's why she and I conceived him the very night before I left."

He laughed as he told the story, and Mensa' was embarrassed to hear so many details from an old man. She met Mbeng's gaze, and saw he was just as embarrassed. But that didn't slow down Champs-Élysées.

"His mother was the one who called me Champs-Élysées, because that's where I told her I was headed when the train came to pick us up in Ongola and take us to France."

"The train?" Mbeng asked.

Champs-Élysées wasn't listening.

"His mother was a very beautiful woman, with *otou*,[‡] two little commas tattooed on her cheeks," he said dreamily. "Light-skinned, just like you."

---

* In Ewondo, "All is well."

† In Ewondo, "The country where all is well."

‡ These traditional beauty marks were, of course, forbidden by the German colonizers.

"My father was a tirailleur," Mbeng explained to Mensa'.

"A beautiful woman," Champs-Élysées went on. "Do you know that in our language, *mbeng* comes from *ambeng*, which means beauty? That *mbeng* means both what is good and what is beautiful? I must say that my son Mbeng has good taste!" His eyes lit up when he looked at Mensa'. He tilted his head and raised his flyswatter before continuing, "Mbeng, that's his name and his nickname." He was laughing, revealing all of his teeth. "Both at the same time."

With a quick wave, he chased away a fly.

"*Mbeng* also means both good and beauty in Bazou," Mbeng said, looking to Mensa' for her approval, which she gave him with a quick squeeze of his hand.

"Good! Beauty!" Champs-Élysées cried. "When we walked down the Champs-Élysées, I was still young. We were led on by an ideal. Liberty! Brotherhood! Equality! De Gaulle was in front of us. Of course, Leclerc, who'd led us all the way from here, was there as well. I was in the first division of tirailleurs that left Yaounde in September 1940, with General Dio, who is still in Yaounde. He often comes to pay me a visit. The first division of tirailleurs that marched into Paris in 1944. With all those Bassas, like Hebga, Philothée the Stutterer, and the others!* Among us Cameroonians, we usually spoke Bassa instead of Ewondo. You'd have thought it was a tribal army, except for all the Chadians. The *mafis*, you know. Black like the bottom of a pot. Ah, it was a beautiful thing to arrive in Paris, how great it was! We're the ones who liberated France—we did it! The Champs-Élysées, Pigalle, the Latin Quarter—in all those places, no one was speaking anything but German until we got to town! All the French came out to greet us! The Frenchwomen are beautiful! They all came out from where they'd been hiding to kiss us, to kiss this Ewondo son, *menyu n'ewondo*. Can you imagine! Me, the son of Charles Atangana Mballa, and all those flowers they tossed. The Champs-Élysées was covered in roses!"

---

* Their story is told in *When the Plums Are Ripe*.

With another quick wave of his hand he swatted a fly, but didn't lose track of what he was saying.

"The French called us all Senegalese, but we knew who we were: we were Cameroonians, Bassas, Ewondos, Bamilekes. We were one big family." He leaned on Mensa''s arm, like he was telling her a secret. "There was a Sawa who told me that where he came from, down by the coast, *Mbeng* means the North. He told me about river people who'd come down in pirogues to the port, where they'd board ships, which took them across the Atlantic Ocean and on to Paris. He said that for them, France was Mbeng, and that they were the first from Cameroon to discover the white man's land." And then he added, his voice rising louder, "But we crossed the Sahara. We didn't just discover the white man's land, we liberated it!" His pride was contagious. He beat his fist on his chest. "Ah! The Tripolitan! We did what we had to do! I saw men die in the middle of the desert, eaten alive by scavengers. I saw some whose heads just exploded under the sun, burned to the bone. And then there were Germans hiding in the sand, lying in wait. *Guten Morgen, mein Lieber!*—Hello, my dear! And there were Italians, too, ready to ambush us. *Ciao!* All of them with the most advanced weapons on earth. The panzer division was no joke, huh! All of them lined up against the sons of Yaounde. But we beat the Nazis. General Dio is still here. He is my witness."

Mensa' looked at him, sitting back in his bamboo armchair, waving his flyswatter in front of his face. It was as if the battlefields he was talking about were unfolding right there in front of his eyes, as if the plums were ripe once more, and as if suddenly the beautiful women of Paris were right there in that courtyard. She was captivated by his words, and soon realized that the son was talkative, just like his father. That thought amused her. As he spoke, Champs-Élysées squeezed her hand, but his eyes sought out those of his son, who also squeezed her hand when he whispered to her. There was clearly a real complicity between father and son, and a special sense of pride that the father did not try to hide. He wanted to transmit all of his courage, which had enabled him to stand up and face the most unbelievable dangers, to his son, who was now a subprefect in a troubled zone. You see, for him, Mbeng was the fruit of his battle. Because, he said, raising his flyswatter again, "France owes a debt of blood to the Cameroonian people. We're the ones who freed her from barbarity." That the debt be repaid as a civil servant's salary, after his son was hired by the colonial administration, seemed to him the most natural thing in the world. He didn't say thank you, but he did enjoy vicariously through his son the fruits of a war in which he'd risked his life. That was the source of the pride he felt in seeing his offspring named subprefect. He took a philosophical view of the fact that his son had been caught up in the bowels of another war—philosophy being another name for fatality.

He talked to Mensa' and Mbeng about himself, his wonderful life, and that country where the ground was covered with flowers. It was as if he were giving his blessing to this accidental couple with his enchanted words, giving them a glimpse of paradise. *Go on*, he seemed to say, *my children, the world is yours! Go on, because there is no battle worth more than that of the heart, of beauty, of all that is good.*

"It's going to rain," Mensa' said suddenly.

The wind was lifting up clouds of dust and rustling tree leaves, the sky was growing dark.

"I'll take her home," Mbeng said to his father.

"You'll come back, my daughter?" he asked, suddenly worried that he hadn't said the most important part.

It was Mbeng who replied, "Yes, Papa, we'll come back."

The rains in Yaounde are treacherous, but Mbeng couldn't really complain. As he dashed out of Champs-Élysées's courtyard, he holding Mensa''s arm, and she the flounce of her skirt, small drops were already falling from the sky.

I should have asked the chauffeur to come and get me, Mensa' thought. But did she really want him to? Yaounde's rains fall without warning and bring everything to a halt. They often pursue you, like the cops chase down a robber. All you have to do to get away is run fast. But this rain was already pounding the ground with her watery fists.

"There's a taxi," said Mbeng, darting out under the rain.

Once in the car, he looked at Mensa' and realized both how beautiful and how calm she was. She was soaked through, and was adjusting her wig with a touch of her hand.

"Etoa Meki," he said.

He would have loved to give another destination, and quickly regretted not having done so.

"Fifty francs," said the taxi driver curtly, when the car stopped in front of Mensa''s gate.

Mbeng watched her get out of the car and run through the rain. She was covering her head with her hands. Before shutting the gate behind her, she turned back and gave him a friendly wave, a smile spreading across her face. That's the image he took with him to Bazou the next day.

That evening at home, Mensa' ate very little. She told her sister, Ngountchou, that she wasn't hungry. Another sort of hunger had taken hold of her, making her whistle tunes from France and hum, *Quand le film est triste, ça me fait pleurer.** The ball at the palace was just a distant memory. The arrival of her older sister in Yaounde had been something both women really needed. For Mensa', it had seemed like a solution for her solitude. As for Ngountchou, she was fleeing the violence that had taken over Bangwa. Even before that night her fiancé had abandoned her, she had told him that she wanted to live in Yaounde. The fire had made up her mind for her. But, in the end, her presence did little to help her sister. Mensa' was sinking into a listlessness broken only by the meetings of the Capable Women.

As for her husband, he was living through the hardest time of his life. He always had to be in the village, back in his constituency, on the battlefield of the civil war. He was so busy with a thousand different tasks that he had no time to miss his wife. He'd been able to recruit Mme Nki'tcha to join him; it was with her, as well as with her husband, the prefect of the western province, that he crisscrossed the region, fishing in the boiling waters of the rebellion. He could also count on the mayor of Bazou, Denis Djonga, who knew the lay of the land better than any-

---

* "When the film is sad, it makes me cry": Who didn't want to be Sylvie Vartan?

one and who had set up militias that patrolled the town. And Mbeng was very busy, too. He'd come back to Yaounde to "catch my breath a little," he said, "so I can see more clearly."

"You need to get married," Mensa''s husband advised him. "It helps in these somber days to be able to count on your family."

The road to Yaounde was dangerous. Ntchantchou Zacharie, Mensa''s husband, never forgot it. How could he have forgotten the assassination of his colleague, Deputy Wanko, or the recent ambush from which Minister Nkwayim had only barely escaped, or the attempted assassination that he himself had dodged? He remembered that mayor who had received a package one morning: the head of his *mafi* bodyguard wrapped in a plastic bag. He could see his car being chased by a crowd with rocks in hand, determined to smash his windshield! Not to mention those soldiers and militiamen whose worm-eaten bodies were found here and there in the bush, sometimes with their eyes gouged out or their balls cut off. "You can't even trust the whores in Bafoussam anymore," people said, trying to make a joke. Yes, how could he forget the permanent danger he was in? Was he just going to hide in the crowd from then on, taking the Dina bus like everyone else? Being a Bamileke deputy was no cakewalk—no! Having Mensa' by his side wouldn't have made him feel any safer. Then he thought of the camps. The villages had been emptied by the army, and the villagers rounded up in resettlement camps. He'd visited several of them, improvised clusters of shelters that he hoped would be temporary. The orders were strict, and he'd been the one who'd had to circulate them: no one was to stay in their village. Of course, there were those who refused, old folks mostly, who were camping among the ruins—first and foremost his own father-in-law! How ironic! As he was pursuing everyone in the bush, he'd had to intervene personally—he, a federal deputy—so that Pastor Tbongo could stay in his home, because "the old man, he's very stubborn"—that was just what he'd said. "Too stubborn, really.

"He doesn't want to leave."

Enoch Nkwayim had sighed. "Our parents!"

Often, when he was on the road, something in the bushes would catch his eye and Ntchantchou Zacharie would think about his own death. He'd think he was seeing men wearing hoods, but it was just the trees.

Like other officials from the West, he was accompanied by a police officer, wearing a colonial cap, who served as his bodyguard, and he had a chauffeur, too. But he was never as vulnerable as when he was on the road back to Bamileke land—*the road home*. He could see the greenery spreading out before him, and suddenly he was afraid. The green hills of this country seemed endless, so beautiful they pained him. It was as if a wound opened up and an ache grabbed hold of his heart, making him struggle to catch his breath. He trembled and thought of his wife. He closed his eyes and the pain of her absence struck him even harder, like a whip. *She is safe back in the city.*

He remembered that day when he'd first seen her, in the middle of the crowd that had gathered to listen to him in the Bangangte market. Her terrified face had stood out to him as he was introducing the young bandits he'd had dressed in hunters' clothes, covered with motor oil, and called "Maquisards." He'd seen in her face a silent sincerity; mostly, she reminded him of her father. *She's the pastor's daughter*, he'd thought. Throughout his speech, he kept thinking of Elie Tbongo, who led services in the church where he had been an elder, before becoming a deputy. Mensa' was listening to him, calmly, but he read a judgment in her eyes. *Maybe she knows the truth?* he wondered. *Maybe she's mocking me?* In that crowd, suddenly one girl, just one, was stripping him bare—he would make her his wife because, after his speech, he couldn't stop thinking about her. Even now, he had just left Mensa' and was still thinking only of her. Like any man, he imagined that she would quickly tell him everything hidden in her heart.

When Mensa' and Mbeng paid a second visit to Champs-Élysées, he wasn't there.

"He must have gone back to the village," Mbeng told her.

"I thought that Yaounde was your village," Mensa' replied.

The man smiled.

"We're in Nlongkak."

She thought about Bangangte. "Maybe it'll be a real town soon, too . . . With electricity?"

"Ongola," Mbeng went on, and smiled, "but now none of us can live in Ongola like we used to."

Except for the President of the Republic.

"Except for the President of the Republic."

Mensa' remembered the night they'd danced. Then, despite herself, she laughed in embarrassment, knowing that she was caught in a trap.

"Mbeng," she quickly asked, "what will my husband say?"

"He won't know."

The man's answer was definitive. Right then, he placed his hands around her waist, as if about to lead her off to a new dance, but he stopped. So she pulled close to him, molding her body to his, while he lowered the zipper of her flowered dress. That's how, one piece after another, he removed all of the clothes she'd bought at the central market: her earrings, her shirt, her slip, her undergarments.

"I can do it myself," she said when he tried to take off her bra. His hands were trembling.

Still, he didn't let her.

"*Ambeng!*" he said. Beauty!

Just a little nudge, and she fell into his arms. He carried her into the bedroom and gently laid her down on his bed. She opened his shirt, running her determined hands across his chest. The lovers disappeared into their shared passion, caught up in a fevered whirlwind; they gave no thought to what they were doing until they found themselves, out of breath, in each other's arms.

"It's raining," Mensa' said.

"Welcome to Yaounde," Mbeng answered. "It rains like this at the same time every day."

They met each day at that same time for a week, for two weeks. When it wasn't raining, Mensa' came by bike; the path from Etoa Meki to Nlongkak was easy. She'd pedal quickly across the neighborhood, her nimble feet leading her to her fevered and secret passion—like her husband, Mbeng would be in town for only a short time. When it rained, she came by taxi. *This is pure folly*, she thought the first time he said, as he was getting dressed again, there in the living room where he'd taken her, "I'm going back to *your* village." That day she'd given herself to him right on the floor. He helped her up. Still naked, she walked to the window and grasped the latch with both hands. She wanted to throw it open and shout how happy she was for all Yaounde to hear, but the thought of the scandal stopped her. She stood there for a long moment, trembling, letting the distant thrum of the city's heartbeat speak to her, until she felt Mbeng's arms slip around her waist and lift her up. She was crying. That's when Mensa' realized how truly alone she was, just as he penetrated her for a second time from behind.

Since she'd refused to join the tribal *tontines*, Mensa' had very few friends in the capital. Her husband was in Bazou, where, in fact, he and Mbeng were supposed to organize a *cadi*.

"Don't leave for Bazou," she pleaded frantically with Mbeng, caressing his neck and his damp cheeks, "stay here with me."

She even shouted. "Can't you just stay here with me three more days?"

"I cannot," he whispered to her, as he put on his underwear. "The war."

"Quit your job," she said.

"The war."

"Exactly, the war."

She said she was afraid for him each time he left, and then spoke of terrorism, of death, of all those things that filled the greasy files piled on his table. Except that she also spoke of passion. She spoke of the attempted abduction of Enoch Nkwayim. He stopped and caressed her neck. He would be the first subprefect in Cameroon to quit "because of terrorists"—what he didn't say, but thought, was *because of a woman*.

"I cannot," he said, and pulled her close.

"Stay in Yaounde," she pleaded again.

"My work," he began; she stared deep into his eyes.

"Your cat eyes." Mensa' didn't say that he sounded like her husband.

She just threw herself at him. She cried as he penetrated her for a third time. And later, when she found herself standing in front of a mirror, she looked at herself and shuddered. "I love seeing you naked," he had told her earlier, "because you are beauty itself."

"I am crazy," she said.

She burst out laughing at the thought of her husband, Ntchantchou Zacharie, who only ever declared his love when he set down in the living room the bunches of bananas he'd brought back from the village. *Love is as mute for the Bamilekes as it is talkative for the Betis*, she told herself. She no longer recognized herself in the mirror; her fingers ran over the ritual scars that ringed her belly button and so intrigued her lover, because Ewondo women don't have them. She had others, as well, on her back and her arms.

What is happening to me? she asked herself, touching her arms, then her breasts and her belly. *I have two husbands.*

Mensa' ran her fingers over the chain that circled her hips, fondling the pendant that hung from it. Her hands were trembling because she suddenly saw the two men of her life undoing the chain at the same time. Her hands moved lower toward her pubis and she closed her eyes.

To me, a Bamileke woman?

Bangangte women are different, she told herself when she opened her eyes again, after her fourth orgasm, and that reassured her: *Nobility, dignity, elegance!*

Three letters!

Free women!

Her mother hadn't flattened her breasts. She looked at herself, full of confidence. It seemed that the discovery of her body, her breasts, by a man who wasn't her husband intoxicated her; she was no longer even aware of the furtive but determined steps she was taking along the *mapans** of betrayal. There she was, walking around her living room and whistling, the evening breeze flowing over her possessed body.

---

* A Camfranglais term for the footpaths that crisscross a neighborhood, but also for houses of ill repute.

Perhaps Mme Eteki had seen that woman, whom she'd met at their monthly meetings, crossing the neighborhood in the evening; or then again, maybe Mme Ngapeth had seen her turn left at Le Restaurant africain by the Etoa Meki roundabout, instead of taking the hill down toward Bastos, passing by without even stopping to say hello, as she did when she'd first arrived in the capital; women from the Capable Women's *tontine* had certainly glimpsed Mensa' climbing back up the road toward Nlongkak on her bike and then knocking on the door of *Monsieur le Sous-Préfet*'s pied-à-terre, as she straightened her dress and her hair.

They had certainly all been scandalized. Starting with a phone call and then a courtesy visit, and even a chance encounter at the door of the Printania department store, these women had certainly had a good laugh as they shared the news. They all got together several times a week because they shopped at the same stores, got manicures and pedicures from the same Vietnamese woman, and passed the time at the Hippodrome, and all their children went to the French school in the center of town to prepare for their studies in Paris. Nothing got past the Capable Women.

Mensa' had no ears for their gossip, and besides, she had no other friend in town except that man, now so far away, whose face she'd feverishly imagine until he was there before her once again. Her belly remembered that man, who had his own way of making her lose control—there was no one she could talk to about that. He took her to a place where everything was good, beautiful, marvelous—she shook her head and smiled.

Mensa' held out her arms and called to him: "Just come to me." She didn't tell him that she was a fountain, that she was the Nkong, or the Maheshou River, that she was the Nde!

"I'm not crying," she'd tell him later, tears running down her cheeks as she drank deeply from the cup of pleasure.

She thought of all that when she got into the bed where her husband was not. She'd wake up with a start, her nipples hard and her thighs yielding to the touch, right in the middle of a dream in which her lover had pinned her to the ground. She thought of all that as she took her morning shower, washing her arms, belly, and vulva with coconut oil.

She thought of all that as she dressed, and went out for a ride on her bicycle, her joyful face whipped by the breeze.

Ambeng!

The word her lover used came back to her time and time again. Her husband never spoke when he made love to her, had never really spoken to her affectionately, trapped as he was in a Bamileke upbringing that said you show love only by giving things. Without wanting to, she started to think of him as the typical Bamileke man, a caricature she made fun of, a stereotype she'd often heard mentioned and who was the personification of a poor sod: For how can one be Bamileke?

Quickly, but methodically, with determination, she began drawing up a list of the things Ntchantchou Zacharie had never done to her—little things that didn't just make him different from Mbeng, but actually ridiculous. She could hear his voice, and even the way he spoke French seemed ridiculous to her: he tripped over his *r*'s, adding a harsh click to words like *French*, *crap!*, and *market*. No, he didn't speak French like any of the French people she'd heard back in Bangangte, or like Champs-Élysées. Without realizing it, she began to detest all the little things that made him who he was. She conjured a despicable image of him, saw him as calculating, sly, and greedy—saw him as a trader, with a wad of bills, so much cash, the ill-gotten gains from all those faked confessions when supposed Maquisards rallied to the government, or maybe from some sort of pact with the Fam.* He was a crook continually mired in shady business, looking up from his mud bath and grunting: he had become a *pig*.†

Sometimes she laughed a little despite herself when she thought about him, about that old, ill-fitting suit coat of his, about the shoes that he never took care of, about how he got so wrapped up in his duty that he

* Fam, that's the Devil in classical Medumba.

† This is a stereotypical association: pigs with curly coats were first introduced into Dschang—formerly a German stronghold—and from there into the rest of the region, where chickens and goats had previously been the ubiquitous barnyard animals. They then became the emblem of the Bamilekes, who, by extension, are seen as pigs—even when they don't stink and aren't dirty. Ironically, pigs can also be referred to as *beauregards*, or good-lookers.

worked like a madman, about how introverted he was, and how he had no friends except those he thought would be useful. Even his favorite phrase, *A mvelou ke nzui ou*—It's your brother who kills you—rang hollow for her; she saw it as a sign of his unhealthy suspicion, his foolish paranoia, because—good god!—just what was he afraid of? What were the Bamilekes so afraid of? Then suddenly she asked herself: *Why did I marry him?*

And she replied, *To get away from Bangangte.*

Then Magni Sa's face came back to her, *To escape from the fire.*

She told herself that she must have been in deep despair to have agreed to marry that man and so chosen to hide in the very source of her misfortune.

She saw Ntchantchou Zacharie swallowed up by a war that he hadn't started, but that he had made his own. She had somehow forgotten that the dividends her husband earned from rallying the people had been transformed into the closetful of clothes in every color that she used to make herself beautiful for Mbeng. Or was this just her way of getting revenge on her deputy of a husband, who was so focused on his work that he forgot his young wife? Mensa' detested him precisely because she was cheating on him. Hatred is a whirlwind. And hatred's accomplice is cowardice, whereas love's companion is courage. The hate-filled man dispatches his enemy with a quick dagger in the back, while the lover must approach his beloved face-to-face, if he wants to conquer her. The deputy's wife was justifying her betrayal, and her betrayal became the pretext for even more betrayals. *Ambeng! Ambeng!* she thought, echoing her passionate cries.

When Ntchantchou Zacharie came back from Bangangte, she gave herself to him reluctantly. He didn't seem to notice; he was so exhausted by the long trip from the village, by his fear of being ambushed, and too eager for his wife's embrace to pay much attention to her mood. He was used to her giving in to him out of duty. He'd married her after paying her dowry in *cash*: "*Me jun yam menzui*,"* he often said smugly. Because

* "I bought my wife."

Mensa' was his wife, he didn't even realize that the woman he made love to was just a shell: a shell of a woman that he loved, although she never let him see the real her; a shell of a woman that he thrust into; a shell of a woman who cried out and shook the house with her fake orgasms. Mensa' did her conjugal duty; she played the part of a wife so well it surprised her, staged the lady of the house with a talent that frightened her. All she had to do was think of her lover and her vagina flooded; the mere mention of the word *prefect* within earshot made her lose her mind. Once, even, when Ntchantchou Zacharie brought up his colleague, whom he called, with a laugh, "your prefect"—"Do you know what your prefect there did again?"—she thought she was caught. But her husband was blind.

The young wife only really came alive when Mbeng came back from Bazou and carried her to his bed like a leading man would do with his new bride. *He is my true husband*, she said to herself when he arrived, when she took off his clothes, when she saw him naked, when she felt his chest hair against her breasts, when she felt him moving between her legs, when she felt him thrusting inside her, taking possession of her soul and whispering those strange, beautiful words that always made her lose control, again, again, and again: "*Ambeng! Ambeng! Ambeng!*"

6

In Bangangte, the family home, even emptied of his two daughters, was anything but calm. Hens, ducks, and goats wandered in the courtyard. Pecking at kernels of corn, grazing on weeds. But Pastor Tbongo just couldn't find his dog. He'd looked everywhere, in the courtyard, behind the house, in the kitchen, the toilets, out in the clearing.

"Where is Kouandiang?" he asked.

He searched in the living room, the kitchen, the bedrooms.

"Who has seen the dog?"

Everyone was looking. Tama' had seen him, but that was several hours ago. Tama' was still living with the pastor, like a new son, a deposit paid in advance of Ngountchou's marriage, whose shadow lingered like an unfilled promise.

His wife, Nja Yonke', pressed her hands to her temples.

"What do you want me to say?" she asked.

The pastor was afraid, but he was also irritated and determined. His wife's fear had taken root in that living room, lifeless now since the departure of her children. Nja Yonke' wasn't really old, but the series of miscarriages that had preceded her daughters' births had taken a toll on her. Her hair had gone white quite suddenly, and that was what was really frightening: her body's brutal revelation of impending death.

Elie Tbongo went to his bedroom and grabbed his jacket, because it was cold outside. He was clearly in a hurry.

"I just hope it wasn't *them*."

"Where are you going?" Nja Yonke' asked.

"Tama'!"

The boy came running. With a quick wave of his hand, he motioned for the boy to follow him.

That's how they disappeared into the mist. And that's how they came to be in the courtyard of the chief's compound. There was already a large crowd gathered, forming a circle in the courtyard where large meetings were held, around the *nlong la'*.* The pastor made his way through the crowd, ignoring the faces of those who recognized him—the men, some of whom doffed their caps, and the women, who clasped their hands in a show of respect. People waved, surprised to see him there. All eyes were focused on him. Elie Tbongo held Tama''s hand, dragging the boy behind him.

"*Passitou*, you are here, *too*?" one woman asked.

"Too?" That word stuck in Tama''s memory. Later, he'd talk about what he'd gone through growing up there, about the sarcasm of Bangangte women, their mastery of the impenetrable art of mockery. History—which had made of him an orphan, although he didn't know that yet, and provided him with an adoptive family, which had torn his guardian away from him and his adoptive mother, as well—kept opening unexpected chapters before his eyes. It didn't matter that he tried to hide, as he would later tell Mensa', history always came looking for him—*kounya, kounya, kounya*—even under his bed, *bam la kounda*. He always ended up standing naked before history, just like when he bared his heart to his cousins.

The pastor's voice cut through the crowd.

"That's my dog."

He came into the center of the circle and untied the dog from the post to which it was tethered.

"Who told you to take my dog?"

No one knew what to say. Kouandiang was trembling, both terrified

* A building stone placed in the courtyard of a compound to represent the authority of the head of the family; often placed at the base of a pillar.

and so, so happy to have found his master in that hostile crowd. He'd pulled his tail back tight between his legs.

"You're making a whole scene," one voice said, "about nothing."

It was Deputy Ntchantchou.

He was standing next to the *nlong la'*. Chief Nono was sitting in front of the door, as he did when he handed down judgments. He didn't move, and kept his long-nailed hands on his knees.

"So, what's this story about a dog again?" he asked.

But Pastor Tbongo was already holding the newly freed Kouandiang. He didn't even listen to his son-in-law, who, with polite gestures, tried to convince him to let it drop.

"We aren't going to hurt it," he said.

"I know," the pastor replied. "You take me for a fool!"

He pulled his dog closer to himself.

"You, too, *Passitou*."

"Tama'," he called out, scanning the crowd. "Let's go back home."

He could be fearless, Pastor Tbongo. Had he waited one minute longer, he would have been even more horrified. After he left with Kouandiang, the crowd gathered at the chief's stayed put. They found another dog, another black one, like Kouandiang.

It was Ntchantchou Zacharie who had called everyone together that day—even Nkuika Tchamba, the chief from Bangoulap, was there. The deputy organized these public confessions all across Bangangte and the surrounding area. He'd decided to obtain one from Tankongan. Fire no longer did the trick. Pastor Tbongo ought to have stayed. He'd have seen his foreman, bareheaded and gaunt, brought trembling into the circle, limping more than ever, to take his place by the *nlong la'* with a basin before him. He would have seen his daughter's husband take action. But he refused to witness this abuse of power, this farce that was for him nothing but charlatanism.

Even if these sorts of ceremonies were organized all over the West, this one was a first, because Jean Nono had agreed to hold it in the chief's compound. He was trying to piece together the glory he'd gotten from his position as lackey, and fell back on his old reflexes of a corrupt man in bed with the government. It was like in the old days, with Jeucafra and the Bamileke Union in the pocket of the French colonists.* He burnished his glorious reputation with his own bad faith. There were other administrative authorities there alongside him; their beige uniforms made them stand out. The ones from Bazou were there—Nkuimy, as well as Djonga.

"Mbeng isn't coming?" a voice asked.

It was Ntchantchou Zacharie who spoke.

"He's in Yaounde."

That surprised everyone. While the deputy kept on talking, giving orders here and there, everyone looked at the new dog.

"Hit the dog!"

The order make Tankongan jump. The animal began to whine softly. The crowd fell silent. A bare-chested fellow, holding two switches cut from a horsetail plant in his hands, walked up to the foreman, who was struggling to breathe, and stared into his eyes.

"Take this!" he said.

"What am I supposed to tell you?" Tankongan began.

He was stammering.

"What are you waiting for?"

The frightened animal looked around. Tankongan struck its back. The animal trembled and turned to look at him, its face filled with fear. That seemed to open the floodgates, because suddenly the foreman fell to his knees, pressed his hands to the ground.

"Confess!" they heard, as a scandalized rumor ran through the crowd. "Confess!"

"I'll speak!" he said. "I want to speak!"

"So speak!"

* Between 1945 and 1951, Jeucafra, the French-Cameroonian youth movement, along with its double, the Bamileke Union, had a stranglehold on politics in Bangangte and sought to block the rebel forces that "threatened the country"; at that time, Dschang was led by the progressive Kumzse.

7

Sometimes Mensa' wanted to take her lover and lead him to the deepest reaches of her body, but she'd stop midway, blocked by that damned Bamileke upbringing. Never had she gone so often to the market or run so many errands. At first it was he who undressed her, but soon she was the one rushing breathless through Etoa Meki, her body hungering, without underpants beneath her *kaba*. The pleasure she felt when she told him, "I'm not wearing panties," was offset by the modesty that flooded back suddenly once they were stretched out in bed. He'd be counting the freckles that ringed her nipples, his eyes gleaming with an insatiable curiosity. She'd cover her breasts with both hands or the sheet. And she'd laugh. How he loved to make her laugh! *The Betis know how to make love to a woman*, she thought.

Then one day Mensa' woke up from this universe of ecstasy in her sister's arms. She'd fainted.

"You're pregnant," Ngountchou told her, "*ou be jum.*"

She had lived her love all the more intensely because she had kept it secret. But the most exquisite love is the one that multiplies—an equation that most certainly makes it public. When she told her husband that she was pregnant, he kissed her joyously, then tried out a few dance steps, a *ben skin*. That day, too, like always, his car was filled with "food from the village." There were bunches of bananas, peanuts from Garoua, eggplants, bushmeat, pistachios, and everything else that he bought either at the market in Bangangte or in Bazou—"because it's cheaper there"—or somewhere else along the road. He asked Ngountchou to prepare some good *bou'len* with *mbitali* for her sister, then thought again and asked her, instead, to make a succulent *kondre* with *sok tchen*, but then he had one more thought and promised Mensa' that she'd give birth in Paris, nothing less!

The woman in love didn't tell her second husband that she was pregnant because she didn't get the chance to. One day she found her husband in the living room, sitting on the couch. He'd come back to town just two days after he'd left. He was holding a letter with both hands. He had ransacked their bedroom, looking for a damning piece of evidence, an evil talisman, a telling bit of proof, the scarlet letter of her betrayal, a trail of crab tracks. He was there in the living room with all of Mensa''s shoes, her dresses, wigs, and jewelry, piled up at his feet; all her beauty tricks lying there in bits. His stare, his eyes, his mouth, his whole body—it was nothing but fury.

"Are you coming back from *his house*?"

His words hit the mark precisely because it was true: Mensa' had just come back from his house, yes.

It was raining that day, and she'd taken a taxi. How did she manage to lie to her husband so expertly when her feet, her arms, her belly, her breasts, and even her mouth still carried the perfume of Mbeng, whom she'd just left?

"Whose house?" she asked coolly, in Medumba. "*Jou we?*"

Your red-hot lover's, was what he wanted to spit at her, but, overcome by anger, his voice failed him, and he began to cough so hard it sounded like a sob. "Tell me the truth!" he went on, his voice trembling; he was losing his mind. "Are you coming back from *his house*?"

The discovery of betrayal leads us into the mathematics of despair, and in her despair, Mensa' grew methodical.

"*Jou we?*" she asked again.

"Read this."

He showed her the note he'd received, scribbled on a crumpled piece of paper, the signature illegible. She took it and read it, slowly, then raised her eyes and looked at him. She suddenly found the self-control she'd had before, when she was questioned by the police, when Semengue's soldiers were searching the area.

"It's the Maquisards who did this," she said in her calmest voice, and in French this time, too. "They want to blackmail you."

She was calm, cool, and collected.

"*Ou len-a ndje ke?*" shouted Ntchantchou Zacharie. How do you know that?

She looked again with a bureaucrat's eye at the note her husband had handed her. Written in a stilted French, it told her husband that he was a *puppet-husband*, and that his wife was "getting balled behind the back of the neocolonial state by a disrespectful colleague."

It was signed: "*Sinistré*."

"What do you want me to tell you?" said Mensa'. "That the child I'm carrying isn't yours?"

"Confess, *mbap*!"

"I did not have sexual relations with that man."

How coolly she said it, with her left hand raised!

The woman who had so often burst out laughing as she stood in front of the mirror and thought of Ntchantchou Zacharie was finally revealed. She threw back in her husband's face all the awful things he'd repeated to himself during his trip, trying to make him see how ridiculous it all was.

She burst out laughing.

"Is it *his*?"

"You are crazy," she said, suddenly growing quite serious. Then she ran to her room.

He followed, but she shut the door behind her.

"*Tchou' nzenda'*," he said in Medumba, pounding on the door, shaking the handle, gasping for breath like the billy goat he'd become. "*Ou nya ke tchou' mba ma' be' nzenda-li!*" Open the door! If you don't, I'll break it down!

On the other side of the door, she cried, frightened by a rage she'd never before seen in Ntchantchou Zacharie's eyes. He pulled back his leg, ready to kick the door down. He stopped only when he heard Ngountchou shout. Dumbstruck, the deputy, covered in sweat and foaming at the mouth, turned around and found himself face-to-face with his terrified sister-in-law.

"That's enough," she told him, "that's enough, Tachene."

The echo of his *ndap* brought him out of his madness. He left the house, his rage still intact, and slammed the door behind him. He walked across the city, under the rain. He realized that Yaounde is a small city for someone who has such a burning volcano in his belly. He walked the path from Etoa Meki to Ongola with a determined step. In the heart of the night, he found himself standing before the central post office, empty at that late hour. The date "1939" was illuminated in white lights. He continued on his way, and the road leading to the central market opened up before him. He opted, instead, to follow the other avenue toward the central train station. He waited there a long time in the dark, staring at the tracks, thinking again about his death. Not the one that had appeared before his eyes that day when he'd escaped from an attack. This time he thought about suicide. He thought, too, of those dismembered bodies that were found on the train tracks in Mbanga, in N'lohe, in Nkongsamba, men the Maquisards had killed and tossed there on the tracks, the cadavers of soldiers abandoned in the bushes.

"*Benzui ngangte', mbadi*,"* he said to himself, nodding his head.

He thought about his sister, who had warned him about Bangangte women. He thought about his mother, and saw her sobbing. He wondered what he hadn't given his wife, what had led her to do this. In his mind, he drew up a list of everything he had given her, everything that his mother, that rural peasant, could have never even imagined having. To think that he had moved Mensa' out of Bangangte after their wedding to protect her from the jealous tongues of the town that unleashed its resentment at his opulence! To think that he'd protected her in Yaounde, ever since that day a zealous stranger, passing by their house, had spat on the ground and—in front of witnesses—threatened to harm her! To

* "Really, those Bangangte women!" They don't have a good reputation among non-Bangangte people, especially after marriage when, it is said, they become too talkative and begin to roam; in other words, they're rebellious, free—you know. And what Cameroonian wants a wife who feels free?

think that he had given her a house in one of the best neighborhoods of the capital, right next to Bastos! To think that he had wanted to have her give birth in France!

"*Benzui! Benzui! Benzui!*" he shouted. Women!

He suddenly felt quite sick, so he sat down on the stump of a banana tree. But there was no escape from the torment his wife had thrown him into. Without wanting to, Ntchantchou Zacharie started to detest his child, and he saw it growing, growing, growing in Mensa''s belly. He heard the child burst out laughing in its mother's belly, and weighed the dimensions of her betrayal.

He struck his forehead, mortified by a feeling that had taken over his heart, body, and soul. He clenched his fists as if trying to keep himself from doing something bad, and he felt his gut tighten and his heart grow stony. The jealousy choked him; it so cloaked his mind that he was blinded. He imagined Mbeng as a drunk—someone who drank *odontol*, homemade brew—who thought only of fulfilling his own impulses, a charlatan of the flesh, and then as an orangutan, who leapt out to rape his lonely wife. He went back home, soaked to the skin, his body clammy; impelled by a desire to protect his wife, he grabbed hold of her hand so hard it hurt.

"You are going back to the village."

The best punishment for adultery was to separate the lovers, he'd concluded.

"No, you will not give birth to that child here in Yaounde," he said in a loud, determined voice, his hands frantically gesturing at the hostility that surrounded them. "You will go back to the village."

Because those words emerged from the red-hot hearth of anger, and because that fury had taken control of his body, Mensa' understood that any resistance to his decision would have revealed her secret.

"You will go back to the village," he repeated.

A hurricane was roiling inside him.

8

How long was Tanou going to keep avoiding his father's eyes because of Marthe? He felt like he was a kid again, sunk back into one of those moments when, knowing he'd done something wrong, he tried everything he could to delay judgment day and the punishment sure to follow. Those moments when he saw only mockery in the eyes of his brothers and sisters, who were all counting up the number of lashes he had coming and running their index fingers across their necks. It brought back memories of hiding the switch back in Bangwa. He couldn't imagine that his father would just ask: "Tanou, tell me, do you think you did the right thing?"

"No, Papa," he'd reply.

Then silence, as his father scanned all around, looking for where his son had hidden the switch, because he knew his son, too.

"So, what will your punishment be?"

It was that same silence that filled the trip back to the house, a silence built up over some thirty years. With his father in the car, Tanou really didn't want to turn on the radio. They'd had a final checkup and the young Indian doctor had found nothing alarming. "Your father is in good health," he'd said, "for his age." One less thing to worry about. Tanou knew that there was another word lying in wait somewhere, but he really didn't want to hear it, because he knew it all too well.

My punishment has already begun. That phrase kept ringing in his ears, sounding the bell for some self-imposed time alone. Back then, when his father couldn't find the switch he was looking for—betrayed by his other children who, in a surprising show of solidarity, said they didn't know where it was—he would turn the physical violence into psychological violence. He'd do nothing, or rather, he'd just say, "Go stand over there."

He would point to a corner of the courtyard where his son would be isolated for what, even now, seemed like an eternity. And hadn't Angela imposed the same sort of isolation on him for his mistake? He'd spent his exile at Céline's, in Big's empty office; at first he'd found the time productive—he'd written a novel—but then his exile from home began to weigh on him.

"Say something," he burst out.

He should have been talking to Angela.

His father said nothing. Tanou might as well have been speaking to that child—his former self—with knees covered in dust and holes in his underpants. Back then, Tanou couldn't even count on his mother's sympathy; Ngountchou took her husband's side. And now he couldn't count on his wife's sympathy, because it was her verdict that had made the world fall silent.

"What really makes me furious isn't so much the betrayal," Angela had said, "as the fact that you take me for an imbecile. Who do you think I am? I am your wife, damn it!"

"Don't tell me you have nothing to say," Tanou snapped.

The father smiled.

"You want me to judge?"

"Yes."

"What should I judge?"

"The mistakes."

"Why do we always need to judge?"

Tanou wanted to say, *In order to punish.*

Here's a stupid question: When does a man stop being his father's son? Never, according to the Bangangte—never!

But Old Papa was tired of punishing. When his son, caught up in his inescapable childhood, turned back into an adolescent; when the son repeated the same old habits born of a guilty conscience—he found he just didn't have the strength for it anymore. Grandfather had lived too long with his own gray hair to call on the reflexes of that man who'd controlled his passel of children with a military discipline.

"Line up!"

The children would line up, with the father on one side, wearing his Sunday suit coat, and the mother on the other, wearing her Salamander shoes.

"In order, from tallest to smallest."

They jumped.

"Tanou, come over here."

He did.

"Stand up straight.

"Attention!

"Ready?

"Now smilies!"*

And then—click! The family photo was taken, the black-and-white one that hung in the living room of 26 Birch Avenue but that embarrassed Tanou because of his shorts and socks. ("My mother made me wear them.") And he could still see Ngountchou insisting, showing him a pair that were too big, saying, "Your father bought them yesterday at the central market," and then making him wear those awful socks.

"But they're not my size."

"Tanou," his mother said, and she reeled off his *ndaps* with that voice that always made him obey, even as he begged her to stop. "When are you going to grow up, huh?"

When he had to shop, his father always bought things in bulk, at the used clothes store if possible. His finds didn't always please everyone.

"It's just for the picture."

"Exactly!" Tanou shouted.

---

* Photographers in Cameroon always get the verb wrong; *sourissez* for *souriez* has become a Camfranglais idiom.

"Exactly, what?"

The photo would be there forever and ever.

"So what?"

"I'll be wearing those socks."

The son had been proved right. The photo, which they had gotten reframed at Jackson Photographers in Princeton, New Jersey, now adorned his own living room, although Ngountchou was no longer. Then he remembered another question his father would ask.

"Is this what they are teaching you in school?" he'd say, although his son was still only studying for the CEPE, the certificate of primary and elementary studies. "Ngountchou, come see what your child has done again."

Angry words flew.

"Do you ever think?

"Use your brain from time to time!" That's what Ngountchou had to say, before she knocked on the child's forehead and insulted him: "*Nsen mbaa mafi la*." As black as a *mafi*.

But he was no longer in elementary school, he already had his PhD! And they were no longer in Bangwa, but in the United States! No longer following paths lined with bamboo fences, but driving down Route 1, heading for Sears. Even a man who teaches white people knows absolutely nothing in the eyes of his Bamileke parents! Though the child may have grown, and may have even earned a diploma thanks to all the encouragement and bullying, he's still just as ignorant as the day he was born: "Seems like your diplomas are no good!"

Tanou tapped his fingers on the steering wheel.

"There are moments when it's good to talk, Papa."

"Even if you have nothing to say?"

"Yes, just to talk."

And so, he talked. First, he asked his father what he found amusing about Americans.

"*Tchip*," his father sucked his teeth.

Silence.

Then, "In a week, you'll be back in Cameroon."

"Yes."

"You'll be in Bangwa."

"Uh-huh."

"You'll see Marianne."

"Yes."

His father's silence was like a lash. If he'd shouted—*What do you want me to say? That you're a bastard, that you're not worth the trouble?*—Tanou would have felt better. Yet, he knew that those words would never come out of his father's mouth; he just sat there next to him, rubbing his hands and looking out the passenger-side window at the landscape flying by. He could have said, *I'm not a woman.* Tanou knew how much he missed his mother. Or even, *What do you want me to say? That Marthe is like Clara? That I'm no different from the deputy? Is that what you're waiting for?* For me to admit that I'm just a man, too?

That would be a step, at least, Papa.

But a step in what direction?

Where was Marianne, his sister, when these two men needed her? She was the one who, after each well-deserved spanking, would come with the broad smile of paternal reconciliation on her lips.

"Did Papa send you?"

"Don't cry."

There in the store, surrounded by the displays of shirts, pants, and shoes, all on sale because it was winter, he suddenly turned to his father and asked, "Papa, who was Nyamsi?"

"Nyamsi?"

"Yes."

His father smiled and traced symbols, arabesques you might say, in the air in front of him.

The translation of that telling silence:

The rhythm of a doctor's life is set by the shift schedule.

9

Mensa' discovered that there were people suffering more than she, when she arrived back in Bangangte. She had spent over a year in Yaounde and had seen her happiness bloom there, but her return showed her how much the village had changed, and her new day-to-day was stamped with the seal of boredom. To tell the truth, there was no village left at all; no more scent of grilled corn coming from hot smoky fires; no more little girls in braids clapping their hands and stomping their feet to the beat of a *mbang*, or dancing with abandon the steps of a *mvah* or a *nkwa* in dusty courtyards!* No more boys, wearing nothing but underpants, chasing after a metal hoop or pushing a toy car they'd made from bamboo. There was not one woman she met who didn't look sad. She walked through neighborhoods where nothing remained but broken corner posts, shattered windows, blackened remains of brick walls, and ashes. And yet her family home still stood, unharmed in the midst of the desolation. When she walked through the grove, past the *nfekang*, the peace tree, and stood in front of the veranda, her heart began to race.

Kouandiang's barks were at first the only sign of life, but, happily, her father soon came out from the living room. Nja Yonke' followed on his heels, tightening the knot of her *sandja* and adjusting her headscarf. The resigned look in her eyes did not escape Mensa', who was used to

* These informal dances were typical pastimes for young girls; the first combines rhythmic clapping and stomping, while in the two others, you are tossed in the air by a circle of friends.

seeing her with her head held high, as if trying with a show of nobility to negate the disaster all around. She had suddenly become a *village woman*. Mensa' hugged her parents. The dog jumped around, licking her fingers, legs, and feet.

"*Bi ke tchou nda gi?*" Pastor Tbongo asked. Aren't you coming into the house?

Ntchantchou Zacharie had stayed in his car, a Peugeot 404, a rather surprising move that didn't escape the mother, who knew well that man's pride.

"Tachene," Nja Yonke' insisted, "won't you come in?"

She spoke to him in French, because her son-in-law was in the car with his chauffeur and bodyguard. Nja Yonke' was so happy about her daughter's pregnancy, now visible beneath her *kaba*, that she tripped over her words.

"I have work to do. I'm very busy," Ntchantchou Zacharie replied.

That was certainly true. As soon as he got to Bangangte, he always had to forget about his "vacation in Yaounde."

Mensa' noticed that her father was in mourning.

"Tankongan," he said; the features on his face were drawn.

It took her a moment to remember Tankongan, the foreman who'd built the *Tchunda*, who had designed the walls of the crypt in traditional Bamum style; he and the pastor had met many times in their living room to discuss the project. How could she have forgotten that man with whom her father had built so much?

"He's dead," the pastor added.

"When?"

Nja Yonke', trying to bring the pastor back to a happier topic, brought up their daughter's pregnancy, pulling her flowing *kaba* to the side to reveal her belly.

"Was he sick?" Mensa' asked.

"I didn't want him to go to the camps," the pastor said. "Not to Penka Michel.* I didn't want him to go."

* One of the first resettlement camps; it grew into a whole village.

"*Zit camp-a?*" What camp?

Mensa' soon saw firsthand the houses of Bangangte reduced to ashes; she saw how the fire's passage had incinerated people and things. Tama''s words reminded her of the lives that had been extinguished; he pointed out ruins, roofs razed by the flames, blackened piles of all that remained of the burned-out lives, everything now soaked in mud from the rains.

"The Ndjong Mbap family lived here, do you remember?"

"This is where the shop was, did you forget?"

Of course she remembered, but she no longer dared to ask where the people had gone, because the answers were always the same:

"In Yaounde."

"In Douala."

"In Nkong."

And sometimes, "They're dead."

Back in the city, people said that everyone wanted to flee Bangangte, that parents were giving their daughters away in marriage without even asking for a dowry! "It's that serious!" There were those who laughed about it, saying, "The women over there are free!" Or, "They just give themselves away in marriage, *njo'o*! For free!" Yet what Bamileke likes the idea of free women? Let him raise his hand and be counted!

Suddenly, in the midst of the ruins, she recalled the image of Magni Sa's body, with Kouandiang licking her calcified skull. Mensa' also saw firsthand the misery of the camps her father was talking about. He went with her to visit Tankongan's family so she could find out more about the foreman's trial; she found them in a hut surrounded by barbed wire. She was stunned by the shelters made of woven mats. Tankongan's first wife, whose *ndap* was Mami Tong, was sitting in front of a shack, her flattened breasts hanging in the breeze as always; she was cooking some *bôn*, couscous, with one hand pressed to her left cheek while the other stirred around and around in the blackened pot. Her co-wives sat beside her, just as miserable, shelling peanuts or nursing an infant. Mami Tong stood up when she recognized Mensa'. She hugged her as if she'd found her own daughter, or a long-lost sister. Then she looked at her belly and hugged her again.

"How many months?" she asked.

"Four."

Her joyous explosion brought her co-wife Ntchankou' out from the bamboo shack; she was the same age as Mensa', with big wide hips, like so many women here. Her joy revealed the beauty hidden in the ruins and made the deputy's wife forget their destitution, although their shaved heads let all know of their recent loss. Children appeared. They seemed frightened by their mothers' ululations. They hid behind them. One of the kids, maybe six years old, was sucking on his finger; a tear had left a somber trace across his cheek. Given his swollen belly, you'd have thought he was pregnant, too.

"He's the little *passitou*, little Elie," said the kid's mother, Tankongan's third wife. "*Ou lakdii gi?*" Have you forgotten him?

The child had been named in honor of the pastor, Elie Tbongo, to acknowledge an act of kindness. Mensa' took the infant from its mother's arms.

"Elie's my next-to-youngest," the mother added. "I gave birth in the camp, but that was after *he'd* left us."

She pressed her hand to her cheek and tears welled up in her eyes. Mensa' hugged her close; she was overwhelmed, it felt like she was cuddling her own sister.

"The government put us all here," the woman went on. "The French put us here. They did it. They say the Maquisards won't kill us if we're here. But then, who killed my husband?"

She wiped her eyes with the edge of her pagne.

"*Jou' a bou ben zui Tankongan-a?*" Aren't they the ones who killed Tankongan?

"*Me tchoup-a mbe ke?*" Mensa' asked, her eyes looking all around, trying to find some support. What can I say?

Later she'd learn that Tankongan had been killed defending his wives. The militia had come to take him away one day, "even though he'd already confessed that he had no more connections with his Maquisard brothers."

"*Ke ghe mba pitié mbang lou ke.*" They had no pity even though he limped.

"*Ne ne ne.*"

They took him away, after ransacking the house, raping his wives, and setting fire to his fields. Who was responsible for all that hatred? Mensa' didn't dare ask because, as she gazed at the infant in her arms, her eyes were filled with horror. Tankongan's wife saw Jean Nono behind all these evil plots, but she would say no more than that. Mensa' would learn the details of the *cadi* only much later. That day her father just said that, were it not for his position in the church, he would have had to make a public confession, too, and then he and his "old wife" would have certainly been sent to the camp as well.

"What was there to confess?" she asked.

The story of the Tbongos unfolded before her

"It's the Saras, the *mafis*, who come to take people away," her father said, "the Chadians," he added in French. "You know they're the tirailleurs, right? *Bou ben nse', ou nya ke ghe jou ze bou ko la, mba boua' labou.** They're the ones who behead people," he went on, closing his eyes. "They do that because they're not from Cameroon."

Waving his grief-stricken, powerless hands, he showed her how wide the violence that took his friend's life had spread.

"A Cameroonian could not do that." That was the first time his daughter had seen him really angry.

"You can't run from your brothers and sisters!"

"It's your brother who kills you"—that's what one voice said. It belonged to a tall thin woman, whose child, just as skinny, was sucking noisily on her flattened breast like a cannibal.

"They say that when the war is over, we can go back home."

"When will the war end?"

"What home?"

"They set fire to everything, didn't they?"

* "They come and whip you when you don't do what they want."

"They went from house to house, spreading the fire to each roof."

"Even sheet metal burns."

"They pour gasoline in the courtyard and then set it on fire. It all burns."

"Too bad for whoever hasn't already fled from his home."

"The villages are all gone!"

"Here's my child," one woman said, pointing to a kid. "He was just a baby when we came here."

"People are already starting to build houses with bricks," a man added.

Some people found that amusing.

As they walked by shacks where dozens of people were packed in, men and women came out to greet Pastor Tbongo and his daughter. The word *Passitou* was carried from courtyard to courtyard, and soon there was a whole crowd in front of them. Women who exclaimed over Mensa''s pregnancy, and men who shook the pastor's hand, shivering as they told him bits and pieces of the tragedy that had befallen them. Several people begged Mensa' to ask her husband to help them. "Are we in a prison camp?" they asked. Their eyes were transformed into pleas that pursued Mensa' long afterward.

She came out of that visit with her heart in knots, filled with anger at those responsible. "All those wasted lives!" she murmured. "All those lives shot down!" Mostly she grumbled about her husband: "He did this." And she took in all those thousands of eyes begging her to speak to *Monsieur le Député*. In her mind, he was as small as the soul within him; *The bastard! The pig!* she thought. She forgot that Mbeng was the subprefect for Bazou and that he was also responsible for everything that was happening.

How can a human being do this to his own brothers? I've never seen such a malicious man!

In fact, it was systematic, well planned and methodical, and, as she said, put into action "by minds working for evil." She felt dizzy, and that's when Mme Ngapeth's words came back to her. "The weight! The weight!" Fam became the name she used for her husband. Fam, like the Devil.

The suffering of all those people gave Mensa' even more reasons to think of Mbeng as her savior. She remembered that old Banoumga* woman in the market who was offended by all her young male neighbors telling tales of their *litique*† exploits, and so addressed the woman next to her in French, saying, "*Obeye*, do you remember Makeki?‡ He told people I'd become a whore in Douala, remember? Then, one day he told those same friends—the ones he'd been bad-mouthing me to—that he was the one *licking my ass*, do you believe it?" The scandal of her words made the young men jump. They turned toward her, but swallowed their insults, embarrassed at the sight of all of her wrinkles. She went on. The young men plugged their ears. She didn't stop, but kept repeating the phrase "licking my ass," and saying it in the most serious tone. Soon the loudmouth men began begging her to stop with her story, to tone down her crazy talk.

If the wife of Deputy Ntchantchou Zacharie had told her story, could she have elicited some compassion from those eyes staring daggers at her? Could she have found one understanding ear among those who would be left dumbstruck by the confession of her mistake, if only she told them how much she hated her husband? Who would be her friend? She hadn't told Mbeng that she was pregnant. Yet he'd been telling her lately to leave her husband, to move into his pied-à-terre; one day he went on and on about how much more wonderful that would make their life. He called it "coming out of the Maquis"—well aware of the irony carried by that word; he also spoke of "rallying." Because they had

---

* A Bangangte dialectal group.

† *Litique*, a Camfranglais term for sexual, a calque on the French *lit*, or bed.

‡ *Obeye* means "my friend," in Banoumga pidgin, while "Makeki" is the name the Bangangte use for the "Everyman" in all their dirty stories.

started referring to their parallel life, and more specifically the house in Nlongkak, as "the Maquis."

I'm joining the Maquis, Mensa' would say to herself, as she crossed Yaounde on bicycle, urged on by the image of the lover who was waiting for her, pacing back and forth in the living room, excited by the ardent promise of sex. He had stopped carrying her into the bedroom, sometimes it was there on the living room rug, or even in the dining room, that he undressed her, that he made love to her.

"Stay with me, Ambeng," he said.

When he didn't see her for two days, Mbeng grew impatient. Yet he didn't go knock on her door, because he saw her husband's car parked in the courtyard. He was surprised that the deputy had returned to Yaounde after only two days away, but he quickly understood. He learned that Ntchantchou Zacharie had taken his wife back to Bangangte.

Mbeng knew that it would be dangerous to go find his love in that small town where everyone knew each other, and especially the deputy's wife. Still, he scribbled a note to her and addressed it to "Deputy Ntchantchou Zacharie, from the subprefect of Bazou." He wanted his chauffeur to give it to Mensa', but then he realized what a crazy plan that was.

I have to find some way, he told himself.

And then added, *It's not that I'm lacking courage!*

Another time, he drove past the family house and saw her sitting on the porch, shelling pistachios and chatting with her mother. His chauffeur and guard were with him then. He wanted to stop, but he realized that the look on her face would give away to her mother the secret of their Maquis. *Let's imagine*, he said to himself, *that her face blanches with happiness, that she unconsciously reveals her love, right in front of her family!* Or what if—and this thought frightened him—she looked at him coldly and pretended not to know him, *like a whore who happens to see one of her clients unexpectedly, while she's taking her children to school.*

Why did I think "whore"? he wondered, reproaching himself for thinking of his lover in those terms. *I don't pay her, after all!*

And yet, society—"the Bamilekes," he said—would think of her in those terms, as a whore. For the first time Mbeng really thought about

Mensa' as Bamileke, and that thought horrified him, because he felt the oppression that came along with it, and the chains it placed on their feelings and their relationship.

The freedom that Yaounde had given to Mensa', the latitude Ongola gave their love—he knew that would be impossible to find in her hometown. If in the capital they could use a foreign language to bind them together, here, Bangangte, would impose its own rules. Never had he hated that town more; now a ghost town, it took away all the places where he might have met Mensa'. Putting the people in resettlement camps had asphyxiated their love.

Things can't go on like this, he said to himself.

He came up with elaborate plots, wrote novels that went like this: He would go to church in Mfetoum* and, by chance, meet her as they were leaving. He'd tip his subprefect's cap and say, "Hello, *Madam Federal Deputy*!" And then, when everyone was talking about the civil war that was ravaging Bamileke land, he'd whisper in her ear, "My *chérie*, my sweet, can we screw tonight?" But he quickly forgot that scenario, because just then he remembered the day he'd started to call her his wife.

"You are my real husband," she'd said that day, "you are my husband, you know."

"And you, *Madame Mbeng*," he'd replied, "you are my wife.

"I trust you," he said.

"Me, too."

"Totally."

Totally? *Bebela*. His father certainly never would have said that word to one of his wives. "Don't ever entrust all of your treasure to just one woman."

"Totally."

"My marriage to Ntchantchou Zacharie was a mistake," Mensa' went on. "But you, my husband, you're the one I love."

And she shaved his testicles just as he, in turn, shaved her pubic hair.

"And I love you, too, Mensa'."

---

* A neighborhood in Bangangte.

Never had he imagined that she could say those words—"*Je t'aime*"—only to a man in French, and what's more, only in a town other than Bangangte, where she was a foreigner: Yaounde! He remembered what she'd said to him the day they'd made love for the first time, at his house; she had insisted on knowing whether the house they were in belonged to his father. She'd told him that the Bangangte believed that screwing in your father's house would "dry up a girl's vagina." He'd laughed at that tale, but was also surprised that she, a married woman, still believed it.

How old traditions die hard among those people, he'd thought.

"Happily, I am not Bamileke," he'd said to her, quite amused, then took her in his arms.

"Happily?" she asked; she'd given an uncomfortable, embarrassed little laugh, whereas his laughter shook his whole body.

He'd moved on to a different topic.

Now he imagined novels where she would come knock at the door of his office, dressed in her most beautiful dress, covered in lace, just as he liked, a broad yellow hat on her head.

"Hello, *Monsieur le Sous-Préfet*," she'd say. "May I speak to you for a moment?"

"But of course, *Madame Beauté*! Of course!"

He'd close his files about the Maquisards and the fake Maquisards, about the resettlement camps and severed heads.

"Now fuck me," she'd say. "Fuck me!"

But he shut that novel out of his mind, because it seemed absurd. Why would she come knock on his door if she had already stopped coming to their "Maquis"? Still, he woke up the next morning hot, covered in sweat, and horny, because in his dreams her sex had been right in front of his face. The sugary sweet of her vagina stayed with him the whole day. There were moments when his passion made him lose his mind. Dressed in his khaki uniform, he'd tighten a black bulletproof vest around his chest, hide his head under his military cap, and drive through Bazou like a man possessed. He'd circle Bangangte and climb the hills of Bangwa, sitting in the back of his black Peugeot 404, his left hand thrust deep in his pocket, trying to bring his *bangala* back into line. His love had been locked away in a Maquis in Yaounde and now, like a bewitching perfume, had suddenly dissipated in Bangangte.

Was it witchcraft?

Like a dog on the prowl, he circled the neighborhood where *his wife* was being held captive by her legitimate husband, intoxicated by the solitude imposed upon him. He circled, and circled, but never once defied the ministerial order, which stipulated that *on administrative tours one must always be accompanied by a chauffeur and at least one armed guard.*

10

WHAT DO THE BAMILEKES WANT?

A civil war is always complicated, and La Presse du Cameroun *did nothing* at all to make it comprehensible.* How easy it would be if the answer were as clear-cut as Blacks against whites, terrorists against the French, Betis against Bamilekes, Anglos against Francos, or, what else? Muslims against Christians, perhaps? Mensa' just wanted to understand the workings of this whirling reality that had brought her crashing back to earth. Had anyone explained the steep paths that led from Tankongan's shivering confession during the *cadi* to the story of the Extraordinary Villager or Ernest Ouandié, she would have thought about the pistachios she had to shell and pressed a hand to her temple, too. More as a distraction than because she was actually collecting the stories told to her, she went into the camps that her husband had built, studying the interiors of the shacks, the remains of people's lives, and always promising to help.

She thought about the Capable Women and the *tontines* they organized for charity. *If I let Mme Ngapeth or maybe Mme Nki'tcha know, that could make a big difference in the lives of many refugees*, she said to herself. She wanted to be organized about it. *For example, I could focus on how*

* It's interesting that in 2017 this was again the major headline of *Jeune Afrique*, a pan-African magazine based in Paris ("Cameroon: Que veulent (vraiment) les Bamilékés?" by Clarisse Juompan-Yakam, *Jeune Afrique*, April 12, 2017, https://www.jeuneafrique.com/mag/424038/politique/cameroun-que-veulent-vraiment-les-bamilekes/).

women were suffering. But she hesitated before the unfathomable depth of the job ahead. *No, the children. Children are the real victims.* Compassion is an ineffectual balm for someone who suffers and who understands the sources of their misery as well as solutions for it. But doing nothing may just kill you.

"So, what are you going to do there?" Tama' asked her. "You're going to borrow other people's troubles?"

"Minister Nkwayim asked that we build a prison," Ntchantchou Zacharie announced to her one day.

He was rubbing his hands at the thought of this new endeavor, happy at the thought of the money he would get by rigging the bidding for the work.

"Too bad it's going to be in Bazou!" he'd added, shaking his head.

But he didn't stop there.

"That *Mbeng* has done it to me again!"

He pronounced the name Mbeng with all the hatred a man could muster. The only thing that soothed her husband was the idea of making money. She knew he'd walk over cadavers and smirk if he could grow his investments—adding to his bookstore, coffee factory, gas station—by using unfair laws for his own gain. Taking her to her parents' so that she give birth back in the village amounted to a divorce. When he came by the house, he never went into the living room. It was in the courtyard that he talked to her, bringing her the traditional ration of foodstuffs given to wives, and always telling Nja Yonke' that he'd come back "sometime soon" to share a meal with them. Then he'd head back alone to what ought to have been their family home, in Badiangseu.*

Nja Yonke' wasn't fooled. The old woman had seen many incomprehensible things happen in the village these past years, but she saw through the dirty tricks of a man who was avoiding his pregnant wife. Why? she wondered. But Mensa' was evasive, always changing the subject. The pastor didn't complain about his son-in-law's newfound "forgetfulness"—he used to bring him packs of cigarettes from Yaounde, one of the

* A neighborhood that borders on Bangwa.

pastor's few luxuries. He just went back to his usual tobacco, to his pipe, and didn't make a fuss about it.

"*Ntcha ke' be*,"* Mensa' said reassuringly.

Asking Ntchantchou Zacharie to take her to visit some of the resettlement camps was a way for her to get out of the prison she'd been locked in. Mme Ngapeth's words showed her the path forward: "Suffering doesn't make you more sympathetic, just more vulnerable," she remembered her saying. "Action is the only way out of the vicious cycle of self-flagellation." And she could see her mentor clapping her hands and repeating the call to action in Camfranglais, "*Actons! Actons! Actons!*"

She went to see Mademoiselle Birgitte at her orphanage. The Norwegian woman hadn't left. The troubles had just bound her all the more tightly to the shattered lives of families on the High Plateau. Orphans were born almost every day. It wasn't difficult for Mensa' to take her sister's former place and become the assistant of that woman, who was now seen as a saint. It was in the children's courtyard, surrounded by their tears and laughter, in the smell of their excrement, that she began to make a new life for herself in Bangangte. Cries from the newborns now dictated her every step, setting the rhythm for her pace, even if she had to stop to catch her breath as she walked up Badiangseu Hill, her mind open to the echo from the far-off cliffs. Mademoiselle Birgitte let her know what the whites thought about the civil war: "She opened my eyes to the reality of this world," she often said. All she had to do was to listen. She'd sit on a rock, breathing in and out. All she had to do was listen to what the wind had to say.

"Just don't get involved," she heard.

Who said that? She looked around and saw a group of whites, those who'd come around several times before and seemed quite confident.

"That's what the UN is for."

"The UN was already in Cameroon, until 1960," a white man was saying. "Have you forgotten that, dear madam?"

"And what about what happened in Congo!"

---

* "There's no problem," a typically Bangangte dismissal.

"What did happen in Congo?"

"Oh, that bullshit with Patrice Lumumba! It makes me puke just thinking about it."

"Back then, I was a missionary in Katanga."

"In Katanga?"

"Yes, madam. I lived through it all firsthand. You want me to tell you about it?"

"No, thank you."

"That's why I say, let them sort out their problems on their own."

"They're not children anymore, come on!"

"They are independent!"

"In-de-pen-dent!"

"Aren't they?"

"France is behind all of this. France organized the Bamileke genocide. It's her!"

"Just like Belgium."

"Who?"

"Fraaance, I'm telling you."

Are they already normalizing everyone's suffering? Mensa' wondered.

Spending her days at Mademoiselle Birgitte's was the only activity her husband allowed her, and even then, each time she went to the Norwegian's, she had to have Tama' go with her. Ntchantchou Zacharie found every pretext he could to keep her under his thumb. How long would this go on?

Yet it hadn't taken long for Mbeng to find out where his Dulcinea was spending her days. For a starving heart like his, Bangangte is just a small village, and Bangwa his neighborhood. Besides, his profession gave him a freedom of movement that he could exploit for his passion. *The goat grazes where she's 'tached*, he thought.* Nothing could be done to keep that

---

* A schoolteacher would have corrected him: *attached*, ignoring the common Camfranglais joke, mimicking the typically clipped Bamileke pronunciation.

subprefect in line, now that he'd tasted the Bangangte taro sauce, seasoned and stirred as it should be; from then on, he had nothing but pistachios on his kepi-covered mind.* One might have said that, from danger to prohibition, everything was conspiring to thwart his pleasure.

An identical obsession had taken over Mensa''s heart. The energy she was putting into her new job was just a way to compensate for his absence, a strategy to quiet her fevered body, which sometimes woke her in the middle of the night with a dream where she was being torn limb from limb, and that led her to touch her breasts, massage her sex, and cry because she was alone. She counted the number of people she'd helped, but in truth, what she was counting were the days of their separation, the days since she'd last seen her lover: the measurements of that love that had become a silent torture. Surprisingly, her efforts to distract her body allowed her to focus her mind, to put all her energy into measuring the precise quantity of potassium permanganate needed to clean a wound, or to listening to the unbelievable story of someone's escape from a military raid. She'd use her scarf to wipe the beads of sweat from her brow and her cheeks, while her body, her whole body was concentrated on completing a task for which she wasn't even paid! She learned the true value of giving one's time.

"Hey," a woman said to her, "you should rest a little, shouldn't you, mama?"

But Mensa' didn't listen to her; her head tilted to the left, she kept scrubbing a pot, scrubbing and scrubbing.

"There's no end to work."

Mensa' had no ears to listen; she saw only the job before her, which was important because it silenced the thumping of her heart.

"It will still be there tomorrow, won't it, my sister?"

But she needed to do everything right then, in that sublime moment when pain and pleasure commingled.

"This isn't *njokmassi*, you know."

"Volunteering is volunteering!" people said.

---

* As we've said before, *pistachios* are a symbol for female genitalia, and obviously, subprefects should have thoughts of nothing but the Cameroonian Constitution under their kepi!

She listened only to her soul.

The children around her cried, jumped, played—the mirror image of the active child in her belly who responded to their excitement with his own, flooding Mensa''s body with pulsations she could not control. Sometimes she needed to stop, open her mouth wide, and breathe, in and out, just to calm her racing heart. But then she just threw herself even more determinedly into her work. Sometimes she'd stop for a drink of water. Never had *that odorless and colorless liquid* dripping on her feet seemed like such a powerful remedy as when she was gulping down those mouthfuls; it flowed through her veins, irrigating her soul, and with tremors and throbs, it soaked between her legs. Her head spinning, she'd go back to Mademoiselle Birgitte's living room and collapse on the couch, breathing in and out, wiping the sweat from her neck, her arms, her underarms, her entire body.

Tama' would find her there at nightfall, when he came to bring her home after work.

"I'm going to stay here tonight," Mensa' said one evening, and he didn't insist; he could see the exhaustion on his sister's face.

"*Mbat li, mba di*. It's the hill, right?"

She didn't need to say anything more.

That's how Mensa' started spending her nights at the orphanage where Ngountchou had been the assistant before. No one at the house at Bangangte saw any problem with that.

"You can sleep here," Mademoiselle Birgitte said, and showed her her own bed, covered with a flowing mosquito net.

"No, that's your bed," Mensa' said with a laugh, "if you sleep in the *other room*, the mosquitoes will kill you."

"Are you sure?"

"Yes."

The "other room" was the one for her assistant, a small bit of room that had been enough for Ngountchou, but where the Norwegian had trouble imagining the wife of the federal deputy Ntchantchou Zacharie would sleep. But that's where she was when, one night soon after, someone knocked on the window, calling out in a voice that quickly set Mensa''s whole body atingle, as if she'd just climbed Mount Cameroon, as if she'd gulped down not just a goblet full, but all the water in the Maheshou River.

"Mbeng," said the voice. "Mensa', it's me."

The woman rose, found a match, and lit the oil lamp, but then quickly put it out and stood there in the dark, breathing in and out, and trembling.

"It's me," the voice insisted. "Mbeng."

It wasn't the window or even the door that Mensa' opened, but her heart, her body. The subprefect's wanderings had left him so aroused that, once he saw her in her sleeping pagne, he didn't take the time to say one more word to Mensa'. His lips quickly closed her mouth, his hands slid over her sweat-drenched body, while Mensa', returning to the pattern set during their affair, led him, moving backward, step-by-step, to the bed, where she sat down, then lay down, grasping on to his head, which she led, as she had so often in her dreams, beneath her belly, now visibly round, to the temple she had raised in his honor a hundred times before, that she had prepared for him a thousand times or more, had anointed for him with oil a million times, and offered to him a billion times, and where, on her mons veneris, he discovered a soft tuft of new-grown hair. Then the subprefect began a conversation with his child, while its mother, who had so longed for this, closed her eyes and reached with her hands for something to hold on to, the sides of the bed at first and then the wall where shadows played, and then finally Mbeng's head. She wrapped her arms around his head, then around his shoulders, and his hips, urging him along until he penetrated her.

"This is my first time," he said, gasping.

"What?" the woman replied, panting in and out.

The man was smiling in the darkness.

"Making love to a pregnant woman."

"I hope it won't be the last time," said Mensa'.

They came together more than a dozen times that night, in a number of gymnastic positions imposed by the woman's belly. One position led to another, and their dance continued joyfully until they heard a rooster's cry in the distance. Mensa' felt like she'd swallowed a whole sea of waves.

"I have to go to work," Mbeng said.

As he dressed in the early morning light, Mensa' realized he'd been wearing his uniform, with stripes on his shoulders. She dozed lazily in the bed, stretching out and pulling the covers up under her chin, which left her toes peeking out below.

"*Monsieur le Sous-Préfet*," she said, pointing at his hat, "today I will rest."

He didn't put his cap on, but when he carefully tightened the bulletproof vest around his chest, she snapped awake.

Mensa' was with her husband in Mademoiselle Birgitte's courtyard when Tama' announced the terrifying news.

"Nsoup,"* he said, pale and trembling, "they found the subprefect dead in the bush over there."

"What?" was all the deputy said.

Next to him, his wife screamed and collapsed into his arms.

When they found his car in a ditch, riddled with bullets, with his chauffeur slumped over the steering wheel with a hole in his neck, his bodyguard collapsed on the seat, and he himself sitting in the back, his military cap still on his head but his face torn to shreds, as if chewed off by a beast, everyone was scandalized, but no one blamed him for having disobeyed orders. No one. Mbeng was going to a work meeting with the mayor of Bazou and, people learned, he had taken the Bangangte road "because he had things to finalize with Deputy Ntchantchou Zacharie." His bulletproof vest was still intact, pulled snug over his uniform.

Yet the crime was surprising and the Sinistrés had left no mark: no drawing of boots or a hammer, even if his execution did look, point by point, like one of those ambushes that had brought down so many officials in Bamileke land recently. Ntchantchou Zacharie stamped these three cadavers as the work of the Maquisards, and everyone believed

* An honorific title.

him, even if they also recalled that the subprefect hadn't been there on the day of the public confession.

Ngountchou learned that Nithap was alive and staying in Bangangte. She received a letter from her father written in Bagam script. Very few people could have read it, which was for them a blessing. The letter from Elie Tbongo weaved its way through the civil war without awakening any suspicions. His daughter received it in Yaounde, trembling as she read it. Only its signature, which included the symbol for *Tchunda*, convinced her it was true. It had been three years already since she'd had any news of Nithap. She had stopped waiting. Instead, she had filled her heart with resentment, jealous of her younger sister who had passed her by, and was even pregnant already.

Ngountchou was even more frightened at the idea of returning to her parents' home than of going back to the war. In her silent acceptance of humiliation, she had discovered the other side of love. She was living in Mokolo, the Bangangte neighborhood in the capital, with a cousin who was a prostitute. In the miasmas of those stunted houses and cancerous courtyards, she opened herself up to the wonders of her reawakened breast, to the resurrection of her body. She put the letter to her lips, but couldn't keep tears from flowing down her cheeks. She read the words aloud, speaking to fill the absence that had until then been filled with her resentment:

The toad who does not walk will have nothing big.

Ngountchou read her father's phrases hesitatingly. She paused over each symbol. The letter was a trail of crab tracks, and its promise enchanted her:

He who fled has now come home. The horse is back in its stall.

There are instants of happiness that bring a family back together, and this was one. She wiped her tears. Each word, each symbol, brought her comfort:

My dear—be happy at this revelation that shows us that hope is our condition. Now you will stand like a tree in the courtyard, you will sleep as long as you like, everyone will encourage you to rest, because, like your father, happy you are. The clothes you will make, the walking cane, the arrow, will be looked upon with envy. My dear, the ground where you will sit will tell you that all is well, the house has found he who was missing. The father—O, Ngountchou—and the chief can no longer contain themselves before your happiness.

When she finished deciphering these symbols, she folded the letter in quarters, pressed it to her breast, and gazed out onto the street with eyes filled with happiness.

"He is alive," she said.

"Who?" asked the cousin.

That was a useless question. She didn't reply. It was as if the past months, the years of suffering just evaporated. She rose and walked across the living room, and then down the paths of the neighborhood. The music of her soul resounded within her. She could also hear the whimpering of an infant, the one who'd always been waiting in her belly to be conceived, and who was lost each month in a sea of blood. Then she heard the moaning of a woman in orgasm. The letter had made her into *a wife*, wresting her from that house of fornication that each night moved her further from her destiny.

Ngountchou had opened up a sewing shop, Chez Singer; that's where she spent her days. The work allowed her to chase away the demons from her life, which she considered failed. She had sewn dresses for her sister several times, but that was before Mensa' had discovered ready-made clothes and Parisian couture. Sewing, creating something beautiful for the women she dressed, made her happy, but nothing had captivated her soul as much as the symbols her father had written on a piece of paper. She stared at those arabesques, symbols of her joy, and then pressed them again to her breast, smiling, because it had been worth the wait.

It was in the *Tchunda* that Ngountchou met Nithap again. She arrived at night and, instead of stopping at her parents' home, followed the well-worn path. And there, from the shadows of a window, she heard the man's voice, that voice she knew by heart, because she had heard it in her dreams for so long.

"Ngountchou," Nithap said.

That one word made her tremble, reawakened her body.

"Tatumba, is it you?"

Then she stood for a long moment in the crypt's courtyard, shivering, unable to believe it was true. Nithap came to her.

"It is me," he said, "don't you recognize me?"

She nodded but did not move. Nithap laughed. Dressed like a peasant, he had become someone unfamiliar. That *sandja* that hung down from his hips, his bare chest, the biceps on his arms—he'd grown strong in those three years. He hugged her tight.

Ngountchou's heart was beating wildly. He led her to a room inside. The Sinistrés let them have a moment alone. Many had their wives with them, or had taken a new wife in the bush, but there were a number of others who had also left their families behind.

"You are alive," Ngountchou repeated, as if trying to convince herself.

"And you, too."

They just stood there for a long time, holding hands and telling each other everything that they'd lived through until that moment.

"If you knew," Nithap said.

Ngountchou paused now and again to wipe away a tear. The words of this book are the words of brothers and sisters, of cousins who, years later, gathered in a living room to mourn and bury this woman, whom we see here coming back to life. The words of this book are Nithap's story, for he will know how to compose a symphony about the woman who was to become his wife. They are summed up by a status Bagam posted on Facebook, after he discovered the pastor's letter, and shared it on his page, with the title "*Nkoni! Nkoni!*" Love.

"Why are you crying?" Nithap asked. "I'm here now."

"Because I'm happy," Ngountchou answered. "I'm happy that you are *really* back."

"Did you doubt me?"

"Never!"

"Ngountchou," Nithap said, "we couldn't just go on living, ignoring that people were dying all around us."

His words were almost a supplication.

"You have always lived like that," she answered. "You're a doctor."

"But this is different," he said, looking at the moon moving swiftly across the sky. "Our happiness wasn't enough to keep us together in a *sea of blood*. It was impossible."

Nithap realized the violence of his words when he saw the tears on Ngountchou's face. She didn't talk to him of the sea of blood that flowed from her body each month, proof of her interrupted marriage, of his absence! She lowered her eyes, as if offering a silent and suddenly useless reproach. She didn't talk to him of the pain in her belly, the ache born of his unending absence, which transformed into little drops of envy whenever she saw Mensa', into seeds of avarice in the face of her little sister's success, and which finally grew into flowers of spite on that fateful day. When Ngountchou, standing in the suffocating kitchen, heard her sister's husband explode with joy at the news he would be a father, come give her orders, as if she were her younger sister's slave, and then head back to the living room to talk about giving birth in Paris, her evil heart caused her to curse her failed life. With trembling hands, she wrote a treacherous note that she slipped into Deputy Ntchantchou Zacharie's Peugeot.

Puppet husband
Wife screwed behind the back
of the neocolonial state
by a disrespectful colleague.
Sinistré.

"I'm so sorry," Nithap said, "this war has changed us all."

Ngountchou's chest rose and fell.

"But it has no right to destroy us. Nor to turn us into monsters."

"I'm not a monster," he answered.

"I know, Tatumba. *But what about me?*"

He wasn't listening, he didn't hear the start of her wail, he just closed her mouth, *lock nshou*.

"I don't kill, I cure."

"I know."

"You are lucky that you lived through the war with your family. At home with your father, and your sister. It's really fortunate." He paused. "I know that no one told you what happened in Foumbot, or in N'lohe, or Tombel."

Nithap wanted to say *the pogroms*, but fell silent, because he suddenly thought of Clara.

"I know that no one told you about the napalm they used against us, the fire that fell from the sky." He laughed as if he were mad. "The sky suddenly on fire, everything burning. The mountain that turns into a volcano, although there's no mouth; I saw that on Mount Kupe. The bush that starts to burn, although we're in the forest. The pigs and dogs who feed on cadavers. We barely escaped with our lives." He said *we* out of modesty. "No one told you about the towns that were razed, the villages sacked, the skulls in the streams. No one told you about the Chadians who signed up and were brought here as tirailleurs. The *mafis*. And

I'm sure no one told you about *France*, which does all the dirty work in Cameroon for Ahidjo."

He clenched his teeth.

"You are really back," she said, as if everything he had just said was less important than his return.

Her story was different, but she didn't tell him about the spiral of waiting, the cycle of depression and madness. She didn't talk about France, or Mount Kupe, but about Mademoiselle Birgitte who had saved her life, about the sacking of the village and her departure for Yaounde to live with her sister, about her life in the city. She looked at him with tears flowing from her eyes. She knew he wouldn't understand that she hadn't been living "safe and warm." She wiped her cheeks and told him that she had been brave, but she didn't tell him about her *sea of blood*, and just kept caressing his hand to calm his anger. "Yes, I like Yaounde. Remember, I always said I wanted to go to the city."

She told him she had never lost hope that he was alive, but didn't add that she hadn't buried a banana tree, as people customarily did to put a dream to rest.

"I became a seamstress!"

"I know you'd been wanting to go to Yaounde for a long time," he teased her.

"At least they don't have troubles there, like they do in Douala," she said, a smile spreading across her lips. "Papa told you about Tama', didn't he?"

He and the pastor had talked of other things, Nithap admitted. *Oh, men!* Ngountchou thought.

"Tama' has really grown up!" she said. "You should see him, you'll hardly recognize him."

She laughed.

Many young people had been taken in by families, but this was different. Nithap told her that Tama''s parents were probably dead.

"I saw them in N'lohe," he said, "before the *pogrom*."

He said the word *pogrom*, and shuddered.

"Tama''s home is with us," she answered. "We're his family."

"Bamileke values," he said.

"Papa's house is a safe harbor!" she insisted. "Like this crypt. We learned how to hide in the belly of the panther. That's why we can be together tonight."

"But we're surrounded by suffering," Nithap said, "the suffering of Bamileke land. The campaign isn't taking place just on the battlefront anymore. They're waging war against an idea. In combat, there are rules and laws. But here, no, there's just a brutal reality, and the only law is silence. We are in the middle of a civil war. And here, the campaign is being waged against a whole people. The campaign is waged against the Bamilekes. The pogroms are waged against a specific group. The pogroms are waged against the Bamilekes, and the mass killings are perpetrated with the help of government soldiers. They are perpetrated against the Bamilekes. It's planned and put into action. It is a *genocide*, plain and simple."

Alas, he couldn't show Ngountchou the damning calendar he had drawn to fix in his mind the relentless criminal spiral that had swept up Bamileke land, ensnaring it in madness. He would never be able to show anyone that damning chronogram, leaving his own history bereft of the evidence needed to prove it, for he lost the trail of its most telling witness, Clara. Yet he insisted on the word *genocide*, punctuating it with a long moment of silence, as if trying to curb the anger that had built up during those years of wandering through the elephant grass, shivering in death-filled shacks, and seeking the shelter of a barren womb.

"Why did you come, Ngountchou?" Nithap suddenly asked, now standing in the shadows behind the woman. "Why?"

"To see you," she replied, as her shoulders slunk down, a reflex born of the shame that led her to hide when she undressed. "To be with you, to stay in the Maquis with you."

She caught herself before she said the words *Because I love you, Tatumba*. Even then censured by convention, by pure Medumba convention.

"*I am your wife*," she said in a rush. "Don't you remember?"

"Look at the danger you're putting yourself in." He took her in his arms.

"We are all Sinistrés," she said, placing her hands on his. *"All of us."*

That word echoed in his soul, the echo of a terrible and distant history, composed of many actions they had each taken and about which they kept silent.

"All of us."

The only sounds were those of nocturnal birds. He helped her take off her shirt, her bra, and placed her clothes on the ground beside them. He spoke quietly into the crook of her neck as he lowered her skirt. Nithap stopped asking questions when he felt her scarred hips beneath his fingers, her bushy pubis, and soon the warmth of her sex enveloping his finger. He had left a young girl, but the one he had found and saw then was a woman. He wanted to ask her if there had been another, but stopped. Did he suspect that she, too, had a bloody story to tell? He had first loved her when she was surrounded by children, and now she was there, in the *Tchunda* that others had left to protect their intimacy, this woman who had spread her thighs and rubbed oil on her vagina month after month, waiting for him. That night, when she wrapped herself around his body, when in her belly she felt no longer a finger but his sex, she said, *"I want a child!"*

The next day, Ngountchou came back to the *Tchunda*, dressed like a village woman, a hoe balanced on her head. Tama' was walking in front of her, carrying a pot of *koki* with bananas that she had made for Nithap and the *tsuitsuis*. She made that trek through the bush several more times, telling the men—who could no longer bear their daily rations of guavas and raffia weevil grubs, and who were entranced by the scent of her dishes—how she'd dodged the militia by hiding behind burned tree trunks.

"I just crouched down, like I was peeing," she said.

Nithap said nothing, at once horrified and amazed by the example of courage she set for his young nephew. He sometimes watched them coming, the young man walking ahead, each with a pot on their head.

He's becoming a man, he said to himself.

"I've been covering my behind with a pagne," Ngountchou told him. "The militia didn't dare touch me. They're local boys. They know us. They know I'm the pastor's daughter. And that Tama' is our son."

She burst out laughing.

"They *couldn't* touch us!" she said, stressing the *couldn't*; the materialization of her matrimonial dream had given her courage she didn't know she had. "*Bou lou ke fit!*" They couldn't.

"You're going to stop me from going to the fields?"

How could they do that? The army had no other way of feeding the Bangangte than to let the women continue farming as they had for centuries.

Another time she wrapped a scarf around her head as if it were her *nja*:* "Even the *mafis* are afraid to touch someone else's woman," she said.

A woman in love is ready to do anything, and the twists and turns of her time waiting had emboldened Ngountchou's heart. Courage isn't passed down through blood, but is born of the promise of happiness to come: *I have a husband! I have a husband!*

"*Boulou' courage-a ya?*" she asked. Where will they find the courage?

"*Yam mejou*," Nithap replied, full of admiration. "My dear thing. *Yam nkoni*, my love."

"*Yam ndjou*, my husband," she answered.

Nithap didn't find it funny that his wife was capable of facing bayonets for him, and even death—for one day she arrived shivering and pale. She had seen a cadaver lying alongside the path, a *mafi*'s body with head and sex cut off. She pictured her husband using his skills on that soldier's body, severing his essential parts. But even then, she didn't lose heart. No, her fertile imagination quickly transformed him into the saint the *tsuitsuis* needed, that Bamileke land needed.

The Toungou valley was a sanctuary that enchanted her mind. Sleeping in her husband's arms, waking up with the sunlight as the spar-

---

* A scarf that symbolizes betrothal.

rows and weaver birds chirped, bathing in the clear waters of the Maheshou, surrounded by fish she could catch with her hands, with sometimes a squirrel, sometimes a gazelle as her furtive companions. Making love in the bushes, her clothes scattered over the mimosas and the daisies. This was how she became pregnant with her first child, a boy, born in the Maquis, who died in the Bangwa hospital. She would never get over that loss, even if she'd later say that she lived the best moments of her marriage in Toungou: "Our Maquisard honeymoon."

A photographic memory inscribed in her mind: Nithap with his feet in the water, chanting and dancing. "*Oyo yo! Oyo yo! Oyo yo, eh!*" She never asked him whose name he was singing.

11

The Tchunda *had become Ernest Ouandié's headquarters. It was there, in the* Toungou forest, that he trained his fighters, disguised as masons. They sat on benches that they'd built themselves when the leader held what he called "ideological sessions." He promised that with support from the villagers—Bazou, Moya, Bangangte, Bafang, Bafoussam, and primarily Bamileke—they would build a New Cameroon; that was his ideal. He even dressed like a contractor himself. They'd come down from the village at daybreak, leaving their houses one by one, following tracks and streambeds, skirting along backyards, and coming together at the work site, where they'd put their backs into their work all day, raising corner posts and building walls. Sometimes at nightfall, they'd still be at the work site, and then the moon, cutting across the sky, would reveal their ghostly silhouettes. For them, rain was as much a blessing as night, because it didn't put a stop to their work.

Ouandié didn't use a blackboard, but he might as well have, for he'd walk between the benches where they sat, those men who'd been pupils long ago and were now accidental builders, talking to them as he used to talk to his own pupils. The first time that Ngountchou brought cooked yams, she simply set them down in front of her husband; he opened the pot and the men came running. They plunged their hands into the food, licking their fingers. I won't give a list of all the different *taks* she brought—cakes of peanuts, beans, and others—but never had such joy spread across their faces as when Ngountchou brought them *kouakoukou*!* She kept hold of "her man" through his stomach. Nithap swallowed down her love with balls of couscous, sitting around her pots into which the *tsuitsuis*, one after the other, plunged their hands.

Nithap watched Ouandié's army gather around the supper plate and fall under her spell: *touabassi*.† He remembered that first time in Bangwa when he'd seen Ngountchou in Mademoiselle Birgitte's courtyard. He fell in love with her all over again. Love is a perpetual beginning, but this time only the thousand animals of Toungou were witness to his happiness. The War Girl became a myth, present in the memories of all those who would confide in Tanou later, because no soldier would ever forget the woman who'd fed him in the bush, that's for sure. They imagined her crossing through the burned remains of neighborhoods, where embers still glowed on piles of debris, to reach their hideout. They composed hymns to Ngountchou, the Woman of the Hearth Fire, but in their minds, they sang of Mama Cameroon.

Neocolonialism is a system the French and English use to exploit Cameroon—that's what Ouandié taught them, and each of his pupil-fighters listened, eating all the while.

The French can't behave in France as they do in Cameroon, because in France people are citizens.

He looked at the faces, kept alert by their dinner. He was calm, his gestures measured. Life in the Maquis had transformed him. As he spoke, he paced back and forth, punctuating each word with a step. His hair had gone white, giving him a dignified air that imposed respect on all around. He kept it cut short, but let his beard grow. Here, they no longer called him the leader, but Comrade Émile. Nonetheless, people still behaved around him as if they were standing before the President of

---

* Please don't make me translate *kouakoukou*, I'd die of hunger!

† Hold on a minute! Ngountchou, who had just come back from Yaounde, must have learned that spell when she was there, because it is said that only Eton or Douala girls know it, and use it to keep their men faithful. As you can see, she had the whole regiment charmed.

the Resistance: le Président de la République du Cameroun Sous Maquis. Except for the hemorrhoids, for which he still needed Dr. Nithap's care, he never fell sick.

"The French come to our country because it is rich in resources," he said to the soldiers.

His voice echoed across the work site. "They take our resources and kill the people.

"Neocolonialism is a system that brings the French into a country and makes the people work without pay.

"The soldiers of the revolution are not thieves. It's France that exploits Cameroon. We are Cameroon's soldiers."

Ouandié said that an armed soldier who has nothing in his head is just a brute. And he knew that brutality was what those men were experiencing; they needed to be liberated from it. He showed them the destruction all around, which had led many of them to join his ranks. He spoke of how the villagers were mistreated, and how that had transformed them into dissidents. He reminded them that the raids and the beatings were not accidental but the actual backbone of the colonial system, adding, "Who is it who works in Melong?"

"People from Bangangte," said the voices around him.

He reminded them of the construction of the train line; everyone there could recall the violence.

"Who does the *njokmassi* in N'lohe?"

"They're Bamilekes."

"Who do they kill in N'lohe?"

"They're Cameroonians!"

He used what the people knew to make them into the fighters that he needed. He had learned to rely on concrete examples. From Martin Singap he had learned that you have to meet the people where they are in order to lead them toward their chosen path. From Pastor Tbongo he had learned that revolution is no more than a gust of wind unless it's inscribed in an autonomous set of beliefs. He added these lessons from his various masters to what he had learned from his courses in Eastern Europe and in China. He emphasized the lived experience of people in

Bangangte, in that village whose language he spoke. He spoke to the people in Pidgin; even better, he spoke to them in Camfranglais, he spoke to them in that *invented language* that he had adopted, as had others before him, to create Cameroon.

"*Na fô Cameroun wi di wôk*," he said. We work for Cameroon.

He knew that this people who had gathered around him had accepted him as their leader—Comrade Émile!—that they had given him everything they held most dear, just as the pastor had offered the *Tchunda*, convinced that they could build something even grander, more beautiful, more worthy. He was of this people—the Bamilekes!—and he knew that they saw themselves as the engine of the Cameroonian nation. Without intending to, he had adopted Singap's tribalism, but only in order to lift it up, to make it serve an idea that had escaped the commander: Cameroon! There in the forest, Ouandié listened to the villagers, who spoke to him in a language he understood, Medumba, and which he used to reply, as well.

"*You bi avant-garde*," he said, "*avant-garde fô Cameroun, avant-garde fô kiakde wè*." You are the avant-garde of Cameroon, the avant-garde of independence.

If he had been unsettled by the poor quality of Singap's soldiers—in truth, many of them were thugs—he was happy to see before him farmers whom, word by word, he had transformed into fighters. These volunteers, accidental masons—he knew he could make soldiers of them. Except that he lacked weapons. There were some hunting rifles they fought with. Among the villagers, there were also a number of blacksmiths who had fashioned makeshift weapons. But he never received the weaponry promised by Czechoslovakia; the "specific package" had never arrived. Had the UPC supporters from Ghana forgotten him? Had the courier Fenkam Fermeté been arrested? Ouandié had stopped waiting for him. But while that undelivered package didn't drain the courage of the volunteers, it did isolate him. That unfulfilled promise hung over the heads of those *new men* and *new women*, who had accepted hunger and privations, who were ready to face danger, but who had to confront soldiers while armed only with wooden rifles or, like Ngountchou, with their bare hands.

It was in Toungou that they planned the attack on the chief's compound in Bangwa. One night, in just the same way as he would lead his ideological sessions during their midday meal, Ouandié presented the map of the compound to the fighters. He had gotten it from the Extraordinary Villager. Clara's husband had reminded him of the old dispute that had resulted in No Tchoutouo's exile and sent thousands of Bangwas down the path toward Anglophone Cameroon. Ouandié was still a schoolboy in Dschang when Jean Nono—the chief the French had installed on the throne in Bangwa in 1922—shook up the entire West of the country with a plot that had poisoned a dozen people, including local chiefs, but from which he curiously emerged unscathed. No one here liked him. That collective hatred had stewed for a very long time. For the *tsuitsuis*, this was an opportunity. Bangwa was an open wound, the chief's compound the very heart of it.

They'd been joined by many of the carpenters and masons who had built the structures. They drew up detailed sketches of the place. They waited for the dry season, because it would be their ally. By then the elephant grass would have turned yellow and the fires would leave scorched earth behind them.

The days that followed were far from routine, even if they were all focused on the coming attack. One day, Nithap watched a silhouette move through the tall grass, slightly bent, walking slowly. It was Ouandié.

Everyone there was used to the leader's pensive stance, the pipe held between his teeth, how he walked. Fighters hurried after him, and there was more commotion ahead. But when he spoke to his personal doctor, he didn't talk about his own health. What he hated most about Cameroonians was their inability to defend their own rights. "A Cameroonian doesn't attack head-on," he'd once said to Nithap. "He'll go talk to your boss, your wife, tell them you're a bastard. He takes advantage of the big things for his own little schemes." That's what Ouandié wanted most to change here, in the Maquis. He wanted to create a new type of Cameroonian.

"You really don't want to do any target practice?" he'd asked the doctor a few days earlier.

"Comrade Émile," the doctor replied, sheepishly. "Are we going to have that conversation again?"

Ouandié looked at him and smiled. He had a smile that spread across his whole face, revealing an enigmatic joy.

"You know you are the only one here who isn't armed?" he said.

This wasn't the first time they'd broached that topic. Each time, Nithap had replied: "I don't kill, I cure."

"I know," Nithap conceded that day.

"I'm not asking you to kill anyone, *ndocta*," Ouandié said, placing his hand on top of the other man's and looking straight into his eyes, "just that you protect yourself against *our enemies*."

"By doing what, exactly?" Nithap replied.

Ouandié paused. He pulled back his hand and stood for a long moment, lost in thought. For the first time, Nithap watched him work out the solution to an existential equation before speaking.

"We're not killers," he said.

"The opposing camp thinks otherwise."

Nithap had spoken too quickly. He wished he could take it back.

"It's what *you* think that concerns me."

With one phrase, he had roused the fighter.

"What you think."

A good question: Just what did Nithap think?

"What I think doesn't really matter," he said, "as long as I'm doing my duty."

"Precisely," Ouandié replied, lost in thought once again. He took a long draw on his pipe before continuing. "That's why you need to protect yourself. You're not wearing your doctor's smock anymore, you know."

It was true. Since he had joined the Maquis, Nithap had of course dressed differently than the fighters, but how could anyone besides the Sinistrés recognize him as a doctor? Should he cross the region as he used to, dressed in a white smock? What foolishness! He dressed in traditional

Bangangte style, in a flowing *tayangam* over which he layered a *sayong*,* which stood out starkly among the buttoned shirts and shorts of the *tsui-tsuis* or the ragged *sandja* of the villagers. He even shaved his head as Bamileke soldiers had done long ago, with a ponytail in the back, which he tied up in memory of Clara; it made him look like a *megni*,† and that's just what he wanted.

This time he took the pistol that Ouandié handed him. He had come to see the futility of his arguments.

"Well, now, Nzui," the leader said to him, using the nom de guerre he'd given Nithap. "Nzui, this is how you hold it."

He talked to Nithap as if they were colleagues in the teachers' lounge, and he showed him how to aim; it was such a paradox to see this doctor, whose outfit, as well as his education and his conscience, rejected the weapon he held in his hand, but who still let the mathematics teacher give him a lesson.

"No, not like that."

Nithap's hand trembled.

"Don't forget that you are a surgeon."

His hand, as well as his eye, focused on the task.

"Shooting is an act of precision," Ouandié told him. "You just have to really focus on the *goal*."

He talked with the pipe clenched between his teeth, which turned each of his words into whispers. Nithap closed one eye and stood still for a moment.

"Now fire."

Nithap fired. The sound was a dry crack. The pistol wasn't loaded.

"See, it's simple," Ouandié said, adding "self-defense," in English.

Later, Ouandié pulled him aside to speak in private.

"*A sabi sé*," he said, speaking now in Pidgin. "*You hét di tchèk plenti. Na so mi tou a bing bin tam wé wi dong inta fô bouch fô mil neuf cinquante cinq. Mi a bi tchitcha you bi ndocta. Tsuitsui na sèns. Tsuitsui di tchèk bifo i*

* A garment that hangs down midcalf.

† An herbal doctor, a seer.

make some ting. Ènè tam wé tsuitsui di chouti gôn, i di tchèk bifo i choutam. No bi na fô skia sé i di fia. Na fô skia sé win ô môsi spol laf. Ènè Cameroon man wé wi di kècham, wi môsi jôsi yi ana wi si sé i dông fôl lowa. Tsuitsui môsi tchèk bifo i kili man. Wi môsi make sé gomna fia wi ana sé pipi dèm bin wéti wi. Fêt wé wi di fêt na fêt fô ndocta." I know that you are trying to understand, but that's how I was, too, when we formed the Maquis in 1955. Me, I'm a teacher, and you are a doctor. Being a *tsuitsui* requires intelligence. A *tsuitsui* thinks before doing anything. Before shooting, the *tsuitsui* must think. It's not because he's afraid. It's because he pays attention to what people think. We need to win over the Cameroonians, and we need to act in ways that make them love us. A *tsuitsui* must think before killing. We need to make the government fear us so that the people will be with us. The war we are fighting is a war of the mind.

Nithap didn't reply.

"That's the difference between us and them," Ouandié said, now speaking in French. "The war we are fighting is surgical."

"*Dêm don tichi sondja fôr Semengue fôr kilo Cameroon pipi,*" he continued. "*Na plaba condrê fachin. Bifo kiakde, dêm wôk bing bin na fôr shouti gôn. Frôm fôr bikin'am fôr jaman tam, dêm wôk na fôr kili Cameroon pipi. Tam wé dêm di louk wati man, dêm di shouti gôn fôr bouch, but dêm gôn nô di jam hét fôr pôpô dêm mblala. Na so dêm dé. Na De Gaulle di gip dem ôda. Bicôs sé Ahidjo na tchidang fôr French-pipi. Louk all dang French sondja wé dêm dé fôr yi kôna. Na dêm di wôk. Ôl dang wan fôr kili Cameroon-pipi! Wi wi bi pipi fôr fêt!*" We are the resistance. The new resistance. We protect ourselves, and that's why, from the very start, our fighters have understood themselves as Sinistrés. It's a question of our humanity, of our dignity, even. We defend our brothers and sisters from the criminals who batter them. They teach Semengue's soldiers how to kill Cameroonians. That's our problem. Well before independence, their only goal was killing people. Since the Germans were here, their only job was to kill Cameroonians. When they faced a white man, they shot into the bush, and they only found their courage when they faced their own people. That's how they are. De Gaulle is the one giving the orders. Because Ahidjo is only a French lackey. Look at all the French soldiers who are with him.

They're the ones doing the work. They're the ones who are always killing Cameroonians. We are the children of war. We're fighting for the people. We're fighting for our country.

That night, the doctor slept with his gun beside him, close at hand. In truth, he didn't really sleep. He couldn't stop looking at his weapon; once, he even spoke to it. He talked about people he hadn't been able to defend and who had disappeared beneath the ruins of a destroyed town, N'lohe. "They died without proper mourning!" He spoke of Clara's beauty, of their love that he still sometimes felt at the end of his sex when he thought about her, and of her talent for figuring out the problems that made his belly ache. He spoke about the calendar that, in his mind, replicated the cycle that linked her body to the moaning of this country. He spoke of his sister and brother-in-law, Tama''s parents. He spoke of the dead lying alongside his path, of those bodies, sometimes dismembered, that he'd had to bury, of that young man whose face, with eyes wide open, stared out at him from the heart of the bushes. He realized that his voice was trembling and that tears were running down his cheeks. "I'm bleeding": he remembered Clara's words and then stood up, aware that he knew nothing about the sea of blood. He discovered that a deep rage had taken hold of his heart, of his arms. He looked at his hands. They weren't trembling, because he remembered his wife's courage; he could see Ngountchou's silhouette before him. But it was Clara Ntchantchou's face that filled his night, the sensation of her vulva squeezing his hard penis, her legs wrapped tight around his hips, her breasts against his chest, and her strong arms circling his neck. He got up and walked out into the bush, his eyes lost in the expanse of king grass, and he cried.

"They can't kill us all," he said to the weapon in his hands.

It was because of his love for two women that he slung a pistol from his hip, and also because of his son—he didn't want it to be easy for him to become an orphan. He tied it on just as the warriors of the past had carried their cutlasses.

"Miracle!" Ouandié said when he saw him.

There was no other word to describe the transformation of the doctor into a *tsuitsui*. He fell asleep singing a song—a poem, really, that was also a prayer.*

Dear brothers, dear umbilical cords
Come out of your bushes
So that together
We may begin to hunt
So that together we may push them back
To their lands and liberate our own
When at last my eyes were opened wide
They hung us
Like grilled meat on spits, we were hung
When at last daybreak came
They stood us in front of firing posts
And mercilessly cut us down
But know that the hour has come
War is upon us
The belligerents crawl ahead
While in the background
Machetes and rifles clank
And fearless
The girls of the land are everywhere along the front
They bring refreshing water to all
Our valorous mothers go through the bush from Maquis to Maquis
They hide beneath their robes
Messages for the fighters.

The attack took place during the dry season. It was carried out by just a few of Ouandié's soldiers. But he chose the most battle-tested of his fighters. He

* "La Chanson de Nithap," a poem written by Jean-Martin Tchaptchet. How, there in the depths of the bush, did the doctor get ahold of this poem, which he knew by heart and even recited there in Céline's kitchen in Pennington, while Tanou listened? There are things in this world that remain mysteries.

knew the symbolic value of this act and wanted, even more than taking terrain, to strike at the heart of the system of servitude. In the middle of the night, a dozen men came out of the sacred woods where they'd been hiding. The imposing buildings of the chief's compound rose up before them: sculptures with stories to tell. It was easy to see through the bamboo walls. The orders had been clear: It was imperative to avoid killing women and children. Like Ouandié said: "We must not alienate the people, but convince them." So the women's quarters, which were the first they reached, were spared.

"The other buildings belong to the war," he'd told Nithap. "The goal is to capture Jean Nono. *Dan fingwong*." That traitor.

They wanted to use him as currency to trade for the many imprisoned Sinistrés. Five gunmen took their places, one in front of each house, while the others edged along the wall around the living quarters.

"That's the house," one of them whispered.

The chief was sleeping surrounded by his wives. The chief's compound was the site of an endless series of parties, and the attack took place the night after one of them. Nono told himself that by giving party after party, he could win over the hearts of the locals. To make himself beloved, he had opened a bar in the compound where the men came each market day to get drunk on raffia wine. But they weren't going to be duped; the transformation of their suffering into a farce made them laugh, but it didn't change their minds. The legitimate chief of Bangwa, who'd been sent into exile in Dschang, had died there. To avoid rekindling fond memories, there'd been no mourning ceremonies for him in the chief's compound. The death of Dr. Broussoux hadn't cut down on the number of parties, either, but there were more public confessions and more civil guards in the courtyard.

They were the ones who sounded the alarm and roused the sleeping.

"Fire!" they cried. "Fire!"

And the universe erupted with the sound of women's ululations.

Raffia is a friend to flames. Many times, even before the civil war, the compounds of chiefs in the West had burned to the ground. The first palaces in Foumban, for example, were destroyed by fire in 1911. It's very difficult to fight fire here, because in the dry season, flames spread with the speed of a bullet. Later, the Maquisards will be blamed for these infernos, and historians will talk about their lack of concern for preserving examples of Bamileke engineering. It will be said that, carried away by communist rhetoric, by the bible of the Third World, they had fallen into an iconoclasm like the one that had led Stalin to destroy centuries-old churches. There are also those who will say that the fires that burned down chiefs' compounds during the civil war were the start of a cycle of persecution of the Bamilekes, who were made to pay the price for their retrograde feudalism.

Ouandié was truly a son of the West.

But do those historians know the sadness that overcame Comrade Émile when, there in the classroom of the village school, he laid out the plans to burn down the compound of the chief of Bangwa? Do they know that what gave him pause was precisely the thought of seeing that work of living art go up in smoke? They forget this: If the people accept as their chiefs the lackeys imposed by the administration, they are spared. Otherwise, the national army will burn down their chief's compound in the name of national cohesion, in the name of the nation, in the name of nationalism! Because they will have become rebels! *Maquisards!* "The problem," Semengue had said, "is the people."

The *tsuitsuis* saved very little from the fire at the chief's compound, only the chiefly garments that Jean Nono never had the courage to wear, and which he'd kept piled in a room. Just touching those garments sent the men into a frenzy. No one dared to put them on; all stood frozen at the sight of the strands of ceremonial Venetian beads. This expedition was Nithap's baptism. From then on, he was the living, breathing incarnation of the age-old traditions of the West. He had arrived at the end of a very long journey.

The inhabitants of Bangwa had for the most part abandoned the chief's compound to the usurper, and, like the Extraordinary Villager, joined the Maquis. They knew they'd be condemned for that fact alone. A wooden house in which a pillar of colonialism resided, a simple trader made chief by the colonial authorities, at the expense of the banished legitimate ruler: that defined the space of their damnation. It was as obvious as the suffering of the Muscovites when their invaded capital was devoured by Napoleon's flames! It was the people of Bangwa who set fire to the chief's compound, just as it was the Muscovites who set fire to their capital! The flames swept up the entire universe in their whirlwind.

The ten men who were waiting, armed and ready, at the doors of the living quarters, were all from Bangwa, and their rage boiled as hot as the flames that licked the walls of the houses. Nithap was with them.

"*A nô fit mis hi*," one of them said, his hand on the trigger. He can't escape me. He meant Jean Nono.

The others thought it was funny to watch the women and men rush out of the compound, wearing nothing but a *fiek* or a *bila*.*

"*A tèk am*," said one gunman. I'll take him.

A man came out waving his machete and screaming like a madman. The loud crack of a gunshot. His head exploded like a watermelon. Another man spread out his arms toward the night and fell backward. A third would be found dead, his pants filled with his own excrement, and his face disfigured by a bullet shot through his head.

"I got him!" a voice cried out.

Gunshots were coming from every corner of the bush, their echoes sounding out across the valley. Caught off guard by the flames, the inhabitants of the compound hunkered down in ditches, slunk away between the reeds.

"*Tsuitsui!*" they heard.

"*Tsuitsui!*"

Morning rose over the ashes and ruins of what had been the compound of the chief of Bangwa. Jean Nono wasn't dead. He had stayed hidden in his wives' sheets throughout the fight.

Ouandié will never know that the chief owed his life to Ouandié's decision to spare the women's quarters. The next day, Jean Nono rode in

* *Bila*, an article of men's clothing; *fiek*, a garment worn by women that covers only the sex and a part of the thighs and is commonly called a "loincloth."

a jeep driven by a French soldier and inspected the compound. His expression was a stark contrast to the defeated look of his men who'd fought the flames. They showed him the cadavers lying on the ground, covered with banana leaves. He came nearer and realized that one had his belly sliced open and another a bullet hole in his forehead. An exploded face made him close his eyes. He went into what remained of his palace. In the corner, a skull was lying right on the ground, surrounded by bits of calcified wood—all that remained of the House of the Ancestors. He walked through what was left of the houses.

"We will get revenge," he said.

Silence was his only reply.

"We will get revenge."

12

Mademoiselle Birgitte often wondered why she had been spared by the rage that had consumed Bamileke land and devastated all the courtyards. The only white woman who'd stayed at the Bangwa hospital, now a military camp, she was in charge of providing bare-bones medical care, even as her orphanage was expanding and taking over other empty residences. She never imagined that by sending Ngountchou to be her assistant, Nithap had become her *tsuitsui* guardian angel, because it was he, her colleague, who became Ouandié's personal doctor, who had made her house a sanctuary. He had an argument no one could contest. It wasn't that he'd met his wife in her courtyard, or that she was his colleague: "She is Norwegian."

"White."

"Not all whites are the same," he snapped back. "She's not French. *Nuance*."

He knew his friend too well, knew that she wasn't, as rumor had it, "a collaborator." He could still see her, surrounded by her orphans (whose numbers had grown dramatically), and he knew she was doing humanitarian work. It was his silent friendship that gave her the confidence to stay when all the other whites were leaving, one after the other. "What will they do to me?" she asked all those who reminded her that fire was spreading over the Bamileke hills. "These are their children." And she pointed to the toddlers for whom she'd become a mother, whom she clasped to her breast, whom she pampered, and to whom, for fun, she sometimes taught a few words of her incomprehensible language. She turned her eyes away from what was happening in the offices occupied by the military, and she never learned what had happened to Nyamsi.

When she was found with her throat slit, lying under her mosquito netting, everyone kept the children away and blamed the militia. The first to point a finger toward the bush was Ntchantchou Zacharie.

"My lord," said the deputy, "will this never end?"

He was desperate because of the growing number of cadavers that filled the courtyards of his constituency. And especially since the dead woman was beloved by all. He couldn't get over it. His accusatory words amplified a thousandfold the rage boiling all around. Who didn't know Mademoiselle Birgitte? Chief Nono had even given a *ndap* to the woman who was for all the "Godmother of Love"—Makokwa—and she had earned it. Her death hit the community like a bolt of lightning; it was a setback for the *tsuitsuis*.

"How could they?"

"Why?"

Deputy Ntchantchou Zacharie accused Ouandié, just like he had accused Djonga, the mayor of Bazou, of the murder of Joseph Mbeng. Jean Fochivé, the chief of police named by Minister Enoch Nkwayim, led the inquiry.

"Get out of my office," he shouted when the deputy came to tell him how angry he was. He stood up from his seat, over which loomed a large portrait of Ahmadou Ahidjo, and waved his hand. "Get out or I'll have you arrested right away. You Bamilekes, what are you trying to prove in this country? Do you want to kill me, too? You're a plague! We'll see about this. I'll have you all arrested! You people think that you are Cameroon!"

His anger was a sign of the country's boiling rage; it had found in the Bamilekes the scapegoat its history needed, the justification for its age-old violence. Yes, after the death of Joseph Mbeng, Yaounde was shaken, the Bamileke neighborhoods rattled. The cousin from Mokolo had gone into hiding, and many other Bamilekes like her had taken refuge with relatives. The memory of the pogroms in N'lohe and Bamendjing was still fresh in everyone's mind.

"What is going to happen now?" they wondered.

"It's the dance!"

"The dance of death, you mean, *nessa*."

"I won't stick around to see."

"I'm going back to the village," one frightened woman said. "I'm going back to my parents."

"But in the village, there are even more killings, *me yam menzui*, my dear wife."

"There's no village left."

"The militias control the place."

"They set fires."

"They kill."

"They rape."

"Who?"

"Their own brothers."

"*Ne ne ne*, it's really true."

"Everyone in the West has been sent to resettlement camps."

"What can we do?"

"Leave Cameroon."

"Yes, leave Cameroon."

"Anti-Bamileke hatred is our daily bread in Cameroon."

"All against one."

"The stone in the shoe of Cameroon."

"Get out of Cameroon any way you can."

"To go where?"

"Anywhere."

"To France."

"It's the French who started all this."

"Lamberton."

"The French aren't the solution, but the cause of the Bamileke problem."

"So where can we go?"

"Lamberton, that's in what part of France?"

"It doesn't matter where, just get out of the country."

Exile had already sent the Bamilekes into forced labor camps, had created in Mungo the first community of the Bamileke diaspora, and had forced thousands into the poor neighborhoods of Yaounde, Douala, Mbalmayo, Tombel, Kumba, and in neighboring countries as well, in Gabon, Nigeria, Mali, all across Africa. The massive exodus filled the cargo holds of ships and planes, forcing the Bamilekes onto the streets of South Africa, Europe, the United States, China, all around the world. "Invaders," they were called to chase them away from here, and there, "*came no go*," to chase them along again. "Bosnians." The people of silent wandering. People of the path.

The turbulence that shook Bangangte left everyone in Elie Tbongo's home anxious. The fear that had thrown thousands of men onto the paths of exile played out in the pastor's living room in a very particular way. Never had he written so much, but that was because the destruction all around had left his home isolated, transformed it into a hermit's cabin. His hedge had grown wild and thick, isolating him even more. His neighbors had been led off to camps. There was no more air in the neighborhood, only the silence of abandonment! Ngountchou had taken charge of the kitchen, throwing herself into the work with her mother and Tama' as her helpers. And Mensa', too—at least with lighter tasks like peeling plantains or crushing tomatoes. The pastor's daughters had returned grown women, each followed by stories whose echoes concerned him. Mensa''s belly was growing bigger and bigger and, though Ngountchou was secretive, he often overheard chuckling that made him smile. Tama''s voice was the only one that ever broke through the monotony of the living room's parallel monologues, because sometimes, from the depths of the conspiracy, the boy pulled out a joke.

"I have two mamas," he said. "What is the French word for that?"

But his cheerfulness wasn't enough.

"You're the one going to the white man's school," she said. "*Ou nya ke len, ou lock nshou'ou, oh*." If you don't know, be quiet.

Happily, Tama' never kept quiet. The arrest of Ntchantchou Zacharie shook up all of Bangangte, like a bomb exploding in the middle of the market. It hit that living room hardest of all, and put on hold the translation of the Bible that the pastor had started working on again to distract his wandering mind.

It was Fochivé who had him arrested. Because he was Bamum, people blamed it on their rivalry with the Bangangtes.

"The Bamum are jealous of the Bamilekes," they said.

"They're two-headed snakes!"

"Seriously!"

And everyone listed off the names of the Bamileke officials who'd fallen into the hands of the police. People remembered Daniel Kemajou, the chief of Bazou who was still living in exile.

"They want to kill us!"

"All against one!"

"They will kill us!"

Mensa' was the most shaken by the news. For the third time, she fainted.

"She's going to give birth!" cried Ngountchou. "Let's take her to the Bangwa hospital!"

"That's impossible."

"Why?"

"There's a roadblock."

"Since the fire at the chief's compound," Tama' declared, "not even dogs get through."

"It's not a hospital anymore, it's a military camp!"

"A prison!"

"Since Mademoiselle Birgitte's death."

So Mensa' stayed at her father's house while her husband was taken to jail in Bangwa. Surrounded by her sister, her parents, and Tama', in whom she discovered a sympathetic ear, she fought back a double-sided fear: the specter of a Bamileke plot that was driving popular opinion and her fear about the words of the unborn child growing in her belly who knew all her secrets. She remembered their passion, but mostly she thought of Mbeng; she saw him between her legs, chatting with his child. Because Mensa' was convinced that the child she was carrying in her belly, and that kicked her so hard, was Mbeng's. She remembered their clandestine love and thought about her room, their Maquis, and then of Champs-Élysées. She thought about Yaounde and the neighborhood of Nlongkak. But she told no one here any of that: it was her secret.

Lock nshou.

She didn't even breathe a word to Tama'.

Mensa' didn't want her child to bear her husband's name, Ntchantchou. Could she name him after the man she'd loved? Mbeng! Bamileke? Beti? One shame was enough, and that one would be too much. Ah, her torment had no equal but the violence of the child in her belly, who was kicking and punching, making her breathe in and out, while in the camps around town, everyone was talking of nothing but the arrest of the deputy, telling each other how he'd been led across the market road in handcuffs, with two gendarmes behind him and photographers in front.

It was said that Fochivé, with his policeman's flair, had been able to trace a line that, from fingerprint to fingerprint, pistol to pistol, bullet to bullet, drop of blood to drop of blood, death to death, connected the assassination of Joseph Mbeng to that of Mademoiselle Birgitte, and both back to the deputy. A *sea of blood*: he had ironclad proof. Those who'd done the killing were two common criminals; namely a certain Nkuindji, from Tonga, and someone named Yitna François, both escapees from Bazou, whom Ntchantchou Zacharie knew from his distant and disavowed past as a UPC supporter. He'd used them several times as fake Maquisards, but, in reality, they were the actual accomplices the deputy had paid to liquidate "a sexual rival" and the "troubling witness" that the Norwegian had become despite herself. There are, of course, a thousand different versions of this affair,* each one wilder than the next, but neither Mensa' nor Ngountchou would ever challenge this one.

---

* According to one version, the motive for the crime was economic and was connected to the sale of schoolbooks—because to get a Bamileke interested, there has to be some money in it—just *ngkap*, you know. Another version holds that the weapon used in the crime, here one single-barreled rifle (not double-barreled), had belonged to Chief

Nithap didn't come to help Mensa' give birth, because as it spiraled further into violence, Bamileke land had no room for fairy tales. Ngountchou let him know what was going on in the house, however. He wrote out for his wife all the stages of a birth—in Bagam writing, of course—and so it was under his silent instruction that the War Girl was transformed into a midwife in her paternal living room. It was with those orders that she became his beloved assistant. To encourage Mensa' to push, breathe in, breathe out, and push again, Nja Yonke' distracted her with a children's rhyme, telling her the story of the hyena who walks at night, calling out to the children and eating them, one by one, *ngangoum, ou nya ke katte ou ke yen mbwo chou!** Elie Tbongo did the pacing for the father of the child, whose name he refused to mention, and whose name he will actually never know! Tama' ran to the well to fetch water, and then more water.

To her newborn daughter, Mensa' gave the pastor's name: Tbongo, as well as the given name that she remembered Champs-Élysées used for all the beautiful women in Paris: Marianne. Ngountchou will take the little girl and raise her. In that way, she erased all traces of the actual parentage of Tanou's sister, even as she drowned the echoes of her own guilty conscience in the family's silence.

Lock nshou.

*Deputy Ntchantchou Zacharie was executed in the market square in Banga*ngte. Loudspeakers had roused the whole village. November 19, 1965, at ten o'clock in the morning. His nocturnal confrontation with Djonga, whom he accused until the end of the murder of Joseph Mbeng, was used

Nkuika Tchamba of Bangoulap, who, when brought to trial about his weapon, which the deputy had borrowed, was sentenced to twenty-seven years in prison for taking bribes. A third version—well, it's up to you, dear readers, to show that you have the fertile imagination of the Bangangtes.

* "Hyena, if you don't walk, you won't find any good things!" The song sung by the panther to draw out the hyena.

against him (even if that ultimately didn't save the mayor of Bazou, who died under torture). The mayor simply asked him, as calmly as possible, to explain just why he would have killed a man who was "in Yaounde with the deputy's own wife.

"Explain that to me, *Monsieur le Député*."

"You're not going to take that calumny seriously!" Ntchantchou Zacharie snapped back.

Fochivé was used to taking words said under torture very seriously. But Djonga couldn't speak at all after his sessions on the swing. He coughed, as if trying to say something, to give one final confession. Fochivé leaned his ear close. The man died, spitting out, "Your mama's ass!"

Why would a Bamileke kill a Beti? That was the question that everyone in Bangangte was asking. Why would the Bamilekes start a war? The repercussions of such actions were always horrific; Bamendjing, N'lohe, Ebolowa still weighed heavily on the Bamilekes. Why would they do this? Djonga didn't have the strength to express his convictions, to lay out his political beliefs, which the deputy often categorized as lunacy. For example, this one: "The civil war? It's the alignment of the North/South axis in this country. You see, power will go to the Northerners after the Southerners, and to the Southerners after the Northerners, and so on, because the Northerners and the Betis form the majority in Cameroon. That's the problem the Bamilekes face. They are a minority. So they are the country's guilty conscience." He didn't have the time to express his hopes, like the peaceful coexistence of the Cameroonian tribes, which he wanted "based on a balance of forces."

At one point he spat out, "Someone carrying a basket of eggs on their head doesn't start a fight."

The federal deputy representing Bangangte, who was one of the most respected men in the region and in Cameroon because of his previous post as a schoolteacher and bookseller, because of his position as a church elder, because of his efforts to rally Maquisards, and especially because of his campaign for the expansion of the *cadi*, wanted to be seen as the victim in this affair. He had buried his UPC membership card beneath his banana trees far too long ago to feel guilty about it now, although he often said, "Who wasn't a member of the UPC when they were eighteen?"

What would you do in my place? he wanted to ask Fochivé, man-to-man, while he was driving him to Bangangte in his official car. *What would you do?*

He wanted to talk about his wife lying in Mbeng's arms; he wanted to talk about that *nkwa'* who had spread out his wife while he was gone.

Ah! he wanted to shout. *If someone was balling your wife, what would you do?*

He looked at Fochivé, trying to see a man in him, a brother.

"You understand me, don't you?"

But Fochivé didn't hear anything he said.

"My wife!"

Fochivé was thinking about what Djonga had said.

"*A tchou yam menzui!*" He screwed my wife!

Fochivé didn't understand Medumba.

He held in his hands a note from Enoch Nkwayim that gave him orders to *stage the public execution of the guilty party in order to enhance its psychological effect on the population.* The minister of territorial administration had spared himself from witnessing this spectacle, even though it took place in his own village, and had at center stage a man he knew well. So it was actually in the market square in Bangangte that the deputy finished making his argument, for he had arrived in a car with the three coffins intended for the condemned stacked on top. Semengue was waiting for him there. He'd already had his soldiers tie the Maquisards that Fochivé's men had arrested to the post.

Ntchantchou Zacharie jumped when he realized that there were only two of them, and then he quickly recognized Nkuindji and Yitna. After all, he was the one who'd recruited them. Scattered around Nkuindji's feet were the thirteen hundred francs he'd received as a bonus for hiding the pistols used in the crime on a coffee plantation; the weapons were also lying there in front of the condemned.

"There are three posts," the deputy said to Fochivé, who was cleaning his teeth with a bit of root as he got out of the car, clearly quite pleased with the large crowd that had gathered and that included children in school uniforms.

"Yes, sir," Commissioner Bayiga replied, after giving a military salute. "There are also three coffins."

And with a snap of his fingers, he ordered the civil guards to get the coffins off the car. Ntchantchou Zacharie quickly did the macabre calculation and arrived at the logical conclusion.

"We're missing a person," he said.

"Indeed," Fochivé said, then spat a bit of the root he'd been chewing out on the ground. "Indeed."

Just then, Ntchantchou Zacharie saw his own civil guards step forward and surround him.

"The third convict," Fochivé said calmly, then spat out another bit of root, "is *you, Monsieur le Député.*"

Yet Semengue's soldiers did not tie Ntchantchou Zacharie's hands behind his back, because he protested: "Just where would I run and hide?"

Indeed, Bangangte stretched out before him in the hundred or so curious faces who all knew him, who knew his *ndaps* and his story, who'd often come to his house to get fresh water "from the pump," which was then something of a miracle in Bangangte. They led him to the third post, the scandal of his arrest visible on the faces of the crowd in that market, now plunged into an endless mourning.

"That's Ntchantchou Zacharie," said one woman.

"No, it's his twin."

"It's the deputy!"

"No, it's his double."

Semengue's soldiers took aim at the condemned men.

"Wait!" shouted Ntchantchou Zacharie. "I have something to say."

Semengue went up to him.

"Say it fast."

"Is my wife here?" asked the deputy, who hadn't seen his wife for quite some time, who had spoken to her only at a distance, and whose story he hadn't heard. He'd looked for her face in the crowd before him, the same sort of crowd he had riled up himself several times, and where he had noticed her for the first time, before deciding to make her his wife.

"She was invited," Bayiga said. "But she refused to come."

"Why?" he asked, filled with outrage.

"She just gave birth," was the answer.

"A boy or a girl?"

"Girl."

"What is her name?"

"Tbongo."

Ntchantchou Zacharie sighed heavily as he heard this second death sentence pronounced right in front of his face. He, who had only ever done his duty, discovered love in all its blinding glory.

"What's her given name?"

"Marianne."

"I want her to come here."

"Who?"

"My wife."

"She has to take care of the infant," Semengue told him.

"No," Ntchantchou Zacharie replied. "She will take my place."

"Then who will take care of the child?"

"I can take care of *my child*," he said, but Semengue didn't understand this shift in tactic. "I am a deputy. I am the representative of these people. She must take my place," he insisted. "I have the means. I can feed *my child*."

"Oh really?"

"I'll give her my breast."

As he said "my breast," he feverishly tore open his shirt and showed his chest. Semengue guffawed. *Bebela*, he said to himself. *You'll see everything in Bamileke land!*

"Your breast?" he asked.

"Yes, my breast."

He squeezed his nipple. The military leader couldn't believe it.

The Bamilekes!

But the deputy wouldn't stop talking. Even as the firing squad took aim at him, he kept raising his voice, saying that there in the crowd he'd recognized a doctor from the Bangwa hospital.

"Manganchet was also there with us," he said, "now I remember."

"Huh?"

"Who is Manganchet?" someone asked.

Semengue ordered the squad to put an end to this nonsense.

The soldiers carried the three cadavers away with them, and buried them, no one ever knew where. For three days, the heads of the three men adorned the main market square.

The head of the federal deputy seems to be there even now—at least his cry is still heard.

Even now.

Like a refrain.

13

Colonel Semengue's reputation for chopping off heads had preceded him. It hadn't escaped him that Ntchantchou Zacharie's spouse had been absent during the deputy's public execution. Hadn't the man asked that Mensa' take his place? So the colonel ordered that they look into this story more closely, and that's how he ended up at the pastor's home, his hands still dripping with blood—no, I'm not exaggerating—and his legendary smile on his lips. And let's not mention the sarcasm that always accompanied it. He aimed his sarcasm primarily at those who thought they were smart—everyone knew that. But what irritated him the most was men who were taller than him, as Elie Tbongo learned that very day. He wore all of his medals pinned on his chest when he went to call out the enigmatic prelate.

"You are disobeying orders," he spat out from the courtyard.

His soldiers followed him, as did Fochivé.

"My daughter just gave birth," the old man replied. "She's still confined to bed."

They could hear the child's whimpers, and soon Mensa' came out, holding the newborn in her arms.

"The child of the *rebel*," Semengue said, taking note of the famous breast that had forced the firing squad to hold fire.

The way he said *rebel* made them all jump, because he was speaking, after all, about a newborn. Fochivé went into the house, followed by a dozen armed men. He found Nja Yonke' in the living room. She'd been busy cooking the midday meal and wiped her hands on her dress.

"What's going on?" she asked, frightened.

Ngountchou appeared behind her.

"Nothing," said her husband.

"Have they come to arrest us?" she asked, speaking now to Ngountchou.

Fochivé burst out laughing.

"Of course not, madam!"

Semengue picked up a yam from the table, peeled it, and took a bite, then blew on his fingertips.

"It's hot!" he said, as he chewed.

He wiped his fingers on his trousers. He knew that it was only the protection of the distant Ministry of Territorial Administration that had made an exception of this house. Not that Enoch Nkwayim had ever given the order outright; but the fact that he had previously supported the building of the *Tchunda* had lingered in everyone's mind, a sign of the government's patronage. Yet what Elie Tbongo didn't know was that Fochivé wanted to use the fact that this house hadn't been evacuated against the minister in Yaounde, by linking him to Ntchantchou Zacharie and to what would be called "the Great Bamileke Conspiracy" on the front page of all the newspapers.

"It's always them," said Fochivé to whoever was listening.

To think he never learned Ngountchou's secrets! Still, he did ask where the documents were, because every republic relies on written proof, even if it fabricates what it needs to justify its decisions.

"What documents?"

The pastor jumped.

Fochivé certainly didn't notice. But Elie Tbongo's mind was like a boiling pot filled with *koki* wrapped in banana leaves: the implications of his explosive family tree were on the verge of spilling over. He pictured his son-in-law with Ouandié and sighed; that thought led him to the deputy, whose execution had brought all these armed men into his courtyard.

He knew that one day his deep roots in the bloodied soul of this land would be revealed. He thought of the plot hatched in the *Tchunda* and knew he was already condemned. He'd been told that when Ntchantchou Zacharie was tied to the execution post, he'd asked to be replaced by the pastor's own daughter. He could see Bangangte scandalized by the thought, women pressing their hands to their temples—but was there really any room left for scandal in this village left empty by the resettlement camps? Shooting a pastor wouldn't be the last folly committed in these mad days that had stripped a deputy of his immunity.

"Look what we found," said one of his uniformed men, coming out into the courtyard. "These aren't skulls!"

"This house is a treasure trove of documents!"

That realization was the start of a celebration for Semengue, who crowed, then peeled another yam and asked, "What's this?"

"The Bible," said the pastor.

There was a whole trunk full of papers spread out before him, dusty red manuscripts, notes from the intensive work that, until that moment, had drawn Elie Tbongo to that table every day.

"I'm translating it."

And Semengue smiled.

"Into Bamileke?" he asked sarcastically.

The pastor tried to explain the principle behind his work, the structure of the Bagam alphabet, the significance of the relationship between line and point, the elaboration of the fractals that soar, higher and higher, evolving into a metaphysics of life as well as of writing; he wanted to start with the obvious, to tell him that there is not one Bamileke language, but several, even if they share a common matrix, *tchun*, and that he wanted to produce a text that would be a touchstone, but he stopped when he realized that Semengue really didn't give a damn about such work, and that his men were carrying away his manuscripts, one by one. The pastor realized how foolish it was to expect someone who cuts off heads to respect the work those heads produced. The question asked by that man who had hundreds, no, thousands—and some would say hundreds of thousands—of Bamileke deaths to his name let him know it was futile, and so, until the soldiers had left the room, he said nothing more. *Lock nshou.* From then on, he never said another thing, but instead just sat on his veranda to pass the time. What else could he do, he who had always dedicated his efforts to the translation of words, when his work was taken away from him? It was as if his own body had been stolen from him, his home whisked away.

Pastor Tbongo wasn't killed, but the loss of his manuscripts was the blow that ended his life. From then on, his daughters would watch him staring blankly, counting the passing minutes. A game of chess might occupy him for a moment, but it was clear that an era had ended.

"They didn't arrest me," he said, "but my Bible."

Sometimes he laughed about it.

"Are they going to arrest truth?"

He'll never know that his papers were abandoned to the humidity and the roaches in the cellars of the Valley of Death. He'll never know that the pages of his Bible were used as toilet paper by the soldiers of the President of the Republic. For the moment, he imagined an officer in the archives—CEDOC, the Center of Documentation, leafing through his translations with greasy hands.

What is this? the man would ask.

If they could only read those texts! Tbongo would say with a sigh.

It never entered that man's mind that the goal of Semengue and his men was not their own education, but just causing trouble. What the colonists hadn't forbidden in Bamileke land, they had made it their mission to erase. He couldn't imagine that this was the beginning of his own destruction. An empty shell, he wandered through the house, rejoicing in his new life as a grandfather, but knowing that it was not enough. The child's cries irritated him, even as they reminded him of his happiness, and even as the presence of his two daughters reminded him that death occurred elsewhere, but not in his home. In the evening, every evening, he gathered his family around him, as was his habit, for their daily prayer, his gaze focused on the table in the living room and its absent Bible. He would clasp the hands of each one there with all of his might during these prayers, their incantations offered to the heavens that now loomed empty above his head, above everyone's head, and he'd chant those verses he knew by heart, having said them thousands of times. He wanted God to hear his prayer, the prayer of this bloodied land, of this family whose very heart was caught up in the pulsations of a country. He wanted to feel God's presence and, if needed, for God to plant there in his living room the roots of a nation: Ba-mi-le-ke!

14

The execution of Ntchantchou Zacharie plunged Bangangte into a stupor that further emptied out the already empty courtyards. But where it struck worst was in the *Tchunda*. Fewer and fewer peasants came there. One day the sky over the hill where the school sat was lit up by the glow of a fire. It was as if the clouds were falling. Planes cut through the night, raining down a hellish payload on the buildings and all around. Napalm! Soon the walls were aflame. Down below, the ululations that spread from hill to hill were punctuated by cries of, "The mountain is burning!" *Wo mbwok, oooo!* Everyone raced outside. The fighters who raced down the hill were picked off by the bullets of the soldiers hidden in the bushes, lying in wait, weapons leveled; the circle of destruction had closed in around the dream that had given meaning to Pastor Tbongo's life and had given Ouandié a secret place where he could train his fighters. The end of the utopia was thunderous. The world smashed into oblivion: *nathin!*

No one knows how many died under the burning rain, or how many were arrested as they fled. The morning broke over ruins, over blackened corner posts and bits of walls, over collapsed roofs. The fire had raged all the way to Bazou, the inhabitants of which were already shut away in resettlement camps. Semengue's army wanted to crush once and for all those who had set fire to the chief's compound in Bangwa. In retaliation, the army had set fire to all the hills at once, to teach them a lesson. They burned entire villages, so that no Bamileke would ever think of rebellion again. A spectacle of desolation: but those soldiers had come to destroy. *Nathin!* Happily, Ouandié escaped those flames. He had enough time to make it down to the valley and disappear into the bush. It was Nithap who saved his life; that's what Old Papa would tell his son. He had dragged the leader off toward the stands of bamboo, down in the hollow between the hills of Bazou, that lead to the Moya valley. He knew the Toungou woods, having followed that path several times with his father-in-law when they were building the *Tchunda*. The two men had hidden there, among the suffocating stalks, as the morning mists rose. How long did they stay there?

"They've gone," Ouandié said.

How many of them were left? Nithap, Njassep, and a few others, a dozen men. Once calm had returned, and while the horizon was still dark, they snuck through the walls of miscanthus and reached the shores of the Maheshou River.

"I don't know how to swim," Njassep said, staring at the bunches of sugarcane stalks growing up through the water and at the shoots of daisies.

The men looked at each other.

"That water is deep."

And that was true. So they disappeared under the umbrella of thorns and made their way through the swamp. Catfish, toads, and all sorts of river fish kept them company. Grasshoppers awoke and circled the sky. The slicing sound of helicopters set the rhythm, imposing its order all around.

"What luck, no crocodiles today," a voice said.

That was the only thing those men really feared.

"Let them come," Nithap said. "We have bullets."

The canopy of banana leaves offered them the shelter they needed. Death hadn't stopped prowling across the sky, racing down the hills. A burst of gunfire shot across the water and another shook the woods. There was a cry, that of a man shot through. The clear waters ran red with that wasted blood. How many dead had been swept away by those swift waters? The shores will never be able to say. They are counting on Nithap to tell their tale. They are fused into Bagam's messages, into the words of this novel, and they hide beneath stalks of *macabo* and potatoes.

The fighters walked, some behind Ouandié and others in front, rebuilding the protective shield they'd adopted for their leader since Mount Kupe. Their lives—they put them on the line for him. They spoke very little, and when they did, they whispered along the surface of the water, which carried their words.

Another burst of gunfire across the water. Ah, how long did they stay in the river of grass? Thorns pierced their feet, and the daisies sliced their hands, and yet the water offered them protection, keeping death at bay, even as dragonflies and butterflies flitted about before their eyes, tracing phosphorescent swirls of light. They measured the hours by the shifting colors of the sky and the moon, by the lifting of the mist, and the drying of the dew. From time to time they heard a noise in the distance, a noise that shook the ground, and they wondered what other horror Semengue's soldiers had unleashed on the people of Bangangte. They would never know for certain, but they kept their ears perked for that distant rumor that might be the cries of dying men, or the wailing of a village in mourning. There came a moment when even the toads fell silent, and the crickets paused their pastoral symphony to make way for a stunned silence.

"Our deaths will not be in vain."

It was Ouandié who said that.

"Our deaths will not be in vain. The people can't be silenced."

Vegetation grows thick in the West, as thick as in a fairy tale. Even today you can follow the riverbank where the *tsuitsuis* hid, all the way to Nkongsamba, all the way to Melong, and retrace our hero's final path: his passion play. The Bangangtes showed the Narrator the exact place where Ouandié was found. All it takes is to speak to them politely and with a modicum of respect, which may be the most difficult thing to do in this country named Cameroon; but because the Bangangtes respond instinctively to flattery and praise, it is enough just to tell them that they are noble, dignified, and elegant. They will lead you to the Maheshou River, whose waters are still so clear that you can watch the fish flitting away in its depths.

"That's the place," they'll tell you, pointing to a spot in the rapids, among the rocks. "That's the place."

"Semengue's soldiers were caught off guard."

For how could they know that beneath the water's green surface, beneath the cover of leaves, men were hiding? There are those who say that the river was transformed into a sea of blood, that it became an unmarked mass grave, but what do they really know? Still, anyone from Bangangte will tell you that the place where Ouandié was found is easy to recognize, you just have to be patient and, most of all, lucky. If you are there at dusk, when the sensitive plants, *Mimosa pudica*, close up and the daisies weep, when the setting sun transforms the universe with its golden glow, you will see a red crab come out of the water at the very spot, and open its mouth three times, as if breathing in and out.

"Ba-nga-ngte," that's what he's saying to you, "ba-ha-nte'."

It was thirty years later that Nithap returned to the site of the disaster. In 1997. He made that trip with his son, but without explaining the meaning of it to him. Minister Nkwayim was then mobilizing the Mandjos, which he had transformed into Bamileke Development Committees, CODEBA, to rebuild the destroyed villages of the West.

Can you believe it?

15

Can you believe it?

When they came out of the bush and returned to Bangangte, the pastor's family made their way through nothing but debris, nothing but cries and tears. What until then had been spared from the fury of the sky had now been carried away by the flames. Not even the miscanthus had escaped the fire. The hills, their slopes now covered with nothing but detritus, rose up in an apocalyptic spectacle. Only a few sheets of corrugated metal remained to suggest the durability of some of the houses, because no earthen walls had withstood the heat. Calcified chairs stood on verandas—the telling, petrified remains of lives frozen in place—and there were also smashed-in windows and toppled corner posts, reminders of where a palace might have stood, or perhaps just a large house.

The haggard populations dragged themselves from wherever they'd hidden for the night and formed a tattered procession, retracing their steps like frightened animals. Because in the forest there were wild beasts. Here a child opened his mouth, but his cry faded away under his mother's empty stare. That woman, that child, they had waited for calm to return so that they could go back to their house, which had disappeared, but mostly they had waited for the end of their fear. But could there be an end to fear in Bamileke land? The pastor's family hadn't gone so far as to hide in Toungou, but had they made their way to the *Tchunda*, they would have found the same spectacle of destruction. No Bangangte town had escaped, no village, no hamlet. The forests had been delivered over to an incandescent rage, so that even the trees' roots would know of the army's fury, and hear the ricochet of Semengue's laugh.

Ngountchou led the procession, and behind her came her sister, clasping to her breast her infant, who closed her eyes so she would not see, and whose mother did not want to show her what they had lived through, either. Could there be an end to fear? Mensa' thought of her father, whom they had left back in the living room, because he had refused to leave: "What would I be fleeing?" He had come as far as the veranda, and she could still see him waving his hand happily and smiling; Nja Yonke' had accompanied them as far as the courtyard, telling them that this time would be no different from the others.

"They are local boys," Elie Tbongo called to Ngountchou. "We have lived here with them during this whole war."

"Don't worry about us." And Nja Yonke' mentioned one of them, whom Ngountchou certainly knew, now the leader of the militia.

She'd forgotten his name.

"But you know him, the guy who's a bit *confoozed*," she'd said. "He wanted to recruit Tama' into his thing there. So I asked him if that meant he'd go in his place to fetch water from the spring for me."

She found that amusing.

"Do you realize!" she added, shaking her head. "He told me Tama' was already old enough to carry a rifle."

She really couldn't get over it.

"Tama', a soldier?" Her body shook with a deep sonorous laugh that tickled her even more, lighting up her face like never before. "But he's just a child!"

And yet, this time the stubborn old couple hadn't escaped. Mensa' and Ngountchou went into the living room, now in ruins, stepping around the calcified tables and chairs, the scattered plates and cooking pots. They were roused from their stupor by the dog's welcoming barks, because although Kouandiang was frightened, he still jumped to greet them, licking his mistresses' hands, wagging his tail and his whole body, jumping left and right.

"Where are they?" Ngountchou asked.

Tama' found them when he broke down the door to the bedroom, which had remained shut despite the fire.

"*Bou baa noum koun n'da.*" They're on the bed.

Pastor Tbongo and his wife had been lying in each other's arms when the flames took them, consumed by the madness of the universe, which had left behind only charcoal. Ashes and dust were all that remained of them, of their bed and their home—that's all that remained of the Bamileke civilization that, since it had once vanquished Bamum slavery, believed itself eternal.

Can you believe it?

Following the Maheshou River, Ouandié made his way out of Toungou. He walked all the way to Melong, where he turned himself in to Semengue's forces—who, for ten long years, hadn't been able to capture him, or to vanquish his battalions. He was condemned to death after one of those trials that are still all too common in Cameroon today, and then executed, shot in the public square on January 15, 1971. Twenty years later he would be named a hero by the very same state that had killed him.

Yes, can you believe it?

What Is a World with No Utopia Worth?

JFK International Airport is not very comfortable to someone who has just watched his father disappear into the customs and immigration lines. Tanou took out his phone and sent a quick message to Angela: *Everything went well.* He didn't want to call because, at that hour, Marie was certainly already in bed, fighting sleep. In any event, they'd already spoken, he told himself. He took a moment to send Bagam a message, too, reminding him about Old Papa's flight information. *Please remind Marianne*, he typed, as he walked. He almost ran into a few passengers running to catch a flight. "*Sorry*," he said in English, without looking up, because he was still staring at his phone, checking Facebook and his news feed. Really, it was just a distraction. A few years ago, he would have lit a cigarette, no doubt, but those days were gone. "A world without distractions is almost unlivable," he murmured as he got into his car. As soon as he turned the ignition, music filled the air. It was a New York station he really liked, because it played mostly pop. FM 102.7. Taylor Swift, "I Don't Wanna Live Forever." He let himself relax for a moment in his seat, before slowly heading out to the highway, his lips opening to sing along, *o hooo, oho! o hooo, oho!* Because he had an E-ZPass, he didn't have to wait long at the tollbooth, no need to shift his mood or even to stop skipping through the songs on the radio playlist, which he knew by heart, since they played ad nauseam every time he got behind the wheel. In truth, the songs kept his mind busy, filling up a space in his head as big as the plane that was taking his father away. His mind was as much caught up in the music as in the hectic pace of his life these past days, past weeks, past months. He heard Old Papa's voice, even though, all of a sudden, the man was out of sight, as if death had taken him suddenly, and whose voice would return tomorrow at the other end of a line from the far-off depths of Bangwa. He could still see him in Céline's kitchen, laying out the unimaginable twists and turns of his life, of their life, their memories, and he suddenly realized that illness can be a blessing, an opening toward freedom. Because you see, he told himself, if Old Papa hadn't had to extend his stay, if he hadn't had that unfortunate accident, he wouldn't have been there when Tanou's own marriage was falling apart, and so he wouldn't have had to answer those few simple questions that had led him to unfold the events of his distant past, which was less the story of a family than that of a nation—*ba-ha-nteh*—or an intercontinental country—*Ba-mi-le-ke*—or of Cameroon itself. Tanou thought of his aunt Mensa' (whom he'd call the next day to say his father was on his way) and then of Ngountchou; suddenly he saw them both, his mother and his aunt, there in the living room of the house in Bangwa, and then on the veranda of the house in Bangangte. He saw those times that he didn't live through, and yet that he needed to understand if he was going to unravel the knots of his own existence. He saw Ouandié and he saw Singap, furtive figures who had changed so many things in his life. He saw Nyamsi, repeating his own name, which had been changed when he was young, and wondered if he shouldn't shift back the clock, call himself Nyamsi once more; it would be easy to do in the United States—yes, he could do it: Tanou Nyamsi.

That's when the radio suddenly switched to ads, going on about cars for less, deals for less, "just $125.55." He reached out his hand and pressed a button: first he heard Franco Luambo, the Congolese singer, and listened for a moment to "Coller la petite." A smile spread across his lips—"Marthe"—and then he quickly switched to another song. It was a makossa he liked, a mix by Épée & Koum that took him back to another place and time, pushing him back into his seat and expanding the space of the Cherokee around him as he upped the volume. Now, because he had known the words of those songs for so long, too long, he sang at the top of his lungs, viscerally, bopping his head, tapping his fingers on the wheel, opening his lips to let out a cry that, he suddenly realized, was a sob; he was carried away by something he thought he had under control, but that now grabbed hold of what was deepest within him and projected him back into that evanescent world, a world that disappeared long ago. Right then the phone rang—Angela. But he didn't hear it because his mind was far away, plunged deep into his country, in that place that had taken away his father and that, there on I-95, made him shake his head, wipe away tears, and drive. He looked left and right, because he was free, yes, free: free from all those stories, all those dirty tricks, that age-old tradition of *lock nshou*; free from the tyranny that, in some sense, had kept his family in captivity. And then he made himself promises. Big ones: to bring Bagam over, for example, because "that little guy really deserves it," and to build a house in the *Tchunda*, as his father hoped to do. And little ones: to take Marie to Cameroon, maybe that summer, since he hadn't been back himself for four years. And even simpler things, too, like to pay attention to what Angela asked him to do: "Please don't forget to buy some milk." He kept on humming along to the song, then leaned to his left and shook his head as he passed a Lexus, driven by someone who could only be middle-aged: "Old drivers." He saw the sign DRIVE SAFELY fly past, written in bold letters.

He was driving with just one hand.

ACKNOWLEDGMENTS

This book is a novel, that's to say, a work of fiction. Yet it wouldn't have been possible without the choral writing of Facebook that, since 2011, has allowed me, along with my compatriots back in the country and elsewhere, to launch a political endeavor I couldn't have imagined, and to benefit from the unlimited intellectual generosity of hundreds of people, thus giving me a public work space. But it also allowed me to begin a dialogue on the question of tribalism, of *tode* in Medumba: the most pressing question of our day and which otherwise would have remained cloaked, taboo, even as it continues to cause thousands of deaths in Rwanda, Côte d'Ivoire, Mali, and elsewhere, and in Cameroon, of course—in Bamileke land. This novel would not have taken shape but for the violence elicited—in the past as well as in the present—by any mention of the Bamileke question, whether here or in Cameroon, and the duty this violence has imposed upon me to make my reflections public, in my role as Caretaker of the Republic. I thank all of those who have in various ways helped me to write it.

Alongside the prayer "Nya Thadée" by Namy Jean de Boulon, these documents were telling, speaking volumes precisely where witnesses fell silent. First, *Short Notes on the Syllabic Writing of the Eyap—Central Cameroons*, which introduced an article by L. W. G. Malcolm, and "The Lost Script of the Bagam," by Konrad Tuchscherer, as well as "Towards the Decipherment of the Bagam Script," by Andrij Rovenchak, of the Ivan Franko National University of Lviv, Ukraine—these were all revelations to me. Andrij Rovenchak also graciously provided me with the font for the Bagam script. Then there were the photographic archives of the Basel Mission and the Protestant Mission, Défap; the prehistory *Main basse sur le Cameroun: Autopsie d'une décolonisation*, by Mongo Beti, and the monumental *Kamerun! Une guerre cachée aux origines de la Françafrique, 1948–1971*, by Thomas Deltombe, Manuel Domergue, and Jacob Tatsitsa; the irreplaceable *Nation of Outlaws, State of Violence: Nationalism, Grassfields Tradition, and State-Building in Cameroon*, by Meredith Terretta; *La Marseillaise de mon enfance* and *Quand les jeunes Africains créaient l'histoire*, by Jean-Martin Tchaptchet; *Cameroun: Combats pour l'indépendance*, by Marie-Irène Ngapeth Biyong; *Femmes Bamiléké au maquis*, by Léonard Sah; *Le Chien noir: La Confession publique au Cameroun*, by Gilbert Doho; "Autochthony and Ethnic Cleansing in the South West Province: The 1961 Tombel Disturbances," by Piet Konings, published in *Neoliberal Bandwagonism: Civil Society and the Politics of Belonging in Anglophone Cameroon*; the seminal *African Majesty: A Record of Refuge at the Court of the King of Bangangté*, published in 1939 by Clement Egerton; *Bamiléké! La Naissance du maquis dans l'Ouest-Cameroun*, by Noumbissie M. Tchouaké; the film *Bangwa, hôpital de brousse* (1957), by Daniel Broussous; as well as many books and individual testimonies—too numerous to mention here, as this book is neither a work of history nor a doctoral thesis, but quite clearly a novel, and so a work of imagination.

And yet I cannot forget to mention the pamphlet "Les Noms et les titres de noblesse dans le Ndé," by Joseph Nkammi, which laid out methodically for me the elaborate system of given names, praise names, forms of address, and titles among the Bangangtes, and *Poésie et luttes de libération au Cameroun*, by Gilbert Doho, who gathered and transcribed for me songs by Martine Kengne, Florence Madé, Marie Magne, and Monique Tshingoum, who, along with Clara Nya, are the still unsung mamas of our citizenry. The oral testimony of *Nkamtan* Jean-Martin Tchaptchet, as well as his wife, *Tchankou'* Florence, recorded in Geneva, has proved priceless for the writing of this novel. I beg that they—as well as those whose lives I altered in order to make the truth of their era understandable—take this book as my entirely respectful homage to what they did to create our present. May my father, *Takwa* Joseph Nganang ("of Pesquidoux"), and my mother, *Makena* Rebecca Kemi, my wife, *Mako* Nyasha Bakare, Catherine Mauger-Williams, C. K. Williams, my aunt *Njanou* Julienne Yonkeu, Mathieu Njassep, the last of the maquisards, Sandjo Mambo Pierre Roger (aka Lapiro de Mbanga, who holds a PhD in *Camtok*, or the language of Mboko), the patriarchs John Eboung Epié and Simon Ngwesse Epié ("The Boy No Well"), Papa Daniel Nkuikeu, Jeanette and Divine from Tombel, the notables Isaac Komé, Jacques Ngolle Malaka, and Hans Njoumé Eboténé, as well as Teddy Tembe and Daniel Ndjoumè Komè of N'lohe, Papa André Noumbi ("Njangou") of Bangou, Bertin Ngouleu and Raymond Kwatcha, aka *Le Sommeilleur de Bangangté*, Jean-Marie Teno, Chief Mila Assoute, Daniel Poupessie, Célestin Ngoa Balla, Koko Ateba, Omar Mefire, Mounkambouh M. Youssouf, Michel Mombio, Aline-Léonie Chouapi, Serge Ngassam, Armelle Touko-Ngassam, Seme Ndzana, Jacques Mbakam, Roger Nouck Nouck, Romuald Hervé Momeya, Bana Barka, Daniel Tagne, Dieunedort Wandji, Jacob Tatsitsa, Almut Seiler-Dietrich, David Wanedam, Ali Ouba Mohaman, Odette Ngamen, Edmond Mfaboum, Gilbert Fumtchum, Francis Domo Sango, Théophile Nono, *L'engin* Fidèle Nguenssi, Jeremy Tatja, Marcel Nana, Ambroise Kom, Bergeline Domou, Gérard Kuissu, all my friends from *Tribunal Article 53*, the volunteers and supporters of Generation Change, Manuel Domergue, who placed all his historical knowledge at my disposal, Daniel Delas, Nicolas Martin-Granel, Laure Pécher, Pierre Astier, and my editor Anne-Sophie Stefanini, who all read drafts of this book and gave me constructive feedback, the Fondation des Treilles, which allowed me to work on this text in peace and calm, as did the village of Tourtour, which offered me shelter and the warm welcome of southern France—may they all find here the expression of my deepest gratitude. The Anglophones now at war each showed me that this story cannot be written in the walled-off solitude of self-flagellation, but only with the open generosity of all. That is why I dedicate this novel, which completes the Triptych of Njoya—the first two parts of which are *Mount Pleasant* and *When the Plums Are Ripe*—to my daughter, Nomsa, my *Bwonda'*, to whom for now I can only explain who I am by telling *tolis*, while waiting, of course, for the time of the *nou* that is our subject here.

Patrice Nganang

Hopewell, New Jersey—Kupe-Tombel, 2013–2017

Translator's Note

I first "met" Patrice Nganang through our friend Mboudjak, the canine narrator of *Dog Days*, which I had the good fortune to translate in 2006. Our collaboration on that project led to what I can only describe as an epic journey: the trilogy composed of *Mount Pleasant*, *When the Plums Are Ripe*, and *A Trail of Crab Tracks* led us across oceans and deserts, and along many dusty roads and forest trails, from the nineteenth century to the twenty-first. As he knits his plots with strands of History, lore, and stories—or *nou*, *toli*, and *tcho*—Nganang examines the patterns in what we do and do not know in order to remind us of how voices and languages call us together to listen, remember, and share. *Crab Tracks* is an explicitly political novel, deeply invested in understanding the past so as to shape the future, but it is also an extremely personal reflection on family and community. I am grateful to Patrice for trusting me with this book; I hope I have done it justice, and apologize for those places where I dropped a stitch.

As the novel unfolds on both sides of the Atlantic, let me first thank those in Paris and New York who worked to bring not just this novel but the whole arc of the trilogy to fruition. Pierre Astier and Raphaël Thierry at Astier-Pécher and Jonathan Galassi at FSG recognized Nganang's talent and the importance of the hidden histories these novels recount. Working with FSG's team of editors, publicists, and designers has been both a pleasure and, frankly, humbling; I am indebted to their collective wisdom and attention to detail. And my heartfelt thanks to Katie Liptak, whose patience and insight were crucial to capturing the nuances of Nganang's writing, especially in the last rounds of editing.

She never lost sight of our goal, and her appreciation of the author's humor helped me to keep things in perspective.

I want to acknowledge, as well, the generous support I received from New College of Florida, which allowed me to focus on this project during the summer of 2019, thanks to a grant from the Faculty Development Fund, as well as the following spring, when I was on assigned research. Colleagues and friends in the Humanities Division and in Gender Studies helped me to balance this project and teaching responsibilities; *un grand merci à tou·te·s.*

While this novel is about the politics of memory, specifically the consequences of censuring stories about Cameroon's civil war for our present, when fires again rage on the hills of the West, it is also about family, about how languages, writing, and digital communications shape the conversations we have with those we hold dear—lessons all the more poignant as we come through the long expanse of the Covid pandemic. May Jacob, Miriam, and Ben, my children and companions in lockdown, always know the place they hold in my heart. And here's to reunions to come with my far-flung family and the fierce friends on whom I count every day—you know who you are.

Amy B. Reid

Sarasota, Florida, 2021